Praise for Gregory D. Williams

"In matters of the heart, a single lapse of judgment can prove fatal. In this wise and tender novel, a young man finds out if he can live up to his father's reputation and his own expectations of himself. Greg Williams is a terrific writer!"

— Ron Carlson, author of the *At the Jim Bridger* and *Return to Lone Pine*

"In the tradition of great physician writers like Chekhov, William Carlos Williams, and Walker Percy, Dr. Greg Williams proves himself to be a master chronologist of both emotional and physical matters of the heart. With a diagnostician's keen eye for telling details, he brings the novel's scenes into vivid life. He shows his beautifully drawn characters the same empathy, I am sure he once showed his patients. Sharply honed as a scalpel, *Open Heart* is mesmerizing and profound, a superb novel that is guaranteed to bring pleasure and a deeper understanding of the human condition to those who read it."

— Daly Walker, author of *Surgeon Stories*

"An actual heart beats in this novel from the first line to the last. Make no mistake about it, with care and grace, and an urgency you'll feel on every page, Greg Williams has written a beautiful and evocative novel about a young man's singular and authentic quest to make meaning of life."

— Billy Lombardo, author of the *The Man With Two Arms* and *How to Hold a Woman*

" . . . a story about the boundaries of love, and how terrifying it can be to face up to our own emotional shortcomings."

— Clint McCown, editor of *American Fiction*

" . . . a tale that holds both surprise and inevitability, and evokes laughter even as it veers into pathos and tragedy."

— Peter Selgin, judge of the *Arts and Letters* Fiction Prize

"*Open Heart* is a gentle coming of age story that leaves readers wanting more, yet gives them a sense of comfort as they reach the end."

— Rabia Tanveer, for Readers' Favorite

"From his physician father's ability to save the day, which turns into an impossible legacy for his son to fulfill, to the career and love choices that create turbulence and complications in a son's life, Gregory D. Williams does a fine job of capturing the changing options and challenges facing a young man who breaks others' hearts because his own is being wrung by life circumstances and family ties. "

— Diane Donovan, for Midwest Book Review

"

OPEN HEART

Grand Canyon Press

233 E. Southern, #27733

Tempe, AZ 85285

www.grandcanyonpress.com

Cover Design © Erin Seaward-Hiatt

www.erindesignsbook.com

Names: Williams, Gregory D. (Gregory David), 1954-2020 author.

Title: Open heart : a poignant and gripping historical novel about the enduring power of love / Gregory D. Williams.

Description: Tempe, AZ: Grand Canyon Press, [2020]

Identifiers: ISBN: 978-1-951479-10-7 (paperback) | 978-1-951479-12-1 (Kindle) | 978-1-951479-13-8 (ibook) | 978-1-951479-14-5 (ePIB) | 978-1-951479-11-4 (epub) | 978-1-951479-15-2 (pdf) | 978-1-951479-16-9 (audiofile)

Subjects: LCSH: Medical students — United States — Fiction. | Bildungsromans. | Reconciliation — Fiction. | Operating rooms — Fiction. | United States — History — 1969-Fiction. | Romance fiction, American. | Medical fiction. | Psychological fiction. | LCGFT: Historical fiction. | Romance fiction.

Classification: LCC: PS3623.I55667 O64 2020 | DDC: 813/.6--dc23

Publisher's Note: This is a work of fiction. Names, characters, places, and incidents are a product of the author's imagination. Locales and public names are sometimes used for atmospheric purposes. Any resemblance to actual people, living or dead, or to businesses, companies, events, institutions, or locales is completely coincidental.

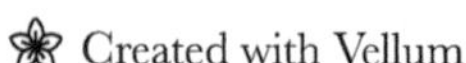

OPEN HEART

A poignant and gripping historical novel about the enduring power of love

GREGORY D. WILLIAMS

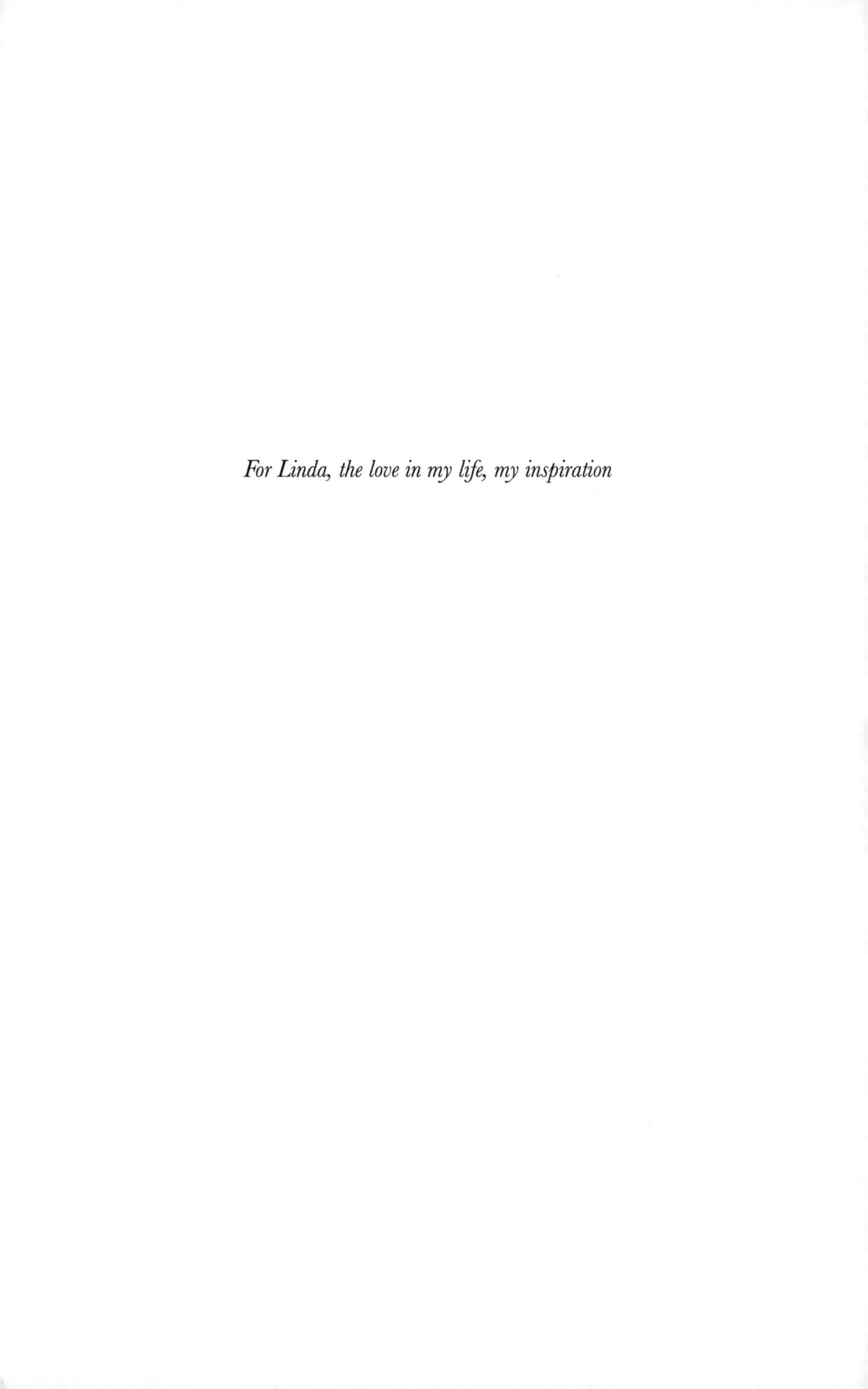

For Linda, the love in my life, my inspiration

CONTENTS

The silence is broken: into the nature
My soul sails out,
Carrying the song of life on his brow,
To meet the flowers and birds.

When my heart returns in the solitude,
She is very sad,
Looking back on the dead passions
Lying on Love's ruin.

I am like a leaf
Hanging over hope and despair,
Which trembles and joins
The world's imagination and ghost.

— Yone Noguchi

Chapter One
HELP

August 1965, Huntington Beach, California

Years before Gene would hold a girl's heart in the palm of his hand, at a time when love was still a singular thing, he lay awake, unable to push thoughts of the accident from his mind.

Eyes closed, he was picturing his father running full speed away from their station wagon, and then Gene heard a muffled cry. He whipped his head toward his older sister, curled up in the other bed. Amber light, slicing through a break in the motel room's curtains, cut across her back. "Suzanne?" he whispered. She didn't respond. Unlike him, she was finally asleep, her rhythmic breathing riding the distant, breaking waves. She had been crying earlier tonight. Gene could tell by the sniffing and the way her shoulders shook after she turned away.

Slipping from his bed, he tiptoed to the door separating their room from his parents' room and pressed his ear against the panel. His mother was crying. Not his father. Gene had never seen him cry. There was talking. He couldn't make it out. When he shifted to the other ear, his knee knocked against the door. He held his breath. Uh-oh. Footsteps. Gene jumped back into bed, pulled the covers up, and turned his head. The door creaked open. "Gene," his father whispered. "Gene, you okay?"

Gene played dead. But not really dead. He made sure his chest moved so his father knew he was okay. After the door clicked closed, he waited several minutes before he faced the brown stain on the popcorn ceiling. It looked like blood. He shut his eyes. Then shut them a little tighter.

Earlier, his father had said, *We're on vacation. Let's try to forget the whole thing.* But Gene couldn't. Eyes closed or eyes open, he couldn't stop reliving the day.

It had begun that afternoon. Gene rested in the far back of his parents' Chevy II station wagon as the vehicle sped west across the Arizona desert toward the beaches of southern California. The hum of tires on hot asphalt bled through the vehicle's frame, through the four-inch foam bed he'd helped his father fit precisely to the space, and through the green corduroy bedspread, which covered the foam. The vibration tickled his bones. Sometimes his bones ached at night. *Growing pains* his mother once assured him. He hoped so. He wanted to be bigger. He wanted to be older than eleven. Someday, he wanted to be just like his father.

For now, he'd like to be as old as his sixteen-year-old sister, although today their mother said she was acting like a sulking child. Suzanne flopped into the car at sunrise. During the breakfast stop in Wickenburg, she said she wasn't hungry. And now, despite having the whole bench seat to herself, she leaned her head against the window behind their father and pouted. She was missing a party at Saguaro Lake later tonight. All her friends would be there. But Gene knew this was about a boy. He'd seen Suzanne making out with Rodney in the backyard by the orange trees. At night, Gene sometimes exited his second-floor bedroom window to the slanted roof below. There, if the conditions were just right, he could pull in the San Francisco Giants play-by-play on the Heathkit short-wave radio he and his father had built.

This roof-top privilege came with stipulations, one of which he broke on occasion by venturing onto the roof after his parents were in bed. The hours after midnight felt like a place beyond his horizon. He had yet to stay up all night, but the night he made it to one thirty was the night he discovered a clear line-of-sight to Suzanne and Rodney kissing in the backyard. He had no intention of squealing. He would like to be Rodney, but of course not with his sister.

Cool air from the air conditioner flowed between his parents, over Suzanne's seat-back, and settled onto his face and thin, bare arms. Gene drifted on the vibration and the A/C's drone.

"You kids have to pee?" his mother said. "Rest stop one mile."

"No," Gene said.

"Suzanne?"

"I guess not."

"You could get a Butterfinger from the machine."

Suzanne didn't answer.

Gene touched the ceiling with his fingertips. The sun, hidden from view, rained its heavy heat through the hood of the wagon. He sat up and squinted south across the barren, thirty-foot median. For as far as he could see, maybe a hundred miles to the gray, jagged mountains, an army of saguaros flexed their arms to the cloudless sky. His father called this *no man's land.* Which was why Gene's space in back was crowded with a thermos of water, a Craftsman toolkit, jumper cables, two gallons of antifreeze bungeed together, and a plastic crate loaded with motor oil, flares, belts and hoses, and of course his father's black doctor's bag. The bag held a stethoscope, bandages, a plastic box labeled *Suture Kit* in block script on a piece of surgical tape, and an instrument his father said he used in the operating room everyday called a laryngoscope.

He'd helped his father load the wagon the day before, placing a tick by each checklist item with a carpenter's pencil. Then his father closed the rear hatch and said, "I think we're covered." Gene liked the *we're* part of that. On a trip last summer, somewhere in the desert near Blythe, he'd helped pack icy-wet rags around the steaming carburetor. They were treating something called *vapor lock.* "It's the same as when air gets inside your heart," his father said. Gene had nodded as if he understood.

"Look at that," his mother said. "One hundred and three and it's not even noon." She tapped the dial on the gauge he and his father had installed. Gene rolled his eyes, lay back down, and lip-synced her next words: "This is my last summer in Arizona."

"You know," his father said. "I'm putting that on your gravestone."

"Carl, I'm serious."

A gust of wind buffeted the car and the thermos rolled into Gene.

"That was a big one," his mother said.

Gene set the thermos upright and braced it with the doctor bag. He opened the bag's mouth a smidgen and inhaled. Something about the hospital smell pleased him.

"I changed my mind," he said. "I have to pee."

"Too late," his mother said. "We just passed the exit."

"Who's that?" his sister said.

Her voice was different. Gene sat up and followed Suzanne's concerned gaze out the window. A woman in a yellow sundress raced back and forth along the median. She tugged at her raven-black hair as the wind whipped her dress. She appeared to be screaming.

"There's someone on the ground!" Gene's mother said. She turned the music off.

They zipped by so fast, Gene didn't see the person on the ground. But he kept his eyes on the woman as the station wagon slowed, jostled across the scrubby median, and picked up speed again. As they approached the scene, Gene noticed a white pickup truck parked off the shoulder on the right. The driver's door was open. He looked back for the woman. She was kneeling over the person on the ground. Suddenly she ran away with her hands on her head as if something had bitten her.

Gene's mother screamed. "Oh my God. Carl. It's a child!"

Suzanne shrieked.

They passed a Cadillac canted in the median. An elderly woman in the front seat held a towel or shirt or something on the driver's face. The station wagon skidded to a stop just past the Cadillac. Gene caught himself against the back seat. His father bolted from the car. He ran across the hardscrabble earth toward the child, a bouncing tumbleweed crossing his path. Gene had never seen his father run like that — his arms pumping in his white t-shirt, the soles of his favorite traveling Hush Puppies kicking gravel and plumes of dirt high behind him. He ran about twice the distance as from home plate to second base, and with his back to Gene, knelt next to the child. A man in a black cowboy hat was already crouched there. Gene's father must have said something, because the man ran toward the rest stop across the highway.

Gene's father leaned down. Gene couldn't see his father's face or the child's, but he was sure he was breathing into the child's mouth. A couple years before, in their living room, he'd taught Gene and Suzanne how to do this. He had them practice on each other. Now, his father seemed to push on the child's body. It was hard to tell. He could only see the child's foot and pink sock.

"It's a girl," Gene said. "I think she had the wind knocked out of her." It had happened to him once. He thought the pushing might be another way to help her breathe.

After several seconds his father leaned over the girl again. The pattern repeated — breathing, pushing, breathing, pushing. Over and over and over. Gene grabbed the doctor bag and crawled across the seat back, nudging his sister aside. He pulled up on the door handle.

"No! Stay here." His mother's face was twisted.

"What if he needs this?"

"Stay."

Gene rolled down the window. The heat curled into the car like a wave. Other cars had stopped. People were shouting and running, while others stood around Gene's father, protecting their faces from gusts of sandy wind. Everyone looked confused. Several feet away, the woman in the yellow sundress was on her knees. She threw her head back and screamed again. Another woman ran to her.

Suzanne was crying. "Please, please, please."

His father continued: breathing, pushing, breathing, pushing. It went on and on as more cars stopped, but nobody helped his father. They stood or they knelt, but he was doing all the work. Was he getting tired? Maybe he needed some water. The cowboy-hat man ran back from across the highway. His hat flew from his head and tumbled across the desert. He was waving his arms and shouting. "They're coming," he said. He was so out of breath he could barely speak. The man bent over and vomited. Gene said, "Gross," and briefly closed his eyes. The girl still wasn't moving, but he was sure that at any moment she would sit up and take a deep breath just like he had done. Why wasn't anyone helping? Maybe he could do the breathing.

Finally, his father stopped. He rested back on his heels.

In a voice Gene had never heard from his mother, a voice balanced on a thin wire, she said, "Oh God, no. Please. No." She put her hand over her mouth. Her eyes were wet.

"He needs help," Gene said. He grabbed the doctor bag and thermos, vaulted over the seat, and opened the passenger-side door. His mother screamed his name. He ran as fast as he could with the heavy load jerking his arms. He was almost there, when his father turned and shouted. "Gene. Stop."

Gene obeyed, as much from the odd tone of the command as from the command itself. "Stay right there." His father said this calmly, stood, and trudged over to Gene. He knelt and took the thermos and bag from his hands. "Let's go back," his father said.

Gene looked past his father to the girl. Below her cutoffs, her bare legs resembled question marks. One foot had a white sneaker; the other, only a pink sock. Her tattered yellow shirt laid open, and her chest was flattened. Except for smudges of blood around her mouth, her face was the color of an eggshell. One eye was half-open.

His father grasped Gene's waist and gently turned him away. Gene looked at him for several hard seconds — at the smudge across one lens of his black-framed glasses (his father's flip-up shades were missing) and at the sweat blooming across his forehead and dripping off his nose, but mostly at the blood drying within the morning stubble above his lip and on his chin. His father swiped his mouth and looked at the blood on his fingers. He poured water from the thermos and wiped his face, hands, and glasses. He took off his sweat-soaked t-shirt and used it to wipe his chest. "Here, take this."

He rolled up the shirt. "Take this and the thermos back to the car. I've got to check on her mother."

Again, Gene looked past his father at the girl. Someone had covered her with a beach towel, but the wind tossed it aside. Gene's shoulders began to shake. His whole body shook and the tears that erupted seemed as far from his control as the shaking.

His father pressed Gene's cheek to his waist. "It's okay," his father said. "It's okay." The steady rub of his father's thumb against his head and the gentle, deep voice slowed Gene's breathing. Then, with a hand firmly on Gene's shoulder, his father walked him back toward the station wagon.

Gene wiped his eyes. He looked up and squinted against the harsh sun glinting off his father's head like a halo. "Dad," he said. "I feel — "

Then everything went dark.

Chapter Two

THE HEART ROOM

Summer 1974, Phoenix, Arizona

DAMN. He's going to be late. Gene glances up to his rear-view mirror and accelerates his yellow Jeep ten miles past Central Avenue's posted limit. He's practically the only car on this normally busy thoroughfare at…he checks his watch…5:07 a.m. The light at Camelback turns yellow…damn…he stops. Damn. Damn. Irene, Dr. Harrington's private scrub nurse told Gene on the phone last night, practically threatened him, not to be late. "It's not like baseball," she said. "With Dr. Harrington, one strike and you're out."

He's supposed to meet Irene by the scrub sink outside the open-heart room by five thirty. This job was a favor. Actually, it's a volunteer opportunity to shadow Dr. Benjamin Harrington until August, a man Gene's father called the *godfather of open-heart surgery in Arizona.* Normally the only outsiders allowed in the Heart Room were fifth-year surgical residents from Tucson. That Gene, a soon-to-be junior in college, had been granted this opportunity had everything to do with genetics.

On the Jeep's radio, KCAZ's disk-jockey introduces the next tune — "Only Love Can Break Your Heart." Gene shakes his head.

The whole world must be conspiring to ruin this day. He turns up the volume and recites the lyrics in his head, something he couldn't have done before Love-You-With-My-Whole-Heart Patty McLellan cut out his with a weed whacker last spring. But it isn't just this song. Every song seems to tell his story of love, loss, and longing.

The light turns green, and Gene floors it. Up ahead the lights are timing out perfectly. He might be a couple minutes late…okay maybe more than a couple…but being Carl Hull's son is sure to buy him a little time.

Then a red bulb between the speedometer and tachometer lights up. Gene slumps in the Jeep's bucket seat. He might just be back to painting the trunks of orange trees this summer. "Damn."

He slams the steering wheel with his open palm. The steam curling around the hood evaporates his imagined, glowing letter-of-rec from Dr. Harrington. So much for medical school.

Gene angles into the parking lot of Karsh's Bakery and unlatches the hood. A dripping hose dangles next to the water pump. Why now? Why today? The bakery door is locked. He pounds on the glass, but nobody comes. A mile down, a Union 76 station lights the dawn. Gene's hard-sole shoes clack along the sidewalk as he runs. A blond, curly-haired kid is opening up the small office. Not the owner, Jerry.

"Hey," Gene says. His chest heaves. From behind the counter, the kid startles. "Sorry. You got a clamp for a water hose? '65 Jeep."

"Gimme a sec."

The kid fiddles with a ring of keys, testing them one by one on the cash register.

"I'm kind of in a hurry," Gene says.

The kid doesn't speak. He shakes his head and saunters into the bay.

Gene taps his fingers on the counter. Come on. Come on.

The kid returns with five clamps. "One of these might work."

"What do I owe you?"

"Come back with the others and we'll settle up."

Gene turns to run back but stops. "Can I use your phone?"

The operator connects him with Desert Valley's switchboard.

"Surgery, please," Gene says.

"You mean the OR desk?"

"Yes, I guess. I'm looking for Irene. She works with Dr. Harrington."

"Excuse me. Are you a physician?"

"No. I'm Gene Hull. I'm supposed to meet her there today and —"

"Dr. Hull's son?"

"Yes."

"Please hold."

The line is busy.

He calls back. The operator connects again. Still busy. Gene slams the receiver down. "Sorry."

"Hey, don't stress, man." The kid plops a two-gallon kitchen pail onto the counter. "Radiator water's by the last pump."

"I owe you." Gene runs back to his Jeep, water sloshing onto his cuff and shoe. He slithers under the Jeep. "Shit!" How could he forget? A screwdriver.

He rifles through the back of his Jeep and his glove box. Nothing. His father always had at least a small set of tools in the car. Not Gene. He left his in the garage. Think. Think. Run back to the gas station? He looks up. The distant light deflates him. Think. A dime. He checks the ash-tray. No dime. But maybe the penny. Working mostly by feel in the dim light, the third clamp he tries fits. Thank you. The penny fits as well. He tightens the screw as best he can, but the penny slips, and he fries the meat of his hand on the engine block. "Shit!"

He pours a little water onto his hand and the rest into the open mouth of the radiator. Without a funnel, some of it steams off the engine. It will have to do. He tosses the other four clamps on the seat and wipes his hands with an old rag stained with tree-white.

GENE SCREECHES into Desert Valley Hospital a nose behind the sun. He parks in the staff lot adjacent to the muscular cooling plant which, even at first light, rumbles and hisses, sending swirling columns of steam into the dry, tepid air. He angles into a space close to the coolers. Their shadow, as long and wide as a gymnasium, will delay the sun's inescapable intrusion upon the canopy-covered cockpit of his Jeep. Still, by late afternoon, the steering wheel will be hot as a skillet.

He races across the asphalt and slows as he reaches the back entrance. When he steps on the rubber mat, the electric doors swing out with a hiss. Still the same.

Gene is familiar with the hospital's six-story layout. So many Sunday evenings he waited in the lobby while his father made pre-op rounds. Never, in all those years or after, did Gene venture inside an operating room, much less the Heart Room.

He quick-steps down a gleaming, windowless tiled corridor which bends right, a space he remembers as being larger and louder, crowded with people in street clothes or white coats, a din of conversations bouncing off the walls. Now, at this hour, his shoes click and echo along the cream-colored linoleum. The service elevator is just around the corner near the kitchen. Clanging of dinnerware and muffled, good-natured banter permeates the hall, as well as the odd aroma of bacon and rubbing alcohol.

He presses the elevator's UP button in rapid succession until he hears the carriage mechanism's stark whine. Beginning with six, the red numerals above the door count down as the carriage makes its maddeningly slow descent.

Irene told him on the phone: "There's a chance this may not work out. A lot depends on you and, unfortunately, on Dr. Harrington's mood on any given day." She went on to explain that the previous spring the assistant administrator's son arranged to observe a case one day. They'd just opened the chest when the kid walked in. Without looking up, Dr. Harrington said, "Son, perhaps your father has some menial office task you might perform that does not require punctuality. Have a nice day."

The elevator dings, drawing Gene's eyes to the lit numeral one. There is a pause, a silent moment when Gene's heart almost stops.

It just has to open. But the carriage whines and ascends…two, three, four…

"Damn!"

He exits the stairs to the fourth floor, pulling air liked he'd just finished a set of first-to-third sprints. A corridor leads north and south to patients' rooms. On the east side of this intersection, the rising sun beats against the reflective coating of a large picture window centered in the alcove's waiting area. Across the corridor, double glass doors lead to the operating rooms. The lettering on the glass is still the same — *Operating Room Attire Only*. He walks around to the left of the electric doors to a small window and taps lightly to get the attention of a woman dressed in scrubs and shower-style cap. A bead of sweat trickles down his chest. She has her back to him and is chatting with someone else, a man similarly dressed, who seems upset about the workings of a long instrument the size of barbecue tongs. He tips his chin toward Gene, and the woman turns around in mid-yawn. She slides the window open and grins.

"So, what happened?"

Gene dressed as his father would have — slacks, short-sleeve dress shirt, and tie. But they're a grimy mess now. "Radiator hose."

"Eugene? Right?"

"Gene."

"Irene's been asking about you."

"Did surgery start already?"

"Harrington cuts at seven." She spins around and looks at the clock. It's not quite six. "Irene's been here since five thirty."

Gene's father usually left for work at about five forty-five. At least that was the time on the bedside clock when he opened an eye to the touch of his father's hand on his forehead and aroma of his cologne.

"My God, you have your father's good looks. More hair, though. I'm Darlene."

She extends her hand, but Gene holds up his dirty mitts and shrugs. "Sorry."

"We were devastated. Everyone loved him."

"Thanks. Do I go through this door?"

"The place just isn't the same. How's your mother doing?"

"She's off to New Hampshire."

"It's got to be tough."

So, this is what he was in for, even though it's been nine months since the crash. Gene's moved on. "I'm kind of running late."

"Okay, okay. Scrubs are inside. Don't forget the booties." She stands and looks down through the window.

Gene looks at his dress shoes.

"They'll fit over those," she says. "There are masks in there, or grab one by the scrub sink. Pin the locker key to your pants, and don't lose it. Any questions?"

"Irene filled me in."

"And work on those hands...and your chin."

Gene starts to reach for his chin but stops.

"There's a smudge up there as well." She smiles.

A buzzing sound comes from the door. "Just push it open," she says.

The buzzing stops before he can open it. Darlene takes something from the man behind her and looks back at Gene. "Another thing. Use one of these." She passes the same style cap she's wearing. "You'll need this to tame that gorgeous, dark hair of yours." The door buzzes again. "Hey, there's coffee in the doctor's lounge."

Gene pushes the door open. "No thanks. I don't drink it."

She tips her Styrofoam cup to him and says, "You will."

Crap. Look at all this. The scrub pants and shirts, the color of dried moss, come in sizes double extra-small to triple extra-large. After washing his face and hands, it takes Gene more time than he can spare to sort out his size, and in the end, he settles on medium tops and bottoms. He sits on a bench and fumbles with the paper booties. Then, instead of the nurse's bouffant cap, he tries on a regular doctor's cap, but Darlene was right: his hair's too long. From the boxes of masks, he chooses one like the masks he's used in the metal shop, pinches it at the bridge of his nose. He takes a step back from the mirror over the sink and sighs. He feels like a freshman wearing a varsity uniform for the first time. Like an impostor.

Gene hurries through the heavy door to the cool, empty doctors' lounge. Scattered across a long coffee table are plates of half-eaten sandwiches and cigarette-filled ashtrays. Sections of the previous day's newspaper cascade from vinyl-padded chairs onto the industrial carpeted floor. The carpet tugs at the bottom of his paper booties.

Irene said to meet outside the Heart Room. The doctors' lounge exits to a tiled corridor, a space as cool as the lounge. It's empty of people but crowded with equipment. In front of him stands a line of stainless-steel shelving packed with supplies mostly unfamiliar to Gene except for bags of intravenous solutions, boxes of syringes, and a stack of blankets next to more bouffant caps. As he walks toward the glassed-in OR office, he passes gurneys, stainless steel carts, IV poles, an oscilloscope similar to those in his electrical engineering lab, and another device on wheels that stands about chest high. He recognizes it by the green oxygen tank: the large glass cylinder filled with white granules (although a layer at the bottom is a purple color) and the black corrugated tubing. It looks like the anesthesia machine he's seen in an old photo of his father taken during his medical training.

"Gene." Darlene leans out of the open office door. "Irene's down there." Gene stands near the glass entry doors. The *OR Attire Only* warning is now inside out. "The Heart Room is all the way down at the end." She points past Gene to his left.

IRENE WASHES her hands at one of two deep porcelain sinks in an alcove. She works the nails of one hand with a soapy brush in fierce, rapid strokes, a nest of brownish-orange bubbles growing on the tips of her fingers. She's short and sinewy, not what he expected from the sound of her voice on the phone. The cuffs of her pants are rolled up a turn or two. Above the sink hang shelves stocked with boxes of hats and masks. She wears the same style cap as Gene. A disposable mask, the kind with two sets of ties, the kind Gene isn't wearing, hides her face except for her eyes. Maybe he chose the wrong mask. She looks over at him.

"You're late."

"My Jeep overheated."

She gives him a hard look while continuing to scrub. "You're late."

If this had been baseball practice in high school, he'd be running laps now. She looks at him again, a long look that makes him uncomfortable. Here it comes. She's sending him packing.

But her eyes soften. "You're definitely Carl's son."

"Was he late, too?"

She shakes her head, and he knows she's smiling.

"Not only do you have his eyes, you have his voice."

She steps on a stainless-steel pedal. Water pours from the gooseneck faucet. She rinses each hand and then foot-pumps more liquid brown soap onto the brush and begins scrubbing her arms.

"I think you're even taller than when I saw you at the service," she says.

His mother told him that Irene had been Dr. Harrington's private nurse as long as he'd been in practice. She must have come through the line at his father's memorial service, but Gene doesn't remember. So many doctors and nurses had offered double-handed condolences that after a while they all blended into the same sorrowful face.

"Your dad was quite a guy. Like I said on the phone, we're not in the habit of taking on college students, but your dad was special."

Gene knows she means well, but he has the sickening feeling that in the belly of her compliment is a warning not to let her down…or his father.

"Be in the doctor's lounge dressed and ready to go by six-fifteen," she says.

"I thought you said five-thirty."

"That's just for today. I was going to teach you to scrub, but we'll hold off for now."

"Sorry."

"The girls and I start setting up at five forty-five." She looks at the clock. "Although more like six today. Depending on the case, there's about an hour of prep before Dr. Harrington cuts at seven. He can be late. You can't. This isn't college."

"Yes ma'am."

She explains that the team performs two surgeries a day except on Tuesdays and Fridays. On those afternoons, Dr. Harrington has his office hours. Gene can't shadow him then. Teaching would just slow him down. But, if Gene wants, he can follow Dr. Harrington on rounds in the afternoons when he sees his post-ops and the admits scheduled for surgery the next day.

"You might want to consider sneakers." She nods toward his bootie-covered dress shoes. "You'll be standing a lot."

That's some good news. His feet already ache.

"Have you met Dr. Boswell? He's our anesthesiologist."

"No."

"You'll be standing with him, just watching for the first week. If all goes well, Dr. Harrington will let you scrub in next week. You can do small things, like suction blood while he works."

She eyes him. "I hope you're not squeamish."

"Not at all." He fainted once while watching his father sew up a gash on Suzanne's knee, and of course after he saw the dead girl. But that was ages ago.

"If you feel faint, sit.

"Got it?"

"Don't try to be brave."

"I'll be fine."

He had envisioned this job, if that's what it was, as just tagging along, retrieving forgotten charts or x-rays, hanging a few steps back from the profession's edge before diving into medical school. He hadn't planned on actually helping during surgery. That would look great on a med-school application.

"You've never been in the OR."

It isn't a question. "No."

She smiles. "You can lower your mask." He complies and wipes a layer of moisture from his upper lip. "You only need to wear it in there." She tilts her head toward the Heart Room door.

After a rinse and more scrubbing, she says, "You'll only scrub if you're going to be gowned and gloved at the OR table. And then you'll stand by Dr. Pereira. He's our First Assist. I'm sure he'll help you out. He's such a sweetheart. But then you know Rui," she says. "He was quite persuasive."

Years ago, Dr. Pereira and Gene's father trained at the same hospital in Galveston, Texas. He's from Portugal and still carries an accent. For years, when Gene thought of Dr. Pereira, he thought of his passion for the Cincinnati Reds and more recently his twelve-cylinder Jag. He loved to work on cars, always wearing surgical gloves to keep grease from getting under his nails.

Early last May, Gene called Dr. Pereira and asked if he could spend the summer shadowing him. Gene had taken a disastrous early stab at the MCATs, and according to Gene's counselor, his grades were more than a tick below the level of Cal Poly students previously accepted into medical school. She suggested he abandon the premed track and focus on engineering, a discipline where he excelled. Combining the two was challenging even for someone who hadn't missed time because of a death in the family. No. Her recommendation was basically horse shit. He's wanted to be a doctor for as long as he can remember.

To improve his chance for medical school, he needed work experience and a glowing recommendation from someone who could attest to his character and aptitude for the career. Rui had listened to all of this over the phone and suggested Gene pin his summer and his hopes on Dr. Harrington instead. "He carries considerable weight with his surgical brethren down south at the University of Arizona. I shall speak to him. I am sure he will be receptive."

About a week later, on a Sunday afternoon, as Gene and his roommate Doug worked their way through a six-pack of Anchor Steam beer while burning Patty's letters and photos, Dr. Harrington called Gene. The conversation was short and to the point. He was in. Irene would handle the details. What stuck with Gene was the last thing Dr. Harrington said in his slow Virginian drawl: "It will be an *honah* and a privilege to have a *youngstah* of your caliber at my side." His caliber. Until recently, Gene had rarely questioned his caliber.

Irene rinses her hands and arms one last time and moves away from the sink, holding her hands at head level, arms away from her body. Then she nods to a white coat hanging opposite the sink. "That's for you. Wear it over your scrubs whenever you leave the surgery area."

Gene holds the coat at the shoulders. Red cursive stitching over the left breast reads *Desert Valley Heart Team*.

"We all have one," she says.

Then he notices C. Hull printed on the collar's tag in black ink. Gene recognizes the block script and swallows hard.

"Thanks," he says. He tries the coat on. It feels a size too large, the sleeves reaching to mid-palm.

"Maybe you'll grow into it." Irene walks across the hall and leans her back against the door to the Heart Room, her arms held high like the Pope in greeting. "Put it in your locker, and then come on in."

THE HEART ROOM is even colder than the hallway. Gooseflesh rises on Gene's arms.

"Sandra, Betty. This is Gene, Doctor Hull's son," Irene says. The masked women are opening packs of instruments onto Irene's two long, draped tables, but pause to shake his hand.

"I adored your father," Sandra says.

He recognizes her. "You spoke at the service, right?"

Sandra nods.

Gene sits on a rolling stool at the head of the empty surgical table, while Irene points out what Gene can't touch, which is most everything. Ceramic tile comes halfway up the walls. Gene asks, "Why's it so cold in here?"

"I don't want Dr. Harrington sweating into the patient's chest. Here. Put this on." She hands a surgical gown to Sandra who holds it open like a tailor waiting for Gene's arms.

A man walks in wearing a five o'clock shadow and a custom cap decorated with Valentine hearts. He introduces himself as Roger, the pump tech.

"I heard you'd be joining us. Your dad was the best."

He invites Gene to slide closer to the heart-lung machine and explains how the device works as he sets it up. Open heart surgery involves letting a machine do the work of the heart and lungs while the surgeons fix the problem. That's bypass — the heart and lungs are bypassed.

Roger guides clear tubing through the roller pump, fills the tubing with saline, and then taps at the tubing with a clamp to move any bubbles up toward a stopcock. "Air in your blood is like air in your car's fuel line," he says. "Not a good thing."

"Vapor lock," Gene says.

"Exactly."

Betty, the older (and considerably wider) of the two circulating nurses marks off a checklist as Irene runs her fingers and eyes over orderly rows of glittering instruments. Irene calls off, "Kellys. Two, four, six. Mayos. Two, four, six, and one on the floor makes seven. Scissors. Straight. One, two. Curved. One, two...." It goes on and on. She counts what must be a hundred instruments as well as a stack of four-by-four gauze pads, laps (Dr. Pereira used these to wax his car), and every suture, every needle, everything that is on either of her tables or adjustable tray, right down to small, cotton bullets called peanuts, which are gripped by the tips of long clamps. "We'll count at the end of surgery as well," Irene says. "If the counts don't match, we'll search until they do. Don't want a patient taking hospital property home."

Sandra, probably the youngest in the room except for Gene, continues to move back and forth from the operating room to center hall — the area in the middle of the U-shaped surgery configuration. That's where things are sterilized and stored until needed. Sandra moves about with confidence. She opens sterile packs of gowns and gloves in a prescribed way meant to insure there is no breach in sterility.

Soon, he realizes that his attention is focused on her eyes. As a matter of fact, all he can see of anyone's face is their eyes. The caps and masks frame them. Sandra's eyes aren't like Patty's. They aren't blue, much less a blue you could swim in. Hers are olive with long mascaraed lashes. She's taller than Patty, closer to Gene's height. As she collects an armload of unopened supplies, a ribbon of her brown hair escapes her bonnet. Does her conditioner smell like Patty's? When she backs up to the door leading to center hall, she catches Gene staring. Her eyes smile. He gestures to indicate the loose hair. He's sure she mouths *Thank you.*

A moment later, the OR door opens, and a stocky man strides in. "I see y'all rounded up a new anesthesiologist?" he says.

Irene turns. "Gene, this is Doctor Boswell."

He shakes Gene's hand. "Call me Boz. Darlene said you were here. So, you're trailing Dr. H around this summer?" He rolls a red Craftsman cart closer to the anesthesia machine, opens a drawer and lays out some syringes.

"It's only for eight weeks until he goes on vacation," Gene says. "Is that cart from Sears?"

"Yes." Dr. Boswell pulls vials of medications from another drawer and begins drawing the liquids into the syringes. "Irene," he says, turning. "Since when does Harrington go on vacation?"

"He tries every year, Doctor."

Dr. Boswell adjusts some dials on the anesthesia machine, holds a mask near his face and presses a button, causing a blast of air from the mask. "Ah, Halothane," he says. "Breakfast of champions." Gene catches a whiff of something pungent. Dr. Boswell then lays out a couple of instruments and an endotracheal tube on top of the cart, items familiar to Gene from his father's doctor bag. "I'll explain things once we get going," Dr. Boswell says, "but I suspect you know most of this from your dad."

He doesn't. Why exactly? He's not sure.

Sandra walks in from center hall carrying some kind of black paddles in her gloved hands. "Sandy, darling," Dr. Boswell says, "I'm going to need an epi drip for later."

"Okay." She hands the paddles to Irene, snaps off her gloves and scans the room. "I'm off for the patient."

Several minutes later, with the help of an orderly, Sandra wheels a half-asleep man into the room and transfers him to the table. The patient is already hooked up to an IV. Sandra attaches the electrocardiogram pads. The oscilloscope's green line comes to life — *beep, beep, beep*.

Dr. Boz straps a black rubber mask to the man's face, injects medication into the IV, and says, "Say goodnight, Irene." After another syringe of medication, Dr. Boz grips the mask and squeezes the black breathing bag. With each squeeze, the man's chest rises.

As soon is the man is out, Dr. Boz inserts the breathing tube — the endotracheal tube — through the man's mouth into his windpipe and tapes it in place. He also tapes the man's eyes closed and wraps the man's head with the towel.

Dr. Boz inserts a cannula into an artery at the man's wrist, something Gene's father must have done thousands of times. A second wave now bounces in synchrony under the EKG. Finally, Dr. Boz inserts an IV in the man's neck vein using a kit Gene had not seen Betty prepare. It just appeared. The teamwork is impressive.

"Okay, Sandy," he says. "Work your magic."

In seconds, Sandra strips the patient of his blanket and hospital gown, revealing a man as large and unshapely as Camelback Mountain. His naked body doesn't draw a glance. Using her gloved hands, Sandra lathers the man's penis and testicles with a sudsy pink solution. She pulls the man's penis upward and slides a lubricated catheter through the slit. Gene winces. Sandra bundles the items she's been using and throws them into a large receptacle in the corner. Irene aligns instruments on her adjustable stand. Roger once again taps on his bypass tubing. Gene hardly knows who to watch. Like warm-ups before a game — hitting, fielding, throwing — every player is prepping for the first pitch.

After scrubbing the man's skin with more of the pink solution,

Sandra paints his mountain of flesh with Betadine. Now he is orange-brown from his chin to his knees. Small bubbles slide along the slope of his landscape and then pop. He looks cold.

Dr. Boswell writes in his anesthesia record, pausing every few seconds to glance at his monitors. Sometimes he injects a medication. Sometimes he adjusts a dial on the anesthesia machine, raising or lowering a bullet-sized float in an amber tube. Gene sits on a stool next to him. Each time the ventilator hisses, the bellows drop and the patient's chest rises. As a boy, Gene asked his father to explain what he did at work. "Well," he said, "I put the patient to sleep and then wake them up when we're done."

This is a bit more than put them to sleep. He should have pressed his father more. He should have asked to watch him work. Too late now.

Gene recognizes Dr. Pereira as soon as he backs into the operating room. Water and suds drip off his elbows. Irene hands him a sterile towel.

"Boz," Dr. Pereira says, his mask billowing. "I see the administration has taken my advice and assigned a young man of impeccable character to monitor your activities in the operating room." He dries his hands and arms while he looks at Gene over the top of his half-frame glasses. He's run a length of white tape from earpiece to earpiece over the crown of his surgeon's cap. "Gene, a delight indeed to see you again. How did you fare with your final exams?"

"A draw at best."

"I have no doubt you will emerge the conqueror. So glad to have you with us." He drops the towel to the ground and kicks it aside with his foot.

"But I feel for you, Gene. For the next four hours you must suffer the company of the good Dr. Boswell."

Irene snaps open a sterile gown. Dr. Pereira inserts his arms into the sleeves.

"I take it you've got some history with Rui," Dr. Boswell says.

Gene nods.

"That's a shame."

While Sandra ties Dr. Pereira's gown, Irene curls her fingers under the cuff of a latex glove and stretches it open, the fingers dangling.

"Boz," Dr. Pereira says. "Have you heard this one: How do you know elephants have been making love in your alley?" He thrusts his hand into the glove.

"Gene," Dr. Boswell says. "Do you know anyone telling elephant jokes anymore?"

"Gene?" Dr. Pereira says. "Care to hazard a guess?" Dr. Pereira notices Irene waiting with the second glove and obliges.

"Give up?" He releases the tie-string at his waist and holds it out to Irene, who grasps it while Dr. Pereira pirouettes 360 degrees, drawing the full-length flap around his back. He takes the tie from Irene and ties it in a bow. "All your trash can liners, they are missing."

Gene smiles. His father sometimes prefaced a joke at the dinner table with *I heard this at the hospital.* Gene assumed he meant the doctors' lounge or the diner. He envisioned the operating room as all business. At least it was on television.

When Dr. Harrington backs into the heart room, the chatter halts. He accepts a towel from Irene, and with an elephant's grace and power moves to the X-ray view box, where he examines the films already mounted there. Dr. Harrington has several years on Dr. Pereira. A neat line of silver hair protrudes an inch below the back of his surgeon's cap. Physically, he could have been a former home-run hitter twenty years past his prime — still the broad shoulders and massive forearms, but thick through the middle. "I trust the patient is surviving so fahr," he says in his hypnotic, Southern way.

"Cruising at thirty thousand," Dr. Boswell says.

Dr. Pereira moves to the side of the table opposite Irene. She hands him green towels the size of kitchen towels, and he cordons off a rectangle of skin the length of the man's breastbone. Then they cover it all with what looks like brown-tinted cellophane. With Irene's assistance, Dr. Harrington gowns and gloves. He takes his position next to her and accepts a folded drape. Together, he and Dr. Pereira unfold it the length of the patient, the near end taken by

Dr. Boswell and affixed with clamps to IV poles on either side of the patient's head.

"Gene, you know what this is?" Dr. Boswell says, running his hand along the back of the drape. The top edge comes to Gene's mid-chest. "We call this the blood-brain barrier — the blood on their side, the brains on our side."

Dr. Pereira grins behind his mask. He attaches handles to the two alien-spaceship-looking lights overhead. "Gene, here is a sad truth. Were it not for Dr. Boz's hands, he might be a surgeon today." He focuses the beam of one light onto the man's exposed skin. "But, alas. The cost of manufacturing custom gloves with ten thumbs proved prohibitive."

Using a lap, Dr. Pereira wipes the illuminated narrow rectangle. Dr. Harrington palpates the notch at the top of patient's breastbone — the sternum. "Eugene," he says. "This unfortunate man nearly expired while raking his pink-rock lawn in Sun City. He has elected to have us bypass two blockages in his coronaries so that his dear wife can once again place a rake in his hands." He looks up and laughs, the eyes behind his thick lenses as large as quarters. Then he holds out his right hand. Irene snaps a scalpel's handle against his palm.

In a single, swift stroke Dr. Harrington incises the man's flesh over the length of the sternum down to the bone. Seconds later, the skin and fat bleed. Dr. Pereira touches a wand-like device to the bleeding vessels and steps on a foot pedal. The wand buzzes but nothing happens. "A little higher, if you will, Sandra," Dr. Pereira says.

Sandra turns the dial on a gray box near the foot of the bed. When Dr. Pereira presses the pedal this time, the blood bubbles and pops. As he continues to cauterize the bleeding, a swirling column of smoke rises like an apparition from the charred tissue into the surgical light. The smell is like fat burning on a grill. Gene breathes through his mouth. Dr. Harrington sews the thick skin edge back away from the underlying sternum. Irene then hands him a stainless-steel jigsaw with some sort of guide on the end. The saw connects to a black tank behind him via an air hose.

Starting at the patient's neck, Dr. Harrington angles the saw's blunt tip under the bone and pulls up. When he presses the trigger, the saw whines. He rips along the length of bone, a rooster tail of bone dust trailing the saw as the sternum splits in half. As Dr. Harrington exposes one edge with an angled instrument, Dr. Pereira uses the cautery to char the bleeding marrow. It simmers and pops, the smell like nothing Gene has ever encountered, far worse than an eighteen-wheeler's burned-out brakes. More like the stench he imagines from still images out of Vietnam — naked, smoking, burned-out bodies in a charred village. Breathing through his mouth isn't helping, but Gene doesn't budge from his standing position, looking over the drapes.

The surgeons switch roles. Now, Dr. Harrington begins long continuous torches along the bone's edge.

Jeez, the smell must be entering through his ears.

"Gene," Dr. Boswell says behind him. "You feel okay?"

"Yes, I'm fine."

"Take a seat if you need to." It's Sandra. She's moved behind him with an IV pole and hangs a bottle.

"What's that?"

"Saline." She attaches the tubing and studies him. "Should I hook this up to you instead?"

"I'm fine, okay?"

Irene passes a medieval-looking device to Dr. Pereira. "This is the chest spreader," Dr. Pereira says. Dr. Harrington positions it under the edges of the split sternum, and with a few turns of the crank, the man's chest opens like a carpet bag. The tapered edge of each lung surges from the periphery of the gaping chest, nearly meeting in the middle, before retreating.

Suddenly, heat floods Gene's face.

"You're not a smoker, are you, Gene?" Dr. Pereira asks.

"Smoker?"

"Observe this man's lungs… There… One might postulate he worked in a coal mine."

"What? No."

"To have lungs young and pink. It's a beautiful thing."

"Gene?" It's Dr. Boswell. "Slow your breathing."

"What?"

"Sandy!"

Gene is turning, falling backwards down a narrowing tunnel. He reaches for the IV pole. It falls with him. Someone grabs his arm.

"Gene!"

In an instant, Sandra's masked face, her worried, green eyes fade to darkness.

WHEN HE AWAKES, Sandra gives him some orange juice. He sits against the wall by the OR door as surgery continues in hushed tones and clinking of instruments. Kneeling next to him she says, "That's a new one."

"Fainting?"

"No. We've never had anyone go to ground and take the patient's IV with them." She tells him the glass bottle shattered into several large pieces. Fortunately, he didn't pull the IV catheter out of the patient's arm. Instead, the tubing pulled apart at a junction point. The patient lost a little blood on the floor, but after a short delay, while she and Dr. Boswell hung a new IV, everything was back on track.

"You still look a little pale." She replaces a cold wash cloth on the back of his neck. "You eat this morning?"

"Not much."

"Just sit here for now. We're on bypass."

"I'm sorry," he says.

As the team focuses on their tasks Gene feels invisible. At least to everyone but Dr. Boswell, who calls out from his position behind the blood-brain barrier. "Welcome back, Chief. Glad you could rejoin us."

After a time, Gene rises and sits on a rolling stool by the phone. Between calls for instruments by the two surgeons, who are head to head, hunched over the patient, Irene glances his way.

"Gene," she says.

Her stern tone cuts right to his fear.

"Go home. I'll call you tonight."

He dresses and drags what's left of his dignity back to the Jeep. The black vinyl seat threatens to seer through his slacks. Let it burn, just like his last chance for medical school crashed and burned today. No doubt, Irene's call will be to dis-invite him from the Heart Team. He rests his sore palm on the steering wheel, forgetting it's as hot as a branding iron. "Shit!"

He starts the engine and angles back, but before he shifts into first, before the red dashboard light blinks on again, he spots a large puddle of fluid where he'd parked, as if the Jeep had wet its pants. This isn't how the summer was supposed to start.

The sun presses down with near maximum heat, ricocheting off chrome and glass, and all around the full lot, not a single beating heart, except for Gene's, dares to loll in this no man's land between one air-conditioned sanctuary and another. But he loves it. The superheated air feels like the blank slate of his best summer days. He reaches into the glove box for sunglasses and notices his tattered Citrus Care scheduling book. He pulls it out, flips to August 14, 1971 and reads the entry. And to think, he didn't even know her name.

Chapter Three
WHEN I SAW HER STANDING THERE

August 14, 1971, Phoenix, Arizona

A BEAD of sweat dripped off Gene's stubbled chin and plopped into the can of tree-white paint. He moved the can aside, balanced the wide bristle-brush across the top, and sat cross legged under the navel orange tree's canopy. On the tinny transistor, KCAZ announced the time as four o'clock, the temperature 101, and warned of a possible dust storm. Gene wiped his face and bare chest with his folded t-shirt. After an unending succession of cloudless days, the summer air, usually as still and dry as loneliness, was quickening. Dark clouds stacked one atop the other on the eastern horizon. They were moving west.

For the last couple days, he'd been painting citrus trees on this small tract of new homes. He still needed to meet the owners next door. They hadn't moved in, but it should be soon. The front and back yards were graded, a couple queen palms framed the sidewalk, and the orange trees had been trimmed. With their bare trunks, they looked embarrassingly naked next to Gene's white-clad army. Now, a boss Sapphire Blue Mustang was parked in the drive. Must have arrived while he was taking a piss. After this last tree he'd head over.

He hoisted his thermos and drank the remaining water in long, eager draws. Across the street on the Grant Elementary School ball-field a group of boys yelled *mine, mine, mine* as a fly ball arched their way. A small black dog barked and scampered from batter to fielders. Gene had played the same game — 500 — during his grade school summers. In less than a month, he'd begin his senior year of high school, and this summer, like the previous two, he painted trees. He called his little business *Citrus Care.*

His subdivision and the surrounding neighborhoods had been carved from thirty-year-old orange and grapefruit groves, the surviving trees' canopies trimmed unnaturally to the hip, exposing the trunks. Without a coat of paint, the bark would burn. When he was fourteen his father put him to work on their trees — a small grove of nine in back and four in front.

"These are your trees now," his father had said. "Own them."

Gene had. The immediate neighbors noticed the job and hired him for their trees. Over the summers the business grew from the edges, his services spilling from house to house, and soon included fertilization three times a year. The work was simple and mindless, but he loved the way he felt after a shower, scrubbed of dirt and salt rings, his swollen veins coursing up his arms before diving deep to his heart.

Gene moved his equipment to the last tree. To protect the new grass, he draped an old *Johnny Quest* bedsheet around the trunk's base. Using his father's yellow-handled shop brush, he broke off the suckers, whisked away loose debris from the bark, and then sprayed the bark with a hard stream of water. He applied masking tape eight to ten inches out each main branch and then laid on a thick coat of paint from the base to the tape. When he was done, he peeled the tape away and stood back, admiring today's work, the trees resembling stout young men in white t-shirts, their sleeves bulging at the biceps.

Overhead, the leaves began to rustle. He removed his paint-spotted wide-brimmed hat and looked north toward a solitary, three story eucalyptus — the Big Tree — rising from where the street ended and a dirt path began. The branches at the crown swayed west. This storm would strike soon, but it didn't smell like rain. He wished it did. More likely he was in for a towering dust storm, a fifteen-hundred-foot-high wall of dirt scooped from the surrounding desert and dumped into his family's swimming pool, which he'd have to clean. Better roll it up.

After loading his gear in the rear of his yellow Jeep, he climbed in back and sat under the vinyl canopy, making an entry in a small scheduling notebook.

A cry came from the direction of the ballfield. "Hey, mister! Can you give us a little help?"

Gene looked over and saw the batter tapping his bat on the grass. "I was just getting ready to go home."

"Your dog took our ball," the boy said.

"My dog? What dog?"

"The dog under your Jeep."

Gene hopped out and crouched down. Under the driveshaft, a muscular ink-black mutt the size of a large Chihuahua lay panting with the baseball between its white-stockinged paws. Gene grabbed his lunch pail and enticed it out with a chunk of his mother's apple crisp. He threw the ball back to the kids.

The dog padded in place and licked his chops. No tags. Not even a collar. His belly was caked with mud. Gene gave him the left-over corner crust from lunch and water in a plastic cup. Maybe the Mustang owner knew the dog.

Gene picked him up and hustled to the front door. He rang the doorbell and knocked several times, but nobody answered nor could he see anyone through the window. He jogged to the side of the house, where the gate for the redwood fence had yet to be installed. A gust whistled through the orange trees and whipped his hat from his head, sending it tumbling through the open fence into the back-yard. With stabbing strides, he trapped the hat with his foot. When he looked up, standing at the edge of the rebar-lined pool…was a girl. Her eyes were closed. She fingered the hem of her peach-colored sleeveless top, while the frayed strings of her cutoffs patted her thighs. Her thick dark hair rippled behind her like a beckoning flag. She just stood there as if hypnotized, a slight smile on her face, her slender body braced against the gusts. Later, he would recall that moment as if it were the movie poster for a love story.

Gene called out, "Are you okay?"

She startled and turned.

He shouted again over the wind. "Are you okay?"

She sidestepped to put more of the pool between them.

"I'm looking for the owner. I'm Gene. I was painting trees next door." She took another step back. He looked down at the dog in his arms. "I live about a mile from here." He nodded to the north. "I found this dog. It's lost." She remained silent, studying him.

"You live here?" he said.

"Not yet."

"Do you know who he belongs to?"

She shook her head.

The gusts thrashed the newly planted queen palms into a frenzy. "This is quite a storm. You want to get under cover?" He stepped back, trying to appear less threatening.

She faced the wind. "I love this weather."

"Yeah, it's nice." Gene sidled under the cover of the patio, the house a welcome buttress against the storm. "You go to Central? I don't recall seeing you?"

"We just moved."

Her hair whipped across her face and she swept it back. She was about a head shorter than him. The dog squirmed and barked once.

"Sure you don't want to get out of the wind?"

She shook her head.

"You a senior?"

"Yes"

"Me too!" He smiled and petted the dog's head. "That's got to be tough. I mean moving to a new school your last year."

She looked past him. Gene turned, expecting to see someone

through the Arcadia door, but the family room beyond the glass was empty.

"Hey, I could show you around. You know, before school starts."

She twisted her mouth.

"Just meet there sometime," he said.

"Sure."

"Right on." Gene stepped off the patio, shifted the dog to one side and extended his hand. "I'm Gene, by the way."

A dust devil blasted across the yard. They both turned their backs to the onslaught. Then she rushed past him and onto the patio. He followed and shook the dirt out of his hair. "You okay?"

She nodded while coughing.

"You really should get your Mustang in the garage. I'll give you a hand."

"It's my father's." She tilted her head. "He's working inside on the closets."

Gene looked through the glass. "That's great. I wanted to ask him about painting your trees."

She turned to the yard.

"I paint the trunks white," he said. "To protect them from the sun." He placed a hand on the door.

"Wait," she said. She touched his hand and recoiled as if he was on fire. "Wait here."

"Does he need a hand?"

"Let me check. He's going to be awhile."

"I could give you a lift home. I mean if you don't want to wait."

Uneasiness clouded her blue eyes. A timid smile. It worried him. Maybe her father was a bit of a hard-ass. But Gene was happy to wait. He'd wait forever if it meant driving her home.

"I'll just be a minute," she said and closed the door behind her.

The sky darkened. He looked down at the dog. "What do I do with you?"

He faced the backyard. The storm was peaking, every molecule in the air replaced by dust and leaves and paper debris, reducing his squinting view of the pool to a mirage. The orange trees raked and screamed in gale-force spasms. One of the young queen palms along the fence uprooted and landed at the pool's edge, precisely where the girl had been standing. He smiled, thinking he could tell her he practically saved her life. He leaned against the wall and waited several more minutes before peering through the glass with cupped hands. No movement. Nothing. He checked the sliding door, but it was locked.

"Jeez." With the dog tucked under his arm, he ran around to the front.

The Sapphire Blue Mustang was gone. He stared at the spot where the car had been. A fleeting notion, a desperate hope really, entered his mind: maybe she'd be right back. Then he heard flapping. The Jeep's faded black-vinyl canopy, ripped from its moorings except at one corner, waved in tattered surrender in the waning breeze. Gene placed the dog on the passenger seat and checked the back of the Jeep. The paint-splattered bed sheet had blown against the house next door. He collected it, untied the canopy, and tucked both under the heavy paint can in the rear. Then he brushed dust from the driver's seat and climbed in. The dog, trembling, let out a yip.

Gene felt something new and inchoate, a connection to this girl, so profound and illogical that it must be love. He'd dated other girls in high school — homecomings and proms, a rented tux, close dancing, and a goodnight kiss. But he'd never had a girlfriend. For it seemed the girls he'd been attracted to were either too tall, too beautiful, too full of themselves, or too attached to someone else to give Gene more than a friendly glance. He was the guy they talked to about their guy-problems.

No longer the shortest kid in school, he was just the shortest on the varsity baseball team, embarrassingly listed on the roster as a five-foot-nine, hundred-and-twenty-five-pound pitcher and second baseman. He was, he thought, not unattractive; certainly not a cleft-chinned homecoming-king type, but pleasant enough to be within the margins of this girl's sphere. But what was her sphere? Did she like sports? What were her hopes and desires? He didn't know anything about her, except that she was a senior and ran from him. Was it fear or timidity? Either way her escape was brilliant. And those eyes. He'd seen blue eyes before, but not this color blue. Eyes so blue, if you dove in, you'd never reach the bottom. But more than the color, her eyes ached, practically pleaded for help. And it wasn't just to escape him.

Gene pulled out his scheduling book and wrote a note. He had a feeling he'd want to remember this date: August 14, 1971. The day I first saw…

He looked over at the dog. "I don't even know her name."

Ears cocked and looking at Gene with pleading eyes, the dog whined.

"Mom's gonna have a cow when she sees you," Gene said. But what could he do? Abandon him?

Gene rattled the Jeep's stick into neutral, then completed his entry…*the girl I'll someday marry*. He pressed the accelerator and turned the key. The tachometer leapt.

For the next three weeks, each afternoon after painting trees, Gene ran past her house hoping to see her again. But each day her blue Mustang failed to materialize.

Then on the Saturday of Labor Day weekend with school beginning the following week, he left for his run in the mid-morning. He'd never been much of a runner but had settled into a routine. Already he felt in better condition for the upcoming baseball season. He turned at the dirt path, ran past the Big Tree and skirted around the red and white striped barricade and onto Third Street. Up ahead, at the curb of the girl's house, two men unloaded a couch from the truck of a small local moving company. A woman stood at the front door directing the two men inside. Gene, sweaty, in running shorts and an old Central High baseball practice t-shirt, ambled up the front walkway. He waved to the woman as she accompanied the men back outside. In an instant, he recognized the similarity between the girl's and this woman's dark hair and blue eyes.

She looked suspiciously over Gene's shoulder and then back at him. "Yes, can I help you?" Smiling now.

"I'm Gene Hull. I don't know if your daughter told you about me, but I paint citrus trees. Fertilize, too. I've done the other four homes on this street, and I was wondering if you'd like me to handle yours."

"Oh, so you're the young man who scared her."

Gene's tongue thickens. "I didn't mean to — "

The woman placed a hand on Gene's shoulder and laughed. "I'm kidding. You hardly look the threatening type."

She stepped past the porch and looked left and right down the block. "I wondered why everyone's trees were painted white. Something about the temperature?"

Gene nodded. "It's not so much the temperature. Well, it is the temperature, but also the sun's angle." He used his tanned arms like a drawing compass and pantomimed how the low winter sun skirted under the tree's canopy and struck the trunk.

"You know your trees."

"Yes, ma'am."

"How much?"

For a date with your daughter, he thought, I'll paint them and pay *you*.

"Four dollars a tree. Three to fertilize."

She looked past him. "That was quick."

Gene turned. The Mustang was pulling into the driveway.

The girl eyed Gene a moment and then exited the driver's side and opened the trunk. The rear door opened. A surly-faced boy got out and immediately reached back in for a box.

"Dennis," the woman said. "Put that in the living room for now until they have your bedroom furniture unloaded."

He passed Dennis, a little bulldog-of-a-kid who looked Gene up and down.

"Why does Patty get the biggest room?"

"March," his mother said.

So her name is Patty.

Dennis huffed away. "He's going to be a sophomore." She

pointed to Gene's shirt. "You play baseball at Central? Dennis wants to try out for catcher."

"I'm sorry," he said. "I'm Gene Hull. I didn't catch your name."

"It's Gloria McLellan."

Patty McLellan. Beautiful.

Patty, wearing a tie-dyed t-shirt that fell just short of her knees, carried a stack of hangered clothes.

"Let me help you," Gene said.

"No, I've got it."

"There's more in the trunk if you want to lend a hand," Mrs. McLellan said. Then she called back to Patty. "Are you drinking water?"

"Yes. I'm drinking water," Patty said. She sounded as if she'd been asked that question a hundred times.

Gene, Patty, and Dennis emptied the loaded Mustang of boxes, clothes, and odds and ends, while Mrs. McLellan directed them to this room or that, including Patty's bedroom, one of the rooms that looked out to the ballfield across the street. The powdery aroma of Patty's perfume rose from the armload of clothes he deposited atop her naked mattress.

They made three more trips to empty out a nearby short-stay apartment. Gene sat in back. During one of the drives, Gene asked, "So where's your dad?"

Patty and Dennis looked at each other.

"Probably with his girlfriend," Dennis said.

"Dennis!"

"Jerk," Dennis said.

Patty gave Dennis a hurt look.

"Not you. Dad."

A wave of heat spread up Gene's neck. He looked up at the rear-view mirror. Patty averted her eyes.

"He's in Van Nuys," Dennis said. "Mom divorced him."

Turning to look between the seats, Dennis said, "You're on varsity at Central?"

Gene nodded, thinking about the day of the storm, the day Patty told him her father was inside the house.

"What do you play?" Dennis said.

"Pitcher. Second when I'm not pitching. Your mom says you're a catcher."

"Catcher. First base. I'll play anything to make varsity."

"You may be a year from that. We have a pretty good catcher and first baseman."

Dennis turned back to face straight ahead.

"How about we go to Sluggers sometime?" Gene said. "It's a batting cage."

Dennis glanced over his shoulder. "Right on."

In the rear-view mirror, Gene caught Patty smiling at him.

After he'd carried in the last load, Patty's mother offered a tumbler of ice water in the shade of the porch. "Thought you might like this." And then she passed one to Patty.

"Thanks." He downed the full glass and handed it back. Perspiration bloomed across his back.

Patty held out her full glass. "You want mine?"

"Patty, you should drink that," her mother said.

Gene sensed he shouldn't take it. "No, I'm fine," he said.

Patty handed the glass back to her mother, who then gave Gene an exasperated look. "She's felt a little dizzy lately and — "

"Mom — "

"I was just going to say you're probably a little dehydrated. This heat and all."

"I'm fine. See. I'm standing."

Embarrassed, Gene looked out to the front yard, the newly planted grass, and the five mature orange trees. "About your trees," he said.

"Oh, yes, I'm sorry. Gene. Things are bit chaotic right now. Maybe next summer."

"How about I come over next week and give these in front a quick coat. Just the lower trunks. Free of charge. Move-in special. The ones in back are fairly well shaded by the neighbor's oleanders."

"Well, that's sweet of you. Okay." Her hands rested on Patty's shoulders. She looked at Patty who kept her eyes on Gene. "I don't suppose you'd want to paint this door while you're at it?"

Gene wasn't sure what to make of her request.

"I'm only kidding," she said. "The builder likes it. He calls the color russet." She ran her finger along the door's edge. "I'm just happy we found the place." She looked down at Patty again. "Should we start unpacking?"

Mrs. McLellan went inside. Patty stopped the door from closing behind her. "I gotta go, too," she said and stepped into the air-conditioned entry.

"Patty." Gene stepped forward, and then seeing her shrink away, pulled back. "Would you like to go to a movie or something this weekend?"

She hid behind the door, drowning him with her lagoon blue eyes.

"How about Big Surf? Have you been there?"

She hesitated and shook her head.

"Maybe after school starts," he said.

She gave him a coy smile. "I don't know."

"So maybe, then?" he said.

She eased the door to only a sliver of an opening. "Maybe."

But Gene heard *yes*.

MEETING up with Patty during the school day proved difficult. They didn't share any classes, not even the same lunch period. But knowing her schedule, Gene came up with a plan. As a player on the varsity baseball team, he had PE last period during the off-season. All week he loitered outside the double-wide entrance to the boys' locker room and waited for Patty to walk by on her way to orchestra practice.

It wasn't hard to spot her. She walked with her shoulders pulled back. With each step her knees locked for a brief, wonderful instant. Each day, she approached with a smile. While they talked at the confluence of walkways between gym and music, Patty held her flute case to her chest like a shield, but she never rushed off, never gave Gene any indication that she wished to leave his company until the second bell threatened them with detention.

On Friday, he reminded her about his invitation to Big Surf. "It's like a giant wave machine," he says. "Phoenix's answer to Huntington Beach."

She pursed her lips and twisted slowly from side to side.

"C'mon," he said. "Bring Dennis if you want."

She laughed and tossed her hair back. "Okay, two conditions."

"Name them."

"First. No Dennis."

"That's easy."

"Second. Not until you paint our trees. Remember? You promised you'd paint them this weekend."

"I'll be over at sunrise tomorrow."

BIG SURF WAS CROWDED. The last day of the season and it seemed every junior high and high school student was here celebrating the end of a short first week of classes. Fifteen feet from the water, Gene found an open patch of sand and spread out their beach towels. Patty removed her jean-shorts and gauzy white cover-up. In the powder-blue bikini, her toned figure looked even better than he'd imagined. She put on oversized sunglasses and sat looking out to the water.

That morning he had painted the trunks of all five orange and caught her stealing a glance from her bedroom window. And now, here they were.

"Tic tac?" he said. He held the container out to her.

"Is that peppermint?"

Gene looked at the label and nodded.

"No, thanks. I'll start sneezing and can't stop."

He hoped to kiss her when he took her home, but not with peppermint on his breath.

A six-foot swell grew from the front of the wave-wall painted to look like the ocean's horizon. The wave powered forward, never actually cresting but rolling toward shore as several surfers caught the bump and wobbled on their boards. Every few minutes another wave made its debut, and another row of surfers set off, dodging the bobbing heads in the water.

"Looks fun," she said. "You ever try it?"

The first dew of perspiration stippled her forearms.

"Only on a raft."

She nodded and smiled toward the action in the wading section. Mothers with toddlers raised and lowered their charges as each remnant wave died in ankle deep water. Young girls emitted roller-coaster screams as their boyfriends invented ways to touch and tackle them in the water. A whistle blew from one of the two life-guard chairs, followed by a gesture from the tanned guard to a reckless surfer to paddle over for a lecture.

"You want to cool off?" she said.

Gene left his sunglasses and flip-flops on the towel and waded into waist deep water where a line of orange buoys demarcated surfing from swimming. Patty shivered. "Colder than I thought it'd be," she said. Gene wanted to take her hand, but his courage failed to crest in time. She dropped to her knees, chin deep in the water. "There, that's better."

As they crab-walked parallel to shore, someone bumped into his side and rose, sputtering to the surface.

"Sorry," a guy about Gene's age said. A girl surfaced ten yards away and yelled back. "I win."

"No way," the guy said. "I was interfered with."

"Hey, you bumped into me," Gene said.

"I know," the guy whispered. "But interference means a do over." Then louder toward the girl. "Do over."

"No way. You owe me a Coke."

The guy moved toward the girl. "Sorry, babe. Do over."

Patty waded close to Gene. "What's that about?"

"I think they were trying to see who could swim the farthest underwater."

Patty studied them a minute and began to hyperventilate. After a few seconds, she said, "Like this?" She torpedoed underwater the length of home to first before she surfaced and flipped her hair straight back. "See if you can top that."

Gene soaked up her smile.

As he started to submerge, she called out. "You may want to hyperventilate first."

"No need," he said and took off. He lasted a body length beyond her and blasted to the surface. "You owe me a Coke."

"Hey, we didn't have a bet."

"Do over then. What will it be?

Patty considered this for a moment, looking to their towels on the beach and then out to the facsimile of the southern California sea, as if the answer lay beyond the painted horizon. She looked back tat Gene. "Loser pays for the movie tonight."

Gene straightened. "You asking me out?"

Patty bumped him with her hip. "If your name is Eugene Hull."

Gene wiped away water dripping from his chin. "How'd you know my full name was Eugene?"

Patty's neck reddened. She put her hands up to cover her face and shook her head. Then peeking through her hands, her blue eyes apologized. "Sorry. I looked you up in last year's yearbook. In the library."

It was a moment. Only four weeks ago she'd ran from him. Now she was nudging his hip. Prodding him on.

"You're on, Patricia."

Her eyes widened.

"Wild guess. That's all."

He shook her hand. "You first," he said.

"Hey, that's not fair. You'll have something to shoot for."

"My surf. I'm the home team. I bat last."

She punched his arm. "I'm warning you. Flute players have tremendous breath control." She began her hyperventilation routine.

"I'm warning you. Guys who grow up in Phoenix spend all summer underwater in backyard pools."

She took a last, deep breath, and sped off underwater. Her

strokes were controlled and graceful, her rippling image growing less and less distinct as she moved away. There was no way Gene would win. He wouldn't allow it. It was why he wanted her to go first. As she swam farther away, the water's glare hid her shimmering form, but the movements of other bathers, pointing down, or hopping out of the way, identified her position. Finally, she popped to the surface, waist deep, and whipped her hair back with her hands. She spotted Gene and waved, a gleaming, affectionate smile on her face. In the next second, her smile sagged. She put both hands to head for an instant, and then her eyes rolled upwards as her arms dropped and she sank below the water like a wounded ship.

"Patty!" he screamed. Then to anyone and everyone, "Pick her up! Pick her up! Pick her up!" His heart threatened to burst from his chest as he powered toward her, sloshing through the water. The moment felt like a horrible nightmare, the water's weight preventing him from running at full speed. A lifeguard blasted his whistle again and again. Gene reached her first and grabbed an arm, pulling her head out of the water as a middle-aged woman lifted Patty's other arm.

"Patty. Patty!"

She sputtered and coughed. Her confused eyes looked right through him. She coughed some more. Between heaving breaths, she said, "My head."

A male lifeguard arrived, and with Gene's help, carried her to the beach and their towels. She was breathing normally and tried to sit up, but the lifeguard told her to lie back. Stretched out and breathing normally, Patty rubbed her temples.

"What happened?" the guard said. Bathers formed a circle. The lifeguard stood. "Everybody, please move on. Give us some room, please. Everything's fine." As the crowd dispersed, the lifeguard knelt again, and took Patty's pulse.

"She was swimming underwater," Gene said, "and when she came up, she collapsed."

"My head hurts," she said.

A female lifeguard arrived with a beach umbrella and positioned it to give them shade. "Hyperventilation syncope?" the woman asked.

"The male lifeguard asked, "Did you take a lot of deep breaths before going under?"

Patty nodded. Her eyes were closed. "I think it's a migraine. I feel kind of sick."

"You have migraines before?" the man asked.

Patty nodded again. "Where are my sunglasses?"

Gene found them in her shoulder bag and handed them to her.

"You shouldn't hyperventilate like that before diving. Do it long enough, and you'll faint. We've seen it before."

Gene never had, but his mother had given him the same warning years ago.

"Can that bring on a migraine?" he asked.

The lifeguard shrugged. "I suppose it could."

"I just need to lie down in the dark," Patty said.

Gene collected their belongings, ran them out to the Jeep, and drove up to the turnstile exit, where Patty was sitting on a bench, slouched, yet aided by a lifeguard. Gene dropped the passenger seat, and Patty got in. On the drive back to her house, with her eyes closed behind sunglasses, she said, "Gene?"

"You okay?"

"I will be. I just wanted to say, I owe you a movie."

He couldn't speak. Moment by moment he was falling more and more in love with this girl.

STEADYING her with one arm around her back and his other hand under her elbow, Gene walked Patty to her front door. She felt weak in his arms. The door was locked, but after ringing the bell, her mother answered. She smiled, then quickly sagged. "Oh, Patty. Not again."

Together, they guided Patty to her bed. Gene stepped back into hallway. Mrs. McLellan removed her daughter's flip-flops and whispered, "I'll be right back with a washcloth, Honey," and turned out the light.

Gene sat at the breakfast alcove. Minutes later, Mrs. McLellan joined him and offered a soda. He accepted and gazed out the window. The swimming pool had been recently filled and reminded him of the moment he'd first seen Patty. Mrs. McLellan poured herself a cup of coffee. "Gene, I wasn't thinking. Would you prefer coffee?"

"No, thanks," he said raising the can of Fresca. "This is great."

She sat opposite him and looked out to the backyard, her hands cradling her cup. "A few months ago, I thought we'd beaten these migraines." She took a sip and sighed. "But apparently not."

She carried the conversation, looking at Gene only occasionally, not out of anger or disappointment, Gene sensed, but because she was picturing moments in Patty's life he'd yet to know. And he wanted to learn it all. So far, he only knew that her parents had divorced, she had migraines, and peppermint gave her sneezing fits.

"Maybe it was the move," Mrs. McLellan said. "Or the divorce. I guess you heard about my divorce."

Gene nodded.

"Ever since we moved to Phoenix, Patty's headaches are back in force. She's weak. Sometimes faint. I keep thinking it's the heat. She's getting tired of me constantly pestering her about drinking more water. My God, my sister said it was hot, but she also said I'd get used to it." She took another sip of coffee. "I'm not so sure. Don't get me wrong. Apart from the heat, I love it here. It's not nearly as congested as Van Nuys, and the cost of living is less, and we're near my sister and her family, which is nice for Patty and Dennis, but I wonder if I would have actually moved here if I'd visited Peg in the summer." She tapped her index finger on the table to some inner rhythm. "Of course, I would. It's what my kids wanted, and what is love if it's not sacrificing for your children." She gave Gene a trembling smile. "So, tell this loving mother what happened."

Gene recounted the day and the suddenness of Patty's decline, wondering if Mrs. McLellan blamed him as he blamed himself for the silly underwater swimming game.

"I'm glad you were there." She studied Gene for a moment. "There are some people in life, whom, from the moment you meet them, you feel comfortable. I can't explain it, but it's a kind of trusting presence. And you have that."

Gene's face flushed.

"I'm probably way out of line here," she said. "But I have a feeling you're good for my daughter. You're exactly who she needs in her life now." Mrs. McLellan's expression became stern and inward looking. "The total opposite of her creep of a father." She took a deep breath and looked to the ceiling. After a moment, she shook her head and wiped tears from her cheeks.

"I should probably go," he said.

"What time is it?"

Gene checked his watch. "A little after four."

"Close enough." She retrieved a half-full bottle of wine from the kitchen counter along with two juice glasses and returned to the table. She poured. "You're nineteen, right?" She winked.

"No thanks."

She drained half her glass. "I divorced Husband-of-the-Year Frank after I found out he was having an affair. Turned out scuba diving wasn't so much his hobby as running around with a blonde from the office."

Gene shifted in his seat.

"I'm sorry," Mrs. McLellan said. "I shouldn't…" She took another sip and then tipped her glass toward him. "See. There's something about you. You're too good a listener."

Gene offered an embarrassed smile.

Suddenly, Mrs. McLellan's eyes widened. She looked past Gene. "Patty, what is it?"

Gene whipped around. Dressed in her nightgown, Patty stood in the middle of the family room holding her head, her face contorted and pained. She tried to say something, but her words stretched loose and wobbly as putty. Mrs. McLellan rushed toward her and together they collapsed to the floor. She screamed, "Gene!"

He jumped from his seat, sending soda splattering against the wall. Patty's gaze ratcheted across the room. She moaned with each quick breath. Her mother held her head and wailed. "Call an ambulance! Call and ambulance!"

Gene fumbled with the wall phone and dialed. On the other end it rang once, twice…Please be home. Please be home….a third time. "Dad! Patty's in trouble."

"Who's Patty?"

"A girl, Dad. *The* girl."

Chapter Four

LIKE A PLUNGE INTO AN ICY LAKE

Just before noon, Gene unlocks the back door from the garage to the kitchen. Apollo greets him with frantic tail wagging.

"Hey buddy," Gene says. "Bet you didn't think I'd be back this soon." Apollo pads in place on the tiled floor. "Me either."

Part Chihuahua, part honey badger, Apollo is twenty pounds of muscle wrapped in a short, black coat. He has slept between Gene's feet each night since he returned home from Cal Poly for the summer, just like he did the day he rescued him, the day he fell in love with Patty. After no one claimed him from the lost-dog fliers, Gene kept him and named him for the space program. His mother said, "So you take care of him for a year and go off to school. Then he's my problem." Just like her to lay on a guilt trip.

After slinking from the hospital, Gene topped up the radiator and then sweated out his disappointment, anger, embarrassment, whatever it was, at Sluggers in the expanding heat. He needed some time in the cage, blistering fastballs past the pitching machine. It was something familiar. Like painting citrus trees. He wishes now he hadn't sent that "retirement" letter to all his clients. No doubt Irene will call tonight, give him a nice-try speech, but tell him he didn't make the team.

Gene sets his keys and tie on the circular oak breakfast table. He hangs the white coat across the rail of a ladder-back chair. His dress shirt, still soaked, sticks to his skin. He pauses. Brings the coat's collar to his nose, hoping for whiff of his father's aftershave. Nothing.

He checks the answering machine on the kitchen secretary. One message. He holds his breath and hits Play.

"Gene, I don't know where my head is, I forgot a couple important things. That Arcadia door in the kitchen sticks. You've got to really force it to close that last little bit. We don't need to be cooling down all of Phoenix. You should see my electric bill as it is!

I almost forgot. Did you bring that trap home with you? I'm tired of that damn cat leaving headless birds all over my backyard. It's like some kind of Hitchcock movie. Apollo brings them inside. He thinks he's doing me a favor. Last week I found one in my tub. I wish I'd remembered to ask you. I really wanted to see it. It sounded fascinating. An infrared activated trap. And your invention to boot. You're a marvel.

I'll write and send pictures of little Carlton. Hope you had a good first day. I'm sure you did. This will be good for you…working with Rui and Dr. Harrington. You'll stay busy. Maybe a nurse's aide will steal your heart, and you'll finally forget about Patty.

Okay, my flight is boarding. For thirty years, I've wanted to get out of the heat. Finally. Finally. Love you."

Gene clicks the off button. She never accepted Patty for reasons only her twisted brain understood.

He looks down at Apollo. "Catch any cats lately?" At the word "cat" Apollo freezes and cocks his head. "Don't worry. We'll get her cat." And send it to her.

He pours a tall glass of ice water, sits and rereads the three pages of instructions written in his mother's impeccable cursive. No stone unturned, she liked to say. She said plenty this morning while scurrying about in preparation for today's flight. Her nonstop chatter made it impossible to concentrate. By now she should be pestering Suzanne and Rodney.

Let's see, there's the trash schedule, the pool maintenance and lawn mowing (his chores through high school), the freezer contents (spaghetti sauce, briskets, those horrible steak sandwich things you like), how the washer worked, which soap to use, how the milk was no longer delivered to the front door, when the sprinklers come on, the watering schedule for the hanging plants on the patio, Apollo's feeding schedule, including where to place the bowls, and a list of specific cleansers for just about every different surface in the kitchen. It goes on and on.

He skips to the last item: Don't forget to check on the irrigation. You know where the board is. It posts every seven days. An hour of water seems to be enough. We're lucky to be on a weekend schedule now. But if you happen to be at work, maybe Doris next door can open the valve.

That's the one thing he won't forget — water for his trees. He Frisbees the pages across the table. A page flutters to the floor. He looks around the kitchen. A clock ticks two rooms away. Apollo stirs at Gene's feet. "What do you and Mom do all day around here?" Apollo offers a deep sigh. Great. A summer of house chores and silence. His few close friends are out of town, no trees to paint, and no Patty McLellan. Gene downs his ice water.

Might as well stay busy until Irene calls. He picks up the page from the floor. "Let's start with the pool. You swim. I'll sweep."

While Gene sweeps the pool, he tosses Apollo's tennis ball into the water more than two-dozen times. Then they walk down to the irrigation board and sign up for an hour of water this weekend. Worn out, Apollo sleeps under the kitchen secretary while Gene mows the front lawn and puts out the trash can. Finally, now that he has a screwdriver, he tightens the radiator hose clamp and makes a trip to Checker for coolant.

After dinner he takes his live trap out to the patio. While only a simple intro-to-engineering project his freshman year, it saved him some money. His landlord knocked a half month off his rent for clearing out the stray cats around the complex. He looks around the yard. He's not seen any headless birds. His mother is no doubt exaggerating, but he'll catch her cat nonetheless. The nine-volt battery is dead. After replacing it, a wave of his hand across the infrared beam drops the gate.

Damn, he wishes Irene would call and get it over with. Apollo follows him upstairs and plops onto the bed. Gene exits through his bedroom window with a Michelob and folded aluminum chair. He steps onto the roof, to the eight by twelve plywood deck he built in stages during high school. He should have turned the light on in the pool. The shimmering blue glow looks cool from up here. No Giants' game tonight. They played this afternoon in Atlanta. And lost. Figures. Two blocks away, the ballfield lights are on in front of Patty's mother's house. A cheer carries through the hundred-degree air.

He's two swigs into the beer when the phone rings. Gene walks back and reaches through the window to the extension on his desk. It's Irene.

"Gene, I called earlier to tell you not to come in tomorrow, but you didn't answer."

"I must have been outside."

"Good thing. Rui changed my mind."

"Dr. Harrington's okay with this?"

"We have two cases tomorrow. If Sandra, Boz, or anyone tells you to sit, then sit."

"Yes."

"You could have contaminated the field."

"Thank you."

"And eat breakfast tomorrow."

No doubt his father's blood inoculated him from a quick exit. He's just not sure how far that immunity reaches, nor does he want to test it again.

Dr. Boz anesthetizes the patient with the same send-off as yesterday — "Say goodnight, Irene" — and once again tells Sandra to work her magic. With the patient's heel resting on Betty's shoulder, Sandra scrubs the patient's left thigh up to the blue towel that covers his scrotum.

"Sandra," Dr. Boz says. "How much do you charge for that? Gene, here would like to get your card."

"I don't believe that for a minute," she says. "Gene's too much the gentleman."

As she finishes, she looks over and smiles with her eyes. Jeez, he can't remember if he thanked her for her concern yesterday.

When he first entered the room today, Irene reminded him to stay close to the rolling stool in Dr. Boswell's domain. But when Boz arrived, Gene pushed the stool to the wall so he wouldn't be tempted to sit. No fainting today.

Once the draping is complete, Dr. Harrington incises the skin. As Dr. Pereira cauterizes the bleeding edges, Gene begins mouth breathing.

"Here, let's lather you up," Dr. Boz says. He shows Gene a small bottle of peppermint flavoring, and then places a dab on the front of Gene's mask. Patty would have run for the door.

Gradually Gene shifts to breathing through his nose, the peppermint aroma mostly blocking the burning-fat smell. Dr. Harrington takes the jigsaw from Irene, taps his foot a few times, and then exhales sharply. "Sandra, is it your intent to hide the pedal?"

"Sorry." She finishes opening a sterile pack for Irene, hustles around to Dr. Harrington's side, and crouches from view. "It's right here."

Dr. Harrington revs the saw with two coarse bursts and then hooks the blade under the patient's sternum. Gene shifts his weight and swallows hard.

Dr. Boz leans into him and whispers, "*Timmberrr.*"

Gene glares at him. "I'm fine."

Boz slaps him on the back. "Just checking."

Gene rolls the stool a little closer anyway.

The surgeons split the sternum, char the bone's raw edge, and, after several cranks on the spreader, open the man's chest and prepare for bypass. During this time, another surgeon, Dr. Brinkerhoff, a rotund man with bushy, gray sideburns, toils to the left of Dr. Pereira. Curled over the patient's leg, he dissects a vein, tying off the tributary veins as he goes. When he's done, he hands one end of the sixteen-inch vein segment to Irene, who pinches the end with her fingers. Dr. Brinkerhoff attaches a saline-filled syringe to the other end and checks for leaks. After a couple tributary repairs, the long vein bulges, holding firm.

"Looks good here, Lee," he says.

Dr. Brinkerhoff backs from the table. "Have your girl give me a call when you're ready for the next case."

"Brink?" Dr. Boz says. "We still on for Friday?"

"Long as you don't crap out on me again."

"Katie doesn't get back until seven in the evening."

"I don't know who you're kidding."

"As long as she thinks I'm only riding the back roads I'm fine."

"Suit yourself. It's going to be hot — 105. You up for that?"

Gene's not quite sure what kind of ride Dr. Boz is talking about, only that he's hiding it from someone, a wife perhaps. Gene's mother didn't know his father was on the helicopter that crashed.

"Gene," Dr. Pereira says, reaching up to the sterile handle. He focuses the surgical light into the cavity. "Lean in. You cannot see from there. I will give you a tour."

Edging closer, he places his fingers lightly on top of the drape.

"Gene," Irene says, latching onto his eyes. "Careful."

Gene backs off. The woman misses nothing.

Dr. Boz raises the drape another few inches so it comes to Gene's upper chest. "You can look over. Just keep your arms back."

Gene's view of the open cavity is incomplete, but he can see most of the heart. It rests in a kind of tissue hammock. It isn't ruby red like in drawings, but is covered with a thick, glistening layer of yellow-white fat.

"We have already opened the pericardial membrane," Dr. Pereira says. Using long forceps, he points to it — the thing Gene thought looked like a hammock. As he works, Dr. Pereira identifies the anatomy. He and Dr. Harrington insert cannulas, tubes a little narrower than Gene's little finger, into the superior and inferior vena cavas. Using a loop of suture, they fasten each cannula in place and then attach them to the sterile end of the clear tubing running through Roger's heart-lung machine. All of this information whizzes at Gene like ninety-mile-per-hour fastballs. One step blends to the next and the next and the next. Even if he had a notepad and pen, he couldn't keep up with the three pairs of hands moving with the synchrony of a Giant's 6-4-3 double play.

Dr. Harrington punches a hole in the aorta with something like an awl. Blood spurts from the hole. Gene flinches. Dr. Pereira cups his hand over the pulsing jet. In an instant, Dr. Harrington inserts a cannula (smaller than the ones in the vena cavas) into the hole. Again, using a couple loops of suture, Dr. Pereira cinches the cannula secure and then attaches it to another segment of clear tubing.

"There you go, Gene," Dr. Pereira says. "We are ready for bypass."

This is like nothing he's ever seen. Deep within the rib's cage, naked and shimmering under the harsh light, the heart rocks with each beat. The rhythmic motion lends it a sentient quality. A kind of being itself, awake and unfazed by the anesthetic which has rendered the larger being unconscious. The surgeons have prepared this smaller, more resilient soul for bypass, but with the cannulas strapped to its limbs, each contraction looks like a struggle, as if the heart is trying to escape its bonds. It's practically pleading for help.

Dr. Harrington turns around where Sandra waits. While she removes his reading glasses and replaces them with shot-glass-like magnifying lenses, Dr. Pereira asks, "Gene, how is it that while Roger's machine perfuses the brain, the kidneys, and other organs, we can isolate the heart, arrest it, and restart it later? Perhaps you know this."

His father had never explained it to him. Gene shrugs.

"Supply and demand," Dr. Pereira says. "The heart demands oxygen. Its supply of oxygen is delivered by the blood. Stop the heart from beating, and it needs less oxygen. Chill it to ten degrees — that is Celsius, my American friend — and it needs even less. That is a beautiful thing, because we are about to place an embargo on its supply. There are more complicated aspects of myocardial preservation during surgery, but at its simplest, the same principles apply here as when someone is revived after being pulled lifeless from an icy lake."

"We're good here," Dr. Boz says.

"Roger?" Dr. Harrington asks.

"Ready."

Gene glances at Roger. With his clamps in hand, he looks like a drummer poised behind his drum kit.

"On bypass," Dr. Harrington orders.

Roger eases a black knob on the machine, and Gene follows the blood's course as it flows from the patient's chest through the clear bypass tubing, pushing the saline ahead of it, toward Roger and his bypass machine. The advancing red wave circles through the rotary pump and cascades down the large radiator-like canister — the lungs of the machine — and then, after dividing through other devices, merges and ascends back through a single tube over the draped chest before disappearing into the patient's aorta.

After a minute, Roger says, "We're at full flow."

"Cross clamp on," Dr. Harrington says. He ratchets a clamp's rubber-encased jaws across the aorta, pinching the large vessel closed. Just below the clamp, he sticks a needle into the aorta and injects the contents of a syringe.

"Cardioplegia," Dr. Pereira says. "It contains potassium chloride to stop the heart."

That it does, as if responding to a command from a backyard game Gene played as a child: Freeze!

Dr. Harrington pours a pitcher of iced saline into the bowl of the chest. The heart does look like someone at the bottom of an icy lake. Gene lets out a breath.

"The clock ticks," Dr. Pereira says.

"What do you mean?" Gene asks.

"The heart, she can only hold her breath for so long." Dr. Pereira suctions the saline from the well, reaches up, and focuses the light to a fine beam over the heart. "The time on bypass is critical. Too long, and the heart may not start up again. Peanut." Irene already has a stiff cotton bullet clamped into a long hemostat's tip. She slaps it to his palm.

"Then what?" Gene says.

Dr. Harrington lays the vein that Dr. Brinkerhoff had excised across the heart.

"Then we are up to our ankles in alligators," Boz says.

Dr. Harrington cuts off a section of the vein. He and Dr. Pereira are forehead to forehead, nearly mask to mask as they work. There's a distinct shift in their demeanor. They could be defusing a bomb. Gene turns to Dr. Boz. "How long does bypass last?"

"As short as possible."

"How long?"

"For a cabbage? Less than an hour."

"Cabbage?"

"Coronary artery bypass graft. C…A…B…G. Cabbage." He nods to the opposite end of the room. "Sandra's our timekeeper."

Gene looks over to Sandra leaning against the table by the phone. She must have heard Dr. Boz because she unfolds her arms and, like a game show hostess, points to the large analog timer above her head. A cute gesture. The timer's second-hand sweeps silently, steadily around.

Using long forceps, Dr. Pereira names the arteries — left main, anterior descending, circumflex — and points to where the blockages lie. Dr. Harrington sutures a small segment of vein to the aorta using a curved needle the size of a parentheses. Stitch by stitch, Dr. Pereira keeps the suture taught. Then they connect the other end of the vein segment past the blockage in the artery. To get to the next two blockages, they roll the heart to its right and stuff a lap under it, like using a pillow to prop someone on his side.

Hardly a word is said between Irene, Dr. Pereira and Dr. Harrington as clamps, scalpels, and hair-thin suture pass between them. They communicate in a silent language. Gene admires their economy of motion, their focus. Except for Dr. Pereira's comment about the heart holding her breath, it is clear that once bypass begins, they have no time for sentimental thoughts. This heart is an engine with bad plumbing. They had two hearts with the same problem yesterday and perhaps more later this week. It is work to them. The seemingly simple, mechanical nature of the repair is appealing. Their every move is coordinated, practiced, precise, and it carries Gene along by a kind of Venturi effect. He takes a slow breath and shudders at a thought. He would have loved to have seen Patty's heart.

"Cross clamp off," Dr. Harrington says.

Sandra looks at the timer. "Fifty-eight minutes."

The heart, previously motionless, now shivers. Irene hands Dr. Harrington two black paddles that look like salad tongs. He places them on each side of the heart. A dull pop follows. The heart flexes and then begins to beat. But the beats are slow and weak.

"You know how wiped out you feel when you just wake up in the morning?" Dr. Boz says to Gene.

"I usually feel pretty good."

"Well, you're still young." Dr. Boz turns a small wheel on one of the IVs. It begins to drip. "We're going to wake this heart with a little nuclear caffeine." He looks over the drape. "Epi's running," he says to the surgeons.

"Epi?" Gene asks.

"Epinephrine…adrenalin," Dr. Boz says.

Minutes later, after some back-and-forth conversation between Dr. Harrington and Dr. Boswell concerning flow rates, fluid boluses, FFP, and other things Gene doesn't understand, Roger says, "We're off bypass."

Dr. Harrington removes the cannulas from the heart and passes the bypass-tubing off the table. Before the chest spreader is removed, Gene takes a last look at the heart. Its beats are no longer labored. They are crisp, like fingers snapping to one of the upbeat, big-band tunes his father loved.

The surgeons close the chest by looping heavy gauge stainless steel wires around the man's sternum, threading the wire between the ribs and then cinching the two halves of the sternum together. Dr. Harrington twists the wire using a blunt-nose clamp, the ring handle making popping sounds against his latex gloves as he tugs and twirls the instrument until the wire is a tight, six-or-seven-layer twist against the bone. Then Dr. Pereira cuts the waste end of the wire, leaving a three-quarter-inch tag. Using the wire holder, he buries the tag end between the sternal halves.

"Will those come out?" Gene asks.

"Only if we have to," Dr. Pereira says.

Dr. Harrington removes his gown and gloves and lumbers toward the desk by the phone. "Eugene," he says. "If those wires (it sounds like why-yahs) get infected, we'll know who put the hex on them." He sits at the desk and opens the patient's chart. A broad sweat stripe imprints the back of his scrub shirt.

Irene scoots her six-inch platform (a custom job of varnished wood with a black, non-skid surface) over to where Dr. Harrington had been standing and assists Dr. Pereira as he closes the tissue between the skin and bone. Then they pull the sticky drape off the skin, and with a wet lap, Irene wipes the open wound free of blood. She slaps a needle holder in Dr. Pereira's palm, who begins closing the skin. Irene blots away any bleeding ahead of him.

"Your impressions, Gene?" Dr. Pereira says.

"Pretty amazing."

"Surgery?...or that Boz stayed awake?"

Dr. Boz stands. "It's amazing I stay awake during your skin closures."

"He feels I devote too much attention to this last crucial step."

"Crucial?" Dr. Boz asks.

"*Sim*. Days, weeks, or years from now, my young Gene, the patient will gaze upon this fine suture line, this thin, white scar. It is perhaps one-tenth percent of the surgery. But it is the last part. The only visible part. It is the surgeon's signature. And from it, the patient will form a judgment. He will think, What a fine surgeon my doctor is."

"You mean Dr. Harrington?" Dr. Boz says.

"All the more important I leave a favorable impression," Dr. Pereira says.

"Maybe you could put a little giddyap in your signature, so I can get this guy to the Unit." Dr. Boz sits back down and charts numbers and comments on the anesthesia record attached to a clipboard. Then he puts down his pen and looks over at Gene, seated on the stool.

"Congratulations," Dr. Boz says.

"For what?"

"You made it. Skin to skin without hitting the deck."

"I did, didn't I?"

Gene looks up to the EKG. An audible beep punctuates each peak of the waveform. A little over thirty minutes ago the machine was silent, the flat green line the electrical signature of a heart that looked as limp and pale as Gene felt yesterday. Yet when Dr. Harrington applied the paddles and shocked it, the heart beat. It had occurred to Gene that it might not. But something about the tenor of the heart room, the casual confidence maybe, diminished that possibility. There must be times, though, when it didn't. The heart, she can only hold her breath for so long.

Chapter Five

PLUCKING A PEARL FROM AN OYSTER

GENE SPED his father's Saab to the hospital, repeatedly looking in the rear-view mirror. Patty was in back, her eyes closed, her head resting on his father's shoulder. Mrs. McLellan, on Patty's other side, stroked her daughter's arm. They were silent for the most part, except when Patty whimpered and Gene's father reassured her with words Gene couldn't hear. Oh, how he wished he was the one in the back seat with her. At least he'd helped by throwing her bathrobe over her as they left the house. He looked in the mirror again and caught his father's eye.

"Slow down a little," his father said. "We're okay back here."

It hadn't seemed that way at first. Mrs. McLellan was in a panic until Patty's speech miraculously recovered in the minutes before Gene's father arrived. That he was home when Gene called was another miracle. He'd just returned from the hospital after a case. Once Gene mentioned headache and trouble speaking, Gene's father cut him off and asked for directions. He was there in less than two minutes, felt Patty's pulse, asked her Gene's name, the city she lived in, and the year, questions she stumbled to answer in a weak voice. Then he calmly said, "Help me get her in the car."

At the Emergency Room entrance, an attendant was taking a

smoking break. Gene's father called out for him to bring a wheelchair. Together, they wheeled Patty through the double door toward the admitting clerk. "Knudson here?" his father asked.

"All night," the clerk said. She started to hand him a clipboard.

"I need him to see her, pronto." He nodded down to Patty, who sat slumped in the chair, her head bowed to one hand.

"Go," the clerk said. "Room Two. I'll get him." She lifted the receiver on the intercom.

There were perks being a physician in need of help at the hospital where you work. Gene had first noticed this when he broke his arm a few years before. Paperwork could wait. Lines could be jumped.

Gene started to follow his father, Patty, and her mother into the belly of the ER, when his father turned. "Best you wait here." Gene must have shown his disappointment. His father put a hand on his shoulder and leaned in. "Family only at this point. Besides, you need to move the car. I'll be out as soon as I know something."

Gene parked the car and ran back inside the chilly waiting room. For over an hour he paged through every magazine he could find and was back to where he started with a month-old issue of *Sports Illustrated*. The one with Fergie Jenkins on the cover. The TV silently displayed an *All in the Family* rerun. Two seats away, a baby cried as her mother teared and bounced her on her lap. Earlier, a young boy had sat there with his father and pressed a bloodied dish towel to his nose. Each time the door to the exam rooms opened, Gene got a hitch in his breath, hoping to see his father's smile. Please, a smile. The door opened again, but this time it was the boy, now being wheeled out with a schnoz full of gauze.

Gene moved to the soda machine and inserted twenty cents. He gave the Coke button a steady look before choosing Mountain Dew. The can clattered to the outlet.

"Gene."

He whirled around. "Dad!" His father wasn't smiling.

He motioned for Gene to come over and take a seat.

"She'll be staying at least one night. Knudson thinks it's consistent with migraines, but he wants to rule out some other things, like meningitis." He placed his elbows on the metal armrests and tapped his fingertips together. His jaw muscles were working overtime. Gene had seen this countless times before, like when the garbage disposal failed and when the car's engine stalled on a climb through a desert mountain range.

"But you think it's something else?"

"Zem's still in house working on our patient from earlier. I asked him if he'd take a look at Patty."

"Who?"

"Dr. Zemlicka. Chief of Cardiology."

"Her heart?"

"I'm going to run up to the ICU while he's with her. Hang in there." He patted Gene's thigh before striding back through the double doors.

Gene stared at the chilly can in his palm, wishing they'd never raced underwater.

Another tortured couple of hours passed. Just as Gene returned from the men's room, Patty's mother walked through the double doors with Gene's father, his arm around her shoulders while she dabbed her eyes. The sight of her crying hit him in the chest like a fastball. His father mouthed to him — it's okay.

His father and Mrs. McLellan sat on each side of Gene. He looked from one to the other. Then Mrs. McLellan, clutching her tissue in her lap, sat Emily Post straight and took a deep breath. She conjured a brave smile, and patted Gene's bare thigh. "Your father just saved my daughter's life."

His father shook his head. "I didn't save her life. I had a hunch. Dr. Zemlicka figured it out. He did an echo. She has an atrial myxoma."

"A what?" Gene said.

Mrs. McLellan nodded. "That's what I said."

"A tumor in her heart. It's probably been growing for years, but now it's causing a problem. She likely had a small stroke tonight."

"She's too young," Gene said. "I don't get it."

"A small piece of the tumor or a small clot likely broke free and traveled to her brain. It seems to have resolved. Knudson doesn't detect any deficit. The big risk is that it could happen again. A bigger stroke *or worse*."

Gene wasn't going to follow the path to or worse, nor did he want Mrs. McLellan to.

"She needs surgery," Mrs. McLellan said.

Gene looked back to his father. "So they'll cut it out. Game over. Patty wins. Right?"

Mrs. McLellan gave a short laugh. "I like your attitude. You sound like the heart surgeon. He said it's like removing a pearl from an oyster."

"Dr. Harrington was upstairs," Gene's father said. "He came down and examined Patty as well. She's scheduled for tomorrow."

"Sunday!" Gene looked to Mrs. McLellan. She was biting her lower lip.

"Dennis is at a friend's," she said. "He'll stay there tonight." Then she rolled her eyes. "Who knows if her father can get here in time."

On the drive home, Gene's father assured Mrs. McLellan again that the surgery was straightforward. "How can I thank you?" she said. "If you hadn't stuck with your intuition, Patty might have walked out of the ER, and who knows…" She covered her mouth and cleared her throat. "Who knows what might have happened."

Gene walked her to the door while his father sat in the car. After she turned on a light, she faced Gene. "See you tomorrow?"

"Of course."

She waved to the car and paused.

"I'll just keep telling myself 'They cut it out. Patty wins.'"

She kissed Gene's cheek and walked inside.

Later, lying in his darkened bedroom, the gravity of the day weighed on him. Through tears, he wondered how he could feel so much love — and so much fear — for a girl with whom he'd yet to complete a first date.

His father tapped on the door and opened it a crack. The hallway light leaked around his silhouette. "You awake?"

"Yeah."

"I need to make rounds before Patty's case, so I might be gone when you get up. Just wanted to let you know I'll take good care of her for you."

Oh, how his father knew him. It's exactly what he needed to hear.

Gene squeaked out a *thanks*.

"Goodnight," they both said.

So, what was he to Patty? Friend? Acquaintance? Tree painter? Certainly not boyfriend. He hadn't even kissed her yet. Her mother has kissed him though. He smiled and glanced at Mrs. McLellan seated next to him, working her needlepoint project. Then he looked across to Mr. McLellan who yawned while reading a hunting magazine. No, according to this guy, Gene was the kid who nearly killed his daughter. His only daughter. A girl, who will now miss the first quarter if not the first semester of her senior year.

From the sterile silence of this small waiting area, Gene could see the automatic glass doors with *Operating Room Attire Only* printed in threatening, black letters on the glass. He checked his watch (nearly one p.m.) and shifted in the vinyl chair. It complained, triggering another look, or more like a condescending stare, from Patty's father.

After he'd gotten the call from Mrs. McLellan, Mr. McLellan had driven all night from Van Nuys. He didn't have time to shower or shave. And the man's densely shadowed cleft chin rekindled all the anger Gene once felt toward a certain dim-witted upperclassman: a lineman on varsity who validated his worth by hazing Gene with a jockstrap to his face when he was a freshman. At least that's how Gene's father had explained it to him.

Floating in this relationship no-mans-land, Gene had timed his arrival at the hospital to allow the McLellans a private moment before Patty was wheeled across the operating suite threshold. He was there, though, when Dr. Harrington lumbered past. Gene had met the surgeon a couple times, but Dr. Harrington didn't recognize him. In his soothing Southern drawl, he said, "Shouldn't take long. We're gonna open her hahrt and pluck out the pearl."

That had been three hours ago.

"They might at least give us a status report," Mr. McLellan said.

"It doesn't work that way," Mrs. McLellan said.

"She couldn't keep her eyes open," he said. "Maybe the anes-tho-gist gave her too much and can't wake her up." He smirked at Gene.

"Frank!" Mrs. McLellan gave him a hard look. "They're done when they're done. Game over. Patty wins. Isn't that right, Gene?" She smiled.

Gene nodded. Then he dropped his head and whispered, "It's anesthesiologist."

Mr. McLellan leaned forward. "Say something?"

"Nope." Rhymes with dope.

F-wing was at the east end of the hospital, and during the day, the sun's burning rays had heated the room. The floor-to-ceiling drapes were still closed across the room-wide picture window. Using his hand, Gene tested whether heat still radiated through the drapes — only a little — while his thoughts drifted here and there, finally settling on a horrible image: Dr. Harrington taking a seat next to Mrs. McLellan, cradling her hand between his large mitts, and saying, We did everything we could.

Gene blinked the thought away. He turned to Mrs. McLellan. "I'm heading down to the diner. Want anything?"

"Thank you. Coffee. Black." Her eyes were focused on the needlepoint project, music-themed throw pillows for Patty's bed. This one was a large treble clef. The intensity of her stitching made Gene wonder if she had a superstition going: if I can get to the curlicue, then Patty will be fine. It was the kind of thing Gene did before baseball games. If I can make every green light, I'll throw a no hitter. He could never time them perfectly.

"You might want to stop by the lab and get checked for tape worms," Mr. McLellan said. He looked up, laughed, and went back to his magazine. "What's this, your fourth trip?"

"Frank!...Gene, don't listen to him. He says stupid things when he's tired."

Patty's dumbass father turned the page to a photo of a felled buck elk. "I was very tired the night I proposed to you." He smirked, still not looking up."

"And I was drunk when I said 'Yes.'"

He slammed the magazine down onto the floor. "I thought this show was only supposed to take a couple hours."

Mrs. McLellan dropped her hands and needlepoint to her lap. "Why'd you even come here, Frank? Do you even understand what's happening? This is our daughter. Not some fleet truck you're having repaired." She started to cry. Put her hands to her face. Then she sat straight, her face enraged, and pointed to the glass doors. "The doctor could walk through those doors any minute and tell us our daughter is dead. Dead, Frank." Spit flew from her lips. "Did that ever occur to you? Did it, Frank."

Mr. McLellan didn't budge. His face was a wall.

"I didn't think so. Why would a man who ran off on dive trips so he could doink his bookkeeper, and then proudly...no, arrogantly...flaunt photos of his trip to his wife, with this blonde bitch always smiling at the camera, a groping-reach behind him? Why would this man ever consider the consequences of any action?" A sobbing wave erupted from Mrs. McLellan.

Gene put his arm around her, embarrassed, yet relieved there was nobody else in the waiting area.

"Typical," Mr. McLellan said. "Always the theatrics." He picked up the magazine and raced through it, presumably looking for a dead animal.

"Bastard!" The word flew from Gene's mouth like a snap throw to first.

For a few long seconds, the silence sucked all the molecules from the room. Mrs. McLellan raised her head from Gene's shoulder. She seemed to hold her breath.

Mr. McLellan's eyes locked onto Gene's. "Careful, Sonny," he said. "I'm here, ain't I?"

"Be right back."

Gene fumed his way to the service elevators between the waiting area and the surgical suite and pressed Down. His use of this elevator was an unspoken doctor's-son privilege, a kind of legacy perk born from the times he'd joined his father on Sunday evening rounds, waiting either in the lobby where he watched *Voyage to the Bottom of the Sea,* or here on F-wing in the usually quiet, empty Open Heart waiting area, itself a privileged space for family of the patients undergoing the most prestigious surgery Desert Valley Hospital offered. And his father was a part of it.

Prestige. Gene may not have it now, but he would someday. Someday he would be a doctor, and he wouldn't have to suffer the condescension of a burly hunter-adulterer, who no doubt thought Gene wasn't good enough for his daughter; as if he'd caused her heart problem. He wasn't only good enough. He was perfect for her. He couldn't say why exactly, but there was a connection, and right now he didn't have the knowledge or experience to heal her heart of the growth inside, but he cared, just like Mrs. McLellan said Gene's father cared, and Gene would do whatever it took to help Patty through this, once she awakened from the haze and went back to her room. God, how he wanted to stomp back over to that piece of shit, stand firm and announce: I may not be an animal killer, but I know where I'm going, I know who I'm going to be, and I know I'm in love with your daughter, and I will never, ever betray her.

The elevator dinged. Alone in the carriage, he pressed "L" and thought, if no one stops the elevator then.... He held his breath, counting down the numbers...three, two, one. He exited to the hallway where a kitchen attendant waited with two towering lunch carts. Patty would be fine now, confirmed by his silly superstition. Besides, not once had his father ever told him about a patient dying in the Heart Room.

GENE ORDERED a coffee for Mrs. McLellan and a Dr. Pepper for himself, then waited several minutes for the elevator. It seemed to be stuck on four. Climbing the stairs might not be a bad idea.

Exercise always relaxed him, and he hadn't fully cooled down after his encounter with Patty's jerk of a father. But the elevator whined, the red numbers descended to one, and the door opened. It took Gene a moment to recognize his father at the back of the carriage, dressed as he was in a surgical cap with an operating room mask dangling from his neck. He wore a white coat over his surgical scrubs. And he was at the head of a large bed. It was Patty.

"Gene," his father said.

Patty's eyes were closed. A tube exited her mouth, the tape contorting her lips slightly to one side. His father squeezed on a bag connected to the tube. A white blanket came up to her chin, and her dark hair flowed across the pillow.

A nurse pulled on the bed as his father pushed it out of the elevator with his free hand. IV bottles, hanging from a pole on the bed, clanged as the bed clunked across the threshold. A small box at the head of the bed made the beeping heartbeat sounds, Patty's heartbeats.

As the foot of the bed swung around and Patty paused beside him, his father touched his shoulder. "Meet me in the lobby."

Gene looked to the nurse at the foot of the bed. She offered a smile more hopeful than reassuring.

"Sandra," his father said. "Let's go."

Gene walked a step or two by the bedrail as they moved, his hands unfairly occupied with the two drinks. He wanted to hold Patty's hand, just for a second.

"Gene," his father said again.

Gene looked up.

"The lobby."

THE MAN with the tranquilizing dart took steady aim with a long rifle at the leopard in the tree. "He's got one chance to hit his mark," the narrator said. Gene sat in the tan leather couch in the lobby, watching but not watching, listening but not listening to this public television rerun. Something happened during surgery. That grim look when his father exited the elevator. He'd seen that before.

"Gene."

His father, still wearing a white coat, took a seat next to him. Gene hoped for the big toothy smile or a comforting slap on the shoulder. It didn't happen.

"We had a little trouble."

Gene shifted in his seat and stared at the red cursive stitching above the coat pocket — *Desert Valley Heart Team.*

"She arrested," his father said. "Her heart stopped…just before bypass." He touched Gene's knee as his voice accelerated. "But we were able to get her on bypass pretty quickly. Sometimes this happens."

"I don't understand," Gene said. "Is she okay?"

"She's in the ICU. So far so good."

"But you cut out the tumor, right?"

His father nodded.

"When can I see her?"

"She may need an extra day in the Unit."

"Can I go in?"

"Sorry, but it's family only. Besides, she's not breathing on her own yet."

"Not breathing?"

"She's still intubated. A ventilator is breathing for her."

"For how long?"

"When she's stronger. Look, I need to get back and check on something."

It wasn't in his nature to disobey his father and risk losing his respect. But Patty McLellan was no ordinary girl, and he needed to see her.

MONDAY, Gene sat in seventh period advanced English, *The Heart of Darkness* closed on his desk, and watched the second hand above the chalkboard click toward three o'clock. He should have skipped school. How could he concentrate? At three the bell toned, and by 3:05 he was speeding up Central Avenue toward Desert Valley Hospital. Of course, he hit every red light, had to stop twice for pedestrians in cross-walks where there wasn't a light, and parked in the last row, the farthest point in the parking lot from the hospital. He didn't try to shade the seat or steering wheel from the scorching sun, he just abandoned his books and notes and sprinted for the back entrance.

Last night at dinner, his father hadn't had much to say. Only that Patty was still in the ICU, sedated, and the ventilator breathing for her. Fortunately, Gene knew the key to skirting hospital regulations.

At the ICU desk, next to the open door with the sign that read *Family Only*, he said, "I'd like to see Patty McLellan."

"Are you family?" asked the unit secretary.

Gene straightened. "She's kind of my girlfriend." She doesn't know it yet.

"Kind of?"

"We were on a date when she nearly drowned." Maybe not nearly. "I'm Dr. Hull's son, Eugene."

The woman smiled. "Every bit as handsome." She looked over toward the row of six or seven patients with curtains partway drawn between them. "Her parents just went down to the diner for a few minutes. Go right in. Number four."

Gene wandered past beds one, two, and three. Bottles of fluid and bags of blood hung on poles. Monitors beeped while squiggly green lines traced across the screens. Two of the patients could have been mannequins: a bedsheet covered them to their chins; their chests rose with each hiss of a ventilating machine. The middle patient coughed as a woman in nursing whites helped him press a pillow against his chest and encouraged him to cough again.

Gene paused at the curtain separating bed three from Patty. Then he stepped into view.

She was lying in bed, head up a little, and her hands were folded over the covers pulled to the waist of her gown. Her eyes were closed, and her beautiful dark hair spread across her pillow. Her mother had probably combed it. He hoped her face wasn't as pale as it looked in the low light. She had the cutest upturn to the right corner of her mouth. Each breath briefly fogged the green translucent mask. Mask. She's was breathing on her own.

From behind him, someone whispered: "Gene." He turned to see the nurse who'd helped his father transport Patty yesterday. He recognized her hopeful smile. Again, she was in scrubs but without her cap. Her brown hair was pulled back to a ponytail. She stepped beside him and kept her voice low. "I'm Sandra," she said, offering a hand. Then she nodded toward Patty. "She looks really, really good."

Gene gazed at Patty. "Yeah?" he said. "My dad had me kind of worried."

Sandra sighed. "We were all worried for a while."

"He said her heart stopped."

Sandra stared at Patty's serene face.

"He asked me to check on her," she said. "He's in the Heart Room."

"Don't let him know I was here. I was kind of supposed to wait."

"Under the circumstances, I really don't think he'll mind."

Gene winced. "He might."

"Our secret, then."

For several seconds his eyes wandered across Patty's face. Her sweet expression hid even a hint of trouble in the Heart Room. "She could have died. Right?"

They were silent.

"I'm just glad he was there," he added.

"Me too," she said and touched his arm. "I've got to get back."

After Sandra left, he counted Patty's breaths until he lost count. He'd never watched a girl sleep before. It was a strange thought. He stepped closer, leaned over the rail, as if he was Patty's boyfriend, and kissed her forehead. She stirred. Slowly, her lids opened, heavy curtains rising. Her eyes moved laterally and Gene moved easily toward the foot to meet them. She smiled, started to speak, but a catch in her throat stopped her. She made a slow reach with an IV-burdened arm toward her mouth and stopped when her hand met the oxygen mask. She looked at her arm as if it was an alien being and let it drop. Then she ran her tongue over her parched lips, cleared her throat and tried again in a hoarse whisper. "Gene." She smiled a drunken smile. "Been here long?"

Gene wanted to say Only my whole life. But he couldn't get out a word. Not a single word.

Chapter Six

THE LAST DAY OF TRYOUTS

Summer 1974

It's four thirty a.m. and Gene's returning to an old routine this morning. Something familiar. Running.

"Apollo, scoot." Apollo yawns and jumps down from the bed.

With a grand sweep, Gene throws the covers aside. The air conditioner thuds to action, delivering a cool blast of air across his bare chest and legs. He hangs a leg over the twin bed and nibbles the carpet with his toes. Around his room, only one of his high-school posters remains — the Giants' Juan Marichal delivering his trademark high-leg-kick pitch. The modular shelves are mostly empty except for a few trophies topped with plastic batting or pitching figures, and beneath the window, sunlight had dulled the top of the faux walnut desk.

After that embarrassing crash his first day, Gene remained standing the rest of the week. He arrived early each day and stayed out of the way. What more could he do? But Irene has yet to give him any indication that he'll get to scrub next week. There's only one surgery scheduled for today, then the weekend is his, not that he has any plans.

Gene rises and opens the shutters. A few blocks south and east of his house, the lights of Grant Elementary's two ballfields are lit. For a grade school they are quality diamonds. That the lights are on at this hour means Mr. Parker, the PE teacher, is preparing the infields for the first Little League tournament of the summer, a tournament Gene participated in so many summers ago, when his father's cheering could be heard from the bleachers and there was only an orange grove across the street from the school. No homes. No Patricia McLellan.

DOWNSTAIRS, Gene tucks the house key inside his sock, adjusts the fit of his sweat-stained Central High baseball cap and heads out the front door. He runs east on Orangewood, passing under the amber glow of streetlights. The morning air, thin and almost body temperature, seems to flow through his bare chest. He's tried to explain the exhilaration he feels from this uniquely desert experience, but most responses are along the line of that's nice. It is nice. It's more than nice. Like the deep-breath nice of completing your last final exam.

He runs past single level block homes with shake roofs, past sprinkler heads popping up to quench the thirst of the carpet-like Bermuda-hybrid lawns, past acacia and olive trees, and past the citrus trees that were once his obligation, where now, like then, the whoo-whooing of mourning doves announces the coming day.

He turns south onto Central Avenue and a half-mile later right onto Maryland Avenue. He's settled into a rhythm. Each breath sounds like a saw sliding through soft pine. With every few heel strikes, sweat slides down his neck to the divot of his chest. His legs, initially leaden from not running for the past three months, surge with strength.

At Third Place he turns the corner and jogs another quarter mile, before slowing to a stop across the street from the Grant Elementary School's ballfields. On the far diamond, under the harsh klieg lights, Mr. Parker horses the infield grader between second and third base. In the eerie predawn, light from both fields overshoots the school's boundary and bears down on Gene like searchlights. He faces the McLellan house. His chest heaves. His skin is slick with sweat. As he removes his baseball cap and wipes his brow with the back of his arm, two shadow hats and two shadow arms sweep across Patty's empty driveway. No Mustang. She's still not back.

He snugs his cap back in place and walks over to an orange tree by the drive. The largest of the young green fruit are the size of ping-pong balls. He runs his hand over a main branch. The paint, his signature, is fading.

He's about to jog home when the light in her bedroom comes on.

Gene eases behind the tree. In high school, she practiced her flute each morning about this time. A shadow walks across the room. His heart picks up speed. The shadow appears again. Patty? Could she have sold the Mustang? She seems to sit, maybe in her practice chair but he can't be sure because of distortion caused by the wavy curtains. He looks around, then staying low, darts across the lawn to a hedge beneath her window. Crouched there, he spies a slim crack in the curtains. Okay, just a quick glance.

As he starts to rise, the curtains fling open. Shit. He drops to his belly. His heart's about to bust through his chest. He tries to slow his breathing. Then he hears grunting, rhythmic grunting. He shakes his head. Oh, Jeez. So that's what's going on. He rolls over and angles his head enough for a view of the window. The grunting stops and a face appears, hands cupped to the glass. It's Dennis. He's looking out at the ballfield. He's between sets, lifting weights. He always did want Patty's room.

The eastern sky is lightening. Soon the neighbors will be collecting the morning paper. He can't just run for it, so he combat-crawls along the hedge to the property line and the house next door. Then he rises and races home, hungry, hollow, and late for work.

GENE, wearing his white coat, exits the service elevator on four. A lean black guy in scrubs pulls a six-foot cart of breakfast trays up to the carriage. Gene holds the door. A bouffant cap ensnares and tramples the man's Afro. His name badge reads *Jesse.* Gene has seen him on the floor while tagging along with Dr. Harrington between surgeries. They'd exchanged nods a few times. Jesse always seemed to be whistling a little four-bar melody , a sweet, nondescript riff, which he repeats over and over as he moves the cart up and down F-wing. Jesse stops his cart halfway across the transom. "You like waffles?" he asks.

"Sure," Gene says.

Jesse picks up a tray out and offers it. "Four-twenty-six checked out."

"Checked out?"

"Not one of yours, I hope."

"I'm sorry?"

"Died, man. They never tell the kitchen."

Gene doesn't feel right accepting the tray, but the smell of bacon is working on him. After the run past Patty's house, he didn't have time to eat. And the last time he missed breakfast, he fainted in the Heart Room.

"It's okay. Take it. It weren't the food that killed him."

Gene takes the tray with both hands. As the elevator door begins to close, he blocks it with his foot.

Jesse reaches around, punches a button, and the door stays open. "You a new resident or something?"

"Not exactly. I'm following Dr. Harrington around."

"You best follow a little closer. I seen him down in the Unit earlier."

"No, I only follow him in the afternoon, but I'm in the operating room with him all day."

"Heart Team, huh?" He nods toward the red stitching on Gene's coat. "That's heavy shit. Not for me…no way. I seen the scars you guys leave. Like they'd been had with some kind of jungle machete." Jesse looks at something on the clipboard hanging from the cart and then checks it off with a pencil. "I seen a heart…two hearts, once. That was enough."

"What kind of surgery?"

"Weren't no surgery. Saw it in Nam."

"Vietnam?"

"Guess you never been. You got time for a story?"

"Not really."

"Rest that up here. Won't take but a sec." Jesse takes the tray and places it atop his cart.

"We was on patrol once — "

Just then, a barrel of a fellow with a tattoo peeking from beneath his scrub's shirtsleeve, comes up pushing a patient on a gurney. "You got a flat?" he says.

Jesse turns around. "Leo. Where you headed?"

The patient's eyes are closed, and she's as pale as her white hair. A tube exits her nose. "X-ray," Leon says.

Jesse balances Gene's breakfast tray and pulls his cart back. The orderly moves onto the elevator while Jesse releases the hold button. "Send it back."

"You got it, my man."

The doors close. "That woman don't need an x-ray. She need some blood."

Gene checks his watch. Maybe Irene won't notice if he's a couple minutes late.

"This won't take long. Like I was saying, we was on patrol once and came into this village. Place was empty, except for some pigs and chickens and shit. A couple pit fires was still burning. Add that all up, and you got trouble. So, we check things out, hut to hut, following our policy of shoot before entering. We ain't finding nothing. Then outside one hut, we see these two poles, like bamboo, with something stuck on top. Well, you probably guessed it. They was hearts. Big as grapefruit and red as apples. Side by side like that, they looked like a couple old folk waiting for the bus. It was pretty clear what was going on with those hearts. Want to take a guess?"

"Some kind of revenge killing."

"Nope." Jesse's lip began to quiver. "They was just having a heart to heart."

It takes a second for Gene to realize he's been had.

Jesse throws his hands on Gene's shoulders and bends over, laughing. His breath smells like an ashtray.

"Oh, man, I'm sorry," Jesse says. "I'm sorry."

Gene's face flushes. He's never liked being the butt of jokes. "That's a good one."

"You should've seen your face."

The elevator door bolts open, startling Gene. It's empty. "Sounds like you've been there."

"Oh, I did my time in Nam all right," he said, wiping his eyes. "The heart stuff I made up. We was always pissin' on each other like that. Be glad you weren't five years older. You'd 'a' been pissin' there with me."

He presses the hold button inside the elevator. "You're a good sport. Breakfast is on me from now on. I'm usually here by about six, although I'm running behind today. What's your name anyway?"

"Gene."

"Nice to meet you, Dr. Gene. You can call me Jesse. Not Jess. Jess-ee." He hands the breakfast tray back to Gene. "Okay, I got mouths to feed." Jesse puts his weight into the cart and moves it forward. "Man, you made my day. Check you later, Doc."

The door starts to close, and Gene takes a step forward. "Jesse, I'm not a doctor."

"Hey, I know. I know." Jesse smiles and pauses the door. "You dressing like one, though. Shit, that's a start. Stay cool."

Gene hustles away with breakfast. Jeez, he won't even have time to eat this.

CARRYING THE BREAKFAST TRAY, Gene rushes into the doctor's lounge. Dr. Pereira, sitting on a couch, looks up from a quarter-folded section of a newspaper and raises a long index finger to his pursed lips. He nods toward Dr. Harrington. The man's asleep in a vinyl chair by the phone, his doctor's cap untied and slanted on his head. An unlit cigarette dangles from his lips. His head bobs with each sibilant breath. Gene stops and reaches back with one foot to prevent the locker room door from closing with a bang.

For the most part, the Heart Team doctors have the lounge to themselves this early in the morning. The other cases in the OR begin a half-hour later.

"We had to bring yesterday's cabbage back," Dr. Pereira says. He takes a sip from a coffee cup. "Bleeding."

Gene sets the tray on the coffee table and whispers. "What time?"

"About two. Dr. H never got home."

"That's too bad."

"He loves it."

Still standing, Gene raises the heavy lid on the breakfast plate. Steam rises from scrambled eggs, bacon, and toast.

"Oh," Dr. Pereira says. "Irene was inquiring about your presence."

Gene gestures to the food. "You want it?"

"I see you've made Jesse's acquaintance." Dr. Pereira uncrosses his legs and leans forward, looking through his reading glasses to survey the steaming plate as well as the pint-size milk carton. "I consider it my duty to spare you the cholesterol." He lays the paper on the couch. "Studies suggest it is bad for your heart."

"I better see what Irene wants."

Dr. Pereira jellies a piece of toast, takes a bite, and holds up a finger for Gene to wait. "Next time we have a bring-back, I will call you. Once you start scrubbing."

Right. If he starts scrubbing.

"Before you go. Look at this. Do you ever do the Jumble?"

"I used to."

"The first three words, I unscrambled in seconds. This last one evades me."

Gene looks up to the clock. It's almost six-forty-five.

He takes the paper and works out various three letter syllables within the six available letters. "Misfit. I need to go."

"Ah, you saved the day."

The intercom clicks: "Dr. Harrington. Dr. Pereira. We're ready."

It's Sandra's voice, booming from the scratchy speaker. "Is Gene there?"

Dr. Harrington stirs. The cigarette drops from his mouth. He pushes his glasses up to his forehead, rubs his eyes with his large meaty hands, and with some effort rises to his feet, placing the full bulk of his weight on the thin armrests. He plops his glasses down to his nose and looks over at Gene. "Eugene, please alert Deborah that I shall be right along." He lumbers toward the dressing room, but as he opens the door, he stabs his hip on the corner of the Formica coffee counter. "Damn." He stumbles and slams his fist on the counter. "I swear, I'm going to rip that from the wall someday."

Pressing the intercom, Gene says, "Sandra?"

"I heard," she says. "Glad you made it."

Then, through the background country music, Gene hears Dr. Boz's voice. "Hey, Rui, you Portuguese piece of shit, get a move on. The patient's asleep, and I'd like to open up the Harley this afternoon before Katie gets back in town." The intercom clicks off.

"The cowboy has his charm," Dr. Pereira says. "If I had surgery, he'd be my anesthesiologist, but Gene …" He takes a deep breath. "I tell you, I miss Carl's spirit, and I miss his jazz collection playing while we work. A true gentleman."

Gene wavers under the weight and spotlight of Dr. Pereira's admission. If only Gene knew what to say. Something catchy and memorable like Jesse's four-bar phrase. But all Gene has to offer, all he can muster after nearly nine months of trying to understand his feelings on this, or anything for that matter, is: "Me, too."

Dr. Pereira remains silent. He claps Gene on the shoulder again, leaving his hand there until they clear the door into the chilly OR corridor.

Gene leaves the surgeons at the scrub sink and enters the Heart Room. It's even chillier than the hallway. He sits on the stool, and for several minutes, Irene ignores him while she prepares for the case.

Finally, she says, "You're late." Her back is to him as she lays instruments on her Mayo stand.

Gene's father once told him, "When your coach balls you out, and you know he's right, don't make excuses. Just take your medicine and do better next time."

Irene turns. "I wanted to talk to you about next week."

Dr. Pereira backs into the room. "Sandra, would you be so kind as to switch the music to jazz."

"My pleasure," she says.

Irene hands Dr. Pereira a towel. Oh great. Now Gene has to wait a few hours until his bitter medicine. He can sense it in Irene's rigid posture. For her, it's time to work.

While Gene stands behind the blood-brain barrier with Dr. Boz, the team prepares for bypass. Dave Brubeck plays in the background. Roger's Valentine-heart cap bobs with the groove as he taps the last stubborn bubbles from the bypass tubing. Gene recognizes the tune, "Blue Moon," from his father's reel-to-reel collection. Now, Dr. Pereira cauterizes the raw, bleeding edge of the split sternum. Gene's used to the smell and no longer needs the peppermint on his mask.

He folds his arms and looks around. He feels invisible, an outsider to the team, while they work. But it hardly seems like work. Dr. Pereira taps his foot to the music as he cranks the chest-spreader open. Irene yawns behind her mask before passing a needle holder to Dr. Pereira and a long-handled scalpel to Dr. Harrington. Her elbow bumps the stand and an instrument clatters to the floor.

"Sandra," Irene says. "I lost an Alice."

Gene squats down. "No, it's scissors," he says. "Metzenbaum I think." He only knows that because he's watched every instrument count this week. Well, except for this morning.

"My young Gene," Rui says. "A little review."

With a Mayo forceps, Rui points to the heart's anatomy as he and Dr. Harrington begin inserting the bypass tubes. Gene leans his head over the barrier, careful not to touch the top with his hands. One by one, he correctly names the major vessels, chambers, and the pericardial membrane.

Dr. Boz nudges him. "You have been paying attention."

Dr. Boz stands and then sits back down. "Hey Gene-o. Take a look." He pulls up a pants' leg and angles his cowboy boot one way and the other. "Know what that is?"

Gene sits. "No."

"Ostrich. Slow ostrich." Dr. Boz's eyes grin.

"How many different kinds do you have?"

"Dozens." He smooths his pants' leg back down. "Anything that can't crawl, slither or fly away." He stands and peers over the ether screen. "Take a look at this."

Gene stands. As soon as he faces the surgical field, a jet of blood spurts over the drape. He ducks to his left, but the pencil-thick stream grazes his cap-covered ear. Something's gone wrong.

Dr. Boz laughs and slaps him on the back. "Nice reflexes Gene-o. Pretty fast for a doctor's kid."

Gene looks around. Sandra, Dr. Pereira, Dr. Harrington, and even Irene, they're all smiling. Their eyes don't lie. He's been had — for the second time today — and his face flushes.

"Eugene." Dr. Harrington draws out Gene's name as he sutures the aortic cannula in place. "We're all a little sleep depraved…I mean deprived…so please excuse our little prank."

The spurt of blood came from the puncture hole Dr. Harrington made in the aorta, but Dr. Pereira didn't cup the spurt with his hand.

As a freshman in high school, before the results of varsity tryouts were posted, Gene found a cheerleader outfit in his locker. He knew then what he knows now — he's made the team. They've accepted him — even Irene. For an unfiltered instant he can't wait to tell his dad. Gene blinks hard and concentrates on the patient's pitching heart instead of his own. He's Carl Hull's son, not the late-arriving son of some hospital administrator. How could he not make the team?

"Gene," Irene says. "There's a book on the counter for you."

Gene walks over and runs his hand over the hard, green cover. *Principles of Cardiac Surgery*.

"Thanks. When do you want it back?"

"It's yours," Irene says. "We had an extra copy in the office."

"What ya got?" Dr. Boz asks.

Gene hefts the text in Dr. Boz's direction.

"When I was your age, my summer reading slanted more to carnal themes."

Dr. Pereira passes an empty needle holder to Irene, then looks briefly at Dr. Boz. "*The Last Picture Show* no doubt."

"Could have been my life. Dying town and only a single virgin left."

"The details, you can spare us," Dr. Pereira says. Then to Gene. "The book. Consider it a head-start toward a promising career."

Despite the warm feelings, Gene still has much to prove — to others and to himself. All he's done so far is watch. And of course, the face plant.

"We're at full flow," Roger says. Sandra turns off the music. Gene has learned that as ho-hum as the team might appear before bypass, once the heart-lung machine takes over and the clock is ticking, Dr. Harrington (through Irene) prefers a quiet room. But for Dr. Boz, the time on bypass is mostly down time. He turns off the ventilator. For the next hour or two, Roger's machine is the patient's heart and lungs. Once or twice during this period, Dr. Boz will hand a syringe to Roger. "Something to keep the patient from jumping off the table," Dr. Boz has told Gene. But for the most part, Roger seems to take control of the patient's well-being.

"Holding at thirty degrees," Roger says. Here is one area, where Gene's engineering background helps. Without thinking, he knows thirty degrees Celsius is about eighty-five degrees Fahrenheit.

Dr. Boz walks over to where Sandra stands by the phone. Hip to hip, they lean against the desk. When he brings his mask close to her ear, she rubs her tan arms. He tucks a stray wave of hair back under her cap, pats the small of her back, and lets his hand drift ever so briefly across her butt before folding his arms. This isn't the first time Dr. Boz has flirted with Sandra. She never seems to dissuade him. Gene allows his mind to wander…to Patty's sapphire eyes blinking like Sandra's above the lip of her mask while a medical student whispers in her ear.

Dr. Boz catches Gene's gaze. He looks back to the surgical field and then over to the monitor and the flat green lines of the stilled heart.

"Everything look okay, Gene-o?" Dr. Boz says. Gene nods. A lie. The weekend is ahead. That's when he thinks of Patty the most — on weekends and at night — when he's alone and he knows she isn't.

Chapter Seven

I AM YOURS

Senior Year

GENE VISITED Patty in the hospital every day after school. On day three she moved to a regular room and by day seven she was discharged. While she convalesced at home, Gene acted as her liaison, delivering homework assignments and returning completed work. Each day as the sun set, they took short walks along her street. By the time football yardage lines had been chalked through Grant Elementary's baseball infields, she was strong enough to make it to the Big Tree, where they shared their first kiss.

On Halloween night, almost two months after their near disastrous first date, they hung out at Gene's house while his parents were out to dinner with Rui Pereira and his wife. Between dolling out candy to trick-or-treaters, Gene and Patty listened to albums on the living room stereo. Apollo curled at her feet. He had taken to her, buddying up whenever he could, a clear sign that Patty was indeed special.

When the action at the front door mercifully petered out, Gene placed one of his sister's Ricky Nelson albums on the turntable.

He'd driven out to Suzanne's ASU apartment just to pick up the record.

"This is for you," he said.

He dimmed the lights and returned to the sectional. She scooted close.

"It's called, 'When Fools Rush In.'

When the song ended, Patty turned to him. "That is so sweet." Her eyes glistened. "Why wouldn't I open my heart and let you rush in? In a way, you saved me."

Gene wanted to believe that. "My dad saved you, not me."

"You had a part." She brushed her thumb across his lip. "You still do."

He gave her a questioning look.

"The things you do. Like helping with my homework. The way you treat me. The things you say."

Gene rose, lifted the stylus from the record and returned.

He sat on the edge of the couch.

"The summer I turned eleven, I watched my father try to save a little girl who'd been hit by a Cadillac."

Patty's eyes widened. She put her hand over her open mouth and sagged. He laid out the whole story of his father's heroic efforts, every detail, even the part where Gene fainted. How cool his father had acted? Boy was he proud of his dad.

"And then to see him taking care of you, taking you to the ICU after surgery. And to learn that your heart stopped before the surgery started...well, he saved you. You might have died, but he saved you." Gene shrugged. That's who I want to be."

She hugged him, pulled her head back, and said, "No doubt, you will."

She was going to say something else, when the sound of the garage door stopped her. Gene jumped up and restarted the album. Ricky Nelson was rocking when his parents entered.

"Did the candy hold out?" his mother said.

Gene turned the volume down and returned to the couch. "At the end I let them take whole handfuls."

His mother looked to Patty. "So back to school tomorrow I hear."

"Doesn't feel like I missed much school. Gene saved me from having to repeat this semester."

He could kiss the grin she gave him.

"Big day tomorrow for Carl, too," his mother said.

Gene's father walked into the living room from the kitchen.

"Carl, show them the pen Rui gave you tonight."

Gene's father pulled the pen from inside his sport coat and held it up.

"Mont Blanc," Gene's mother said. "Rui said that now that he's got a nine-to-five job running Respiratory Therapy, he needed an executive's pen."

Patty said, "I was surprised when Gene told me you were leaving your practice."

"It's just a sabbatical of sorts," his father said.

She smiled. "Who's going to save me if I need surgery again?"

His father's face was almost grim.

Gene's mother encircles her husband's waist and pulls him close. "It was time for a change, right? For a couple years. More sleep. More evenings at home." She hugged him. "And now you can skip out when you want to watch Gene's ballgames this spring."

"Hopefully, now and then." He checked his watch. "I best turn in." He stepped over to Patty and grasped her hand with both of his. "I'm so glad to see how well you're doing. You look great."

"Thanks to you." She tipped her head. "And Gene."

He placed a hand lightly on Gene's head. "Night all."

After waiting for his father's bedroom door to close, Gene asked, "Dad okay?"

His mother gave a dismissive wave of her hand. "New job. New routine. Like the first day of school. Right?"

GENE's senior year was magical. Patty was never far from his mind or his side. Her devotion inspired him. Each morning, his five-mile run before school took him past her house. Behind her backlit curtains, she practiced her flute. He occasionally left a song lyric under her Mustang's wiper, a phrase penned on a three-by-five card reflecting his burgeoning love for the shy girl from Van Nuys. Nothing gave him more pleasure than her hands-to-her-heart reaction after discovering the notes. In class, his grades excelled, and on the ballfield, seeing her in the stands, often next to his father, was good for an extra hit or a couple miles-per-hour on his fastball. On one memorable spring afternoon, he threw his only one-hitter, and after the game captured a photo of his two biggest fans.

They were Gene and Patty, Patty and Gene, and as the school year ended, their paths were set: Gene to Cal Poly for engineering and pre-med studies and Patty to the University of Arizona's nursing program. If their yearbook had an award for Most Likely to Live Happily Ever After, Gene was sure they would have won.

On graduation night, Gene's father instructed the young couple, dressed in their red cap and gowns, to cuddle up against the short chain-link fence encircling the lighted football field. In the background, white folding chairs extended from the end zone to the thirty-yard line. He took a photo with his Hasselblad, smiled without looking up from the viewfinder, then took two more. His father was so taken with the emotion of the moment, that his voice cracked when he said, "You make a beautiful couple."

THAT SUMMER, they often crawled through his bedroom window at night onto his roof deck. His freshman year, he'd leveled plywood across two-by-four bracing, strung a copper wire antenna, and pulled in the Giants' broadcast from San Francisco. Now, he listened with Patty, instilling in her his passion for the most beautiful game ever invented. After the game they'd make out on a sleeping bag.

One night in early August, as they rested back on lawn chairs, listening to the Giants play the Astros, Gene looked over. It was the eleventh inning. Patty's eyes were closed, and she curled her toes and stretched like a contented cat.

He'd been on a sexual edge since graduation. And now her devotion to hang in there with him through extra innings only amplified his desire. Over the past year, they'd progressed through intimacy as far as two fully clothed lovers could. Although hesitant at first, she allowed his caresses through her clothing — thick cotton sweaters in winter progressing to fewer and thinner layers of fabric as the weather warmed, eventually down to a peasant blouse and bra in the high heat of summer. But Gene was eager for more. He'd tried playful finger-walks to her bra's clasp or down her tense abdomen to the edge of her denim shorts. Patty always halted his excursions with a soft "Gene" in his ear. She wasn't harsh or scolding yet offered no explanation to reassure him that eventually a time would come. There was something measured in her demeanor, something other than shyness that guided her. But she never explained. Tonight, he simply staked his position.

"Patty?"

"Hmm," she said.

"I want to make love to you."

She turned onto her side and sighed. She held out her hand. "I know."

"Well?"

"Soon."

"When soon?"

"Gene, I'm not ready." She squeezed his hand.

"Is it your scar?"

"What?"

"Your scar. Are you embarrassed about your scar from surgery?"

She kissed his knuckles. "Gene, I'm just not ready."

What could he say? Soon was better than no.

He convinced himself that soon meant before she left for college at the end of the month. The next day he began expanding the roof-deck with another four-by-eight section of plywood. He worked shirtless in the invigorating heat. As he cut and drilled and fastened the planks, he recalled anecdotes of previous high-school couples consummating their relationship before heading off to college — in the back of vans, at an older sibling's apartment near ASU, in their parent's camper shell stowed in the backyard.

Gene smiled as he laid down a thick coat of spar varnish on the completed project. Then the final touch, something he'd "invented", a light dusting of fine sand to make the surface less slippery. Before crawling back through his bedroom window, he turned to look at his creation. Perfect.

Two days before Patty drove to Tucson, she called. "I have something for you. Can you come over?"

Her mother's car was gone when he arrived.

"Where's your mom?"

"Oh, evening shift."

"Dennis?"

"He's at the movies."

She curled her lower lip between her teeth and took his hand. She guided him through the cool air of the house to her bedroom. "Sit there." She motioned to the bed. "Close your eyes."

Gene's heart pounded.

"Now give me your hand."

He held it out, felt something light, and opened his eyes. A manila envelope.

"It's a kind of going away gift," she said.

He removed the envelope's content, expecting a clever map or maybe a modified reprise of the first lyric he left on her Mustang, something like, I'm ready to open up my heart and let you rush in.

But it was an eight by ten copy of the graduation photo his father had taken. He'd given each of them one. Gene's heart slowed to a trot.

"Check the back," she said. She sat next to him and turned the photo over.

On the back, in lavender ink, she'd written, *Love you with my whole heart — Patty*.

He turned the photo over and examined their faces. He remembered hoping they would succumb to passion that night. It was evident in his nervous bearing. Patty's expression was less expectant, entirely at ease with the boy whose shoulder her head tilted toward.

"You said, soon. We only have two days," he said.

"I know."

"Well?"

She looked down. He didn't want to have to convince her.

"I'm outta here."

"Gene."

He strode to his Jeep and in the TV version of this moment she would run after him. Then she'd lead him by the hand to her bed and turn out the light. He sat in his Jeep, engine running, and waited. He was about to pull away, when her door opened. She just stood there under her porch light, hugging the manila envelope to her chest and piercing his heart. He killed the engine and walked back to her.

She studied his eyes for several seconds. "Have you had sex before?" she said.

Gene took a half-step back. "No. Of course not. I mean —" He stopped. "Have you?"

Her serious expression didn't change. She shook her head. "No." And pressed the envelope to his chest.

They stood silent for some time, suspended in the still, dry air of summer's end. So, this is all she needed to know. That he wasn't some hound dog on the prowl. Why would she ever have that impression?

"I should go in," she said. She squeezed his hand and turned.

"Wait!" Gene tightened his grip. "That's it?"

She pulled her hand away. "Don't."

"So, you go back to your room and write in your diary *Gene's a virgin*?"

She pointed to the envelope. "I mean every word in there. Every word."

"I bet you do."

"And what about you, Gene. Do you love me with your whole heart? Or only with something else?"

He slammed the envelope to the porch. "Keep it." He walked backwards mimicking her voice from almost a year before, "Oh,

Gene I'm so lucky. You saved me." He waved. "Call when you're ready to reward your hero."

HE'D SAID some dumb things in his life. But this was Olympic caliber self-destruction. He sat on his roof deck after returning home, wondering what the hell had gotten into him?

He called the next day. Her mom answered and simply said, "I understand you two had a fight. Give her some time."

At least it appeared Mrs. McLellan didn't know what Gene had said.

"Tell her 'I'm sorry'."

Two days later, without a goodbye, she and her mother drove to Tucson. Patty was gone.

A little over a week into her classes, Gene received an envelope from her — their photograph. To his surprise his head hadn't been scissored out. And on the back, she'd underlined *Love you with my whole heart*. She included a short note.

> I'm sorry, too. Can we start over? I hope you can come down to Tucson before you leave for school. I do miss you, Gene. Call me.

He dialed before his next breath.

SHE LIVED IN AN ALL-GIRLS' dorm on the University of Arizona campus. He arranged to crash on the apartment floor of a former Central High teammate. The thought of being separated from her by seven-hundred miles for the next three months frightened him. Or something close to "frighten." Whatever it was, he pushed it aside and thought only of this weekend. He had a sleeping bag in the well of his Jeep and a speech in his head; a speech filled with respect and desire. He'd emphasize the respect, but the desire felt like an expanding balloon in his chest. When she's ready, she's ready, he kept saying to himself. And if that was tonight, well, he had protection in his pocket.

A desk clerk called up to her room and instructed him to wait in the lobby. When the elevator doors opened, she ran to him, dropped the sleeping bag she had under her arm, and gave him the passionate kiss he'd hoped for. "God, I missed you," she said.

He hugged her again. "Oh, I missed you." He pulled back and looked down at the sleeping bag. "What's with this?"

"Let's go camping," she said. "The Catalinas. It's six-thousand feet. Cool. Pine trees. And the stars will be fantastic." Gene must have looked befuddled. "You brought a sleeping bag, right?" she said.

She loaded her bag in the back of the Jeep and they headed toward the Catalina Mountains looming on the far north edge of the city. They stopped at a Sizzler along the way for dinner. Between bites of coconut shrimp, Patty talked about her classes, including Intro to Astronomy. But she was most excited about her nursing classes. She recounted the tour of the hospital, the pep talks (as she calls them) from nurses; not only those that worked on the floor, but those on obstetrics, the ICU, the operating room, recovery room, and even research. She hadn't fully considered the range of opportunities available to her.

"I'm flying, Gene. I'm flying. Your dad was right. He said I'd love the medical field. I can tell it's for me. I can't wait until clinicals."

Gene had finished eating. He thought only of the hours ticking down until he'd drive away from Tucson and not see her again until Thanksgiving.

"Patty, I'm going to miss you."

"That's so sweet." She grasped his hands across the table. "It's only three months. We'll write. We'll call. I'm so busy right now, the time will fly by." She raised off her seat and leaned over the table. "Come here." She pulled his face close and kissed him like she owned him. "I could squeeze the stuffin' out of you."

It was dark when he parked his Jeep in an isolated camping spot in the densely wooded Catalinas. They zipped the two sleeping bags together in a small clearing between Ponderosa pines. Gene doused the headlights. Then they slipped off their shoes and jackets and crawled into the Coleman cocoon.

"Don't you love that smell?" Patty said. She inhaled. "It smells like vanilla." They were lying on their backs, Gene gazing at her profile. She pointed skyward, aiming at an opening in the trees. "Vega."

Gene looked up. It was a sea of stars.

"That bright star," she said, pointing. "That must be Vega. It was on a quiz yesterday. It looks so much brighter up here."

Enough of the stars. He kissed her hard on the mouth. Her lips parted and he rolled partially on top of her. As soon as his hand charged across her sweater, she placed an open palm on his chest and gently pushed him away. He'd hoped tonight would be different. Should he push back? Maybe that's what she wanted, what she needed. Let passion take over. But he couldn't. His eyes, now fully adjusted to the quarter-moon's light, saw in her eyes the same vulnerability, the same wariness from a year ago when she had escaped into her nearly completed home and out the front door. He rolled off of her.

She sat up. "You know what day it is?"

"Does it matter?"

"One year ago today, you saved my life."

Gene ran a calendar in his head. "Big Surf?"

"You pulled me from the water. You took me to the hospital. You waited in the emergency room. You waited with my mother while I had surgery. You pulled me through that first semester. And you were patient. Mostly."

Her hands disappeared inside her sleeves for a moment. In the near darkness, he couldn't make out what she was doing… until she pulled her light-colored bra through one of the sleeves. Gene sat up. She took his hand in both of hers and guided it under her sweater, inhaling sharply as the weight and warmth of her full breast settled into his palm. It felt like a gift. An offering more tender and intimate than anything he'd ever experienced. A token of trust.

Gene froze. His heart threatened to slam through his chest. She held him there in the way she'd once clutched her flute case to her chest — his hand her shield now. He was about to ask the next question and the one after that, when she answered both with four words she exhaled into the crisp night air: "I started the pill."

Gene was beyond the breech. He pulled her blouse over her head and then removed her jeans and panties. His long-sleeved shirt got hung up on his watch until he yanked it free, the sleeve's button flying off into the dark. She unbuttoned his jeans and tugged them off as he raised his hips. The elastic waistband of his boxers caught on his erection. He freed his shorts and went for her socks, but she wasn't waiting. They made love in the clunky way two kids might attempt to ride a tandem bike, over-sized for their age: starting rough, straining to reach the pedals, and then swerving out of control. At most a couple of frantic minutes from start to finish.

A few moments after, with their chests colliding, Gene started to roll off of her, but she held him in place. "Don't go anywhere, you. I want to remember this." She ran her stockinged foot along his calf. "I want to remember making love with our socks on."

In the morning, with the sleeping bag's edge cuffed to their ears, they lay on their sides locked in a deep gaze. The air was damp and smelled of vanilla, the sky a soft gray slate above the trees. Sometime in the night, they'd both removed their socks. Patty rubbed her bare foot down his shin to his bare ankle. "Sorry," she whispered.

"Sorry?"

"I needed to be sure."

"Sure, that I'd taken my socks off?"

"You're impossible. I'm serious. I needed to be sure you were the one."

"The one what?"

"You're playing with me now," she said, smiling. "The boy who wouldn't leave me a day, a week, a year after I shared my body with him. Someone who would love me with his whole heart. Someone unlike my father."

"What changed your mind?"

"More like who."

"And…"

"My mother. On our drive down, I asked her if she'd ever get married again. She said, sure, if the right man came along. And I said, well aren't you afraid he might say he loved you, like Dad, and then go out and fool around. She said, oh it's possible, but if I loved the man, and I thought he loved me, I'd take the chance. She said, not every grape on a vine is sweet. Occasionally there's a sour one but you don't throw out the whole bunch." She turned onto her back and stared up to the light blue sky. Her face saddened.

"You okay?"

She sighed. "You grow up thinking your parents will always love each other. I was so naive." She turned her head to him. "I need to tell you something."

Her voice unsettled him. Gene braced.

"The year before we moved to Phoenix, I came home early from school. Another migraine. That's what we thought then." She looked back to the sky. "I heard a laugh and thought my parents were home. When I turned the corner into the hallway, I saw my father and another woman in my bedroom.

She took a deep breath.

"They were on the floor. Naked. Doing it like dogs. Saying things."

She began to tear. "He tried to cover up and started for me, saying, 'I can explain.' I was terrified, and I ran."

Gene placed a hand on her shoulder.

"He thought buying me the Mustang would shut me up." She shook her head. "He had no idea how humiliating it was for me. I wasn't going to tell anyone, particularly my mother. I thought it would destroy her. But she sensed something was going on. I wasn't eating and couldn't sleep. Eventually, I lost it, and told her what I'd seen and made her promise not to tell anyone."

Gene kissed the top of her head. "I'm such a shit."

Patty pulled back. "No, you're not. Driving down here, she asked if I was worried that you would hurt me…not physically I mean but betray me if we ever married. I said I didn't think so. There was a time when she thought Dad wouldn't betray her. But she said the one thing she's gained with age is a good bullshit meter.

She said from talking with you, from seeing how caring you are, the needle on her meter doesn't even budge. She also said, 'Look closely at his eyes. There's an old soul in there. A gentle soul.'"

Gene swallowed the guilt in his throat. "I can do better."

She smiled and looked from one eye to the other. "She's right. A gentle soul."

Gene's voice cracked. "As soon as I get back to Phoenix, I'm going to thank your mother for convincing her daughter to make love to me."

Patty poked him in the chest and arched with laughter. "Don't you dare." He laughed and she laughed even harder and then they were silent. Bluejays called and fluttered about in the trees. He combed a strand of her lush hair from her lips. "You haven't asked to see it," she said.

He pushed the cover aside, exposing her tense breasts to the crisp air. But his eyes quickly settled on the pink line running between them, and his heart ached, recalling all she had endured. He ran his finger along the full length of the scar. "It's so thin," he said. A year ago, she'd passed out and sunk beneath the water, and twenty-four hours later, she'd had this. He traced the scar back to her chin. "You know, had you really been drowning that day, I could have breathed for you."

"Really?"

"Mouth to mouth."

"Like Sleeping Beauty." She crossed her arms and puckered her lips.

"I'm serious. "My dad taught me."

Patty raised herself to her elbow.

"I was in third grade. We had just put our swimming pool in, and he wanted us to know what to do if someone was drowning. He didn't have a mannequin, so he had Suzanne and me practice on each other."

"You're kidding?"

"It's embarrassing now."

"How old was Suzanne?"

"She would have been about fourteen. Now that I think about it, I can't believe she put up with it."

"What you're telling me, is the first time you French-kissed a girl, she was your sister?"

"Don't even say that." Gene grimaces and rolls to his side facing Patty. "It's pretty amazing to feel someone breathe for you, though."

"So, let's say you pulled me out of the water, and I wasn't breathing."

He smiled.

"Lie back."

Naked and kneeling at her side, he said, "Breathe through your mouth." Then he placed his fingers under her chin. "That's it." He pinched her nostrils lightly with his other hand. "Inhale...That's right...Now exhale slowly, but don't breathe in again. I'll do that for you."

As she breathed out, Gene breathed in. He placed his mouth over hers, lifted her chin, and gently exhaled. For a second, she resisted. But she relaxed, and it was as if a door swung open. The force of his breath flowed into her, and her chest rose to his cheek. When he separated his lips from hers, her chest recoiled, their warm, shared breath parting around his face. With his eyes closed, he repeated the cycle again and again, and soon the forest fell away. There was only the sound of his breath roiling through her lungs. Only his breath stretching her ribs like a yawn. She didn't shift her weight, cough, or lick an arc of her sweet saliva at the corner of her mouth. She lay still, dependent on Gene's breath for life. He shuddered and raised up.

Patty opened her eyes and blinked. "Wow."

She pulled him close by the small of his back and kissed his nose, and then each closed eye, before kissing his lips. His erection returned in a slow, steady rise. It crept across her abdomen, and he could tell by her sudden stillness that she felt it, too.

"Maybe we should put our socks on?" she whispered.

It became their code.

Chapter Eight

CAMP GENE

Summer 1974

GENE DRIVES his Jeep up Central Avenue. He has a plan. Eventually Patty will drive up from Tucson. When she does, and she finally hears him out, not only will he look older, but she'll learn that he's part of an older world now, stronger of mind and body, and taking giant strides toward medical school. She's got to see that they're still perfect for each other. Hell, he's a member of the Heart Team, not some kid who spreads *Johnny Quest* sheets around the base of orange trees. The first step is to look the part.

He pulls into Sal's, a barbershop located on the first floor of an eight-story building in midtown. He's not been here since his high-school freshman year. Nothing's changed. Since it's Saturday, the corner TV is tuned to the Baseball Game of the Week and the reception is still poor.

"So, what's it gonna be," Sal says. Above the mirror, a half-dozen drawings demonstrate haircuts from crew cuts to something approaching the early Beatles. Gene's shaggy hair is off the map. He points to one that resembles Dr. Boz. Most of the ear shows. Sal beams and says, "That, I can do."

Gene stops by Enzt-White on the way home, the hardware store where he bought the plywood and two-by-fours for his deck. Now, he loads up on sections of threaded steel pipe, elbows, flanges, and tees. He should have worked out the design at home first, taken some measurements, but given that the trusses are two feet on center, he visualizes a structure that's sure to work. And it does. By mid-afternoon, he's installed a chin-up bar under the second-floor eaves, next to his roof deck, but still out of sight from the street. He finds a roll of medical tape in his high-school bat bag and wraps the pipe where he grips the bar. He tests it and fatigues at nine reps. Then he thinks of Patty's new boyfriend, remembers what he can of that bastard's face, and surges through three more pull-ups. He follows that with two more sets, three sets of push-ups, sit-ups, and a milkshake blended with two eggs. On lined notebook paper, he sketches a checkerboard calendar and records his workout.

Later that afternoon, Apollo follows him to his father's study off the master bedroom. The dog whines, the tip of his tail shivering.

"I'll feed you in just a minute."

He powers up the flush-mounted amp and flips some toggles. He runs a finger along his shoebox of tapes. Led Zeppelin, Gordon Lightfoot, Derek & the Dominos, Crosby, Still, & Nash, Rod Stewart, Loggins and Messina, The Beatles, and more. It seems that every album contains at least one song that triggers a memory of Patty: a look, a laugh, or a kiss. Particularly *Chicago VI* with "Just You 'n' Me:" their song. But that's not the mood he's looking for.

Finally, he selects Crosby, Stills & Nash. The driving melody of "Suite Judy Blue Eyes" has always felt like the beginning of hope and possibility. He clicks *play*. The opening riff pumps throughout the house and sends a chill down his arms.

In the master closet, three of his father's suits still hang on a bare rod. Under the suits, thirteen office storage boxes are stacked in twos — medical books and journals as well as a few other books his mother thought Gene might want, books about woodworking, the history of baseball, or automotive repair. Next to those, a wooden crate contains his father's jazz collection on seven-inch reels. It's practically all that remains of his father's stake in the house. His mother wanted Gene to haul it back to school last January. "I can't bear to look at any of it," she said at the time. But even if he'd had enough room in the Jeep, he would have refused just to spite her.

Gene carries a pad of ruled paper and three books into the kitchen — Gray's *Anatomy*, Grant's *Atlas of Anatomy*, and Dorland's *Medical Dictionary*. Each tome has his dad's signature on the inside front cover. The script reminds him of the signatures on the Declaration of Independence — significant in their grace and legibility. Using the flour and sugar canisters as bookends, he stacks the books on the circular oak table along with the surgical text Irene gave him yesterday.

Gene steps back and admires his set-up. It's a medical boot camp — Camp Gene. He grasps *Principles of Cardiac Surgery* by the three-inch olive-green spine and lays it flat on the table. He flips through a few of the thousand or more pages, pages thin as onion skin. It's an imposing volume of schematics, tables, and diagrams surrounded by columns of tiny print, interspersed with black and white photographs, stark in their honesty. Gene turns to the inside front cover and writes his name, the script remarkably similar to his father's. Someday he'll add the M.D. at the end. Or better yet, Patty can do it for him.

For now, he'll start by studying the *Atlas*.

MONDAY, five thirty a.m. sharp, Irene turns the corner from the women's dressing room and marches toward Gene. No way was he going to be late today. She eyeballs him. "Tie your watch into the drawstring of your pants." She lifts her mask over her nose and secures the strings with a bow at the crown of her head. Gene does the same. She faces the deep sink, one of the side-by-side pair across from the Heart Room.

"Stand here next to me. This is just practice. Tomorrow you'll scrub-in for your first case."

The steps are orderly, precise, and timed. "No shortcuts," she says. "Ten minutes. You won't get this from many of the others, especially the younger ones. They'll stop after half that time, but what's five extra minutes if it could save your patient an infection down the line?"

The idea of a patient being in any sense his seems ludicrous and he smiles, but Irene's piercing eyes say otherwise. They aren't unkind, just pointed, and they pin to his chest the realization that he is part of something important, something older. He can't screw it up.

THAT AFTERNOON, Dr. Harrington is hunched over a chart at the fourth floor nursing station, looking as weary as a water buffalo after a thousand-mile migration: his normal look. He's had his usual smoke and brief nap in the doctor's lounge after the last case. He pushes the chart aside and rotates the stainless chart-carousel. Then he sighs and checks the binding of other charts scattered on the Formica counter. Clearing his throat captures the attention of a nearby nurse who is writing in a chart. "By chance do you have Mrs. Perkins' chart," he says.

"Yes, Dr. Harrington. Would you like to see it?"

Dr. Harrington takes in a slow breath.

"No, no. I just wanted to be sure all the charts were accounted for." For an instant, Gene thinks she believes him, but when the Harrington gaze burns a hole through her cranium, she jumps from her seat.

"By all means…yes…here, Dr. Harrington. I'm sorry sir. I was done anyway. Here. Thank you. Is there anything else?"

He snorts and begins writing. She rolls her eyes at Gene and backs away, eventually storming into the hall. He gives her a little shrug, hoping to convey his distaste for the way she was treated. What more can he do?

Outside room 426, Perkins/Harrington is written on surgical tape attached to a placard next to the door.

"Mrs. Perkins," Dr. Harrington says. A petite white-haired

woman wearing a robe turns from where she stands looking out the window. "This is my assistant Eugene Hull."

Mrs. Perkin's expression shifts from bemusement to a smile before she shuffles over and shakes Dr. Harrington's hand and then Gene's. "I didn't recognize you at first," she says. "Those green pajamas and that cap threw me off."

Dr. Harrington nods in the practiced way of someone who has heard that before. "Indeed," he says. Dr. Harrington says little during these pre-op visits — a brief review of the surgery he will perform (mitral valve replacement in her case), the number of days she'll be in the ICU and the hospital, and that the anesthesiologist will be in to see her. Gene witnesses the confidence she, like all his patients, seem to have in Dr. Harrington. It comes through in their eyes, in the way they lean forward while listening to the hypnotizing timber and cadence of his voice.

"You won't forget to speak to my daughter-in-law after surgery," she says.

"I have the memory of an elephant, my dear."

"She's all I have, you know."

Dr. Harrington bends down and cradles her hand between his large mitts.

"Let me do the worrying. When you wake, your heart will be twenty again."

The man's like Jekyll and Hyde.

Tuesday morning, Gene is waiting as Jesse's four-bar-whistle and breakfast cart ascend to the fourth floor. He wants to be well fed and well hydrated. No fainting today.

"Man," Jesse says. "I hardly recognized you with that new doctor haircut you got going. Makes you look...official. What you doing here so early."

"I'm scrubbing in today."

Jesse checks his clipboard. "Little harder when you catch me before my rounds, 'stead of after." He runs his finger down the list.

"Looks like a full house today." He hangs the clipboard back. "Oh, well, someone's bound to have moved on overnight." He slides a tray out. "Take this. You like oatmeal?"

"Not particularly."

"You hungry?"

"Starved."

"You like oatmeal then." He hands Gene the tray. "You know the score of last night's game?"

"Very funny."

"Bet your ass you know the score — Dodger blue, man, twelve to two. I'm surprised you even showed your face this morning." Jesse gives Gene a little wave and pushes on. He whistles "Take Me Out to the Ballgame" as he rounds the corner.

"There's always tonight," Gene shouts.

GENE ENTERS THE HEART ROOM, arms bent, palms turned up chin high. Water drips from his elbows as he waits for Irene's attention. His hands, as naked as they'd ever felt, glow warm in the chilly room. So far, he's done everything right: pinned his watch to his scrub pants, secured his mask, scrubbed his hands and arms as proscribed for a full ten minutes, and backed his way through the heavy door without contaminating himself. Dr. Pereira stood next to Gene at the scrub sink, but abbreviated his handwashing and is now gowned, gloved, and draping Mrs. Perkins' chest with blue towels.

"Gene," Irene says. She hands him a sterile towel to dry his hands. "Lean forward. Remember: fingers to elbows. Don't let the towel touch your scrubs."

Although Gene met Mrs. Perkins yesterday afternoon, with her eyes now taped closed, head wrapped, and endotracheal tube protruding from her mouth, she is just another pear-shaped patient.

Having dried his hands and arms without screwing up, Gene drops the towel to the floor, just like a surgeon. Irene snaps open a sterile gown and holds it out as Gene carefully inserts his arms into the sleeves. Sandra ties his gown at the neck and waist while Irene stretches a latex glove open. He starts to insert his right hand.

"Other hand," she says.

He inserts his left hand, Irene pulling the glove's cuff far up and over his sleeve. On the second glove, he botches it — two of his fingers slide into a single glove finger and his thumb stumbles outside the glove. He reaches down with his other hand to fix it.

"Don't." Irene snaps the glove off completely. "You'll just contaminate yourself." She then turns to Betty. "Seven-and-a half, please."

"Gene-o." It's Dr. Boswell. He's clipping the end of the top drape to the IV poles. "I hope you don't have this much trouble with condoms."

Gene exhales and waits obediently for a second try.

He manages not to mangle the second set. "Dr. Pereira, where should I stand?"

"Right here next to me. And call me Rui."

In a swift stroke, Dr. Harrington makes a deep incision the length of Mrs. Perkins' chest. Rui cauterizes the bleeding skin edges. Irene passes the suction wand to Gene and directs his hand. He keeps the tip a couple inches from Dr. Pereira's cautery tip and sucks the smoke before it can curl up to the lights. He does the same after they split the length of the patient's sternum with the jigsaw and cauterize the bone. He's thrilled to be contributing, to be trusted, to be part of the team. The bone burning completed, Gene rests the suction wand on the patient. It slides off toward him. Gene reaches down for it and feels the iron clamp of Irene's grip on this arm. "Don't move!" Gene freezes and looks up to her dagger gaze. "You're contaminated."

"Gene-o," Boz says. "I thought you were going down again."

"Back away and wait," Irene says. "Sandra."

Sandra instructs Gene to hold his arms out. She removes his gown and gloves. "Keep your hands up."

"Tell me, Boz," Rui says. "Why do elephants drink so much?"

"No. No, *senhor*. We're done with that. No more recycled elephant jokes."

Irene hands the chest spreader to Dr. Harrington. Then with Sandra's help she dresses Gene with a new gown and fresh gloves. She motions for him to step up to the OR table. "Hands on top at all times."

Gene nods.

Dr. Harrington and Rui struggle as they try to fit the right-angled hands of the spreader under the edges of the sternum. Dr. Harrington hands the chest spreader back to Irene and she hands him a smaller one, which this time, inserts with ease. Rui cranks the chest open and turns his head to Dr. Boz. "Then I will tell you: To try to forget."

Dr. Harrington cranks a little farther. Something cracks. "God bless it!" Dr. Harrington says. "These small women don't make my job any easier."

Irene slaps long-toothed forceps in his palm with a little extra pop.

"Except for you, my dear." Dr. Harrington's eyes never waver from the patient.

Rui reaches up and directs the light, twisting the handle to focus the beam to the center of the chest.

Gene's view is not only different on this side of the ether screen, it is more immediate, like being in the game rather than watching from a box seat.

The surgeons divide the pericardial membrane and suture the edges in place, creating the familiar hammock cradling her heart.

With each artificial breath, Mrs. Perkins' salmon-colored lungs peep into view.

On bypass, Dr. Harrington makes an incision through the heart's left atrium to reveal the stenotic valve. Gene leans in to see what looks like a hopelessly seized plumbing part. What would normally have been two halves of a billowy parachute is now a thickened, yellow-white ring, like cheese-filled tortellini. Dr. Harrington excises the valve and hands it to Gene. It is hard as stone. Irene takes it from him and hands back an artificial valve. It looks like a metal disk that pivots on an axle through its equator.

After the new valve is sewn in place, Dr. Harrington, using a series of continuous loops, closes the thin left atrial wall with a single suture. However, he leaves the last loop of the stitch loose. "Fill," he says.

Rui loosens the purse-string tape around the vena cava. The heart, which looked like a deflated football, begins to inflate. As the chambers refill with blood, bubbles gurgle from the gap of the loose stitch. Rui places his hand under Mrs. Perkins' heart and massages more bubbles free. When nothing but blood exits the gap, Dr. Harrington cinches it closed, ties the final knot, and removes the cross-clamp from the aorta. Mrs. Perkins' heart begins to quiver. Irene hands Dr. Harrington the defibrillator paddles. He places them around the heart.

Rui lifts Gene's hands from Mrs. Perkins abdomen. The defibrillator fires. The heart jumps but continues to quiver.

"Up, Sandra," Dr. Harrington says. He fires the defibrillator again. Same result.

"Again."

"Ready."

Another jolt.

Nothing.

"Epi," Dr. Harrington says.

Irene hands him a syringe. He slides the needle into the neck of the heart and eases the plunger down less than a centimeter. He removes the needle and syringe. Dr. Harrington slides his hand under Mrs. Perkins' heart and delicately squeezes, as if testing the elasticity of a water balloon. He squeezes again and again, contracting her heart at a rate slower than the pulse pounding in Gene's neck.

Dr. Harrington takes the paddles from Irene.

This time Gene lifts his hands before Rui prompts.

The quiet thud of the defibrillator sounds. The heart jumps. The room is silent.

Nothing.

Gene looks up to Dr. Harrington. This can't be.

"One more time, Sandra."

"Ready."

Thump

"There you go." It's Dr. Boz

The heart beat once. A pause. Then another beat.

"Come on, honey," Dr. Boz says. "Pick up the pace."

Dr. Harrington holds out his hand to Irene, "Pacer wires."

A few minutes later, the pacemaker pushes her rate to sixty.

Several more minutes later, Dr. Harrington announces, "Off bypass."

Gene grips the drape. He almost lets out a cheer.

THE ICU IS a long rectangular space on the first floor, with a visitor entrance at one end. A bit farther down the hallway is a double-door patient entrance, through which Gene, Sandra, and Dr. Boz wheel Mrs. Perkins. They park her in slot three of the eight bed unit. Six of the eight beds, all in a line, are occupied by patients in varying states of consciousness, three connected to hissing ventilators, but all with competing EKG and blood pressure monitors chirping asynchronously like a mid-summer evening's cricket chorus. A nurse's aide pulls the side curtains between this bed and the others for privacy. It's what Gene remembers from Patty's brief stay almost three years ago.

Two of the ICU nurses help Mrs. Perkins settle in, as they call it. They are dressed identically in white uniforms, support hose, and white shoes. They measure the blood draining into graduated bottles from the two tubes inserted in Mrs. Perkins' chest. Dr. Boz continues to manually breath for her with the Ambu-bag. He calls out the settings he wants for the ventilator and the IV infusions. One nurse makes the infusion adjustments while the other reads off her vital signs. The respiratory tech connects Mrs. Perkins to the ventilator. The rhythmic *Psst…Prrr…Psst…Prrr* begins.

"Boz," Gene says. "You ever had someone's heart *not* start beating again?"

Dr. Boz answers while he completes the anesthesia record. "Most of the time, patients fly off bypass. Sometimes, like this lady, the engines don't fire up — at least not right off — particularly after a long bypass. We have a few tricks." He looks at Gene. "But you can't stay on bypass forever. At some point it's sink or swim."

THAT NIGHT, Gene completes a workout on the roof and records the effort. Then he heats his mom's spaghetti sauce, cooks some pasta, and whips up a protein shake. After loading a Simon and Garfunkel cassette, he opens the surgical text to the first chapter — Cardiac Anatomy — and reads between bites.

At the chapter's end, he pencils a schematic heart on a sheet of paper and diagrams the flow of blood: The venous blood, returning from the body's tissues, blue and devoid of oxygen, yet full of carbon dioxide, flows into the right atrium via the superior and inferior vena cavas. It then passes through the parachute-shaped tricuspid valve to the right ventricle. When the right ventricle contracts, the blood jettisons past the pulmonary valve into the pulmonary artery, which splits into "right" and "left," feeding the unoxygenated blood to the lungs. There, like box cars, the blood cells unload their carbon dioxide and load up the oxygen. The oxygenated blood emerges from the lungs via the pulmonary veins. The pulmonary veins empty into the left atrium. where the blood flows through another parachute valve, the mitral valve, to the left ventricle. This muscular chamber pumps the blood through the aortic valve and out the aorta to every hungry cell in the body, billions of them.

Gene looks down at his plate. Half the spaghetti remains, the sauce congealing. The music ended some time ago. He closes the book and reheats his dinner. In the stillness of the house, he listens for his heart. It is not so much a sound as a feeling in his chest and his neck. He counts the beats. Fifty-six in one minute. The next minute sixty-two. Rounded to sixty beats every minute of every hour of every day. He does the math on the pad. Thirty-one million, five-hundred-thirty-six thousand beats a year. At least. The textbook said what he feels: It is a marvel of monotony and dependability. *Beat, beat, beat* for an entire life.

Gene considers this and continues his calculations. One trillion, four-hundred-nineteen billion, one-hundred-twenty thousand beats over his father's life. How many beats remained in his father's heart the last time Gene saw him? That was just nine days before his father died. He'd driven back to SLO with Gene last September. On that foggy morning, when Gene dropped his father off at San Luis Obispo's airport, he'd thought about giving his father a hug. But he didn't. They weren't the hugging type.

He will never forget his father's last words after they shook hands: "Maybe I'll give that plan B some thought."

"Like you told me," Gene had said. "*Your life, your decision.*"

Gene swipes the surgical text from the table. It thuds to the floor, causing Apollo to cower beneath the table.

Chapter Nine

BRIDGE OVER TROUBLED WATER

September 1973

GENE and his father sat across from one another in a booth at Denny's overlooking I-5 and the Los Angeles basin. While contemplating the crammed parking lot, his father, in his habitual, rhythmic way, tapped his fingers against an icy metal milkshake cup. As always, his father had wanted to leave at sunrise, returning Gene to Cal Poly for his sophomore year.

Patty's assurance that time would fly by their first year apart hadn't panned out. He'd written letters every few days, and they talked on the phone each Sunday when the long-distance rates were the cheapest. Between the weekly chats, they set up a system called buzzing: if Patty heard her phone ring once, it was Gene sending a silent message — Thinking of you. Patty would reply with a single ring of her own. But the last twelve months had been like a hike through the desert. All the letters and phone calls kept them alive but failed to slake their thirst. That had only been quenched during holiday breaks and the summer recess.

Now, another tortuous year lay ahead.

His father was scheduled to give a couple lectures at a meeting for Respiratory Therapists in San Francisco. Before flying on to the City, his father had thought it would be fun to share a ride to San Luis Obispo, see the campus, and maybe sit in on one of Gene's lectures.

Neither father nor son had said a word to each other since Blythe, except when Gene asked, Ready for lunch? Sure, said his father. They were not at odds. There was no spat between them, no aching divide as existed between some of his friends and their fathers. Part of their silence stemmed from the competing road noise in the Jeep. But mostly, it was just the way they were. Quiet and reflective, Gene's father rested comfortably with silence. Unlike his mother, Gene thought, talk for talk's sake wasn't necessary.

His father stopped clicking his nails against the shake's metal cup, and still gazing out the window said, "Gene, did you ever notice how few women in the world are beautiful."

Gene watched a man and woman walking from their car toward the restaurant. The man said something, and the woman looked up and smiled. Gene examined other women walking to or from the parking lot. Then he assessed the busy noontime diner — the frumpy female patrons, the young girls with too much powder-blue eye shadow, the waitresses in white uniforms, support hose, and nicotine stained fingers — and it didn't take a slide rule to realize the truth in his father's hypothesis, at least on this small sample off I-5 on the outskirts of L.A. Sure, his dad made a shallow, insensitive comment that, if said by Nixon in a press conference, would have been one more nail in the poor guy's Watergate coffin. But Gene had to agree. The evidence was all around him. Still, he felt slightly embarrassed for both of them, guilty even.

"I guess you're right," he said.

His father gave Gene a tender smile. "I know what you're thinking. No, I don't mean face, legs, or whatever. I mean inside. True beauty." His father looked at Gene. "I guess what I'm saying is, I think Patty's one of those women. I can tell from the times we've talked. She's special."

"I think so."

"Don't lose her." He pointed his shake at Gene.

"I'm doing my best."

"I envy you." He removed his glasses, fogged each lens with his breath, and rubbed them dry with the shirttail of his polo. "Your life's a clean slate. You can go any direction from here."

He sipped his milkshake. Gene sensed more was coming.

"I mean you can be anything you want. Now's the time to explore. Sure, you're headed to an engineering degree, but combining that with pre-med courses is not an easy road."

"You really think I shouldn't try for engineering?"

"No, not at all. In fact, you may find some aspect of engineering is just the ticket. Then off you go."

"I feel pretty strong about going to medical school."

"It never hurts to have a plan B. His father tapped on the sweating cup again. "I guess, all I'm saying is don't be a doctor because I'm a doctor. You're talented. You have options. Look around. Your life. Your decision. Nothing's etched in stone."

Gene wanted to say, You're the reason I want to be a doctor. Not because it's expected, but because of the things you do. The things you're capable of doing. The respect you have from your colleagues and friends. Mostly he wanted to say, You're my hero. But just thinking those words tightened his throat. He looked down for a moment. "So, was heading up Respiratory Therapy your plan B?"

"No," his father said. "Not so much a plan as an opportunity." He looked down and then back to Gene." The hospital approached me, and I thought why not. A little change of pace. An opportunity to sleep through the night every day of the week…and I did get to see a few more of your ball games."

Gene grinned. He always pitched better with his father and Patty in the stands.

His father cocked his head. "Actually, I can't say that I ever really had a plan B. But I've had this little notion that I could have been a good pilot."

Gene bent forward. His father rarely opened up like this. "A pilot? Really."

"Yep. I took a ride in a small plane once." He leaned in momentarily and whispered, "Your mother wasn't too keen on the idea."

His mother spotted danger everywhere. Stay out of the heat. Don't go up on the roof. Don't swim now. You just ate.

Gene's thoughts leapt to how he might leverage a pilot-father into more frequent visits to Tucson over the next two years. "Maybe you should go for it," Gene said.

"Dee would have a fit."

"You guys could fly up for a visit on a weekend."

"That may be a little far."

"How about Sunday brunch in Sedona? Where it's cool in the summer. Mom'd go for that."

"She certainly hates the heat."

"You'd make a great pilot."

His father sipped his shake.

"Call it your plan B," Gene said. "Like you say, *Your life, your decision*."

"It's very much akin to what I already do…or did," his father said. "A checklist, a take-off, cruising, and then the landing."

"How do you mean?"

"In the OR I checked my equipment before each case, I drew up the medications, labeled them, and laid them out in a specific order…" He blinked hard, sipped his shake, and cleared his throat. "You get the idea."

The waitress walked up with a plate in each hand. "Can I get you gentlemen anything else."

"No. Thank you," Gene's father said.

Gene prepared his burger and then pushed the condiments across the table. His father poured ketchup over his fries in a prolonged lazy *ess*. Then he stopped and stared at his plate as if he were admiring an artistic design.

"There is one difference," he said. "When a plane goes down, so does the pilot. If a patient crashes, I survive."

"Crashes? You mean dies?"

His father nodded.

"Has that happened?"

"A couple times. Emergencies."

"What was that like?"

"Hard. But there wasn't much hope anyway."

"Like the little girl."

Gene's father paused in mid-chew. "Yes. Something like that."

There it was—another opening. Tell him. Don't be a chickenshit. "You know, that's when I knew I wanted to be a doctor."

His father offered a weak smile. "The operating room is different."

"I wish you were still in the Heart Room. I could watch you work."

His father munched on a fry, thinking.

"What really would have been cool," Gene said, "is to have watched Patty's surgery."

His father took a deep breath and let it out. "Tell you what. Maybe you could shadow Rui next summer."

"That would be great."

"We should get going."

When the credit card came back, his father signed and then studied Gene. "Yes. It'll be good experience. Life in the OR might not be quite what you think."

"I'm sure it's better."

Ten days later, Gene pedaled under a virgin blue sky to the campus post office. The sight of a diagonal line behind his PO box's small window raised a smile. A letter from Patty. Her first since he'd returned to school. He dropped it into his backpack and, arms hanging at his side, cruised his squeaky ten-speed toward his apartment, thinking that when there, he'd pop open a Dr. Pepper, settle into his beanbag chair, and sip every flavorful word, inhale each Estée Lauder molecule lingering on her signature pale-lavender note.

The song "Just You 'n' Me" played in his head. Last summer, while he and Patty drank beer at St. James Infirmary, the same Chicago hit ricocheted through the bar. Gene had just turned nineteen, Arizona's drinking age. He pointed at Patty as the song played and then carved their initials among the other vows of love etched across the booth's wooden top. He scratched a heart around it. Patty added an arrow with two socks hanging from the point.

Now he sang in full voice, mimicking Peter Cetera's high-pitched soul. Who cared if the passing cyclists thought he was a little odd? The late September afternoon was working on him. It was still warm enough for shorts and a t-shirt. The smell of the ocean swelled his lungs, and the letter from Patty lightened his backpack. Yet it was the kind of day that pained him for his inability to share it with her.

Gene approached the two-bedroom apartment he shared with his psychology-major roommate, Doug. Doug's car was gone from his assigned space. The lucky bastard had already left for Santa Barbara to visit his girlfriend. The apartment complex was nothing fancy, resembling a pink Motel 6, complete with kidney-shaped pool. The previous weekend, his father had spent a night on the couch before flying up to San Francisco for his meeting. "There's something to be commended in having a simple life," his father had said while drinking a Michelob and admiring the distant ocean from the third-floor roof. "I have fond memories of those days."

Gene locked his bike to the rack under the stairs of building 5 and heard a phone ring upstairs. He bounded up the concrete slab steps. It was definitely his phone. It just had to be Patty. That would be perfect. She sometimes surprised him with a call between their usual cheap-rate, Sunday-night rendezvous. He fumbled with the key before unlocking the door, lunged for the receiver on the kitchen counter, and blurted *hello*.

There was a couple seconds' pause and then a strained, high voice: "Gene..."

"Who is this?" It sounded like a prank.

"Gene, it's Mom." Her voice veered off into a painful squeal.

"Mom?" He tossed his book bag onto one of the four folding chairs around the dining table. There were distant, mumbled voices on the line, thuds against the receiver. Then another voice.

"Gene, I don't know what to..." It was his sister Suzanne. Her voice broke into sobs.

Gene listened, his eyes darting in random directions. "Suzanne...Suzanne is mom hurt? What happened!"

"Dad..." She crumbled again, and then spoke in a nearly inaudible squeal. "He's gone."

Gone?

"Suzanne, what do you mean?" His pulse hammered high in his neck.

On the other end there was only crying between attempts at words. Finally, through gasps, she said, "We've... been trying...to reach you. When...when can you get here?"

"Suzanne, you're not making any sense." He tried to turn from the panic growing in his stomach.

Suzanne screamed over the phone: "He's gone, Gene. He died!"

This wasn't real. His eyes scanned the room — past Doug's bike leaning against the wall, past the record albums piled under the window, up to a photo on the shelf over the stereo. A photo of Patty and his father after a high school baseball game. They're sitting on the bleachers. She's tucked under his arm. They're smiling.

Gene stepped toward the photo, to the edge of the carpet, as close as the phone would reach.

"Gene. You there?"

"Yeah."

"He was in a helicopter crash...He's dead." Suzanne's words trailed into more violent weeping.

"What!" Gene imagined a crash site, a Vietnam-like bubble cockpit on its side, the rotors akimbo. A wave of heat surged to his face. Lightheaded, he dropped to the tiled floor and rested against a cupboard, the phone on his lap.

"Gene," his sister's voice leaked from the receiver.

A sphere of darkness and silence enveloped him. He closed his eyes. There was only his raw breath and a band tightening across his chest. When he opened his eyes, he saw a narrow tunnel of light. He staggered to the sink and bent his head to the kitchen faucet, knocking over a tower of dishes. At the window, he looked out briefly before stumbling through the door, then up two flights to the roof access. When he burst into the sun deck's bright light, everything in his periphery was still fuzzy and gray. He ducked under strings of party lanterns, wove around cheap lounge chairs, his roommate's hibachi, the weathered mattress, and the sorry couch. At the roof's boundary, he rested his hands on the low stucco wall and blubbered. He stretched his fingers. His hands. They could be his father's hands — the shape of the thumb, the pattern of veins, that little swirl of hairs on the wrist. But his father's hands never trembled like this.

Gene fixed his gaze past the shoulder-to-shoulder roofs, beyond the crowns of eucalyptus and coastal pines, to the ocean's steady, gray ledge. Soon, his gulping breaths eased, and his mind cleared enough to see the next step. He needed to call Patty.

When he returned to his apartment, he picked up the phone's handset. "Suzanne?" Nothing. He tapped the switch-hook for a dial tone and dialed. Please be home.

He pictured Patty rising from the couch, saw her idle walk to the phone, willed her hand to the receiver…but after ten rings, she didn't answer. "Shit."

With phone in hand, he dropped to the floor again and sobbed. Cried until he was drained of tears.

The phone rang.

"Gene, are you okay?" It was Suzanne.

"This isn't real." He took a deep breath. "How's Mom?"

"They're giving her something now. She'll get quiet and then she just goes hysterical."

"Where are you?"

"We're still at the hospital. Some administrator's office." She sniffed. "Dr. Pereira just left. He's pretty upset, too."

"What the hell happened?"

"Apparently Dad rode along to pick up a patient in Globe who needed heart surgery. The thing crashed right after takeoff."

"No. No."

"He made it to the emergency room…." Her voice squeaked to a stop.

Once again Gene stared at the photo of his father and Patty. This couldn't be.

Suzanne took a deep breath. "But he died there. Dr. Pereira said his aorta tore. There was nothing he could do."

Gene pounded the floor.

"Mom's hysterical. She smashed a crystal vase that was on the administrator's desk. I've never seen her like this. She keeps saying, 'He promised. He promised.' I don't know what she means."

Gene rubbed the pain at his temples.

"When can you get here?" Suzanne said. "Rodney's trying to book a flight from New Hampshire."

That's right, her husband's new job with Hilton. She had stayed in Arizona to handle the movers.

"I'll stay with Mom tonight," she said. "But I can't deal with this alone. This can't be good for the baby…" She gasped. "Oh Gene… the baby will never know him." She broke down again.

"Suzanne. Please don't." Jeez, she was due in two months. The first grandchild. He choked up. "I'll call before I leave. Soon."

He sat at the kitchen counter. Rubbed his eyes. What next? Try Patty. Then he remembered her unopened letter and unzipped his backpack.

> Dear Gene,
>
> As I write this, I'm showered and ready for bed. I'm wearing your favorite nightshirt. The one with the *Bear Down Arizona* slogan on the front. I can't wait until Thanksgiving and I see you again. It's getting harder and harder to watch you drive away. Two more months! That's excruciating. But, by the time you get this, I'll be three days closer to having you in bed with me….

Gene crumpled the letter. In less than a day he would be with her. And why? Because his father had died. He slammed his fists on the counter and then kicked a hole in the pass-through wall. Gene had practically encouraged his father to get into that helicopter. His stomach roiled. He bolted for the sink and retched.

GENE DROVE his Jeep east on State Route 46 toward I-5, past vineyards and almond groves tinted a yellowish orange by the setting sun. The *Chicago* cassette was on the last cut. Other cassettes were in a heap on the passenger seat. Hopefully he'd grabbed enough music to get him home.

For any other trip, Gene would have choreographed the music and lined up the cassettes. His father had admired Gene's way of thinking. *Linear* he called it. It was the way Gene remained level. It was the way he coped at school, setting up a calendar for each class at the beginning of the quarter and following a strict study plan each day. By quarter's end, he knew the material. No need to cram during dead week. Planning, charting a course, considering points of deviation and having alternative solutions, those were his strengths. He knew it. And he knew an unanticipated perturbation in his life, like this — his father's death — could send him spinning. It had. But after hastily scribbling a note for Doug — My dad died. Driving back — he now had nine hours to regain his balance. The gas tank was full. He hadn't checked the tires, but they had been fine a little over a week ago.

Mile after indistinguishable highway mile rushed past his headlights, the lit asphalt a backdrop for images of his father. He saw him, fingers hooked through the chain link fence, standing behind the grade-school backstop during Little League night games. He pictured him lying on the couch — reading or sleeping; there was no in-between — or sitting cross-legged in front of his stereo equipment, wearing those gigantic studio-grade headphones. It took him several Saturdays to transfer his prized jazz collection from LP to reel-to-reel. Or the time his father injected something into Gene's IV when Gene was in third grade and had broken his leg. They were in the emergency room. "You're going to fall asleep for a minute," his father said. "When you wake up your leg will be in a cast. You'll feel much better." It didn't seem possible, but it was true. The next thing he knew his leg was propped on pillows. Plaster extended from his toes to his thigh. His leg had felt warm and heavy, but the lightning pain had vanished.

Halfway down the desolate spine of California, he spotted the illuminated, yellow sign for the Denny's where they'd stopped for lunch. He pulled off the highway and gassed up at the Exxon before entering the restaurant. The pay phone was in the back by the restrooms and high chairs. When he called Patty, there was again no answer. He slammed the receiver into its cradle. He vaguely remembered her telling him something about clinical rotations on the evening shift. He scooped the dime from the pay phone and made a collect-call home.

"Hey, Suzanne, I'm outside LA."

"Why didn't you call when you left?"

"I'm doing my best. How are things there?"

"Nobody's sleeping."

"Who else is there?"

"Just mom and me now. The Valium has kicked in…for her I mean. I'm not taking it. We were outside by the pool. I can't breathe inside the house."

"I know what you mean."

"Reverend Collins came over. I've never seen him shaken like this. He was always such a fortress on Sundays. He wants to talk with us tomorrow about the service."

"I've got another six hours, maybe less if I push it."

"Don't push it. We don't need you in an accident."

"I'll be responsible. Isn't that my reputation?"

She laughed. "In spades. Dad always said it was only fair since I'd given him a double dose of consternation. I can hear him say that — consternation. That was during his build-my-vocabulary phase."

Gene leaned against a high chair, which shifted and knocked a stack of boosters to the ground.

"What was that?"

"Nothing. Just me fumbling." Gene let the receiver hang while he re-stacked the booster seats. "Okay, I'm back."

"Look, Gene, there's one more thing." Then she lowered her voice, sounding like her hand was cupped around the mouthpiece. "Mom says they had a big fight about flying."

"Recently?"

"Five years ago. I guess he started flying lessons without telling her. He promised to quit. She didn't know he was on a mercy flight today."

A ride in a small plane. His dad had said that right here at Denny's. Not a flying lesson. But that explained an argument he'd overheard. Suzanne gone off to Arizona State. Gene was a high-school freshman. That's right. Five years ago. He had just stepped out onto the roof, near the back side of the house, taking measurements for his deck, when he heard indistinct shouting from the patio. Then his mother had walked out into the bright sun and screamed, "And I'm tired of this heat. So, what's it going to be?" She looked up at what must have been Gene's stunned expression and said, "Get off the roof. Now." It scared him at the time, but all had seemed fine later.

"Gene?"

"I feel kind of sick."

"Eat something."

He needed to hear Patty's voice. He paid the bill and tried her again on the pay phone. No answer. God, where was she?

Two-hundred-fifty miles later, his Jeep chattered across the bridge over the Colorado River and slowed through the Arizona border agricultural checkpoint. Seventy miles after that, he saw a sign — REST STOP, two miles. Eight years ago, there hadn't been an eastbound stop. Only the westbound side.

Gene scanned the desert median along the feathered edge of the Jeep's headlights, checked his rear-view mirror and eased off the highway. He killed the engine and doused the lights. Across the median, a few trucks slumbered at the rest stop. This was where his father had tried to save the girl. She would have been Patty's age by now.

Gene stepped out of his Jeep and leaned against the warm hood. The engine ticked. A car sped past. Far ahead and far behind, there were only pinpoint headlights.

That first night in their Huntington Beach hotel, the air had felt thick and salty. His mother remained next door while his father passed out milkshakes to Gene and Suzanne in their room. "It's been a long, sad day," he said. Suzanne, freshly showered and in pajamas, pulled the covers up to her waist. Their father asked how they were doing, and they'd both shrugged. After several sips, Suzanne asked him to explain what happened. She'd asked him twice before on the long drive to the hotel, but he patiently explained again. He said the girl had just turned twelve. She and her mother were returning from a birthday trip to Disneyland. The girl had to pee, and the nearest rest stop was on the other side of the highway. The girl's mother pulled over. The girl jumped out and ran around the front of their pickup. She never saw the Cadillac. "There was nothing I could do," his father said. "Nothing." Then he told them not to think about it. They were on vacation.

But Gene had replayed the accident each night on the motel's water-stained ceiling. He saw the Cadillac hit the girl. He saw her fly through the air with an astonished look on her face. He saw his father, his hero, breathing for her, trying to save her life. Each time he pictured the scene, he added more and more detail like her jelly legs and the shoe that flew off, her open eye, and the blood on his father's upper lip. It all frightened him, but he couldn't look away. After a few days he stopped imagining her eye. Then other things changed. He would run to his father's side and help him breathe for her. He could feel his breath filling her chest. She would open her eyes, and he would raise her head and offer her water from the heavy thermos. He continued to think of her when he returned to Phoenix, but less and less as swimming and baseball filled his summer. Still, on the nights he spied on Suzanne and Rodney from the roof, Gene imagined how grateful the girl would have been if he'd saved her. How she might thank him with a kiss on the lips. Seemed silly now.

With the start of sixth grade he'd been eager to tell his friends at recess about the accident. Their mouths hung open. They all thought his father was a hero. They asked if Gene was going to be a doctor, too, someday. Being a doctor wasn't for them, not if it meant getting someone's blood on your mouth. Gene didn't have to think long about that question. The answer had come as easy as leaving out the part where he fainted. "Yes."

He started up the Jeep and pulled away, as sure as he'd ever been about where he was headed.

Several miles later, the cassette of Simon and Garfunkel's *Bridge Over Troubled Water* ended. That was all the music he'd brought. In the churning dark of the Jeep, shadowy hints of saguaro and ocotillo, and the smell of desert creosote calmed him. The lights of Phoenix grew larger by the minute. A few more miles to the Maricopa Freeway. He was almost home. He wished now, he'd thought to bring the photo of Patty and his father. It had steadied him back at the apartment. *How about a picture of your two biggest fans?* That's what his father had said before putting his arm around Patty and handing the camera to Gene.

At the intersection with the freeway he slowed to a stop short of the northbound turn lane. Now, he had only one "biggest fan," and he needed her. He flipped the turn signal to the right, crossed two lanes and entered the southbound ramp to Tucson.

AT THREE-THIRTY A.M., nagging doubts about this detour to Patty rose into the balmy night. Suzanne would be worrying about him, but he'd call her from a gas station and tell her he had a flat; that everything was okay but his spare had been flat as well and it took a while to get help. It wouldn't be like him not to have checked his spare, but under the circumstances she'd believe him. Wouldn't she? Of course not. Not from her cautious little brother.

He parked in a visitor's space at the front of the Sunrise Apartment complex. A couple miles away on I-10, eighteen-wheelers downshifted with a guttural stutter. Guided by the oblong glow of landscape lights, he followed sandstone steps to the residents' covered parking. Patty's Sapphire Blue Mustang wasn't there. God, what if Suzanne had reached her, and she'd gone off to Phoenix without waiting for him? Again, he looked up and down the line of cars parked under the aluminum lid. No Mustang.

Hoping she'd answer when he knocked, he trudged up the stairs of Building B. At the end of the covered walkway, two people stood in silhouette. Gene's heart accelerated. One of the figures was Patty. There was no mistaking the way her leg locked straight as she rested against the apartment windowsill. The other figure was a man. He leaned against the railing.

"Patty!" He jogged toward her. "Patty." His voice shook.

The man stepped in front of her and extended his arm like a traffic cop. Gene expected him to say something, but Patty spoke first. "Gene?"

She ran to him. The words he'd assembled for this moment disintegrated. He embraced her with a crushing hug, burying his face in her neck. He tried to form sentences but surrendered to the sorrow and exhaustion and sobbed.

The man's voice said, "Are you going to be okay?" Gene thought he was speaking to him, until he felt Patty's head nod. "I've got to get back," the man whispered. Gene didn't look up. He couldn't face a stranger. The walkway vibrated from muted footfalls.

Patty pulled her head back and examined Gene. "What happened?" she said.

"Who was that?" He sniffed and then wiped below each eye with his thumb. He wanted to curl up inside her dark blue scrubs.

"Jake. He gave me a lift home. My god, what are you doing here?"

Two sleepless hours later, they were lying on Patty's bed. The first light of day peeked through a thin break in the blackout curtains. The long, white sliver cut across the bed at their ankles. They'd removed their shoes but nothing else. Gene still wore his jeans and green Cal Poly Engineering t-shirt from the drive. Patty's stockinged foot ran a soft line along his shin. She repeated it, over and over. Her head lay on his shoulder, a faint smell of her conditioner filling his nose.

"Suzanne's going to kill me," he said. "I forgot to call."

"I'm glad you came." She lifted her hand resting on his abdomen and pulled him closer.

"I should let her know I'm alive. Shit. How do I explain that I'm here?"

"Do you want me to drive up with you?

"Can you?"

"It's not going to be easy. I have a shift today. I'll call the coordinator's office."

"By the way. Where's your car?"

"It's stuck at the hospital. The battery's dead. The guy you saw tried to jump it. He's a fourth-year med student. We're both on nights in the ER right now. He lives catty-corner from here, so he gave me a lift. I'll have to get a tow."

The number of issues Gene needed to consider were mounting: Patty's dead car, the scare he must have put into Suzanne and his mother, how he'd explained the detour to Patty's place; and, he needed to reach his roommate. Then there were his classes. Jeez. Why'd he taken such a heavy load? "What about your classes?" he said.

Patty traced Gene's lips with her finger. "Maybe I can get Peggy's notes."

Patty's roommate, Portly Peggy, was visiting her boyfriend at Arizona State in Tempe.

"A lot depends on when you have the service," she said. "I might need to come back here until then."

Patty's touch was sending chills down one arm. "You know," he said. "We haven't put our socks on yet."

Patty placed the flat of her hand on his chest. "Maybe you should call your sister."

He rolled to the edge of the bed. "I'll be right back."

Gene sat on the couch and dialed. He could pretend no one answered… "Suzanne, it's Gene."

"We are worried sick about you."

"I'm okay. I'm at a gas station in Casa Grande and —"

"What the hell are you doing there? That's halfway to Tucson… Oh, I get it, you're going to see Patty."

"Look, I couldn't reach her yesterday. I'm worried."

"Gene, we need you here. Your family needs you."

"Dad would want me to go."

"Don't pull that. That's not fair."

None of this was fair.

"Why didn't you call and let us know you were heading to Tucson?"

"I tried. I couldn't keep my eyes open, so I parked at a rest stop to sleep. It was the one near where that little girl died." That would soften her up. "I tried to call, but the phone was dead."

Suzanne's soft breathing felt close.

"I haven't thought of that in years."

"Me either."

"Okay, get here when you can."

"It's an hour to Tucson. Patty's going to be devastated. I hope she can come up with me."

"Have her drive."

When he returned to the bedroom, he lay on his back next to Patty. She was sitting on the bed with her legs crossed. "I guess you heard," he said.

She nodded.

"We have at least another hour before she'd expect us to leave."

Patty pulled her knees to her chest. "You stopped where the girl died?"

"Just to stretch my legs."

"Do you think about it a lot?"

"The accident? I was thinking about him. You know. His life."

She took Gene's hand. "I didn't know it still bothered you."

"No. It's nothing like that. Not like it used to be."

"You're sure?"

Gene shrugged. "That was a long time ago. It's like something I saw on TV."

Chapter Ten

CODE BLUE

Summer 1974

GENE's surprised to find Rui sitting on the couch in the doctor's lounge. He already has the comic section folded into quarters and is working on the Jumble. "Look at this." He holds the paper out to Gene. "The last word."

Gene lowers the tray to the coffee table. Trying not to focus too hard on the word, he squints. He's discovered that by not overthinking, the unscrambled word will float to the surface. And there it is — anyone.

"Bravo." Rui pens it into the spaces

"You're here kind of early," Gene says.

"I covered trauma last night."

"Slept here?"

"*Sim.*"

Gene slowly opens the milk carton. "Rui, were you on call when my dad came in?"

Rui sets the paper on his lap. "No."

"But you saw him in the emergency room?"

"I rushed down as soon as I heard."

"I never did learn any details. Just that he died in the ER."

"We tried our best."

"Oh, I'm sure of that."

Rui stands and walks to the coffee machine.

"Was he ever awake?" Gene says. "Did he say anything?"

With his back to Gene, Rui stirs creamer into a cup, over and over. His body language says it all. He'd rather not talk about it.

"Sorry," Gene says.

Rui turns. His eyes are red. "It was my worst day."

"Mine, too."

Rui smiles bravely. "Today is today." He points to the couch. "Sit. I will teach you how to tie knots."

Rui pushes the coffee table away and brings over a chair. From his pocket, he pulls a pack of 5-0 nylon. He opens the pack, unfurls one of the sutures, and hands it to Gene. Then he unfurls one for himself.

With Gene following his lead, they wrap their sutures around the respective armrests of the chair facing them. Rui is specific in how Gene is to hold the suture, which fingers to use, and the necessity to tie square knots, at least five throws, one atop the other, keeping tension on the suture at all times.

The suture is as slick as fishing line, and what looked easy as he watched the surgeons work in the Heart Room is not so easy after all. But then throwing a curve ball wasn't easy when he'd first tried. "Practice, practice, practice," Rui says. "That's all it takes." He hands Gene the remainder of the pack — eight sutures left. "Take these home."

Rui removes suture scissors from his shirt pocket. "Hold them like this. Thumb and ring finger here. Index finger extending along the top. See?" He moves his hand up, down, side to side. "For maximum control." He grasps the tag ends of the suture, the five-throw knot standing taut from the armrest. "Open the tips of the scissors very slightly. See the small V it forms? Place that around the suture...like so...about an inch above the knot. Gently now, move the scissor tips down the suture until they contact the top of the knot. Angle the tip forty-five degrees...and cut." Rui flips the two strands of freed suture onto the chair and fingers the knot. "A perfect two-millimeter tag. A beautiful thing. Now you try it."

Gene mimics what he's just seen. Perfection will come later.

"What about the way Dr. Harrington ties knots?" Gene asks. Now that's slick."

"You mean the one-handed tie?"

"I guess. His left hand holds one of the suture legs straight up and his other moves like hummingbird wings."

"Flashy, yes. But also necessary in some instances." He wraps another suture around the armrest and blazes through a one-handed knot. "You no doubt have heard of Davey Concepción?" Rui says.

"Sure. Shortstop for the Reds."

Rui used to play baseball in Portugal. His stepfather was American, and while his friends played football, Rui played baseball. He even played one year in the Dominican League. First base.

"I played with him. Before he was a star. Best hands I ever observed. Soft hands — the way he scoops up the ball — soft as pillows. A beautiful thing." Rui hands Gene the longest of the suture remnants, and Gene begins another two-handed knot, counting toward five controlled, overhand throws.

"Davey rarely made an error. The routine ground balls, he fielded with two hands. Nothing flashy. That is a two-handed tie — the controlled way to tie a secure knot. But sometimes, Davey could not use two hands. He had to stretch to one side or the other to make the play. That is the one-handed tie. When it is the only way."

Gene adds the fifth and final throw and examines his work — a monkey could do better.

"A grand first attempt," Rui says.

"Looks like crap."

Rui laughs. "Then you must practice."

By the end of the week, the ladder-back chairs in Gene's kitchen are a vine-like jungle of 5-0 nylon. He's starting to fall into a comfortable routine in the Heart Room. He suctions the smoke and blood, interjecting the tip of his suction wand into the mix of rapidly moving hands without hindering them as they incise, cauterize, and suture. It's like dodging fastballs in a batting cage. And at the end of each case, after Dr. Harrington has left the room, Rui and Gene close the wound: Rui placing the stitches and tying the knots; Gene cutting the tag. He's only cut too close once, requiring Rui to re-tie the knot.

But at the end of Friday's only case, Rui places the first subcutaneous suture, pops off the needle, and angles the suture toward Gene. "Would you do the honors?"

Gene hesitates.

"You've been practicing I assume."

"Yes."

Boz stands and looks down at the surgical field. "Is this our new Friday routine? Motor through the case only to have it downshifted into first gear at the end."

"Are we not a teaching hospital?" Rui says.

"Not really."

Gene accepts the suture strands.

"Remember, soft hands," Rui says.

Gene takes a breath and starts to tie. The suture slips from his left hand. He tries again. The first throw is good. He stumbles through the second, the third better, but all painfully slow in their execution down to the fifth and final throw. Rui holds the suture taut, nods in approval and cuts.

Dr. Boz slumps back into his seat. "Sandra, can you call my wife and tell her I'll be late for breakfast in the morning."

"Ignore him," Rui says while placing the second suture. "Here. Go again. Relax."

"I practiced, honest. I was much faster last night."

"That's what she said," Boz says from behind the screen.

"You are doing fine," Rui says. "Thousands of ground balls it took before Concepcion became the best short stop in the world. With this, it is the same. The same with any skill."

Gene concentrates on the next knot.

"Hey batter, batter," Boz says.

This simple skill is one of hundreds he will have to learn someday. Just what he's witnessed the past two weeks is overwhelming: the anatomy of thorax and heart, all the different surgeries, hundreds of instruments. Even the simplest thing like cutting suture involves four precise steps…to do it right. So much detail. And Gene knows he's been exposed only to the topsoil of this mountain of knowledge. "How can I possibly learn all of this?"

Rui cuts the last sub-q knot. He takes a long nylon suture from Irene and begins approximating the skin's edges with a series of loops reminiscent of baseball stitching. Two weeks ago, Gene never heard the word approximating used this way — to bring the skin edges together.

"A single day," Rui says, "it leads to the next and the next until a week has passed, then the weeks form months, and then years. Don't look too far. It is not my intent to overwhelm you. By the time you complete medical school and residency, you shall be teaching me."

Rui ties the last knot using his needle holder — yet another way to tie a simple knot. Gene is quiet as he cuts the tag.

The more he learns from Rui and Dr. Harrington over the remaining five weeks, the more convincing he will be in an essay or interview. Besides, he wants to earn a glowing recommendation from Dr. Harrington, not just inherit it through his father.

MOST NURSES on the fourth-floor scatter as Dr. Harrington and Gene walk down the hallway. Like Zebras near a watering hole, they maintain a safe distance. As Gene witnessed last week, those whose activities inadvertently clash with Dr. Harrington risk suffering a pointed bite. Nothing fatal, just a warning not to impede him in any way. But today, the King-of-the-Floor is in a good mood as rounds are concluding. His only case of the day went well, the post-op patients are recovering more or less on schedule, including Mrs. Perkins whom Dr. Harrington transferred to the floor from the ICU this morning. And, earlier, Irene reported that his afternoon office schedule will include four new patients. In the way Gene relishes the summer heat, so does Dr. Harrington relish a full office schedule, even on a Friday afternoon. Four prospective hearts to mend. He must be licking his chops.

Gliding along in Dr. Harrington's wake, Gene enters the room of Mr. Roger Elliott, the patient who was on the operating table when Gene fainted. Today, Mr. Elliott is being discharged home. Gene has followed the man's progress throughout: from extubation in the ICU on day two (followed by a coughing fit), taking baby steps down the fourth-floor hallway in gown and paper slippers, his sparse hair a wild nest as the nurse rolled his bottle-laden IV pole with one hand and supported his elbow with the other, to now, dressed as Gene has not seen him before, in slacks and a short-sleeve shirt, sitting comfortably in the chair beside the hospital bed. A Band-Aid covers an IV puncture on his right arm.

"Now that I'm unplugged," he says. "I guess I can go." He stands and comes around the end of the bed. He takes Dr. Harrington's hand in both of his. "I can't thank you enough for the second chance." His eyes water.

"You are most welcome," Dr. Harrington says. "Someone will be in shortly to wheel you downstairs. The nurse has the prescription for your medications. If you have any questions. Any trouble. You call my office. The number's on the paperwork. Otherwise, I'll see you in a week."

"What about my diet? I mean any things I should or should not eat?"

"It's all on the paperwork."

The man pats his abdomen. "Tough way to lose a few pounds." He laughs nervously and then glances at Gene, standing near the sink. Mr. Elliott steps closer to Dr. Harrington. "Listen," he whispers. "How long before...well you know...anything sexual? I don't want to collapse on top of my wife again."

"I thought you were raking your pink lawn."

"Raking. Yes."

Dr. Harrington leans in. "When your pecker is willing, your

heart will be ready." Both men pull back in laughter as an orderly pushing a wheelchair enters the room. "We'll talk in the office," Dr. Harrington says.

With rounds complete, Gene and Dr. Harrington walk silently to the dressing room. Dr. Harrington says, "I think I'll rest my eyes a minute." He opens the door to the doctor's lounge and adds, "See you Monday."

Every morning when Gene pulls into his spot by the cooling towers, Dr. Harrington's Cadillac Seville is one of only a couple cars in the shaded doctors' parking. And every evening when Gene departs, Dr. Harrington's car is still there. It's like the man never goes home.

Before a quick trip to Dr. Harrington's office across the street, Gene changes clothes, slips on the white coat, and heads to the diner for lunch. Irene told him to stop by. She has a heart model he can borrow. "Surgical anatomy is easier to understand in three dimensions," she said. Then he'll spend the rest of the afternoon at Sluggers. His workout clothes and bat are in the Jeep. It will feel good to work up a sweat.

Gene is halfway through a grilled ham and cheese sandwich and raising a Dr. Pepper to his mouth when a tone sounds from the ceiling speakers. He anticipates the female voice in the instant before she broadcasts: "Code Blue. Lobby. Code Blue. Lobby."

He's the only one at the counter. The red vinyl booths are nearly empty except for an elderly couple and two wide-eyed candy stripers staring at him.

The overhead page sounds again. "Code Blue. Lobby. Code Blue. Lobby."

Gene hustles the short distance to the lobby, conscious of his Heart Team coat and the looks from the people he passes. At the information desk, a white-haired volunteer wearing a pink uniform has the phone to her ear and a panicked look on her face. She points in the direction of the gift shop. He expects to find the Code

Team working on the victim. But there are two women kneeling over a girl on the ground. The woman in a tennis outfit repeatedly pats the girl's face. "Becca. Becca!" Gene rushes up to her. The girl on the ground is about his age. Her eyes stare to the ceiling and foamy saliva spills from the corners of her mouth.

Gene recognizes the second woman. She runs the gift shop. "Oh, finally," she says, her voice shaking. "I don't think she's breathing."

The other woman looks at Gene, tears drip from her cheeks. "I don't know what happened," she says, and then, to the girl, "Becca!" Her voice breaks to a high pitch. The girl's lips are the color of a plum.

Gene's heart gallops. Without thinking he kneels, wipes the girl's mouth, places a hand on her forehead and the other under her chin. He takes a deep breath and covers her mouth with his. When he breathes out, the air meets resistance. He lifts her chin some more and his breath enters the girl like he's taken the lid off a vacuum bottle. She jerks and arches. Gene reels back as she coughs, spraying his face. With a quick wipe, he wipes his mouth with his sleeve.

"Turn her," someone says. A man, out of breath and wearing a white coat, kneels by Gene. Together, they turn the girl on her side. Her chest seems to rock. Gene lifts her chin and another whoosh of air enters. He holds his hand there, supporting her chin while she breathes.

The doctor presses two fingers against the girl's neck. "What happened?"

Another man in scrubs appears at the girl's head and places a plastic mask over her face. Gene moves his hand. "I don't know," he says.

The woman who called the girl Becca folds herself over the girl's head and cries while petting her hair. She looks at her hand. "Oh, my God."

The doctor looks at the woman's bloodstained fingers and leans over to inspect the girl's head. "Small laceration."

The gift-shop woman explains that she heard a thud outside the door. When she came around the counter, the girl was on the ground having a convulsion. It seemed like it went on forever, but when the girl finally stopped shaking, she wasn't breathing. "That's when this doctor arrived," she says. "Her face was so blue."

The girl blinks slowly, her eyes searching as if she's trying to make sense of her surroundings. Condensation forms inside the mask.

"Ma'am?" the doctor says to the crying woman. "Are you her mother?" She raises her head and nods. "I'm Dr. Knudson from the emergency room. Your daughter appears stable now, but we're going to take her to the ER." He gestures to an orderly, standing behind Gene with a gurney. Gene moves out of the way. "Want to give us a hand?" the doctor says to Gene. As he helps hoist the girl, Gene smells urine and notices a wet spot on her maroon, ASU running shorts. With the sheet from the gurney, he covers her to her waist.

The doctor looks at Gene's Heart Team coat. "Resident?"

Gene hesitates. The woman brushes her hand across her daughter's brown hair. "I'm working with Dr. Harrington," he says.

The girl's mother removes the elastic band from her daughter's ponytail. "You're going to be okay, baby."

The orderly pushes the gurney while Dr. Knudson leads the way at the foot. Gene hangs back. Holding her daughter's hand, the woman turns toward Gene and says, "Thank you, Doctor."

Gene nods and then runs up beside Dr. Knudson. "Mind if I tag along?"

An ER nurse exits from behind the curtained enclosure and mouths "Ready" to Gene. Dr. Knudson writes in the girl's chart at the work-station counter. "I think they're ready," Gene says.

Dr. Knudson closes the chart's metal cover. On the front, Rebecca Layne is handprinted on white surgical tape. As Gene follows him, the doctor says, "I didn't get your name."

"Gene Hull."

Dr. Knudson stops and turns. "Carl's son?"

"Yes."

He scans Gene's full height. "Quite a guy, your dad." He seems to consider what to say next. "C'mon," he finally says with a slap to Gene's back. Just before they enter the curtained area, he adds, "Say, how's the leg?"

"My leg?"

"First time...well, only time...I'd had a father sedate his own son."

The head of Rebecca's cart is raised about forty-five degrees. Her eyes are closed. An IV In her arm runs nearly wide open. Her mother stands on the far side. Dr. Knudson pulls the curtains closed. Just then, someone makes a retching sound outside the curtains, causing Mrs. Layne to look behind her.

"Sorry. Close quarters here." Dr. Knudson nods toward Gene. "This is Dr. Hull. He's a resident. I'd like him to stay if you don't mind."

"Mind? He saved Becca's life." Mrs. Layne squeezes Rebecca's hand to her chest.

During the interview, Mrs. Layne speaks for her daughter, Rebecca occasionally opening her eyes, blinking, and asking where she is. She recently graduated from Arizona State University with a degree in math. She played club-level volleyball there. She's never had an episode like this but fainted once this past year during practice. That time, she felt her heart racing before she passed out, but she came to right away, and the spell was chalked up to not eating before a grueling workout. Why is a lack of nourishment everyone's first guess?

Today, she'd played tennis with her mother before coming to the hospital to visit a family friend who'd just had a baby. She bounded up the broad flight of steps leading to the hospital entrance, taking them two at time. She held the door for her mother, and as they were about to enter the gift shop, just a few feet away, Mrs. Layne heard her daughter say, Mom. When she turned, Rebecca was staggering to the ground, landing with a horrible thud, and then the seizure.

After the interview, Dr. Knudson examines Rebecca's lacerated scalp. "This will take a few stitches." He then uses two different instruments to peer into her ears and eyes. When he instructs her to follow his finger with her eyes, Gene notices a slight ratcheting motion to her gaze. Her eyes are brown, like Gene's, but with a thin green halo rimming the edge. Her pupils constrict under the scrutiny of the doctor's penlight. Using the fingertips of both hands, Dr. Knudson feels along the length of her neck muscles. She leans forward as he listens to the back of her chest with his stethoscope. "Deep breath," he says. "And again."

Dr. Knudson lowers the head of the cart. He removes the blanket covering her legs and tucks the gown around her upper thighs. A nurse must have removed Rebecca's soiled track shorts and panties earlier. There's still a faint odor of urine though.

"I smell pee." Rebecca says. She starts to whimper.

"It's okay, baby," her mother says.

Dr. Knudson runs his hands along one leg, lifting it slightly to examine the full surface. He cups her calf in both hands and presses his fingers deep into the muscle's belly. "Does that hurt?"

"A little," she says.

He repeats the exam on the other leg.

Using the blanket, he covers her legs to her hips and then raises her gown to just under her breasts. He presses his flattened fingers around different areas of her exposed abdomen. She tenses, and he encourages her to relax. Her abdomen is flat and tan with a fine, downy line of bleached hairs below her belly button.

He covers her abdomen with the blanket and raises the head of the cart to about forty-five degrees again. Placing the stethoscope over the pulse on the right side of her neck, he says, "Deep breath, and hold it…breathe." He repeats the procedure on the left side.

"I need to listen to your heart," he says. He has her pull her arms from the gown and lowers the gown to below her ribs, exposing her chest. Neither Rebecca nor her mother flinch. But Gene, feeling as if he stumbled into the women's locker room, turns his gaze as casually as he can to the EKG monitor, focusing on the green, spiked line of Rebecca's heartbeats moving left to right. Dr. Knudson rubs the bell of his stethoscope vigorously on the blanket.

"See if I can warm this up a little," he says. Gene looks over as Dr. Knudson presses the bell to the right of Rebecca's sternum, below the notch where Dr. Harrington hooks the tip of his saw. He moves the scope to the left of her sternum. Then he places it just under the lower boundary of her left breast, where her tan line follows the arc of her ribs. Other than Patty, Gene has never seen the breasts of any girl, at least in the flesh. Unlike Patty, Rebecca's breasts lay nearly flat to her chest, her dark nipple a nubbin in the chilly ER air. It's just an observation, but he feels guilty. He didn't expect to see her disrobed.

"Gene, take a listen." Dr. Knudson holds the bell firmly against Rebecca's skin. Gene tries to appear as if he's done this before. Leaning over Rebecca's rising and falling chest, he places the earpieces in his ears. But in fact, he has done this before, as a kid, listening to his own small heart with his father's stethoscope. He didn't hear much until his father directed his hand. Now, like then, the sound seems to pound from somewhere behind his eyes. He closes his eyes. Like a gallop, two sounds come in syncopated pairs. He can picture her heart's rocking motion. But unlike the labored twisting of the few hearts he's seen in the last two weeks, her heart seems to bounce on fresh legs.

"Do you hear the systolic murmur?" Dr. Knudson's voice is muffled, but Gene hears him nonetheless, and he hears Mrs. Layne's equally muffled response.

"She has a murmur? Is it bad?"

Gene isn't sure what he's supposed to be hearing. He pulls the earpieces from his ears, stands up, and nods anyway.

Dr. Knudson pockets his stethoscope. He pulls Rebecca's gown up and ties it behind her neck. "She has a slight systolic murmur. Could be mitral valve prolapse. It's very common."

"I've been told I have it," she says.

"There you go. We'll order some blood work and get a chest x-ray. She may have just been dehydrated or hypoglycemic. I'll run through everything with you when we get the results. But because she took a bump on the head…you can feel the lump here." He shows Mrs. Layne.

"Oh my. That's quite a knot."

"I'd like to admit her. Just to watch her overnight. Make sure she doesn't have any occult bleeding in there."

Mrs. Layne looks down to Rebecca.

"I fully expect her to go home in the morning," Dr. Knudson says. "Let's err on the side of caution though."

"Okay," she says. "What do you think, Becca?"

"I have to pee."

He opens the curtain and gestures to a nurse to come over. "She needs the bedpan. Grab a urine sample, too. And I'll need a laceration kit."

It takes five stitches to close Rebecca's head wound. Gene's used to seeing ten times that many sutures or more. As he watches Dr Knudson tie the knots with a two-handed technique, Gene thinks I could do that.

Dr. Knudson and Gene move to the ER's workstation and sit at the high counter. "What do you think?" he says to Gene. "Got a little vagal, BP dropped, and she seized?"

"Probably."

As Dr. Knudson writes in the chart, Gene recalls lying on a cart in one of these stalls before his father knocked him out to set his broken leg. He wonders if the paramedics brought his father through here. There must be a special route so that a patient with only a broken bone doesn't have to witness the pell-mell rush of a crumpled body.

"There is that murmur," Dr. Knudson says. "Could be more than mitral valve prolapse. ASD perhaps or even Marfan. Five-eleven, thin, dysrhythmia. Look at this EKG. Her p-r interval is short. Worth ruling out. Let's get Zem to see her. He'll probably want an echo."

"What about atrial myxoma?"

"Hmm, I hadn't thought of that."

Dr. Knudson closes the chart and offers Gene a handshake. "Hard to believe it's been nine months. Must be hard doing a heart rotation here."

"Everyone's been good."

"Best team in the state."

"I should get over to Dr. Harrington's office."

"Gene. I wish we could have done more."

"You were there?"

"Not at first. I had my hands full with an MI. Luckily, Rui was here. He took the lead. I guess he was pretty upset for a while."

"They were close."

Dr. Knudson nodded. "I'm glad he got help. He's a good man."

Got help? Gene nodded like he knew. "The best."

Chapter Eleven

DO YOU WANT TO KNOW A SECRET?

September 1973, Phoenix, Arizona

As the somber organ echoed, Gene guided his mother by the elbow down the sanctuary aisle. Subtly, she pulled her arm away. The big double doors were open behind him, and portable fans offered minimal relief on the unusually warm September day. The air conditioning had malfunctioned, which only added to the discomfort between Gene and his mother. He looked straight ahead, aiming for the front pew. The collective gaze of the couple-hundred mourners seared the back of his neck, and he reminded himself, breathe. A bead of sweat slid down the furrow of his back. Two steps ahead, his once-petite sister Suzanne steadied herself on hulking Rodney's arm. Acquaintances who knew them only as high school sweethearts — she the scrappy, headstrong soccer star and he the gentle offensive lineman — gave brief smiles in recognition of their fairy tale romance. A few mournful faces blinked back tears when they recognized her seventh-month pregnant state.

Suzanne and Rodney entered the pew first, followed by Gene's mother, Gene, and Patty. His mother folded her hands on her lap. Three days ago, she had buried Gene in silence after he and Patty unpacked the Jeep, her way of punishing him for his detour to Tucson. Patty tried to smooth things over that morning as the three sat at the kitchen's oak table. She apologized, explaining that Gene had been unable to reach her because her car died at the hospital parking lot. "Please," she said. "Don't blame Gene. I'm sorry he worried you. But I'm glad he was able to tell me the news in person." Gene's mother reached for his blue blazer, which hung over a kitchen chair. "This won't do," she had said. "Go see Harold. Have him bill me. I'm taking a nap." Later that day, he and Patty drove to Lad to Dad and purchased the dark gray suit he wore now.

Reverend Collins adjusted his black-framed glasses. The music faded to silence, broken only by scattered coughs and sniffs. Patty placed Gene's hand on her lap, the material of her black chiffon dress soft and soothing. With her finger she stroked the large vein on the back of his hand. She had never looked so steady, so firm, so ready to supply the strength he lacked. He just wished this day were over. Leaning into her he said *thanks*, and hoped she understood that his gratitude was not just for today, but also for yesterday and tomorrow.

"Welcome," Dr. Collins said. "We are gathered here to celebrate the life of Doctor Carl Eugene Hull…."

Reverend Collins' baritone boomed through the sound system with tales about Gene's father. The stories, gleaned mostly from a brief living-room meeting, began with Carl, an upperclassman at Boston University pestering the Dean's secretary with daily questions. Finally, she'd said, "If you want to ask me out, then ask me out." From there there'd been a small chapel wedding, life on a shoestring, two kids separated by Korea, medical training, a move to Arizona, and the Heart Team.

"Whether it was attending Gene's ball games, Suzanne's soccer matches, or loading the family in the station wagon for two weeks out of the heat each summer," Reverend Collins said, "it was always family first. Carl's creed."

Gene's mother made a sharp exhalation, like she was blowing out a candle. Gene looked over. She stared straight ahead.

"Carl's generosity extended beyond his immediate family," the

Reverend said. "I understand during the Christmas holidays he loved playing Santa. Those he worked with in the operating room would find a few bottles of wine or a case of Michelob on their stoop along with a cassette of some of his favorite jazz tunes. This reminds me. Several years ago, he offered, with grand enthusiasm, to act as sound engineer and record a series of my sermons. He later transferred the recordings to cassette and sold them at our church fundraiser. Carl insisted on footing the entire bill. He may have miscalculated the market for my message though, as I still have a few hundred cassettes squirreled away in a closet." Reverend Collins paused and looked over the top of his glasses. "Only $2.29 each if anyone is interested." The congregation chuckled.

Dr. Collins told other anecdotes including Gene's fond memories of Sunday rounds and secret snacks with his father. "Simple moments," the Reverend said, "Simple moments accumulate, one by one with a person, and through them, if we are lucky, we are enriched. I know my life was enriched by my friendship with Carl. By the looks on the faces of you all here this afternoon, I know you feel your life has gained something from knowing Carl. But his wife and children…well, they are the luckiest of all."

Gene's mother, who had remained stone-faced, began to tear. She removed a folded handkerchief from her waistband and dabbed her eyes.

"Carl was taken far too soon. I can understand feelings of anger. Anger at circumstances, anger at those justly or unjustly deemed responsible, and anger at God. God's plan is not always immediately clear, but what I can say is that his plan does not include us carrying anger within us. For what good can possibly come from anger's grip? It does nothing but squeeze the good from our souls. Look around. We are, none of us, perfect…."

The Reverend looked toward Gene and his mother. Her head was bowed. Had she opened up to Reverend Collins in private? Told him of his father's broken promise?

"Every day, in ways big and small, we look to God for forgiveness. He is listening. He hears your entreaties, not just from your voice, but from your heart. His grace will heal you. But what of the stranger, the friend, or family member who seeks your forgiveness? Should you not look to God's example? It is a curious medicine, this anodyne called forgiveness. For if you open your heart and dispense this potent elixir, through God's grace, you too, will be healed…."

Gene's mother straightened and folded her hands on her lap, her profile stoic. No. Defiant.

Carl's son Gene told me a story that exemplifies this. One night, when Gene was beginning fifth grade, he awoke and vomited grape juice and other assorted snacks onto his bedroom carpet. As I understand, the carpet was new. Uncharacteristically for Carl, he flew into a rage, dragging Gene to the toilet and berating his son for his inability to make it to the bathroom. We don't — "

"Sixth grade," Gene's mother muttered. She raised her head and spoke as if hypnotized. "He was in the sixth grade."

Reverend Collins paused and leaned an ear toward the front pew. "Dee informs me, Gene was in the sixth grade." He smiled and the congregation shifted with gentle laughter. She was known as a stickler for detail.

The Reverend continued. "We don't know of Carl's state of mind in the minutes, hours, or perhaps days preceding his outburst. But we know what transpired shortly after. Carl left Gene standing over the toilet, crying. Now, who of us hasn't acted reflexively, in a manner counter to our better nature? But more importantly, who of us has admitted we were wrong and exposing our vulnerability, sought forgiveness. Carl did. Carl returned to Gene less than a minute later, the boy still crying over the toilet, and crouched by his son. Gene said he will never forget what his father said: 'I'm sorry. You deserve better. I can get a new carpet, but I can't get a new son.'"

Gene began to cry. Patty placed her arm around him. His tears turned to sobs, gushing from what felt like the taproot of his grief, which, for the first time since detouring to Tucson, felt profoundly deeper than the joy of sitting with Patty pressed against his side.

"Does anyone have a story they'd like to tell?" Reverend Collins said.

Gene dried his eyes and looked left and right.

"Please, anyone," the Reverend said.

Doctors and nurses approached the pulpit. Gene's father had anesthetized many of them in the years before he worked solely in the Heart Room. His reputation grew from his skill, genuine concern, and easy, confident manner. As one nurse put it, "If you needed surgery, you wanted Dr. Hull taking care of you. He cared."

Dr. Pereira, immaculately dressed in a dark suit, a touch of silver at his temples, took measured strides to the podium. Gene had yet to see him since the accident. "I worked with Carl in the operating room…the best anesthesiologist, the best friend…" His voice cracked. Several times he tried to continue, but could only nod, and say "Sorry," before stepping down.

A young woman moved to the podium. "I'm Sandra. I'm a nurse. Dr. Hull was like a white knight in the Heart Room. If things went south, he came to the rescue. But not just for the patients." She looked down and bit her lower lip. "I'll miss him."

"I remember her," Gene whispered to Patty. "From your surgery."

Gene's mother mumbled something. He leaned in. "Yes?"

"Nothing."

Gene felt Patty's arm leave his shoulder. He looked over to give her a smile, but she was rising from the pew. She climbed the two steps to the dais, stood as straight as her flute, and folded her hands atop the lectern. She smiled at Gene and then looked out to the assembled guests.

"I'm Patty McLellan, Gene's girlfriend. I just wanted to say, that if it hadn't been for Dr. Hull, I might not be here today…."

Patty relayed her story with manifest calm and confidence. Gene thought of their first meeting two summers ago. The demure girl who'd cleverly run from him. She'd grown so much since then. Although in the same grade, she was a year older. She certainly seemed older today. When she looked down at Gene, he gave her a tight-lipped smile, his eyes watering again.

"…Dr. Hull and I would sit in the stands and watch Gene play baseball. Seeing his children succeed at anything was the best part of his life. That's what he told me. I'm not sure I ever told Gene that. But I guess I just did." Everyone laughed. Gene's face flushed with pride.

"Dr. Hull is the reason I decided to study nursing. I had doubts, but he encouraged me, and I'm so grateful. I can't thank him enough."

Gene had an urge to stand up and shout My God, isn't she great!

Patty stepped back, out of sight, while Reverend Collins returned to the lectern. He looked behind him for a couple seconds and then back out to the congregation. Gene craned his neck, trying to see where Patty had gone. Had she become faint? He leaned forward, ready to run to her. Then Suzanne snapped her fingers. She gestured for him to relax and mouthed: She's okay.

Dr. Collins said. "This young lady will now grace us with '*Ave Maria.*' "

Patty stepped forward with her flute. Gooseflesh spread down Gene's legs and arms. A knot as large as a baseball filled his throat. He peered at Suzanne, and the look she gave him meant she knew about this.

Patty played flawlessly. Her sweet notes filled the sanctuary. Gene gave up trying to see through his tears. He closed his eyes and listened. He was weightless. This was his Patty playing this steady, lovely music. All the days before and all the days ahead lit brightly before him, and in every image, he saw her. People often spoke of "the one." She was it. How empty he would be without her. It was a feeling as strong and true as any he'd ever felt.

He inhaled the music.

His mother leaned into him and touched his arm. "It's all sweetness in the beginning."

Gene turned his head and frowned.

"Wait till she breaks your heart."

He jerked his arm away, along with any sympathy for this bitter woman who'd crushed his father's dreams.

THE RECEPTION WAS HELD at their house where meatballs, chocolate covered strawberries, and fond memories were served. As the guests trickled home, Patty suggested that Gene's mother needed some alone-time with her kids.

"I'll drive home with Mom," she said. Then she whispered in his ear. "Come by later?"

He whispered back. "Usual time."

Later, after a casserole dinner, Gene reclined on a lounger by the lighted swimming pool, and tipped back a Michelob. While seated in a patio chair she'd scooted next to their mother, Suzanne nursed a ginger ale. Gene had lost track of the number of Gimlets his mother had consumed. She'd been making the rounds, shaking hands, and saying, "It means the world that you came to remember Carl."

The ice tinkled in the warm night, the sun having finally set on a horrible few days. No one had spoken for several minutes. He wiped a finger along the beer's dry, amber glass. "I miss the heat," he said.

Suzanne propped her bare feet on the chair Rodney had vacated. Her husband was inside working on a flight back to New Hampshire. "This wasn't hot enough for you?"

"No. I mean at school. I miss the desert's dry heat.

"You should try it pregnant."

"I find it relaxing. I wish I could take it back with me."

"You always were a little different."

"Think about it. Sure, it's a bear when the sun's out. But like now, the temp's — " Gene looked behind him at the round, sun-faced thermometer on the wall. " — eighty-nine. Practically no humidity. It's so close to body temperature, we just kind of float along. A kind of neutral, ambient temperature. It's perfect."

"Listen to you," Suzanne said. "Where'd you get that — neutral ambient temperature?"

"Biology." Gene sighed, thinking of the work waiting for him at school.

Apollo dropped a tennis ball by the lounger. Gene threw it toward the orange grove. Apollo hustled it back. They repeated the game again and again.

"Look at him," Suzanne said. "He's oblivious. No clue as to what's been going on."

Gene held the ball aloft while Apollo shuffled and whined, the dog's eyes pleading with intensity.

"I'd like to be oblivious," their mother said, swirling her cocktail in the air.

Gene threw the ball and looked over at his mother and then past her to Suzanne. "What do you mean?"

"I don't mean anything," she said. She rested her drink on her abdomen and flexed her stockinged toes.

"Mom." Suzanne swung both feet to the ground. "You're sauced. No Valium tonight."

"A little cloudy. That's all."

"Either way. No more pills."

Her mother gestured with the back of her hand, shooing Suzanne away.

Suzanne shook her head at Gene. "I'll make sure she doesn't take anything."

"You're not the boss of me," Gene's mother said. Then she cackled, spilling some of her drink. "You used to say that to Suzanne all the time." She swiped at Gene but missed.

"Okay, bar's closed," Suzanne said. Then to Gene, "What say we leave the dishes until tomorrow?"

"All those nice things," his mother said. "People said so many nice things about Carl today."

"Yes, they did, Mom. It was great to hear."

"I feel so bad for Rui. He's taking this so hard. He loved your father like a brother."

Her speech was slow and a little slurred. She closed her eyes and was blessedly quiet for a few minutes.

"Gene," Suzanne said. "Patty's pretty special."

"Mom doesn't think so." He downed his beer while thinking about sneaking over tonight. "She thinks Patty will break my heart."

"She does not."

"Yes I do."

"Mom, sometimes I don't get you," Suzanne said.

"I know her type."

"Oh, someone talented, poised, supportive, and grateful. By all means, Gene, dump her now."

"You just wait. I know how nurses latch onto doctors for their money."

"I'm not a doctor, yet."

"Exactly."

"Go back to sleep," Suzanne said. "I like her. I like her a lot. You were right to go to Tucson."

She raised her glass to Gene. He wished now that he'd not lied to her about the detour to Tucson. Lying to his mother he could live with.

"Just like your father," she said. "Always the hero."

Suzanne looked at Gene and shook her head.

"You should go see her," his mother said. She slurped her drink. "I'm sure she needs you. You've put in your time here. Go. I have Suzanne."

God, he hated his mother when she played these games.

"If someone asked for help," his mother said, "he always stopped whatever he was doing. Some neighbor kid needs stitches? No problem. Come on over." She gave a beckoning gesture with her arm, sloshing her drink onto her blouse. She tented the fabric and licked the liquid. "What's it matter that we were headed out to dinner and a movie."

"Mom," Suzanne said.

"Don't Mom me."

"Let it go," Suzanne said, as if reminding her for the hundredth time.

"He just had to be a hero. Thought he'd fly all over the state saving people. Bringing them back to the hospital."

"You don't know that," Suzanne said.

"Oh, I know that. He's done this before."

"You heard Reverend Collins. He was telling you that you can't blame Dad."

Their mother stared up at the sky. The blinking lights of a jet traveled east across the star-speckled night. "Maybe I should move to New Hampshire."

Suzanne rolled her eyes. "Listen. Mom. Now's not the time to be making big changes." She mouthed to Gene, No way. "Come visit after the baby's born. You may hate snow as much as you hate heat."

"Nothing's worse than this heat," she said. She considered something and scoffed. "And what do I get for my loyalty to stick it out in this hellhole? I'll tell you." She turned her head to Suzanne and then to Gene and very calmly said, "A husband who got himself killed. "Yep. Exactly what I said would happen."

Gene looked at Suzanne and shook his head, their mother semi-recumbent and semi-conscious between them. Always the martyr. Let her drown in her grief.

"Mom," Suzanne said. "What do you think Reverend Collins meant when he talked about not being perfect and forgiveness?"

"Even when he yelled at you," Gene's mother said, "he ends up the hero. I told him he was way too harsh on you when you barfed grape juice all over our new carpet — "

"Will you please just answer my question?" Suzanne said.

"By the way," she said. "Who do you think cleaned up that mess? And I told him to go back in there and apologize to you. I said, 'Carl, have you forgotten how lucky we felt the night after that little girl was killed.' That's right. I marched him back in there. I said, 'It's not Gene's fault. You're the one who let him eat all that crap at the hospital.'"

That must have been only a month or two after the girl was killed. Gene had never connected the two events, thinking now what must have been behind his father's apology — *but I can't get a new son.*

His mother took another swig of her gimlet. "Humph. Don't lecture me about forgiveness."

Gene rose and reached for her glass. "Bedtime."

She pulled it away. "I'm fine." She held the drink out, measuring something, and gulped the remainder like a shot. She threw her head back and gave a short laugh. "What the hell. Why not get it all out? Isn't that what you're supposed to do these days?" She waved the tumbler at Gene, holding it precariously by two fingers. He lunged and caught it just as she let go. "Now sit," she said.

Gene shifted to the seat next to Suzanne. "Now what?"

"I guess you already know about our big argument."

Gene and Suzanne didn't react.

"Oh, sure you do. Gene was spying on us."

Suzanne looked at Gene. "I wasn't spying," he said. "I was building my deck."

"Yes, Mom," Suzanne said. "You told me all about it."

"Oh, there's more."

Man, she was enjoying this.

"Ever since that little girl died on the highway, he wanted to learn to fly. On weekends we could fly here, there, and everywhere. So romantic. And if someone crashed in Timbuktu, he'd flying 'em to the hospital." She waved her arms like a bird.

"Every few years he brought it up, and each time I said, 'No way.'" She pointed at Gene. "That's another thing. The night you puked he was all upset because I was squashing his crazy dream."

"He would have been good at it," Gene says.

"You know Eddie Beamer?"

Gene shook his head.

"Of course, you don't. You were too young. He was an ortho doc. Killed himself in a crash in '62. No way was I going to stand at a grave with a little kid under each arm like Mona had to do."

Their mother let her head drop back. "So, the day 007 here was on the roof, your father took another stab at me. Same old crap about how pilots are just like anesthesiologists. I knew what this was about. I reminded him for the umpteenth time that nothing was going to save that girl except a mother who knew better than to let her run across the highway. He calls me insensitive. Me? Then he stands there, juts out his chin and says, 'I took a free lesson today and signed up for the rest. My life, my decision.' That's what he says, My life, my decision. Like we aren't a team anymore."

She stared out over the pool and then raised her chin to the sky. "I said, 'So you decide you want to risk your life in some flying deathtrap to go back in time and save a girl who couldn't be saved.

Then where does that leave Gene and Suzanne and me after you crash? Who's going to save us when your body's a bag of bones? 'Cause if that's your plan, then I'll leave you now and spare myself the grief.'"

She leaned in and stared at Gene. "I walked out into the sun and told him I'd also had it with the heat. That's when I looked up and saw Gene working on his deck." Her fingers added the air quotes.

"So that's why he was gone," Gene said.

Eyes wide, mouth agape, Suzanne says, "Gone?"

"For two nights. Mom said he was on call at the hospital."

"Two nights?" Suzanne looked back to her mother. "He was gone for a couple nights and no one told me."

At the time, Gene had thought their argument was only about the heat. She was always bitching about the heat, and his father always brushed it off.

"Maybe if you'd called once in a while, I might have brought it up," their mother said.

Suzanne looked up to the sky and pressed her palms together. "Okay. He lives at the hospital for two days. Then what?"

"We made it work."

"You forgave him."

"After he promised never to fly."

Suzanne rubbed her pregnant belly. "I can understand it's hard to forgive him now. I've screamed at him a few times in the shower. But that's not good for me. And holding onto anger isn't good for you either. That's what Reverend Collins is talking about, Mom. In time you need to forgive him."

Their mother shook her head, slowly, back and forth.

"It's late," Gene said.

"It's not Carl he wants me to forgive." His mother began to cry.

Suzanne reached over and placed a hand on her arm. Softly, she said. "Who?"

"I said some horrible things to him."

"I know. You said."

His mother looked from Suzanne to Gene and then to her

wringing hands. "Horrible things after we went inside." She squeezed her eyes and shook her head until she found a small window of composure. "I told him...I told him that if he ever set foot in a plane..."

She bowed her head to her hands. Her shoulders started to shake. Suzanne scooted closer to the lounger and grasped her mother's hand. "What, Mom?"

She swallowed hard and cleared her throat. "I told him...if he ever sets foot in a small plane, I hoped he died. It would save me from having...from having to kill him."

She sobbed in great heaves, her head thrown back, her arms out in a gesture of supplication as if she hoped a lightning bolt would rip into her chest. Gene hoped it would. Suzanne, leaning awkwardly onto the lounger, cradled her mother's head.

"He told me I was selfish. Me. Selfish. I said, You're the one being selfish. Then he left. I thought we were through."

Gene dug his fingernails into the vinyl-wrapped armrests. "You told Reverend Collins all of this?"

She nodded. "It's me he wants me to forgive. Me!"

Apollo was back, whining at Gene's feet with the tennis ball. Gene swept the dog aside with his foot. "Stop it!" Apollo yelped and scurried away toward the back door.

Suzanne turned. "Gene!"

"I don't give a shit if you forgive yourself. I don't forgive you. You are selfish. If you hadn't robbed him of his dream to be a pilot five years ago, he never would have died in a helicopter crash."

Apollo returned. Gene reached down for the tennis ball and heaved it over the stand of orange trees and into the alley

"I'm going to bed."

GENE SAT on the roof deck, the lights out in his bedroom. He spent a half hour in the tepid night until his hands stopped shaking. Intending to look for Apollo downstairs, he crawled back through the window, but his buddy, head raised and ears pulled back, had jumped up on Gene's bed. Gene sat next to him and scratched his neck. "I haven't even said I'm sorry, and you've already forgiven me."

He closed his door and set his alarm for one a.m. When the music woke him, Apollo lifted his head from Gene's pillow for a second before groaning and rolling onto his back. Gene stepped back out to the roof deck, this time carrying his flashlight. He only had to wait five minutes before he spied the once-a-second blinking light from the ballfield. He flashed his light in response. "Stay here," he whispered back through the window to Apollo. No lights glowed from the kitchen or family room. He lowered the rope ladder from the roof, left through the side gate, and jogged easily under a sliver of moon.

As he passed the Big Tree, the light blinked again. He followed it to Patty, who sat on a sleeping-bag island in center field, her red and blue Arizona blanket wrapped tight around her shoulders. In the feathered illumination of his flashlight, she revealed one bare leg and wiggled her socked foot. He looked around the empty field. Darkened houses. No movement. The distant churning of water through an irrigation standpipe. He would take that chance. Gene turned off the flashlight and stripped to his socks, leaving his clothes and roiling thoughts on the trampled turf before entering the calm of Patty's blanket.

HAVING MISSED two weeks of classes, Gene returned to Cal Poly. There was no catching up. Slumped in his counselor's office, he listened to condolences and agreed he should drop two courses and concentrate on a trimmed-down load. But despite his vow to push on, he couldn't focus. The void that had replaced his father was like an aching hunger, which left him both weak and ravenous, starved for his dad's laugh, his cheers, his reasoned mind. Finals were a disaster. He wouldn't know the grades for a couple weeks, but believing he had wrecked his prospects for medical school, he limped back home for winter break.

As Christmas Day approached, icy conversations with his mother chilled the house. She hadn't forgotten his "selfish" comment from the night of the funeral. Jeez, she still hadn't forgiven his detour to Tucson after his father's death. Not that Gene needed her forgiveness. She could wallow in her grudges if she wanted.

But with the arrival of Suzanne, Rodney, and the new baby from New Hampshire, an uneasy truce evolved. It extended through Christmas morning, the carols lilting on the radio, and into the festive meal. When Suzanne raised a glass to her father and wished that his spirit would guide his namesake grandson, Carlton, watery eyes blinked around the table.

"Mom?" Suzanne said. She was staring at a candle.

"Oh, yes," their mother said. She raised her glass. "To your beautiful boy." She sipped her wine.

Two days later, after Gene returned from delivering his sister and family to the airport, he found his mother undressing the house.

"You usually wait until after New Year's," he said.

"My new year starts today." She wrapped three, wax Wise Men in yellowed newsprint and packed them in a small cardboard box. "Time to stop pretending."

Afraid she might chuck it all in the trash, all the decorations and memories of Christmases past, Gene lent a hand. He packed everything into well-worn moving boxes — the train set from around the tree, the garlands, Gene and Suzanne's stockings, actually hung by the chimney with care, Christmas candy dishes, the storybooks his father had read aloud on Christmas Eves — the vestiges of what was once the promise of a never-ending string of joyous years. As his mother handed him the last box up to carry up to the attic, she said, "There. It's done. The closets are next."

She walked past him. "You run along to Patty."

"Don't say that."

He followed her into the bedroom. Purging his father's life from the house, he had taken his father's sports coats from hangers and laid them on the bed.

"Aren't you moving a little fast?" he said.

She held out a gaudy Hawaiian shirt of grass-skirted hula

dancers. "I always hated this shirt." She stuffed it in a half-filled garbage bag.

"Don't," he said, a sharp edge to his voice. "I'll take it."

She tossed it at him. "Just don't wear it around me."

"What's this all about?"

"Now this should fit you." She held up another shirt from the pile. A light blue dress shirt.

"You can't just pretend he never existed."

"It will look nice with your blue blazer."

"Mom!"

She was off in her own world, lifting a shirt, some trousers, a sweater. "You barfed on this sweater."

"Stop it!" He grabbed her arm.

She pulled away, stuffed the sweater in the bag, and flung the bag off the bed. "What am I supposed to do!" Blood surged to her face. "Tell me!"

"I don't know, but you can't just throw everything out."

"Why not? He's not coming back."

"It's a mistake. You'll regret it."

"Mistake. I'll tell you what's a mistake. Getting in a helicopter when you have a wife and two kids that need you and a new grandchild on the way. That's a mistake. When you're my age, you might understand."

"He was trying to help someone."

"I don't want to hear it."

"Jeez. Then do what you want."

New Year's Eve morning, Gene was packed for Tucson. three days shacking up with Patty would put them in a better mood. His mother had nearly emptied his father's clothes closet and study. Most of the stuff was trucked off to charity except for the stereo components, some suits, and boxes packed with books, which Gene was supposed to take back to San Luis Obispo. He'd have to come back for his father's stuff. Until then, he'd let his mother wallow in self-pity.

Patty wanted to go see the New Year's fireworks at Tucson Electric Park. The new year would get off to a brighter start. Then they returned to her empty apartment. A bottle of champagne into 1974 they were down to their socks. Patty's head rested on Gene's shoulder. With her fingers she leisurely combed his pubic hair. She extended an aberrantly long hair to its full length, showcasing it between her thumb and middle finger. "I could identify you blindfolded just from this," she said.

The phone rang.

"Oh, it can't be," Gene said.

Patty answered. "Yes, yes, Mrs. Hull. He's right here."

Gene slipped on his boxers. Patty held out the phone with her hand cupped over the receiver and whispered, "I don't think she can see you."

"Don't be so sure," he mouthed back. Then into the phone: "Mom? What's the problem?"

"You can't go back."

"Back where?"

"To school. Stay here. You can go to Arizona State."

Gene dropped his head. "Mom, it doesn't work that way."

"You have to! I don't know what to do."

Gene heard music and talking in the background. "What's all that noise?"

"The TV. The radios."

"Turn it down. I can barely hear you."

"I can't sleep."

"No wonder."

"My heart. It won't slow down. I can't stop hearing it. Please. Come home."

"I can't." Gene tapped the receiver against his forehead. He was too buzzed to think, much less drive. "Mom, I'll call you back."

Gene found Dr. Pereira's phone number in his wallet. At the memorial service, he said to call him if he needed anything. Dr. Pereira was at the hospital with an emergency, but Mrs. Pereira said she'd drive right over to the house. She was once a practicing nurse, something Gene was relieved to be reminded. Forty minutes later she called back.

"Gene. I think she's fine. Nothing more than a panic attack. I gave her a Valium."

"She still had some?"

"I don't know. I had a few at home. We're good for now. I'll stay here tonight, but you need to get up here when you can."

"Sure. I'll drive up tomorrow. Thanks."

By noon, the Jeep was packed. Patty sat at the kitchen table, still dressed in her *Bear Down Arizona* nightshirt, spoonfuls of Cheerios and milk cascading into her bowl. One bare foot comforted the other. Gene saw this and then turned back to scrubbing the skillet in the sink. These last few moments before he had to say, See you in a few months, were always the toughest. Cleaning her kitchen was his way of delaying the moment of departure.

"It's like she wants you for herself," Patty said.

"She doesn't know what she wants."

"I'm missing out on two extra days with you because of her."

"I hope she's not really flipping out. I can't miss more school."

"Some girls would give you an ultimatum."

"You're not 'some girl.' "

"You make it impossible to have an argument."

She raised her spoon higher before tipping it. Milk splattered into the bowl. "Want to put our socks on one more time?" she said.

"Patty." Gene dried his hands and leaned against the sink. "You know I gotta go."

She looked down to her bowl as if her next ploy to delay their separation would present itself floating in the milk. She looked up. "Maybe just your socks?" She grinned.

He folded the towel, laid it on the counter, and walked behind her chair. He leaned over, his ear touching hers and drew his arms across her breasts. Three months, he thought. Three more months before I remove this nightshirt again. She gripped his wrists. For a second he thought she was going to direct his hands under her shirt, a reprise of the gift she offered two summers before.

"You could transfer." she said. "Not to ASU, but here."

It was strange that the subject hadn't come up before and stranger still that it germinated from his mother's panic, but the idea excited Gene, the way Patty, lounging in her nightshirt, her dark hair falling on her shoulders, excited him.

"It takes time," he said. "We still have the rest of this year to get through. Can you wait?"

"No, I can't," she said. "But I will."

Chapter Twelve

SHE'S GONE

Summer 1974

Rebecca Layne. Gene wonders if Dr. Zemlicka has seen her yet. He cranes his head to the desk clock. 8:05. He yawns and stretches. Apollo arches, hops off the bed, and sighs.

"Sorry, Buddy. I've been ignoring you, haven't I? Okay. Here's the plan. I'll feed you first and then go for a run. Then I've got to make a quick trip to the hospital. But after that, we'll trap Mom's cat, if there really is one."

The Saturday morning silence feels odd. But it's more than the house being empty. Much of his life feels foreign to him now. Sure, the stuff is largely unchanged — his roof deck, the swimming pool, the orange trees. He still drives a Jeep and keeps his high-school baseball gear in the same bag. Yet, it all feels different. It had started when his father died. From that day, something he couldn't touch went missing. To him it feels like the fiber in the pillow has vanished. The interstitium. The support that holds all of it together. It's gone.

While staring at the ceiling, Gene unconsciously reaches into his boxers and scratches his balls. He fingers the aberrantly long pubic hair Patty used to unfurl. The last time she did that, the last time they made love, was New Year's.

Can you wait?

No, I can't. But I will.

He turns to his side.

Across the room, a ladder of sunlight, projected through the shutters near his head, creeps up the wall. One of the rungs reveals a slight difference in paint tone over a drywall patch. You'd hardly know there'd been a heel-sized hole there last spring.

Gene groans and shuffles to his closet. He retrieves a chemistry textbook from a cardboard box and sits on the floor next to Apollo. Between the back cover and the periodic table is their high school graduation picture, an eight-by-ten photograph of himself and Patty in red cap and gown. It's the only photo he kept of her. He even burned the one of Patty and his father. That was stupid.

This photo's eight jagged pieces are puzzled back together with Scotch tape. The first tear had run almost perfectly between them except where her head tips to his shoulder. He removes the photo and turns it over, flexing it again and again as he reads and rereads the inscription she wrote in her loopy purple: *Love you with my whole heart.*

He dresses for a run. Downstairs, he fastens the photo to the refrigerator using a bug-shaped Valley Exterminators magnet. The photo overlaps a photo of his father, who mugs a worried expression as he presses a stethoscope to Suzanne's abdomen and signals *two* with his fingers. So much has changed since both photos were taken. Jeez, that's what Patty said. *Things change.*

GENE JOGS PAST the Big Tree. Patty's semester ended a month ago. Before leaving Cal Poly for the summer, he called her apartment to see when she was driving home, but her roommate answered, called him a bastard, and hung up. His other calls were picked up by an answering machine. He left messages that varied in tone from casual to friendly — *I'll be shadowing Dr. Harrington this summer. Love to tell you about it* — to practically begging — *Just talk to me. Please.*

He has yet to call Mrs. McLellan to find out when her daughter will return. He doesn't want to suffer her pity or her anger. It could go either way. It depends on what she knows.

He slows to a stop. He hasn't given up hope that she'll come home this summer. She just has to. But like every morning since he started running by her house, her Mustang's still not in the driveway. Not even a spot of fresh oil.

Gene leans against the low, chain-link fence bordering the school and catches his breath. Four Little League teams warm up on the two fields. In lawn chairs along the sidelines, a few parents have brought umbrellas as protection from the sun. A coach cracks fly balls to the outfielders. Despite their billowy uniforms, the players mimic big-league swagger with basket catches and crow-hop throws, their too-big-for-their-bodies' feet trampling the earth in shallow center field where Patty and he rendezvoused after midnight countless times.

The days the past two weeks were long, but not while Gene was inside them, his body and mind occupied. He didn't feel the weight of the work, of standing all day, until he arrived home, or maybe on the drive home, as the sun, having traveled the arc of his mostly windowless world, beat against the side of his face, reminding him of summers past, those gorgeously hot languid days. Never-ending days. Now, the weight of these new summer days penetrates as a deep ache in the arches of his feet — or ,maybe that's another symptom of loneliness. As long as he is busy, his mind bends around Patty, but at home, or at work if he stops to breathe, he feels her, or at least the part of her resting in his chest's hammock.

Before jogging home, he turns to take a last look at Patty's empty driveway. Mrs. McLellan, dressed in a bathrobe and slippers, is walking back to the front door with the newspaper in hand. He pauses, unsure if he should speak, and then calls out. "Mrs. McLellan."

She stops and turns. Gene smiles, waves, and immediately regrets his shirtless, sweaty appearance. She takes a step back, squinting, her hand shading her eyes from a dagger of sunlight reflecting off a parked car's windshield.

"It's me, Gene." He jogs across the street. She holds the paper across her chest the way Patty used to hold her books, and Gene imagines the person Patty would eventually become. Mrs. McLellan's posture relaxes, and she smiles.

"Gene, it's so good to see you."

She's not angry.

"Don't you look older."

"It's the haircut." He rubs the back of his neck. "Excuse the way I look. I've been running."

"How's your mother?"

"She's spending the summer with Suzanne in New Hampshire."

"Oh, yes, the new grandbaby. But she's coping okay? I've heard it takes a couple years, you know, to adapt."

"She's better." Gene looks around. "Your trees look like they could use a little water."

Mrs. McLellan looks over at one of the trees. "If I could remember to sign up."

"Maybe there's time. I'm not sure when your neighborhood runs, but our water runs tonight."

"I'll have to check."

"Have Dennis do it."

Mrs. McLellan takes a deep breath. "He's with his father." She toes a small orange leaf on the sidewalk. "What a handful. You probably didn't hear about the DWI."

"Dennis?"

"Fortunately, no one was hurt." She looks Gene in the eye. "I wish he'd picked up a little of your good sense."

My good sense, he thinks.

She taps Gene's chest with the rolled newspaper. "What are you up to? Still painting trees?"

"I'm working with Dr. Harrington at Desert Valley."

Mrs. McLellan's eyes widen. "In the operating room?"

Even if Patty listened to his messages, she didn't tell her mother. "Started scrubbing-in this week."

"Scrubbing?"

"Assisting him and another surgeon, Dr. Pereira."

Her expression confirms Gene's intent — she's impressed. "Dr. Harrington was so good to us. To Patty. To me." She pinches her lips together. "And your father. He was such a wonderful doctor. A wonderful man." She pauses and then rallies with a laugh and says, "Those are some big footsteps to follow."

"I have a ways to go."

"Don't sell yourself short."

"I meant I have many years in school before I'm a doctor."

A cheer erupts behind him. Gene turns briefly to see a player rounding the bases.

"Listen," Mrs. McLellan says. "I should get dressed." Folded newspaper in hand, she gives Gene a congenial hug. "Give my best to your mother. And to Dr. Harrington. Tell him Patty's heart is doing well."

Gene's heart sags a little, knowing Patty's heart is thriving without him. "When will she be home?" he asks.

"With her job there? Hard to say."

"I didn't hear."

"Nurse's aide at University Hospital."

"Maybe I'll give her a call."

Mrs. McLellan is silent.

"I'd like to show her the Heart Room."

She takes Gene's hand, unmistakable pity in her eyes this time. "Gene, I know this feels like the end of the world to you. But it will pass. Some lucky girl will find you. You'll be fine."

You'll be fine. The exact words Patty mothered him with last spring before he'd lashed out at her, sending her crying back to her house. The same phrase everyone dumps on him. Is there some break-up manual they've all read? …console the brokenhearted with the simple expression, 'You'll be fine' for nine out of ten will be fine except for the one who wants to rip the lungs out of the medical student who stole his girlfriend.

"I just need to talk to her." It comes out more pleading than he hoped.

"Gene." Mrs. McLellan's shoulders slump. "Patty's engaged."

He forces his face to remain placid. She shakes her head and gives him Patty's I'm-so-sorry, doe-eyed look. "As of a couple days ago."

He looks past her to her russet colored door. He'll never paint it. Engaged. The word whips his heart, faster and faster. His chest tightens. He feels as if he's buried up to his neck in sand.

"Right," he says in a croaking whisper. "I need to go."

He turns and jogs toward home. At the Big Tree, he stumbles against it and screams: "Fuuuuuck." He slaps his hand against the trunk again and again and cries, "Fuck, fuck, fuck." Then he sprints toward home, maintaining a punishing pace beyond when his lungs burn for forgiveness, all the way to his front door, which he enters and slams shut.

He empties his anger at Sluggers, where seventy-five-mph fastballs sizzle past his wild swings. But he keeps at it, and soon his timing is perfect, and he sends the waist-high balls ricocheting off the back posts like stray bullets. He's never felt such heat bursting from his heart and down his arms, such force crushing the spinning balls, each one Jake's face, smiling beneath his rock-star mustache. *Whack, whack, whack.*

At the end of the third round, he stops and looks down at his hands. His chest heaves. Blood from a skin-rip at the base of his index finger stains the wooden bat's grip. Only now does he feel the pain of a hot breeze blowing across the fresh wound. It's over. She's gone.

"You done?"

Gene turns to see three high-school-aged boys, helmets on. "Yeah," Gene says. He presses the tail of his t-shirt against the bloody wound. "Yeah, I'm finished."

The kids are looking at Gene's hand. He opens the gate and exits the cage.

"Man, you were crushing it," one of them says.

"You play college ball?" another asks.

Gene shakes his head. "No time."

"Too bad," a kid says as he enters the cage. He inserts a quarter, presses the button, and the balls start to fly. He whiffs at the first three.

"You've got to want it," Gene says.

The kid whiffs again.

"You got a girlfriend?" Gene asks.

The kid doesn't turn. "Sure. Why?"

"She's standing behind the plate."

He turns his head, and the ball just nicks his shoulder. His friends laugh and slap the cage.

"What the shit, man," the hitter says.

"If you don't protect her," Gene says. "Who will?"

Another ball whizzes past the batter's empty swing.

"That one really hurt her," Gene says.

The batter settles into a deeper crouch and chokes up. Even from behind he looks determined. The next ball didn't have a chance. The kid crushes it, sending it pinging past the machine.

"Solid," Gene says. He looks at his hand. The bleeding has stopped. A little TufSkin spray and a dime of surgical tape will do the trick until the skin heals.

The batter sends the next ball flying off as well. "Man, that works," he says.

"Took me awhile to learn that," Gene says. "Now all you have to do is be that guy when you're outside the cage."

"What?"

The batter swings and misses.

"You'll see."

Chapter Thirteen

ONLY LOVE CAN BREAK YOUR HEART

February - March, 1974

DOUG KICKED OFF HIS FLIP-FLOPS. "You're going to miss this." His roommate propped his feet on the lacquered cable-spool. "Even a desert-dog like you is going to miss this."

As if Cal Poly knew Gene was planning to transfer to Tucson, San Luis Obispo conspired to lay a spring-like Friday on him in early-February. On his apartment's roof deck, Gene set an ashtray on top of the U of A application and let his head fall back. With the wind from the west, the complex could have been right on the water, instead of a half mile from the ocean. Two seagulls danced and complained overhead.

He was going to miss this. Not the ocean or aroma of eucalyptus — he'd trade that for arid desert nights and the smell of creosote after a thunderstorm — but the classes and the projects. After reading through the University of Arizona catalogue, he feared he'd be memorizing circuit theory and find himself groaning under a mountain of problem sets. At Cal Poly he actually built things. Like a real inventor Gene had designed everything, from the cage to the infrared circuitry, and built from scratch, and then he'd tested, rebuilt, and retested. In the lab when the TA placed a dog treat on the bait pad and released his rat-like Chihuahua, the trap sprang perfectly. Even the tiny victory flag ran up the tiny flagpole, and the pre-recorded voice, imitating Hal from *2001,* said, "Dave, did you know the nine-thousand series is the most reliable trap ever made?" That had been Dougie's idea.

Another beer?" Doug asked.

Gene thought hard on that one. "No. I've got to study."

"That should be on the crest of the School of Engineering."

Gene heard Doug rise and walk away. The door to the stairwell opened and then slammed shut. Just a few quiet minutes and then he'd get back to work. This quarter's schedule was insane — twenty-two credit hours as he tried to make up for last quarter's shortfall in grades and credits. To make matters worse, he'd missed the first week of classes because of his mother's nervous breakdown. And now that he was going to transfer to the U of A, he couldn't be sure all his credits would count. They should, but you never knew. Having Patty's calls on Sunday and the promise of Spring Break just over the horizon kept him paddling against the current. More like treading water. He felt like it took all his energy just to keep from slipping beneath the surface.

Gene woke when he felt a hand on his shoulder. The sun, much lower now, hit him square in the face. "Patty's on the phone," Doug said.

"Patty?" What day was it? Not Sunday.

"She sounds kind of pissed." Doug stood aside and let Gene pass. "Said she's called a couple times. I may have ignored one of them. Maybe two."

In the kitchen, Gene put the receiver to his ear, more confused than concerned. He remembered his sister's call last fall and was relieved Patty was pissed and not crying. "Patty! Sorry. I was asleep and Dougie…well, you know, he hates to be bothered. Couldn't wait until Sunday, huh?"

"There's no way to tell you than to just tell you," she said.

His breathing stopped.

"I'm pregnant."

He exhaled the first thought that came to mind. "But you were on the pill."

"I know."

"You sure?"

"Yes."

"How could you be pregnant, if you're on the pill?"

"I don't know."

"I mean you were on the pill, right?"

"Yes, I'm on the pill, or I was until the end of the pack. But my period never came, so I stayed off."

"But if you're on the pill — "

"Gene, it happens sometimes. That's what the clinic doctor says. Okay? Sometimes it just happens."

Gene turned away from Doug's room.

"Why didn't you tell me sooner?"

"I just found out."

"I mean that you were late."

"I didn't want to worry you."

He took a beer from the refrigerator and sat at the kitchen table. He rolled the can across his forehead as he thought. The phone cord pulled the receiver away from his ear.

"I can't tell my mom," she said.

"No, don't tell her. Please, don't tell her."

"I won't. Okay, I won't."

Gene put his hand over the receiver and walked as far as the cord would reach, peering around the wall to see if Doug's door was closed. It was, but he wished he'd checked a few seconds ago. Gene lifted the phone base from the table and moved just outside the front door and sat against the railing.

"Gene. Gene. Are you there?"

"Yes." He paused when Leo from two doors down came out his door with his ten speed and nodded toward Gene. "Hey, Leo."

"Bitchin' day," Leo said looking at the sky and then back to Gene before rolling on down the walkway.

Gene nodded halfheartedly. "Patty."

"Gene, will you please talk to me."

"Sorry. Look. What did they say at the clinic? Can they take care of it there?"

She is quiet.

"Patty?"

"No. They can't."

"Is there somewhere?"

"They gave me the name of a doctor."

"When can you see him?"

"I haven't called."

"Give him a call."

"I wanted to talk to you first."

"Call him and we'll talk again tomorrow."

"They're closed now. I don't know if they're open on Saturday."

"Are you sure the test was right?"

"Gene. They repeated it. It's right. Okay?"

"It'll be fine. We'll get through it." Why'd this have to happen now?

"I wish you were here," she said. "Gene, I'm scared. I can't breathe. I feel like I'm drowning."

"Can you drive up here? I'm sure we can take care of it here. I'll check."

"I don't know what to do."

"I'll check around here for a clinic or something. You talk to the doctor. Okay?"

"Okay."

"We'll get this behind us. All right?" Gene's mind searched for an image of Patty at this moment, cross-legged on her bed, or knees to her chest on the kitchen chair. Whatever her posture, she was quiet. "Patty, alright?"

She didn't answer.

"For now. For me. Try to reach the doctor tomorrow, and then call me back. Let's start there."

GENE WOKE FREQUENTLY during the night. How could she be pregnant? He wondered if she'd skipped a day or two of the pills and didn't want to tell him. He didn't know exactly how they worked. Exactly? He didn't know at all.

By morning, the weather in San Luis Obispo, so unexpectedly sublime yesterday before Patty called with the news, turned sour. The fog rolled in and parked over the school. This he wouldn't miss. Nor the mildew. He looked up a clinic, drove over, and brought home brochures. the basic information filled in his sadly deficient knowledge of contraceptive pills, ovulation, conception, and the timing of it all. He even read about the stages of pregnancy, morning sickness, when a heartbeat is heard, quickening, all of it. Under the gooseneck lamp, he pulled out a calendar and worked forward from New Year's Eve, the last time they'd "kept their socks on." Six weeks. The brochures said the tests could pick up a pregnancy as early as two weeks after a missed period. But she didn't say when that was. Did she?

He needed to study. He aimed his desk lamp over the biology text, highlighting the illustrations of twisting DNA and the half-ladder messenger RNA growing beads of amino acids into protein strands. Half of his DNA and half of Patty's. A family was what he ultimately wanted, wasn't it? Sure. But not now. A baby?

Concentrate. Midterm on Monday.

His grades were high enough to transfer to the University of Arizona in the fall. However, medical school was his ultimate goal, and his grades needed a boost for that. If he could just get through this bear of a quarter. He needed As like a .200 hitter needed a long hitting streak to break out of slump. Fall quarter had been a disaster and medical school only took .300 hitters.

Gene flinched when the phone rang. It was Patty, and she got right to the point.

"The doctor would like to talk to us."

"Us?"

"He wants to see us together."

"Why does he need to talk to me?"

"You had a part in this, you know."

"Look. There's a place here. It's very nice. If you drove here, I could take care of you after, and this way your roommate would never know. You could tell her you're thinking of transferring and are taking a few days off to visit." Patty was quiet. "Or something."

"She knows."

"You told her!"

"I had to talk to somebody, Gene."

Gene dropped his head and rubbed his eyes. "Patty, you know you can talk to me."

"Yesterday, you seemed pretty anxious to get off the phone."

Gene looked left and right through his window, then up to the sky. Dreary and gray in every direction.

"I have three midterms coming up and a project due. I'm way behind."

"You can fly down. Go back the next day."

"You know what that costs!"

"Then drive."

"Are you sure he absolutely needs me there?"

Patty started to cry. She tried to hide it, but Gene recognized the high-pitched, clipped answers. She'd been so strong at his father's funeral. Now, she seemed to be the girl he'd first met. But he knew she had the strength to handle this herself. He gave her time and said her name a couple times as if he were stroking her hair: "Patty…Patty."

"I'm not sure I should even do this," she finally said.

"Patty. You can't have a baby now. It's not…I mean the timing…You just can't."

"You mean *you* just can't."

"Why are you talking like this? I thought you were okay with…with, you know."

"That's the thing, Gene. We never talked. You assumed."

"Are you serious?"

"We should at least talk about it. Talk with the doctor — "

"We just started college for Jeez's sake. How are we supposed to go to school and take care of a baby? We're not even married."

"So that's it."

"What's it?"

"Your image."

"No. Patty, think about it. The costs."

She was quiet.

"You'd have to quit nursing school. Get some menial job."

"I've got to go," she said. "I'll call you later."

"What is it?"

"I'm tired. I need to rest before my next class."

"Can you wait a week? Ask him. See if he can wait a week."

"I'll call you later."

"Tomorrow?"

"I don't know."

"Ask him. This week is going to be hell as it is."

Patty was quiet.

"Love you," he said. "Patty?"

"Sure."

SHE CALLED Monday while he was taking a midterm and left a one sentence message: "He can wait up to ten days."

That news loosened the band around Gene's heart. For the next few days, he plowed through preparations for the other two midterms. But the tests didn't go well, and he developed an ache in his midsection. The thought of driving to Tucson inflamed his gut even more. He called Patty three times, but each time her roommate said she was out — a shift on Pediatrics, grocery shopping, and the last time, on Valentine's Day, just *out.*

"Please tell her to call me back. I'm worried."

"Oh, are you?"

He wanted to reach through the phone and strangle Portly Peggy. "Tell her I can drive down, but I need to know soon."

But no call came, and the window to Tucson and back closed.

Finally, on Sunday evening, while lubricating his bicycle on the apartment landing, his phone rang at their usual time. Doug wasn't back yet from a weekend with his girlfriend. Gene hurriedly wiped his hands and answered. "Patty?"

"It's done."

"Really?"

"I had a miscarriage. Friday night. You don't have to worry."

"Are you okay?"

"I'm fine."

"That's a relief. What happened? Do you still want me to drive down? I can, you know."

"I started bleeding."

"Was it bad."

"Pretty bad."

"How'd you get to the hospital. Was Peggy around?"

"No."

"Did you drive yourself?"

"No. A neighbor."

"You sound tired. Do they want you to stay in bed or anything?"

"It's up to me."

"I'm so glad everything worked out. I guess we need to be more careful when we put our socks on." He laughed, expecting her to follow. But there was only silence.

"Hey, just a joke."

"That's what I thought."

"Patty — "

"Gene, you need to grow up."

"Hey, I'm sorry. Look, you never called me back. I was ready to drive down there. Why didn't you call me?"

Patty took a deep breath. "Gene. I don't think you should transfer here."

"What? Where did that come from?"

"We need to slow down."

"Patty, I said I was sorry, but if you'd just called me, I'd have driven all night to get there."

"We've only known each other a couple years."

"What are you talking about?"

"We don't need to rush. You like it there."

"On New Year's I asked if you could wait until the end of the school year until I transferred. You said, 'No. But I will.'"

"Gene, I'm late. I really have to go."

"For what?"

"Let's talk later."

He buzzed her phone the next day, but she never called back. On Sunday, she answered at their usual time.

"I forgot to ask," he said. "Did you get my Valentine's card?"

"Yes."

"I didn't get yours yet. The mail's been a little slow."

"Gene."

"I sent in the transfer application yesterday," he said. "I requested an expedited review. At first, I didn't know you could do that. I could be starting by next fall."

"Gene, you shouldn't have."

"It's okay. I told you I'd give up Cal Poly to be with you."

"There's no need to rush."

"Why do you keep saying that?"

"We need to make sure."

"About what?"

"Us."

"Us?"

Gene took some deep breaths, hoping it would slow his heart.

"That we're right for each other."

Gene looked at their photo on his desk. He dropped his head and tapped the receiver against his forehead. "You want to go out with other guys?"

She sighed.

"Oh, no. You already have."

"We'll talk over spring break."

"Who?"

"It doesn't matter."

"Jeez." Gene choked the handset. The pulse in his neck bounded. "Where'd you go?"

"Gene."

"Was this before you knew you were pregnant?"

"We can talk when you come home."

They talked a couple more times before Spring Break, but each time Patty was distant, seemingly preparing him for something he refused to believe could happen. The last call before he drove home was like being hit by a Cadillac. She told him, *Things change* and *His name is Jake.*

On a bright, windy day, the kind of cloudless blue-sky day that make most people look up to the heavens and smile, Gene and Patty, heads bowed, sat against the backstop across from her house. To Gene, the few inches between them felt like the Grand Canyon. He stared at his hands while Patty told him about Jake. There wasn't much to tell as far as Gene was concerned. Once she said his name, his mind whipped back to an image of Patty and Jake in the glow of her apartment's porch light when Gene arrived in Tucson with the news of his father's death. He'd not gotten a good look at Jake, but he remembered the prick had a mustache.

Gene rubbed along the prominent vein on the top of his hand. How soothing Patty's touch had been during his father's funeral. Out across the ballfield's green grass, the chain-link pattern of the backstop's shadow crept toward the pitcher's mound.

"I wasn't looking to meet anyone, Gene," she said. "It just happened."

"So, he just asks you out on a date and you say *yes*, like I don't even exist, like the last two-and-a-half years mean nothing to you?"

"He invited me to church."

"I thought you only went on Christmas Eve."

"It was nice."

"When?"

Patty was silent.

"After the miscarriage?"

"No."

"So before?"

Patty looked away.

"Before you knew you were pregnant?"

She sighed.

"Oh great. I'm gone for a couple weeks, and you go out on a date!"

"It was church."

"Must have been some church." Gene lobbed a rock short of the pitcher's mound.

"I don't know what else to say, Gene. Things change."

"Jeez, you keep saying that. What changed?"

She straightened her back and took a deep breath. Here it was. Gene knew Patty. She was lining up just the right words to make her point, and he knew what that point would be: He should have abandoned his classes and flown to Tucson when she asked. But couldn't she see the pressure he was under? He would have come down the following week, and if she had only returned his calls, he could have gotten on the road, but she didn't, and then she had a miscarriage, and what was he supposed to do then?

"Patty, I love you, and I know deep down you love me. We can have children when the time is right."

He braced for a tearful explanation of guilt for the child who never was.

In the softest voice, she said, "Gene, I feel older. That's what's changed."

"What does that mean?"

"I'm in an older world now. Jake is older. His friends are older."

"You're breaking up with me because I'm in college, and he's a medical student?"

"That's not it."

"In a couple years I'll be in medical school. Why can't you wait?"

"It's not about waiting. I was feeling this even before I learned I was pregnant. I guess I kind of pushed it aside."

"I've loved you since the moment I saw you by the pool. You told me how safe you felt with me, and I've always felt the same with you. I couldn't have gotten through that horrible week my dad died without you. Can't you see what we had? I feel like Jake has put a spell on you or kidnapped you. This feels completely wrong."

Tears slid down Gene's cheeks. He wiped them away. She did seem older, or at least different. She'd cut her beautiful hair. It now bobbed to her chin. He couldn't make out the perfume, but it wasn't the Estée Lauder he'd bought her for her nineteenth birthday. She'd be twenty-one in three weeks, her birthday the start of a two-month period when numerically their ages were two years apart until he turned twenty in June. In the past, she'd joked about preferring younger men.

"So how old is he?"

"It doesn't matter."

"It does to me."

There. That look of pity that made Gene want to rip the backstop from its pilings.

"Twenty-seven."

"Repeated a few grades, huh?"

"No. Vietnam."

Gene stared beyond the mound, to the middle of center field where they'd made love during spacious, black nights the previous summer. "I can change a lot of things, but I can't change my age."

"I don't want to hurt you, Gene."

"I wish I could have been with you. You shouldn't have been alone. Okay?"

Patty looked down and shook her head. "That's just it. I wasn't alone."

"That son of a bitch." He heaved a stone past the infield. "So, he drives you to the ER or wherever. It's not like he had to drive from San Luis Obispo."

"No. But he did drive an hour-and-a-half from Sells."

"It's still not ten hours."

"He works as an EMT there on off-days when he can."

"Such a saint."

Patty straightened and turned, her face reddening. "He came, Gene. He came. I was his priority. Not the money he was scheduled to make." She shook her head. "And before that, when I talked to the abortion doctor, he came with me. I was drowning and he saved me."

"You know I would have saved you if I could!"

"He helped me work through all my options."

"Options!"

"That's what mature people do, Gene. They don't make rash decisions."

"Tell me then. What un-rash decision did you make?"

Patty's body softened. She dropped her head to her pulled-up knees and made circles in the dirt with her perfect index finger. "It doesn't matter now."

For several moments, they were quiet.

"Remember the photo my dad took on graduation?" Gene asked. Patty nodded. "On the back you wrote *I love you with my whole heart.*"

She looked up. The sweetest expression came to her face, one of regret and longing — a smile through pinched lips. Her eyes seemed to inhale his every feature. She began to tear. No sound, just tears. She took Gene's hand between both of hers. She was coming around. He could feel it, and he swallowed hard, his own hopeful smile poised to kiss.

"Gene, that was high school," she began. "But I've changed. You'll always be special. I'll always love you." She patted his hand like a mother pats a child's. "You'll be fine."

He jerked his hand away. "Is that what he told you to tell me? It was, wasn't it? Right after he fucked you?"

Patty rose with a kind of parental dignity.

"I'm surprised he wasn't scared off when you told him you were pregnant. I guess the miscarriage worked out well for both of you."

She looked at him with a disbelieving look, the last fiber of their connection straining under the weight of his words.

"This is what I mean. You need to grow up. Be someone your father would be proud of. Be more like him."

She walked away from the backstop and halfway down the third-base line to the gate. She didn't turn. No last look as she opened the gate and walked through. He stood, cupped his hands to his mouth and shouted, "It was his, wasn't it?"

Patty broke into an arm-hugging run across the street and up the walkway to her house.

"Yeah," he said, his voice quavering. "The baby. I bet it was Jake's."

Chapter Fourteen

NOBODY KNOWS YOU WHEN YOU'RE DOWN AND OUT

Summer 1974

Before eating breakfast, before showering, before changing into his best slacks, shirt, and tie, Gene dials the hospital operator. "Room number for Rebecca Layne, please."

He crosses his fingers.

"It's 626. Should I connect you?"

"No, thank you."

When he enters Rebecca's room, Mrs. Layne sets her book and reading glasses aside and stands to shake his hand. Or so he thinks. Instead she spreads her arms and hugs him. "I didn't thank you adequately earlier. I'm so glad you were there to help."

"I was just around the corner eating lunch."

She points to the red stitching above the pocket of his coat. "What is the Heart Team?"

"The open-heart surgery team."

"She needs surgery!"

Gene reaches out with both arms like he's grabbing someone about to fall off a cliff. "No, no, no. Nothing like that. I just came by to see how she's doing."

Mrs. Layne puts her hand over her heart and bends at the waist. "Thank God."

Rebecca stirs, opens her eyes, and scoots herself up in bed. Her hospital gown falls off one tan shoulder. Her mother pulls it up and ties the ribbon in back. "Becca, do you remember…I'm so sorry, I forgot — "

"Gene."

"Do you remember Dr. Gene?"

"No," he said, "It's Gene Hull."

"Sweetie, do you remember Dr. Hull from yesterday. He saved your life."

Rebecca rubs her eyes. "I'm sorry, Dr. Hull, I don't remember much after I walked into the lobby."

Mrs. Layne nudges Rebecca and sits on the edge of the bed. "While I was losing my head," Mrs. Layne says, "Dr. Hull gave you a breath, and voilà…everything's fine."

"Are you with Dr. Zemlicka?" Rebecca says, She looks around her mother to the nightstand. "Mom, hand me that."

"No."

Rebecca nods, pulls her long, brown hair into a ponytail, and secures it with the band her mother handed her. "I thought maybe you had news about the ultrasound."

"Echocardiogram," her mother says.

Rebecca gestures toward her mother with her eyes. "She never misses *General Hospital.* Mom, can you pour me some water?"

"It's not from *General Hospital!* Dr. Zemlicka called it an echocardiogram. I wrote it down."

Gene pours a cup of water from the pitcher on the table at the foot of the bed. Rebecca leans forward to accept it. "Thank you."

"I'm sure it's fine," Gene says. "You were probably overheated and fainted. Some people have a seizure when they faint. Maybe you were hypoglycemic." He apes everything he remembers Dr. Knudson saying yesterday.

"The ultrasound tech sure saw something. While she was running that cold goo over my chest, she said, 'That's interesting', and then when I asked 'What?' she clammed up."

Gene forces his expression to look as if he's considering the possibilities, but he's remembering the night his father told him the results of Patty's echocardiogram.

Mrs. Layne places her hand on the bedspread over Rebecca's thigh. "Do you know what she might have seen, Dr. Hull?"

"No," he says. "I don't."

But it worries him.

———

GENE STOPS by the Union 76 station where he picked up the clamp for his busted radiator hose that first morning of work. After filling the Jeep, he waits in the small office. It has a swamp cooler instead of air conditioning, but it still feels great. The wind from the unit flows across the back of Gene's sweaty neck, over the counter, past the displays of maps, cigarettes, and fan belts, and through the open door to the two garage bays. In one of the bays, the same kid as before is looking up into the engine compartment of a Corvette balanced on a hydraulic lift. Gene dings the small bell. The kid slides from under the car and lopes to the counter, while wiping his hands on a rag. "What'd you take?"

Jerry, the owner, usually limps out to the pump himself, brushing his dark Fu Man Chu while he memorizes the numbers. Gene takes a few steps outside the door and returns.

"That'll be $5.88."

Gene lays the remaining clamps on the counter. "Sorry I'm a bit late returning these."

The kid smiles. "Right on. I wondered what happened to you. You got her running, huh?"

Gene's pretty sure this blond, curly haired kid is Jerry's son, J.J.. Back when Gene started driving, he usually saw this kid's close-cropped head under a hood or his Converse high-tops sticking out from under a rear axle.

"Where's Jerry?"

"Laid up."

"Laid up?"

"Back surgery." J.J. hits a key on the register. The drawer chimes open. "With the clamp that'll be $6.08."

"He okay?"

"Yeah. Mom won't let him out of the house till after he sees the doctor again."

"Where'd he have surgery?"

"Desert Valley."

"That's where I work."

"No shit. You a doctor or something?"

"I work with a heart surgeon."

"What's that like? I mean, it's like working on an engine, right, except all the parts are squishy and bloody and shit? That's what my old man says. He says we're just like surgeons except for cars."

"You're right."

"I couldn't do what you do. I'm allergic to blood...and to school." He grins.

Gene hands him a five and a one and then fishes his pockets for eight cents.

"But I was thirteen when I rebuilt my first transmission. Shit, I can do it blindfolded now. My dad says I got grease for blood."

"Looks like you'll own this station someday then."

"Pop would love it, but I got bigger plans. I'm going to be the next Dale Inman."

"Who?" Gene looks up and hands him three pennies and a nickel.

"Petty's crew chief."

Gene frowned. The name didn't ring a bell.

"Richard Petty. The King. I don't know what Inman makes, but it's got to be at least twenty a year. That's doctor money." The kid's face lights up. He separates the coins into their respective slots in the tray. "How about your pop? He a doc, too?"

"Used to be."

"Retired, huh? Bet he ragged on you to take over for him like mine."

"No. He didn't push me at all."

J.J. shoves the register tray closed. "You're lucky. I keep telling

Pop I got to march my own drum or beat a different drum. Whatever it is. You know what I mean."

"Your life, your decision?"

"Exactly."

J.J. reaches under the counter and pushes a drinking glass toward Gene, the orange '76 logo facing him. "You bought over ten gallons."

Gene tests the weight.

"Give it to your girl," J.J. says. "She'll love you for it."

It used to be that simple, didn't it?

BACK AT HOME, Gene gulps a glass of ice water from his commemorative glass. Commemorating what? Patty's engagement? As the chilled water slides down his esophagus, he feels his heart flinch. Maybe a person can stop his own heart this way. Ah, the perfect crime — wear Jake out at the batting cage, and then watch him drop after he downs a quart of icy Gatorade.

Gene sweeps the pool and checks the chemicals, pausing periodically to throw the tennis ball into the water for Apollo. When the work is done, he dives in. He makes a slow, underwater haul to the shallow end in one breath. When he pops to the surface, Apollo is prancing at the pool's edge. Gene whips his hair of excess water. At Apollo's feet lies a headless dove.

"Maybe Mom is right. There is a cat." She was right about Patty, that she'd break his heart, just not for the reason she thought.

He towels off and, using a paper towel, dumps the bird in the trash barrel. "What say we get that fucking cat?" He tousles his dog's head. Apollo barks. "Yeah," Gene says. "Let's get that mother fucker."

In the kitchen, Gene replaces the wire-trap's nine-volt battery with a fresh one he finds in the refrigerator's butter compartment. He opens a can of tuna from the pantry. Apollo follows him out to the orange trees. The tree trunk's white paint is fading — the price of irrigating this section of the yard. He should paint them. He loads the trap with tuna fish, and sets the guillotine-like sheet-metal door. Using a dead twig, he breaks the infrared beam. The door starts its free-fall descent but cants and hangs. After a couple squirts of silicone spray, the door drops like a blade.

Apollo looks at Gene, then back to the cage, and licks his lips.

"We're here to trap it," Gene says. "Not eat it."

BARE-CHESTED and still in his bathing suit, Gene feeds Apollo and then makes a quick steak sandwich for himself. After dinner, he tries to study, but the motivation evaporates. He'd needed to practice tying knots. He hasn't missed a day since Rui taught him. Until tonight.

Up on the roof, Al Michaels play-by-play waxes and wanes, and no amount of adjusting the wire antenna evens it out. No matter. He listens anyway. Still in his bathing suit, he powers through three sets of push-ups, pull-ups, and sit-ups. With each set, he uses Jake as motivation to grit through an extra couple repetitions. His muscles burn. Then he hustles down to the kitchen and returns upstairs with a chocolate shake. Apollo, having given up scoring more than a spoonful, curls up on the bed as Gene sets the alarm clock to 11:45.

He strokes Apollo's head. "I guess it's official. No getting her back. I blew it. Just you and me now, buddy."

Gene steps through the window into the warm night and settles into the deck chair to drink his shake and listen to the game. Across from Patty's house, the ballfield is dark, a black void in heart of the neighborhood.

Things change. She was sure right about that.

GENE STARTLES AWAKE. He checks his watch. Shit. After telling Mrs. McLellan her trees could use some water he's almost slept through his midnight-to-one irrigation slot. The Giants game ended hours ago, and the reception from San Francisco is all static. He turns the radio off, and stumbles through his window. The room is dark except for scant moonlight that guides him to his clock radio. Damn.

Still in his swim trunks, he takes the stairs two at a time, cursing himself for not pulling the Alarm pin out. He runs through the house to the garage where he stores his irrigation boots and flashlight. He slips the black boots over his bare feet and jogs out to the far corner of the orange grove. A minor rivulet of water leaks through the dried-out gasket. Gene squats down and torques the round ten-inch steel cap by the handle. It loosens a quarter turn, sending a forceful stream of water through the narrow circumferential opening. Gene spins the disk on its axis ten full turns, opening a four-inch gap between the disk and the concrete pipe protruding just above grade. Water surges toward the thirsty trees, tens of gallons per minute. He stands there in his black rubber boots and swim trunks for a second, watching and listening to the roiling water, confident that there is a high enough pressure head tonight to give the trees a good soak despite losing half of his allotted time.

With a half hour to kill before he has to close the valve, Gene leaves his boots on the patio and grabs a Michelob from the fridge. Beer in hand, he walks back through the house and up the stairs to the landing. "Apollo. Come on down and keep me company." When he doesn't hear the jingle of the dog's collar, he climbs the rest of the way and turns on the light. Apollo isn't in the room. Probably on Gene's mother's bed. But he's not there either, and Gene assumes the dog has slipped past him and is outside doing his business. Gene opens the sliding glass door and steps out onto the patio. He calls toward the grassy area hidden in darkness on the opposite side of the yard from the orange grove. "Apollo. Here boy." Nothing. "Apollo." Gene takes three cautious steps toward the grass and hears a thin bark behind him. He wheels around. "Oh, shit!"

Gene runs barefooted toward the cat trap at the downstream end of the orange grove. He splashes through ankle deep water, ducking around and under the canopy of orange trees. One branch lashes his neck. His eyes are accustomed enough to the dark to make out the form of the trap sticking out of the water and something else. "Apollo!" He's jammed halfway inside, his nose pressed to the top of the trap, straining above the rising water.

Gene reaches under the dog and the trap simultaneously and lifts them to his chest. Apollo yelps. Gene stumbles out of the grove. When he reaches the patio, he drops to his knees and sets Apollo on the cement. Light from the kitchen reveals Apollo to be wedged halfway inside the trap. It's so tight, the dog is having trouble breathing. His pants are shallow and rapid. Gene tries to slip his wet fingers between the trap's opening and Apollo's body, but can't. Blood oozes from a cut on Apollo's coat. Gene tries again. Apollo squeals and tenses and pinches Gene's fingers against the thick wire. Gene yells and pulls his hand back, tearing his skin over two knuckles. He pulls and pulls on the wire, trying to stretch the opening but can't get enough bend to make a difference. Then he remembers.

He runs to the garage storeroom, pulls open drawers, and returns with a two-handed cable cutter. He's able to wedge the tip of the jaw between Apollo and the top wires. He snips them along its length until he can open the top like the chest of a heart patient. Gene extracts Apollo from the trap, taking care not to impale the dog on the sharp cut.

Apollo's breathing deepens, but it's still rapid, and he's weak. Gene carries him inside and rests him on the tile floor by the kitchen table. With a towel from the nearby bathroom, he dries Apollo and examines the cut. It's shallow, a scrape really. Nothing that needs a stitch he guesses. Apollo's sandpapery tongue licks the wounds over Gene's knuckles. With his other hand, Gene strokes his dog's head. After a few minutes, Apollo stands, shakes off the water in a single spasm, and curls into Gene's lap. Gene cradles him, rocks, and cries.

Chapter Fifteen

MR. MEAD

WHEN GENE ARRIVES MONDAY MORNING, Jesse is waiting at the elevator. "Man of the hour, too sweet to be sour," he says. "How's the hero? Hungry I bet from playing Superman. No, no. I see you as more of a Spiderman."

"You heard?"

"You can't fart in a hospital without everyone hearing. Me? I served Mary Jane her lunch Saturday."

"Who?"

"Spiderman's girlfriend. One of 'em."

"She still on six?"

"Nah. Took off after chow. Here. Take your breakfast. I doubled up on the pancakes." He slides out two trays and flashes the roster of fourth-floor patients. "Lots of folks took the night train."

Gene takes the clipboard and sees pencil lines through the names.

"Only one died. Like I say, they never tell the kitchen."

"How about her?" Gene points to Perkins, Mary, the mitral valve from last week, afraid what Jesse might say.

"That sweet little thing? Transferred her to rehab yesterday. I don't usually ask, but I asked on this one 'cause she kept trying to bum a cigarette off me."

Jesse closes up the cart. "Gotta roll." Then he taps a finger to his lips and squints at Gene. "Hope you got her number."

"Mrs. Perkins?"

"Mary Jane, Spidey. Mary Jane. I think she was sweet on you. I know her mama was. You got her number, right?"

"It's not like that."

"Man, it's always like that."

RUI WALKS into the doctor's lounge, tying his wedding band into the bow of his scrub pants. He pours a cup of coffee and swirls the pot in Gene's direction.

Through a mouthful of pancakes, Gene shakes his head *no*.

"Are you sure? Now that you act like a doctor, you should drink like one."

Cool air brushes the back of his neck. Since his haircut, he's been wearing a surgeon's cap. "No, thanks."

"Maybe when you are older," Rui says. "When you are here in Boz's place." He gestures to Dr. Boswell asleep on the couch. "A surgeon though, I hope, waking up on a cold, stiff couch after an hour of sleep, and your patient is in the ICU, and other patients are taking off work to see you in your office — ten, maybe twenty of them — and they are bringing their lists and their eldest daughters have their own lists. Maybe then — " He takes a sip from his cup and cringes, "Maybe then you will appreciate the aroma and backbone of a fine Portuguese Bica." He adds milk and sugar to his cup and sits next to Gene. "Until then, you are right not to succumb to this hospital sludge."

After a knock on the door, a lady backs in with a cart of supplies for the lounge. She starts to drop the newspaper on the coffee table, but Rui reaches out. "If you please."

She cleans the previous day's mess. Gene reads the sports page. Rui considers the Jumble.

"Saving lives, I hear," Rui says.

Gene shakes his head and mumbles through stuffed cheeks, "Jesse's right."

"About what?"

"About farting and everyone in the hospital knows."

Rui laughs. "I saw a consult in the ER just now. Knudson told me."

"I tried giving her mouth to mouth, but it didn't work until I lifted her chin. I think she was always trying to breathe. I just didn't notice."

"Carl taught you mouth-to-mouth?"

Gene nods.

"Quintessential Carl. Your instinct was commendable. That's all it takes — do something and ofttimes, no matter your original intent, that something works. Carl would have been proud."

"Careful Gene-o," Boz says. He shifts and clears his throat. "That's how you end up married. Saving damsels in distress. Right, Rui?"

Rui waves him off. "Boz, you should be preparing our patient. I will give you until I am done here. Ah...*spurn.*"

"It's delayed," Boz mumbles, still facing the back of the couch.

Rui taps the pen against his teeth and then fills in another word.

"Zem has a patient in the CCU he wants Harrington to slip in first...."

Gene freezes. Rebecca?

"...Some guy who crumpled on the golf course yesterday. Now, let me sleep."

Gene relaxes back into the couch.

"Before I forget," Rui says to Gene, "bring a grapefruit to the lounge. I will teach you how to close the skin." Rui scribbles another word.

"A grapefruit?"

"We will cut it. Eat it. Then sew it back together."

"They're not in season."

"Check the diner. They always have them."

Rui returns his attention to the Jumble and after a minute says,

"I got it." He fills in the last word — *quaint* — and makes a list of the circled letters needed to solve the riddle. "So, how was your weekend?" Rui says.

Gene thinks, *about the worst since my father died.*

"My dog almost drowned."

"Apollo?" Rui drops the folded paper to his lap.

"He's fine. It was stupid. He got stuck in a trap."

"Animal control?"

Gene shakes his head. "I'm trying to catch a cat. It's a long story."

"Catch it?" Boz says. His eyes are closed. "Shoot it."

"All is well, then," Rui says. He adjusts his reading glasses. "Boz, help me with this riddle. You are particularly qualified."

Boz turns and throws his arm over his eyes. "I'm sleeping."

"Here it is. The first thing a teenager will do. Two words."

"Jack off," Boz says.

"That was a good Texas guess, but the second word is eight letters."

Gene takes the paper and pen and rearranges the letters over and over in the margin until he sees it. "Turn thirteen," he says and hands the paper back to Rui.

Rui fills in the riddle and shakes his head. "So obvious once it's solved, isn't it?"

Gene washes at the scrub sink next to Rui. On the open-heart schedule taped to the wall, the first name and procedure is crossed out. Now in Darlene's handwriting, it reads: Mead, Howard — CABG/AVR. After a couple weeks, scrubbing has become automatic for Gene. He always remembers to pin his watch to his scrub pants, makes sure his mask fits tight around his nose and under his eyes, and he's able to carry on a conversation while muscle memory takes over the scouring — fingers to elbows, fingers to elbows, rinse, rinse. Today, Gene is thinking about Jesse's *Spiderman* comment. He runs the brush over his injured knuckles and winces.

"What happened there?" Rui says.

Gene rinses a small amount of blood away. "My damn trap," he says.

"Go easy with the brush."

Gene applies pressure with a paper towel, and then starts over.

"I learned something else from Dr. Knudson this morning," Rui says. "He thinks you are a resident."

Gene swallows. "He misunderstood."

"Still, best not to misrepresent your role outside the Heart Room."

Rui could have lashed him harder. Much harder. But he didn't. "I won't."

Mr. Mead is tall. An extension piece has been added to the foot of the table. Gene assists Irene and Rui as they unfurl and secure the pump and suction tubing. He tries to stay focused. What should he do? What shouldn't he do? What's the next step? Like he did in baseball. Before every pitch he'd take in the outs, the runners, what base they were on, and ask a question: If it's hit to me, where do I throw it? Option one. And if I can't throw it there in time, what's option two?

Rui says to the room, "How do you know an elephant's been in your refrigerator?"

Gene accepts the sterile light-handles from Irene and attaches them overhead. "I don't know, Dr. Pereira. How do you know an elephant's been in your refrigerator?"

"There's a footprint in the pizza."

"Oh, great. They're a comedy team now," Dr. Boz says.

Rui taps the top of Gene's gloved hand with his fist.

Dr. Harrington, gowned and gloved by the light box, tilts his head up to the x-rays. "Eugene," he says.

"Yes, sir."

"Over heah, son."

Gene crosses his arms and steps close to Dr. Harrington, careful not to touch him.

Dr. Harrington takes a Kelly clamp off Irene's tray and points at the coronary arteries, gray images that look like rivers seen from space. "This is Howard Mead. Sixty-four years old. Yesterday, he sent a perfect drive off the sixteenth tee at the Country Club. He gathered his tee, took one stride toward his cart, and *wham*...flat on his face. Fortunately for Mr. Mead, the head of cardiology here, Dr. Zemlicka, was playing in his foursome."

He points to three narrows along the arteries' course. Then he points to a second radiograph, tapping over the aortic valve. "A real bugaboo. His valve's shot." He lets the clamp drop to the floor. Gene returns to his position next to Rui.

Of course, Gene did not meet Mr. Mead, and all he can see of him now is a rectangle of brown-painted skin running the length of his chest. Rui leans into Gene. "Good you ate breakfast. We shall be camped here awhile."

———

MR. MEAD's heart is enormous. Like the other hearts Gene has seen, a heavy drape of yellow-white fat nearly covers the red muscle. And like all the other hearts, it twists with each beat, but there is a special agony to it, like a man scaling the oxygen-thin air of Mt. Everest.

During bypass, Dr. Harrington wears his thick, magnifying lenses as he sutures the mammary artery, dissected from the inside of Mr. Mead's chest wall, to points past the blockages in his coronary arteries. Dr. Harrington palms the needle holder in his bear-sized paw. The movement of the needle is controlled and precise. Just a small, sweet bite through the wall of one vessel, regrasp, and another delicate bite through the wall of the receiving vessel, a maneuver repeated a dozen or more times until two arteries, smaller in diameter than drinking straws, are joined. Then Dr. Harrington ties the suture using one-handed throws. The smooth, rapid way his fingers move is mesmerizing. Truly, soft hands.

With the grafts in place, Dr. Harrington opens Mr. Mead's aorta. He excises the diseased valve with a long-handled scalpel and hands it to Gene. The normal valve depicted in Grant's *Atlas* is composed of three rubbery, triangular leaflets covering an opening the size of a quarter. This valve looks like a calcified washer with an opening a soda straw couldn't fit through.

Mr. Mead's new valve comes from a pig. As Dr. Harrington and Rui place a series of sutures loosely through the new valve and the rim of the opening left by the old valve, Gene keeps the rim dry of oozing, timing the interjection of the suction wand between the surgeons' rapidly moving hands.

From behind him, Boz says, "Hey, Geno. Let's say we replace this guy's valve with one that has an opening twice as big as his crusty, old valve. How much will the flow increase across the valve?"

No doubt Boz is by the desk flirting with Sandra.

"I'll give you a hint," Boz says.

Gene keeps his eyes on the field while answering. "Flow is proportional to the square of the radius. If the radius is doubled, the flow increases by a factor of four."

Every engineering student knows that.

Dr. Boz doesn't respond.

Irene says, "Sandra, another suture, please."

"My young Gene," Rui says. "Do you hear that? That is the sound of Dr. Boz with nothing more to say. It's a beautiful thing."

Gene catches Sandra's movement in his peripheral vision as she opens the packet of suture onto Irene's back table. He glances up to see her gesture with a waist-high thumbs-up.

"Gene-o," Dr. Boz says. He returned to the head of the OR table. "You're on the wrong side of the blood-brain barrier."

"The lights are horrible," Dr. Harrington says. "Just horrible. I'd like to God…damn…see."

Rui's hands are busy, so Gene reaches up for the sterile light handle, his chest still puffed from slamming Dr. Boz.

"Stop!" Irene says. "You're contaminated." She reads Gene's pleading eyes. "Your thumb touched the light."

Sandra unties Gene's gown and then pulls both the gown and

gloves from him. As long as he doesn't contaminate his bare hands, he doesn't have to re-scrub. Irene looks over. Her eyes fume. "You'll have to wait a minute." The game continues. Gene waits, chagrined to be a pest.

Sandra steps behind him and curls a finger inside his scrub's waist band. She whispers, "It happens."

Her warm breath tickles his neck's cool skin, only partially allaying his anger.

While the surgeons slide the valve along the dozen or so sutures into position, Irene re-gowns Gene. By the time he's back next to Rui, half the sutures are tied. Dr. Harrington ties the remaining knots, and then holds the tag ends high while Rui cuts each free with precise snips of his scissors.

Dr. Harrington closes the aorta, but does not draw the last stitch tight. He partially releases a clamp, allowing the heart to fill with blood from the bypass machine. Rui places his hand under the heart and massages, coaxing the last bubbles out the tented aortic hole. This is such an important step. A single bubble can lead to disaster. When only a steady arc of blood jets from the gap, Dr. Harrington cinches it closed.

Dr. Harrington releases the cross clamp from the aorta. The heart fibrillates, looking like a squiggling bag of worms. Irene hands him the paddles. He places them on opposite sides of the heart. Gene lifts his hands from atop the patient. *Thwump*. The heart jumps but continues to fibrillate. Sandra turns up the juice, and Dr. Harrington tries again. *Thwump*. No beats. The engine isn't starting. "Lidocaine," Dr. Harrington says.

"Just gave it," Dr. Boz says.

Dr. Harrington massages the heart. He takes the paddles from Irene and tries again. *Thwump*. They wait.

"Ventricular at forty," Dr. Boz says. "Epi running."

"Pacer wires," Dr. Harrington says. Irene already has them on her tray. Dr. Harrington implants the pacemaker leads into the left ventricle. Rui attaches the other end to alligator clips and then hands them off to Dr. Boz, who attaches the clips to the pacer box.

"Sixty," Dr. Harrington says.

"Capturing at sixty." Rui reaches over and turns the dial.

"Flow down," Dr. Harrington says. "Give me a hundred."

"There's a hundred," Rogers says.

Dr. Harrington pushes on the left ventricle with his finger, like he's testing the tension on a balloon.

"Hundred more," Dr. Harrington says.

"Hundred mills going in," Roger says. "Pressure's up to ninety-five. Pacing at sixty."

"Off bypass," Dr. Harrington says.

"Flow coming down," Roger says "…and…off."

"Protamine?" Dr. Boz asks.

"Give him a second," Dr. Harrington says. Gene has learned that heparin is given before going on bypass to prevent the patient's blood from clotting as it runs through the bypass tubing. Once bypass is over, protamine reverses that effect so the blood can clot again. He's never seen them delay.

Dr. Harrington and Rui insert two chest tubes through Mr. Mead's chest. Dr. Harrington rolls the heart slightly to lay the end of the chest tube in the well underneath.

"Mother of God," Dr. Harrington says.

Gene doesn't understand until Irene reaches for the paddles. The heart is fibrillating again. Gene raises his hands from the patient just before the heart jumps from the jolt. "Higher," Dr. Harrington says. The heart jumps again, but it doesn't convert.

Dr. Harrington slams the paddles down on the patient. "On bypass," he says as loud as Gene had ever heard him speak.

"Needle," Dr. Harrington says. He inserts a needle in the aorta and a small arc of blood begins to flow. He massages the heart with his massive hand, stroking along the length of each coronary artery.

Rui leans his head toward Gene and whispers. "Probably air in a coronary."

Now Gene understands. Dr. Harrington's instincts told him to delay the protamine. If they'd given it, they couldn't have put Mr. Mead back on bypass.

A slight sputter breaks the arc of blood emanating from the needle, then a couple more. Dr. Harrington continues to massage until the arc of blood remains steady. He holds out his hands for the paddles.

The heart beats on the first attempt, but even Gene can see it's having a harder time than all the hearts he's witnessed before. This heart doesn't look like an old man with a cane: It looks like an old man crawling on hands and knees, gasping for breath. Dr. Harrington inserts an additional monitoring catheter. He calls it a left atrial pressure line. Then Dr. Harrington, Dr. Boz, and Roger talk back and forth in one-and-two-word responses, most of it just beyond Gene's understanding as they try to wean Mr. Mead from the bypass machine. One thing is clear: although Mr. Mead's heart is beating, it isn't beating well enough to function on its own.

"I've tried Epi and Dopamine. Nipride's running," Dr. Boz says.

"One play left," Rui whispers to Gene.

"Sandra!" Dr. Harrington says.

"I'll get it." She runs out the door, while Irene barks orders to Betty.

"Grilled ham and cheese." The waitress spins the plate a quarter turn as she sets it on the counter. "Anything else?"

"Do you have a grapefruit? A whole grapefruit."

The wall clock reads one-thirty. Jeez, they'd incised Mr. Mead's chest at seven. Gene's still in scrubs. He plops a leg onto the stool next to him and leans forward, feeling the pull in his hamstring, holds that position for a few seconds, and then does the same with the other leg. His feet ache. There's a knot just below his shoulder blade. It's his body reminding him *I'm still here*, now that his mind isn't kidnapped by the Heart Room.

He's felt this after other cases, but today, he also feels a knot in his stomach. Maybe it was from holding his breath each time they tried to start Mr. Mead's engine, then seeing it turn over, only to sputter out again. And when they finally cleared the lines, and the heart kept running, it wasn't running on all cylinders, and it clearly wasn't capable of pushing its normal load of blood around Mr.

Mead's body, or even half a load. Roger's bypass machine was doing most of the work, but Mr. Mead couldn't stay on it forever.

"Here's your grapefruit," the waitress says and wipes her hands across her apron.

Gene eats his sandwich and rolls the grapefruit under his palm on the counter. What if? What if Mr. Mead hadn't been playing golf with a cardiologist? He might have died on the course. What if he'd not been playing golf at all, but had been swimming in the community pool at Sun City? He might have drowned. What if he'd undergone surgery last year, before the shiny, desk-sized behemoth Sandra rolled into the Heart Room — the intra-aortic balloon pump — had been added to the Heart Team's arsenal? Without it, Mr. Mead would be in the morgue right now, instead of balancing on a wire in the ICU.

Sandra, with the help of two others, pushed the device into the OR less than a minute after she ran from the room. The machine looked like photos Gene had seen of NASA consoles at the Johnson Space Center — oscilloscope and knobs and sliders — but this was stainless steel. Rui explained how it worked as he and Dr. Harrington inserted a catheter several feet long through an artery in Mr. Mead's groin, stopping when they gauged the tip to be in the aorta. Once connected, a pump inflated and deflated a balloon, the shape of a hot dog, at the end of the catheter. Somehow that action, timed to Mr. Mead's heartbeats, allowed his weak heart to pump with far less effort. Rui said, "We'll take the weight of the jockey off his back for a time and allow his heart to strengthen from the trauma of surgery. Basically, surgery is nothing more than a controlled wreck."

Of course, Gene saw a wreck once. There was nothing controlled about it and his father was not able to save the girl. How could he have? Out in the desert there were no drugs, no magic potions as Boz called them — epinephrine, Dopamine, Lidocaine. There were no paddles to shock the heart. There were no bags of blood and fluid. There wasn't a bypass machine in someone's trunk or a balloon pump in a rest stop's closet. just in case. No. But in the Heart Room, the team had all these things, and in the controlled wreck of the Heart Room, there seemed to be an unspoken creed — failure was not an option.

But it was a possibility. Until now, Gene hadn't truly accepted that a patient admitted to the hospital today, some saggy-chested man hanging his seersucker shirt in the small bedside closet, might die in the Heart Room tomorrow. And because of what? A bubble so small you could sip it through a straw.

So, what if? What if Mr. Mead had died in the Heart Room? Would Gene have crumbled and gone back to tree painting? He hoped not. He could imagine a somber acceptance filling the Heart Room, a dark voluminous silence devoid of music, the cautery buzz, and the monitor's rhythmic beeping. And then Dr. Harrington would step away from Mr. Mead. He'd write a note in the chart perhaps before taking a slow, lumbering walk toward the automatic glass doors. There would be the *pshhht* as his heavy footsteps landed on the black rubber mat, and the doors flung open. Then a few more steps around the corner to the special room, the Consultation Room where he would deliver the horrible news in a tone both comforting and direct.

The OR crew would turn the room over for the next case. Dr. Harrington would say "On bypass" and the team would work. Their minds would not wallow like Gene's is now. They would focus on each step, from the first to the thousandth, until the next patient was wheeled into the ICU. They'd return the next day and do the same. And the day after that. Day after day, month after month, year after year. It's what doctors did. They accepted that they tried their best, and when their best wasn't enough, they looked for ways to make their best better. Like the addition of the balloon pump.

Gene's father had tried his best with nothing but his hands. An impossible task, Gene understands that more clearly than ever. His mother was wrong. The flying lessons weren't about trying to atone for the past. They were about looking for a way to give another little girl in the future a better chance. He didn't crumble. He came up with a plan, however crazy it seemed, to combine his desire to fly with his desire to heal. But even if his wife wouldn't let him pilot the craft, he could still be on board to help.

Chapter Sixteen

PLAN B

BETWEEN THE SECOND and third case, Rui gives Gene a quick sewing lesson in the doctor's lounge. Instead of cutting the grapefruit in half, he makes a two-inch gash with a scalpel and then demonstrates how to approximate the edges using a nylon suture attached to a straight needle. While Gene takes a go at it, Dr. Boz walks in, stuffing the last corner of a sandwich into his mouth. "So that's why you always smell like citrus. I thought it was some high-dollar European cologne."

"If you please, my young assistant here must concentrate."

Watching Gene, Dr. Boz pours a cup of coffee and downs it.

"Keep practicing," Rui says. "And remember always, the scar you leave will be your signature. Make it beautiful, and forever your patients will love you."

"Or…" Dr. Boz says, "…you could just stalk your appy and take a vow. In sickness and in health." He chucks his cup in the trash, says, "Saddle up, boys. One more to go." He whisks out the door.

Gene wants to ask but doesn't.

"Yes," Rui says, "I am a romantic. And there is such a thing as love at first sight, even as she winces in pain in the emergency room.

My dear Alicia experienced similar feelings, albeit at second sight, and loves me to this day...*sans* appendix."

Gene grins. Now he gets it. Alicia was Rui's patient. "How's her scar?"

"A most beautiful thing."

How does Dr. Harrington do it? The Mr. Mead marathon followed by the two scheduled cases, no lunch, no dinner, rounds complete, and he hasn't slowed down. He hasn't sped up either. Just plods along. He sits at the ICU nursing station, hunkered over Mr. Mead's chart, while Gene stands next to him, nearly zoned-out, feeling like one of the children from *Village of the Damned*, minus the glowing eyes...*leave us alone.*

Mr. Mead is at the far end of the room in bed seven. He's easy to spot with the giant intra-aortic balloon pump sticking out into the room from the foot of the bed. On the other side of Mr. Mead's bed, a tiny face looks at Gene and, with a wave of her tiny arm, beckons him over. Gene points to himself and mouths *me*? The lady nods and waves again. Gene walks over.

"Young man," she says. "Do you work with Dr. Harrington?"

"Yes, I do," he says, looking up to Mr. Mead, who's still unconscious. "Are you his wife?"

"Where are my manners," she says. She extends her hand. "I am Mrs. Mead. And you are?"

"Gene Hull."

"Is that short for 'Eugene' by any chance?"

"It is."

"I have a nephew named Eugene."

She shakes his hand in that cupped half-grip way refined people do. "Dr. Hull, it is so nice to meet you." Even though Rui warned him, the way she speaks his name and advances his medical standing with such a sweet-tea Southern accent, he can't bear to correct her. "My grandson is a physician in Raleigh. Just about your age I think."

From television and movies, Gene lumps all things Southern together — garden parties, thoroughbreds galloping in white-fenced fields of bluegrass, lazy summers on the porch dressed in one's Sunday best. He doesn't know if this is Mrs. Mead's background, but she is "dressed to the nines," as his father used to say. All that's missing is her parasol.

He's taken by her grace and equanimity in the midst of the squadron of machines monitoring her husband's vital organs and keeping him alive — the ventilator, the infusion pumps, a half-dozen IV bags and bottles, the oscilloscope with its three rows of green waves bouncing to his heart's beat and measuring the pressures it generates. That's it, isn't it? Can his heart generate enough pressure to drive blood to his hungry tissues?

An alarm sounds on one of the infusion devices. "That's been a pesky one," Mrs. Mead says.

Gene doesn't know what to do except look over at the nurses' station, but a nurse is already making her way toward him. She scans the tracings on the monitor and checks the settings on the offending infusion pump before pressing a button to silence the alarm. "Same one, huh?"

"Every time," Mrs. Mead says.

"I'll call down and replace it." She kneels and examines the blood draining from the chest tubes into the collection bottles. When she stands, she places a hand on Mrs. Mead's shoulder. "You don't need to sit here all evening. Why don't you get some rest? We'll call you if there's a change. There's really nothing you can do for him. We'll be keeping him sedated all night."

"I know that, dearie. I know that." She says it in a way that sounds apologetic. "Mr. Mead and I are just this way."

The nurse pats Mrs. Mead's shoulder. "If you need anything, I'm right over there."

Mrs. Mead gazes at her husband's now swollen face. Rui explained the swelling is from the liters and liters of IV fluid Mr. Mead required during surgery. Mrs. Mead opens her purse and holds up a Chapstick. "I forgot to ask Dr. Harrington if I could give Mr. Mead some of this."

Gene looks toward Dr. Harrington and says, "I don't see why not."

Mrs. Mead rises from her chair. The bed, albeit elevated some, still comes to her waist. "Mr. Mead always carries a Chapstick in his pocket." She spreads a light layer of salve on his swollen lips, carefully tracing around the endotracheal tube. "Says it makes him a better kisser."

Gene smiles.

She holds the Chapstick up between her thumb and index finger for Gene to examine, the little black tube a talisman in her trembling hand. "You should try it," she says.

As he passes the gift shop on his way upstairs to change, the volunteer from last week moves from behind the register and waves him over. "How's our patient, Doctor?" she says. "Any word on what happened?"

It takes a second for Gene to realize she's talking about Rebecca. "No," he says. "They're looking into a number of things."

"She's still here?"

"Discharged Sunday."

"Must not be too serious, then."

In a way she's right. Patty's echocardiogram results kept her in the hospital for surgery the next day. But still, the tech saw something on Rebecca's echo.

"She was so young and pretty," she says. She moves behind the counter. "It broke my heart to see her like that."

Gene agrees. All the echo tech said to Rebecca was, That's interesting. It doesn't mean she found a problem. He hopes not. His next thought feels foreign to him; more like it's coming from Jesse. If Patty is hopelessly engaged and Rebecca's heart turns out to be whole, maybe Spiderman needs a plan B.

Gene taps the counter. The wobble of a small display catches his eye. "I'll take one of these," he says and selects a Chapstick. "How much?"

"Heavens no," she says. She snaps the Chapstick from his fingers and tucks it in his white coat pocket. "It's on the house. Hero discount."

In medical records, a fire-dyed redhead slaps her hands on the counter. "Whatcha' need?"

"A chart," Gene says. "Rebecca Layne."

"Date of birth?"

"Don't know."

"Discharge date?"

"Saturday or Sunday. I think."

She looks behind her to charts stacked ridiculously high in basket carts. It looks like a Dr. Seuss illustration. "It'll take some time. Can you come back tomorrow?"

"Dr. Harrington needs it."

She straightens. "Give me a few minutes."

Gene sits on a folding chair and leans back against the wall. Rebecca Layne. There's a melodic quality to her name. It should be the title of a song.

He's sound asleep when someone pushes him.

"Here," the redhead says and hands him the chart. She's wearing polka-dot culottes, and for a second Gene thinks he might be dreaming. "Sorry for the wait. Found it in transcription…in the wrong pile, of course. I had one of our girls type out Dr. Zemlicka's discharge summary. Dr. Harrington's going to want it." She rolls her eyes. "Oh, how I know that."

Gene clears his throat and stands. "Thanks." He checks his watch. It's after ten.

"I don't know how you residents work with him and live to tell."

"You have to be quick."

She laughs. "Funny and cute."

"I'll bring it right back."

She waves him off. "Tomorrow's fine. Or the next day. Whatever he wants, he gets anyway. Hope you get home soon. I'm off at eleven."

He sits in his Jeep and reads the discharge summary under the glove box light.

Damn. The tech did see something.

The final section reads:

Assessment: Atrial septal defect
Plan: Refer to Dr. Benjamin Harrington

Gene closes the chart and takes a deep breath.

ASD was one of Dr. Knudson's possibilities. Gene planned to take Jesse's advice by stealing her phone number from her chart. But now? He can't ask her out until this is resolved. Of course, at some point he'll have to admit he isn't a resident. Not even a medical student, yet. That could be tough. What the hell. He opens the glove box and writes her number in the Citrus Care notebook.

Chapter Seventeen

CARRY ON

SANDRA WATCHES him put on the gloves. "With your fingers under the head of the penis, stretch it straight up...that's good," she says. "Now, with your left hand, lubricate the end of the catheter. Don't be shy. Slop it up. Insert the tip into the meatus."

"It doesn't look like it will fit," Gene says.

"That's what she said," Boz says as he injects something into the anesthetized man's IV.

The comment barely registers with Gene. He's too nervous.

"It's not the biggest I've ever seen," Sandra says to Gene.

"Oh, man, you're killing me," Boz says.

Gene slides the catheter down the man's urethra. A couple inches in, it stops. "Don't force it," Sandra says.

"Honey, I am biting my tongue down here," Boz says.

Sandra grasps Gene's gloved hand and, keeping the penis stretched, angles it toward the head of the bed. "Try now," she says.

Gene pushes again on the catheter and it glides in.

"It worked."

"Keep pushing," she says.

Gene slides it to the hilt/

Sandra straightens the penis, the passes it back to him. "Blow up the balloon…like this." She injects the full ten-millimeter-syringe of saline into the balloon port.

"It's not going to pop?"

"Now, pull back until it stops."

Gene gives the catheter a tug.

"There," she says. "You did it."

"Congratulations," Boz says. "Your first one's always special. The others you'll never remember."

"Go scrub," Irene says.

"Good job, Gene," Sandra says. She squeezes his wrist and gives him a light bump with her hip.

As Gene opens the door, Dr. Harrington backs in, followed by Rui, and sudsy water drips from both men's arms.

Irene says, "You're early."

"I do believe I move faster after a good night's sleep," Dr. Harrington says.

"Ah, my good Gene," Rui says. "Success, I see. Thank you, Sandra. You are the best."

"My thought exactly," Boz says.

"Eugene," Dr. Harrington says. "May I have your attention for a moment?"

Gene releases the door. "Yes?"

Irene hands towels to each of the surgeons. Sandra moves her prep tray up to the patient.

"Dr. Zemlicka stopped me in the hall concerning a young lady he saw last weekend. Asked if I had consulted on her yet."

Dr. Harrington drops the towel and holds his arms out for Irene's waiting gown. "I squeezed her in tomorrow," Irene says, barely loud enough for Gene to hear.

"Well…" Dr. Harrington draws out the word like he's unsheathing a knife. "I took a peek at her chart this morning. And apparently, according to Tammy, this was the second time I had requested her chart this week."

Gene feels as if his skin is about to be stripped from his body. Irene snaps Dr. Harrington's first glove in place.

"You see, Tammy informed me that my darling resident…now those are her words…had previously procured the chart on my behalf."

Irene snaps the second glove onto Dr. Harrington's meaty hand.

"I assured her that she must be mistaken. My trusty assistant would not risk his current position on the Heart Team to perform any function without my permission." Dr. Harrington's mask puffs out. "At least not again. That would be an undue test of my patience."

"Yes, sir."

"I believe you've made her acquaintance. The patient I mean. In our hospital's lobby."

"Yes sir."

"So, I assume I am the last to learn of Eugene's heroic efforts."

"Probably, Chief," Dr. Boz says.

Sandra's wink means she's heard the story.

Irene hands folded towels to Dr. Harrington, who begins laying them on the man's chest. "Gene," she says. "Go scrub."

Gene exhales. He gets to keep his skin. Now, how can he tag along for Rebecca's appointment tomorrow?

On the way home, Gene buys a half-dozen grapefruit. Except for being ripe, these Guatemalan pinks have nothing on his backyard stock. While his music rattles the kitchen walls, Gene adds open-citrus surgery to his post-dinner routine. He washes one, cuts it open and chucks the pulp. Using Irene's surplus skin suture, he reattaches the halves. Then he clips it open and repeats the procedure one more time before balancing the post-op orb atop the sugar cannister on the kitchen table. Next, he practices knots — adding another ten pack of sutures to the jungle dangling from a ladder-back chair. Finally, he plops open the surgical textbook to a folded sheet of paper. On it, he keeps a growing list of things he needs to study. Tonight, he checks off intra-aortic balloon pump and atrial septal defect

The intra-aortic balloon pump is an ingenious device that effectively lowers the resistance against which the heart has to pump. The diagrams in the text clarify what he had trouble visualizing in the OR. Atrial septal defect is a communication between the right and left atria, usually present from birth. Most often it closes over. Sometimes it doesn't. Sometimes, if the conditions are just right, or more accurately just wrong, blood clots form and pass across the hole, out the aorta, and up to the brain. Same as Patty, but without the pearl.

This was some kind of bad luck. Would he send every girl he liked to the Heart Room? Bobby Whitlock's pleading voice signals the last cut on the *Layla* album, "Thorn Tree in the Garden." Gene pushes back and listens to the end. He closes up the books. It's getting late. For a moment, in the silence of his house and his mind, Gene imagines picking up the phone and calling Rebecca. It would be natural for Dr. Hull, Dr. Harrington's resident, to check on her, confirm her appointment tomorrow.

Better not.

He clears his dinner plate and then rereads a postcard from his mother. On the front — The Washington Hotel. He didn't expect she'd visit it so soon, or at all. He turns it over. Her schoolgirl cursive uses every available space on the card.

Having a wonderful time with Suzanne, Rodney, and little Kate. So glad to be out of that heat, but it never stops raining here it seems. Don't forget the irrigation. *He wishes he had.* There's a frozen lasagna in the freezer. *He'd already found it.* Remember, you promised to stay off the roof. *People promise a lot of things.* The cat? Did you get it? *No, but he'd nearly killed Apollo.* Do you recognize the hotel? I think the oldest memories are the toughest.

Writing postcards instead of letters must make her feel like she's traveling on the opposite side of the world, or maybe back in time. The Hotel Washington was the site of a romantic three-day winter honeymoon for a new bride about to support her college-student husband on an executive secretary's salary. He's heard the story countless times, and it's a good sign she hasn't thrown out all of the memories. Adding it to the rest of the refrigerator door memorabilia, he slips the postcard under a magnet.

On the garage's workbench, Gene welds the top of the trap back together. Then he modifies the trap's exit door, effectively making it too small for Apollo, but hopefully large enough for a cat to slither in. That done, he carries the trap to the kitchen and sets it on the table.

"Apollo." The dog scurries from under the kitchen table, his ears at attention. "Want to take a walk?"

Using a flashlight, Gene and Apollo walk to the sign-up board where the dirt path from the Big Tree intersects his street. On the way, he hears pops and sizzles and sees sparkling lights farther down the street. That's right: Fourth of July. A holiday for all but the Heart Team, although most of the Phoenix fireworks' displays were canceled because of the particularly hot, dry weather.

Gene signs up for an hour's worth of water. It will come in sometime Sunday. The exact time will be posted in a couple days. When he returns home, he opens a can of tuna and is about to open the sliding glass door when the phone rings.

"Gene?"

It's a woman's voice.

"Yes?"

"This is Sandra —."

Relieved that Irene wasn't calling to chew him out about Rebecca's chart, he relaxes and sits.

"— I hope it's not too late."

"No." He checks his watch. Quarter to ten.

"Good. Some of the OR crew are going to St. James Infirmary after work tomorrow. You want to join us?"

Gene sets the tuna can by the phone. Apollo whines.

"Five. Five thirty. If you have plans, it's no sweat."

Plans? He'd yet to figure out how to see Rebecca tomorrow. Or what time. Hopefully before five.

"Someone's birthday or something?"

"Nope. Just to talk."

"I'll try to make it."

THE SANDRA on the phone sounded different than the Sandra in scrubs and mask. More talkative. She even sounded younger. Kind of nervous. St. James Infirmary. Hopefully they won't sit at a certain table near the statue of Marilyn Monroe.

"C'mon Apollo. Help me bait this thing."

Gene stops. "Hang on."

He retrieves his notebook from the Jeep and sits back down. After a minute he dials. Jeez, if Irene finds out…

"Mrs. Layne? This is Dr. Hull. Sorry I'm calling so late. I just wanted to confirm your appointment tomorrow … Yes, he's very accommodating … Five o'clock then … Could you do me a favor? Please don't mention this call at the office. Someone slipped up. I'm covering for them. Thank, you. You, too. Good night."

Gene hangs up and looks at Apollo. "Five o'clock. Damn."

IN THE ICU, Gene leans against the foot of the bed while Sandra and Dr. Boz begin their report on the last case of the week. "Three-vessel cabbage," Dr. Boz says. "Went slicker than bull snot…." Dr. Harrington lumbers over from the nursing station. He lifts the clear chest-tube tubing and watches blood trickle into the collecting bottle. A nurse gently nudges Gene aside and places a strip of surgical tape with the patient's name atop the footboard.

Carpfinger. An unusual enough name, but in a few days, Gene will remember him by the procedure: the three-vessel cabbage. With eight to sixteen patients moving slowly, yet steadily, toward discharge, their names fade — except for Mr. Mead — the CABG-AVR on the balloon pump.

It has been four days since Mr. Mead's surgery, and today, like every day, Mrs. Mead sits straight-backed in a small chair next to his bed. From two slots down, Gene can see her through a wide break in the curtain. A book, likely from the public library given the clear, plastic cover, lies open on her lap. Her thin lips move slightly as she reads. And at the same time, she strokes her husband's wrist, which is loosely tied to the bedrail with a soft cotton strap. A precaution, Gene learned, against Mr. Mead pulling out his endotracheal tube while in a confused state.

"Time to saddle up the Harley." Boz says to the room. "Enjoy the weekend, all."

"Eugene," Dr. Harrington says. He's crouched by the collecting bottles. "Let me show you how to milk a chest tube."

"Yes, sir."

The flexible vinyl chest tubes are connected to a long more pliable latex rubber tube that drains to a glass collection bottle. There is always some oozing of blood and fluid after surgery. Even a fair amount the first day.

"What we desire is a steady drip, drip, drip," Dr. Harrington says. "But sometimes you'll get a clot above heah." He points to where the tube exits the patient's chest. Listening to Dr. Harrington is like watching a leaf float down a stream. "That's when I get the frantic call from the nurse." The nurse at the foot of the bed shifts her feet.

Dr. Harrington continues in a mockingly high voice. "'Oh, Doctor, Mr. So-and-So was doing so well, but now his blood pressure is dropping. We tried milking the tube.' Then, I come down here and milk the tube myself. And lo and behold." Dr. Harrington's eyes widen. "A clot tumbles into the bottle, a river of blood follows, and the blood pressure rises."

Cardiac tamponade. Rui already explained this risk to Gene while they closed the skin on one of the patients earlier this week. If enough blood collects around the heart, it can't beat, or at least not efficiently.

Dr. Harrington grasps the rubber tubing with one hand and shows Gene how to stretch and knead the tubing in precise steps. Then he has Gene try. After Gene's first attempt, Dr. Harrington says, "Come on, son. Put some hurt on it." Gene strips harder.

"Stop! Like this." Dr. Harrington squeezes Gene's left hand

painfully hard around the tube close to where it exits the skin. "You don't want to pull it out. Try again."

Gene does, fearful it might move.

"That's my boy," Dr. Harrington says. "Now, should you pull it out, just let Irene know that you've decided to pursue another profession."

"Yes, sir.

Dr. Harrington shuffles away.

The nurse gives Gene a pitying look.

As they approach Mr. Mead's bed, Mrs. Mead stands. "I don't mean to be a bother," she says. "But Mr. Mead has an awful time with that tube in his throat. I was wondering…"

Dr. Harrington places a gentle hand on her bony shoulder. "Perhaps tomorrow. Let's see how he looks in the morning."

"He's okay though?"

"Just fine. A real soldier."

Gene is used to seeing the patients extubated and breathing on their own the day after surgery. Mr. Mead is the first exception.

At the nursing station, while Dr. Harrington charts, Gene asks, "Why is he still on the ventilator?"

Dr. Harrington continues to write. "There are certain tests he must pass." He closes one chart and opens another. "The first being, very little blood draining from the chest tubes. I'll give him another day."

"And then what?"

"Think positive, my boy."

Gene looks down the row of beds at Mrs. Mead applying Chapstick to her husband's lips. When she notices Gene's gaze, he pulls a new Chapstick from the pocket of his white coat and waves it like a tiny flag, a partisan to her cause.

Pulling the small green oxygen tank, Sandra walks past and motions for Gene to follow.

"Dr. Harrington, Sandra wants to show me something about the O2 tank."

"By all means."

Out in the hallway she asks, "See you at five?"

"I might be a little late."

"Go all the way to the back. We'll be at a large booth in the corner."

"Who's *we*?"

"Kathy up front, Mike, the coordinator on nights, but he's off tonight, a couple nurses from ortho…"

"Anybody I know?"

She squeezes his forearm. "You know me." As she walks away, there's a certain sway to her hips. She turns. "I'm counting on you."

He's not spent a Friday evening with a woman this summer. Now he's trying to meet up with two girls on the same night. It's going to be tight.

———

WITH ROUNDS complete and a few hours to kill until Rebecca's appointment, Gene loiters through lunch in the diner and then checks out a cardiac surgery textbook from the medical library. In the Friday-afternoon quiet of the doctor's lounge, he reads again about atrial septal defects. The OR schedule is winding down. Very few surgeons pass through. Fewer still sit for any length of time to shuffle through the paper or rest their heads back for a catnap. Then, he flips to the index again, searching for anything else about ASDs, running his finger down the atrials: …anatomy…catheters…contraction…until he lands on myxoma. After Patty's surgery, he never did read about it.

The book states that an atrial myxoma is a tumor in the chamber of the atrium — right or left. It is described as a pearl of tissue that is of no consequence until it grows large enough to partially block the flow of blood from the atrium to the ventricle. Symptoms include fainting during or after exercise. Rarely, a piece can break away and flow downstream. If this happens in the right atrium, the piece will flow through the right ventricle and lodge in the lung. That would be a pulmonary embolism. If the piece comes from the left atrium, it would flow through the left ventricle, whistle past the aortic valve, and if the patient was so unlucky, take the second or third exit off the aorta straight to the brain. A stroke. A complete workup, including cardiac catheterization, is needed to confirm the diagnosis and determine if surgery is needed.

Gene stretches out on the couch and closes his eyes against the fluorescent lights. He almost wishes Rebecca had been diagnosed with a myxoma. Then he could watch the surgery Patty had undergone. Maybe he should have asked Irene if he could join Dr. Harrington in the office. But if she said no, then just showing up today would look even worse. Of course, Mrs. Layne won't mind. Gene saved her daughter's life…

…In his musing thoughts, Gene lifts her chin. Gasping breaths return. Dr. Knudson hands him the stethoscope. Gene leans closer and closer to her bare chest and is sucked through the tubing down to the stethoscope's bell. There's the murmur. It's so loud. *Pshhhh-thump, pshhhh-thump, pshhhh-thump*. Then nothing. Now, he's in the desert breathing for a small girl, now pushing on her chest, now breathing, and it's hard to slow his own breathing. His heart beats so loud he can't hear hers, so he takes a breath, and another, and another, and dives into her heart — but it's Patty's heart. The swimming is hard going. There is a current, a powerful force he swims against with equally powerful strokes of his arms and legs. His heart beats hard against his chest, and he knows he's consuming oxygen at an alarming rate. He hopes he hyperventilated enough. At the bottom of her heart, he finds a pearl. It glistens white among the swaying, kelp-like cords of her mitral valve. Above him, a billowy parachute, lit from the sun above, strains to reach the water's surface. And through the thin fabric of the parachute, Gene can see Apollo swimming back and forth on the surface, his little legs churning. He's looking for me, Gene thinks. The surface looks so far away. For a second, he panics, thinking he's forgotten a knife, but Irene hands him a scalpel, the handle so long and he must back up to reach the target. It should be easy, but he has to tread water while he works, and each time he applies pressure to the blade, a force pushes him back. Equal and opposite reactions. Then he remembers he is late for physics. He has a final today. He's already missed the midterm, and he hasn't even read the book. He wants to cut out the pearl, but if he does, he'll miss the final. If he could just take a breath, he could think. He pushes off the bottom and rockets to the surface, breaking through with a stridulous gasp.

Gene blinks and looks around. The clock on the wall says five thirty. "Jeez!" He leaps up and races down the corridor.

Chapter Eighteen
THE GODDESS OF BEAUTIFUL WOMEN

Gene exits the hospital's front entrance, hustles down the concrete steps, and runs across the street to the tri-level medical complex. He jogs through the atrium, past teak chairs and around a gurgling fountain, and arrives at a large oak door framed by full-length frosted glass. On the door, gold lettering reads Leland B. Harrington, M.D, F.A.C.S. and under that, Cardiac and Thoracic Surgery.

He leans into the door. Bells jingle as it opens. In the cool, dim waiting room, an elderly man, his eyes sagging under the weight of a long life, looks over as Gene walks to the receptionist's desk. A Nat King Cole ballad plays overhead. The man sits on an upholstered chair next to a young woman who's bent over a clipboard resting in her lap. She rubs her bare arms and asks the man a question. He looks at the clipboard, coughs while shaking his head *no* and spits into a handkerchief. The other chairs and the two leather couches are empty. Gene's missed her. He's too late.

"Gene," the receptionist says. "What brings you here?"

Gene looks around the room, as if Rebecca might be hiding behind the grandfather clock in the corner. Dang. He's too late. "Irene said she had a model heart I could borrow."

"She didn't say anything to me."

"It's been a couple weeks."

The receptionist spins in her chair, opens one low cupboard and then another. "Must be this." With both hands she passes the model along with its pedestal to Gene. "Anything else?"

The phone buzzes. "Excuse me, Gene."

He sets the lacquered wood base on the waist-high counter. The heart, full-scale if not a bit larger, rotates on a metal rod. It's made from molded plastic that resembles solidified taffy. The heart itself is the color of raw salmon. The blood vessels (red arteries and blue veins) course like rivers in raised relief over the surface. The great vessels are also displayed: the aorta, vena cavas, and pulmonary arteries.

"What about these numbers?" Gene points to a circled numeral, one of eighty or more. "Is there a legend that goes with this?"

The receptionist looks back to the cupboard and shakes her head. "Let me check with Irene."

The woman with the clipboard comes over. "Here's my dad's information. It's the best I can do. There are some dates he's fuzzy on."

The receptionist leafs through the pages. "This looks fine. Thank you." She presses buttons on the phone, rises from her desk, and looks at Gene. "Don't answer if it rings. We…are…closed."

"I'm kind of late for an appointment," Gene says.

"You want that legend, don't you?" She smiles. "Back in a jiffy."

Gene checks his watch. Hopefully, Sandra will stay past Happy Hour. He bends over, legs straight, and holds a stretch on his hamstrings. Behind him, the door opens. He speaks as he's rising up. "Wow, that was quick."

"Oh, hi," Rebecca says.

Mrs. Layne is right behind her. She gives Gene a worried smile and dabs her eyes with a tissue. "Dr. Hull," she says, extending her hand. "I wondered if we'd see you today."

"I just came by to pick this up." He nods toward the model.

The receptionist returns, waving the legend. "There you go." She hands the sheet to Gene and then turns to Mrs. Layne, standing with her hands folded on the counter.

"Let's look at the schedule." The receptionist flips open a large appointment book. Gene backs away to the far end of the C-shaped counter, sliding the model along with him. He opens one of the three doors to the heart and examines the interior and finds more numerals, ninety-eight in all.

Rebecca places one hand on her mother's shoulder and pats her mother's hands. Gene wonders if there's a husband, a father around, or if this family is like the McLellan's or like his, no father to captain the ship.

"How does the thirty-first look?" the receptionist says.

"I'll have to check with my husband."

"It's either that or after Dr. Harrington returns from vacation."

"When is that?"

"September one…unless he gets antsy and comes back sooner."

Mrs. Layne taps her lips. "Can I call you?"

"No problem." She slides forms across the counter. "In the meantime, if you could read through these, then sign and date. Here, here, and here."

While Mrs. Layne reads, Rebecca looks up at Gene. He smiles and nods and then returns to studying the heart, trying to look engrossed, opening another hinged section to examine the paper valve inside. He mouths the words tricuspid and mitral, as if he were lost in concentration, and looks back to Rebecca's eyes. She's admiring the receptionist's nails. Rebecca's eyes are level with his. They aren't Patty's stunning blue, and the look Rebecca gives him doesn't drip with the disappointment he'd seen in Patty's eyes. Of charity, if he was to be honest. No. Rebecca's eyes are brown and creamy like a Milky Way bar.

"Could I see at that?" she says, raising her chin. She moves to Gene's end of the counter.

"Sure," he says. She lifts the small hook on the left-atrial "door" and opens it. Gene thinks he smells Patty's Estée Lauder. He inhales. It isn't, and that fact registers as a small pang, not of longing, but of disappointment. She traces a spot inside the heart, the tendons of her hand rippling under tan. "That's the mitral valve," he says. He opens the left ventricle's door.

"Oh, my," she says.

"The blood moves through the mitral valve into the ventricle here." He opens the last door. Now, the heart's chambers are fully exposed in a way they would never see it in the operating room. "And then the blood exits here, through the aortic valve." He could go on, but her mother is wrapping things up with the receptionist. She shifts her handbag to the crook of her arm. Besides, Gene feels like he's pressing.

"What's this? This parachute thing?"

Gene smiles because the books described them that way. "The tricuspid valve." He smiles. That just about exhausts his knowledge of heart anatomy, and he hopes she doesn't start pointing to numbers.

"Reminds me of a dollhouse," she says, closing the doors and latching them, except for the first one she'd opened, the atrial door.

Gene nods.

Then she rotates the heart for a more direct view of the open chamber. "So that's where the hole is." Her eyes make a slow tour of the surface before she closes that door.

Mrs. Layne walks up. "I guess we might see you in a few weeks."

"There's good chance." At least he hopes so. The thirty-first is his last day, unless he screws up and is fired before then.

"All right, Rebecca. Shall we? Your father's waiting at the mechanic's."

"Just a sec."

"I'll bring the car around front."

"I can walk to the car."

"Dr. Harrington said you shouldn't exert yourself. Dr. Zemlicka, too."

"Yes, Mother."

Mrs. Layne turns to Gene, shakes his hand, and fast walks out the door.

"I'm not supposed to play tennis," Rebecca says, smiling ruefully. "That kind of exertion."

"My mother's the same way."

"And there goes my lifeguard gig, I guess."

Gene wants to ask where she works and her plans, now that she's graduated from ASU, but Irene comes into the room clutching a chart at her side.

"Mr. Kettlebock," Irene says.

The patient leans forward in his chair, and his daughter holds him by the elbow.

Irene, emerging from the examining rooms with the patient's file in hand, looks surprised to see Gene.

He holds the model in the air. "Thanks. This will help."

She eyes Rebecca, who turns and smiles. Irene's questioning look converts to a nod, before she opens the door and follows the patient and daughter into the back.

"She's all business," Rebecca says.

"You should see her in the operating room."

"She thinks the world of you."

"Really?"

"She said I was lucky you were around that day. Most people panic, but she said you knew what to do…anyway, I don't think I fully appreciated that. Thank you."

There's no hiding the flush spreading up his face and tingling his scalp.

"Do you see many people my age having open heart surgery?"

Only Patty. "A few. They sail through it."

"My uncle had heart surgery for a blocked artery." She runs her finger along one of the raised arteries. "Actually, three blockages, and he called it open heart surgery, but I told him it wasn't because they didn't open his heart. Was I right?"

That had not occurred to Gene. But she's right — Dr. Harrington doesn't actually open the heart of a "cabbage" patient. Only when a chamber is breached, like with Mr. Mead or Patty, is the designation apt.

"Yes," he says. "You are absolutely right."

Rebecca adds, "I'm really not too worried. My mom? She'll be a wreck though, but that's my sister and father's problem. They'll have to deal with her in the waiting room while I'm in la-la land."

No boyfriend in the waiting room? Gene resists smiling. "I'm sure surgery will go well. Dr. Harrington's the best."

"He said closing the hole in my heart is like darning a sock. Simple as that."

"Simple as that."

"I should go," she says. "My mom's idling." She extends her hand. "See you soon." Despite the brave smile, her apprehension transfers through the timid handshake.

"We'll take good care of you."

"Thanks."

As she walks to the door, he looks for something. Her knees don't straighten like Patty's, but still....

Crap. He's late. Gene jumps out of his Jeep at St. James Infirmary and runs toward the bouncer at the front door. He wishes he'd had time to shower and change out of his "doctor" dress-clothes. The bouncer checks Gene's ID and opens the door to the red, barn-like building. A blast of cold air hits Gene's face.

It takes him a minute to adjust to the dim rosy lighting. Nothing has changed since Gene's last visit here with Patty over Christmas break, but he's entered at an uncharacteristically silent moment. And then Led Zeppelin shudders the rafters with "Black Dog." For a few seconds strobe lights bounce off the twenty-foot statue of Marilyn Monroe, a likeness from her iconic subway vent photo, her skirt lifting. Chairs and bicycles and toys from yard sales hang from the beams and on the walls. College students facing the heat of summer school carry two drinks at a time from the central bar to the peripheral booths, thick wooden tables etched with devotions of love. Gene stares at one particular booth where four construction workers with hard hats and sweat-drenched t-shirts laugh over a joke and a nearly empty pitcher of beer. One guy is so taken with a punch line that he pounds the tabletop. That's where Patty etched their initials, right near the end of that table. She carved a heart, complete with an arrow and two socks hanging from its tip.

The steelworker who pounded the table catches Gene's eye. "Hey, Poindexter. You a homo or something? Move along."

He's trying, but memories of Patty rise from every girl's walk and every pleading song, every, and they hover over him like the smoke in this room. He should get moving.

As Gene weaves through the crowd toward the back, peanut shells crunch underfoot, but it's more of a feeling than a crackle; the ear-pounding music makes it impossible to hear. She said meet at a large table in back, but there are no large tables, only a milling throng. Would Sandra wait for him? Maybe not. He's about to give up when he breaks through the crowd and sees a semi-circular booth against the wall.

Sandra lifts a hand. Dr. Boz, hoisting a glass of beer, is sitting next to her.

As he walks over, Gene hopes the shocked look on his face doesn't register. The shifting lights sparkle off the buttons on Boz's shirt. It's a light-colored cowboy shirt with those W-shaped flaps on the pockets.

Boz scoots over. "Gene-o. You made it."

Sandra pats the space next to her. "Coors okay?" She doesn't wait for an answer, but pours the pitcher dry into an empty glass. "Thought you'd jilted me."

"We were having a cozy conversation before you arrived," Boz says. Sandra punches Boz's shoulder. "I'll lasso another pitcher." He slides out and bumps into a girl wearing a tube top. She's carrying a pitcher in each hand. In the din, Gene can't hear what Boz says, but Boz bows at the waist. The girl just shakes her head.

Gene leans in and raises his voice over the music. "I got hung up at Harrington's."

"The crew just left. Boz didn't get here until about forty-five minutes ago. He's been picking up the tab ever since."

"I didn't know he was coming."

"I didn't either, but Katie's out of town."

"Who?"

"His wife."

"Oh, yeah."

Sandra taps a cigarette from a pack on the table. "Suffice to say, she's got her thumb on his neck." She slides the pack his way before lighting up.

Many years ago, Gene's father showed him two slices of lung encased in plexiglass. The width of a holiday ham serving, the nonsmoker lung was dense and pink. The smoker's lung was black and riddled with holes. "Why would anyone smoke?" his father had said. "There are enough risks in life you can't control."

Gene looks at the cigarette Sandra holds between her fingers. "I didn't know you smoked."

"A cigarette or two on weekends when I'm out." She picks up the pack. "I never buy them. I bummed the last couple off one of the girls."

She blows the smoke away from Gene. "You look good with your clothes on."

"So do you," Gene says and smiles. It's a surgical joke he's heard before. But she does look nice. Her sandy brown hair falls just past her collar and frames her square jaw. She has a slight underbite, but that only accentuates her full lower lip, a sensuous feature usually hidden behind her mask. Set off by her white blouse, her skin has a deeply tanned look, and when she twists just so, her blouse's neckline, with the top button unclasped, reveals a striking cleavage.

"What do you think of the view?" Boz says as he sets the pitcher on the table.

Gene startles, ready to deny Boz's implication.

"Marilyn," Boz says. He slides in next to Sandra and nods toward the Monroe statue. "Best seat in the house." He pours a beer for himself and tops Sandra's and Gene's. Then he holds his glass aloft. "To the goddess of beautiful women. May every man find his." He reaches in front of Sandra and clinks Gene's glass. Boz takes a long draw and licks the froth from his full mustache with his tongue. "Damn that DiMaggio. If the most butt-ugly cuss on either side of the Rio Grande could snag her, there's hope for us all."

"I know Gene's not going to have any trouble," Sandra says.

"Thinking of dipping into the kiddie pool?" Boz says.

Sandra blows smoke in Boz's face. He coughs and waves the

smoke away. "Those things will kill you, you know." He reaches for her cigarette, takes a long draw, and hands it back, exhaling three perfect smoke rings, which rise and expand into darkness.

"And I thought all you could do was pass gas," she says.

"Darlin' that's just the surface of my talents."

Boz stretches his arms along the back of the booth, his one arm resting behind Sandra. He looks over at Gene. "I hear you got dumped."

Sandra casts Boz a look that would have cut out the tongue of most men. He turns up his hands. "We're all on the same team. I'm here to say his girl made one badass mistake."

"How'd you know?" Gene says

Boz laughs and takes a swig of beer. "You don't work in your pajama's all day and not know everything about everybody you work with. You can thank Rui for this one. He mentioned it a few weeks ago when he told us you were going to join our little family for a while."

"Drop it, Boz." Sandra says.

Gene thinks his mother must have told Rui, or else told Alicia who told Rui. She can't keep anything to herself.

"That's okay," Gene says. He meets Boz's eyes. "It was mutual."

"Partner, it's never mutual. Believe me. But what matters here, is you. You're doing the right thing. Get out. Have some fun. Don't wallow in your grief. Christ, you've had enough of that lately." Boz clinks Gene's glass. "Here's to your father. He was a good man."

The beer goes down cold and crisp but finishes with a bitter thought: He was a good man, doing a good deed that cost him his life. But likely cost Gene Patty's love. It was a long and crooked path to that conclusion, a path he usually treks in his darkest, drunken moments.

Sandra joins in the toast and then asks, "Your mom doing okay?"

"She's coping."

He cups his hands around his half-empty beer and taps his nails against the glass, recognizes his father's habit, and stops.

Sandra squeezes his hand, refills his beer, and raises her glass. "To better days."

"Right on," Boz says. "To Gene. Someday he'll be a famous gas-passer like the ole man and show that bitch what she could have had."

"She's not a bitch," Gene says.

"Of course, she is. Get a little riled, my boy. What's her name, anyway?"

Sandra reaches for Boz's glass and starts to pull it away.

"No way, sweetheart. Don't start acting like my wife."

Sandra leans into Gene. "Ignore him."

"No secrets, my dear," Boz says. He downs his beer and slops another round into his glass.

Sandra turns fully toward Gene. "Sorry things went sour." She searches Gene's eyes. "It wasn't mutual, was it?"

Gene glances at Boz who appears content to ogle passing coeds. Gene shrugs. "People change. We grew apart." It's a canned reduction of several confusing, tense weeks before spring break. "And to think she almost died in the Heart Room before our first kiss."

Sandra swirls her beer in the glass. "But she didn't."

"You were there. What do you think happened?"

"What do you mean?"

"I've not seen that many cases, but nobody's heart has stopped beating before bypass."

"It's rare, but it happens," Sandra says.

"That's what my dad said."

"Now you sound like a Boz punchline."

Gene forces a laugh.

"I shouldn't joke." She tucks her hair behind her ear. "Any chance of you two getting back together?"

"Now that she's engaged?"

"I'm so sorry." She scoots closer. "Gene, you'll heal. You're just kind of on bypass right now."

"You know. You're right."

THE ALARM CLOCK buzzes at 3:25. Apollo raises his head, looks at Gene, and flops back.

"You stay here. No near-drowning this time."

Wearing only his boxers, he stumbles out to the back patio and the calm, dry ninety-nine-degree night. Sitting, he turns each black rubber boot upside down and whacks the heel a couple times, checking for scorpions. Guided by moonlight, Gene walks out to the irrigation pipe. A few turns of the metal wheel release a fanlike surge of water. At the opposite end of the grove, he moves the cat trap to higher ground. Since last week, he only set the trap at night when Apollo is inside. No takers so far.

For a few minutes Gene watches fingers of water serpentine from tree to tree. In less than an hour, eight inches of water will fill the brick-bordered grove, and he'll close the valve. But for now, the water triggers an urge. He drops the front of his boxers and pees.

Last night, at St. James Infirmary, Dr. Boz finally excused himself, saying he had a ride scheduled for early morning. Gene and Sandra ordered burgers and fries and drank another round while she shared a recent tragedy in her life.

Late in nursing school, she was engaged. This was in Kansas City. But her fiancé was diagnosed with breast cancer. He died eight months later. They never married because he didn't want her to be a widow.

Gene had never heard of a man, much less a man in his early twenties, dying of breast cancer. Of all the ways.

"Near the end," she said, "I took a leave of absence and spent weeks ministering only to him. I'm not sure what's worse, losing someone suddenly, tragically, or watching someone waste away into a form you can hardly recognize. I suppose whatever you're dealt, you come up with reasons to wish it had gone the other way, but eventually, you accept it for the positives. In my case, we had time to prepare. To leave each other without regrets or unsaid words. He suffered so I might have that privilege. And for that alone, he will always have a place in my heart."

Gene understood she wasn't trying to top the grief of losing his father. And if she'd opened up so that he might feel less alone, she'd succeeded. There was silence between them after that, a closeness which kept the music and the lights of St. James Infirmary outside their realm. Sandra rested her head on Gene's shoulder and patted his hand. Close to his ear, she said, "Your father was a good listener, too," and the combination of beer and sentiment surged to his groin. If she'd asked, he would have eagerly followed her home. When she spoke again, she wiped her eyes and said, "Obviously, I finished nursing school. My coordinator counted my time caring for Patrick as clinical experience. 'The best and hardest training any nurse could have,' she said."

Shortly after, they parted, each to their respective cars, but not before she tore a square from a napkin and inked her phone number under the St. James Infirmary logo. "In case you need to talk."

Now, in the moon-shade of the grove, he lowers his boxers again. He thinks of Sandra with her head on his shoulder and the way she said *ministering*. He thinks of her breast's soft gaze from above the *vee* of her neckline, and then his mind shifts to Rebecca and the tendons of her hand and how her delicate yet athletic fingers might feel around him, and finally he seeks Patty, on a particular new-moon night in the ballfield across from her house where she waited for him, wrapped in a blanket with nothing on but her socks, the night after his father's memorial service, when the ballfield irrigation came in, and how, when the first tentacles of water crept onto their sleeping bag, they were too passionately engulfed by the promise of an unspoken future to stop…almost as he is now, too deeply entranced in memory and imagination to register the water lapping over the toes of his boots until shortly, convulsively, he succumbs.

As his breathing slows, he carries the trap to the patio table. He opens the sliding glass door behind which Apollo dances, and the two of them dry the trap with a towel, spray WD-40 on the metal, and replace the battery. Then Gene and his dog sit sentinel-like in the warm night, waiting for four thirty when he'll close the valve.

"I'll tell you something, Apollo."

His dog cocks his head. He's placed a tennis ball at Gene's feet.

"I had a great time with Sandra tonight. Maybe I don't love Patty as much as I thought."

Gene changes into his jogging shorts, tucks the house key in his sock, and runs toward the first glimmer of steel-gray dawn. He's not exactly sure why he's doing this. Maybe he just wants to stand at the curb and gaze at her empty, darkened room one last time, and then bid her farewell before loping away with his memories and his dignity intact, unlike the last time, when Mrs. McLellan broke the news, and Gene careened home wounded and humiliated.

He tracks down the center of her quiet street along a rut of expectations — the newspapers will lie in wait, the mourning doves will soon begin their hidden, shared cadence, and Patty's driveway will be vacant.

Today is no different, except for a vehicle parked at the curb. As he jogs closer, he can see that it is parked by her mailbox. It's not shaped like a Mustang though.

As he slows to a walk, his breathing stumbles and his heart quickens. It's a truck. A late-model Ford truck. Maybe navy blue. He stops a few feet from the bumper. The grill is crusted with bugs. The license plate contains a silhouette of a cowboy waving his hat and mounted atop a bucking bronco. Under the bronco, the embossed letters WYO.

That goddamned son of a bitch. Gene looks to her bedroom window. It's dark, the shades closed. He can't be in there. Can he? Her mother would never allow it. He turns to the trampled ballfield across the street. Gene imagines Patty and Jake coupled on her *Bear Down Arizona* blanket in center field earlier tonight, their naked bodies floating in the dry, ardent air — a celestial experience — while he was jacking off in the grove.

Gene circles the truck. He could lift it from the street and heave it through Patty's front door. He curses and grips the air in his fists, strangling every molecule in his grasp.

Feeble sun-scorched grapefruit, withered green-brown orbs the size of marbles, litter the grass under the trees. He collects a few and flings them against the tailgate. They ricochet off. "You son of a bitch." He collects handfuls more, pelting the truck with shotgun fastballs. In less than a flailing minute he stops. His chest heaves. His shoulder aches. If his ammo has left a mark, he can't tell: There are so many dents on the truck already. Gene sits on the curb, his breathing slowing. The sidewalk is still warm from yesterday. No one else moves about the neighborhood or across the way at the school. Gene leans into his knees and fiddles with his socks. The gray dawn is thinning, its perilous grasp inching toward the full light and heat of the day.

Gene pulls his house key from hiding and walks to the driver's side of the truck. Patty and his initials maybe, inside a big fat heart. It will be his signature.

Through the window, Gene notices a white coat stuffed behind the stick shift. There are other things: maps, gas receipts, concert programs, crumpled fast food bags, cassette tapes, loose change in the ashtray, and frilly baby-blue socks balled up on the floor — Patty's beautiful socks. And if that wasn't enough to crush him, he sees one more thing.

Gene steadies himself with his hands on the roof and hangs his head. He opens the door and sits inside the lit cab. There it is. Tangible evidence. Not words. Not imagined images. Hanging from the rear-view mirror is a silver frame with a small photo of Jake and Patty. It's almost worse than running into them at the mall. Jake, in black and green graduation gown, smiles under his dark bushy mustache while Patty, in a lavender dress, hugs his waist and beams. The same shorter hairstyle she had last spring. They look so much older than Gene feels at this moment. But it's the look in her eyes that devastates him. It's clear. It's the "you're-my-hero" look that had once been meant for him.

Gene exits the Bronco and slumps to the curb. He stares at the key he was about to use to carve their initials on the side of the truck. "You're pathetic." He stands and heaves the key across the street and over the chain-link fence into the patchy ballfield grass. Then he trudges off toward home, gradually picking up the pace to a jog, and then finally sprinting the last quarter mile, before slumping, hands on knees, at his back door — his locked back door. He checks the dog door. Of course, he locked that, too. "Son of a bitch. You idiot son of a bitch!"

THE FLIMSY DOG-DOOR panel was no match for Gene's angry heel. He sleeps late into the day and then nurses a jug of water while cutting the lawn and cleaning the pool. He should study. He should tie knots. He should repair the shattered dog door. Instead, after dinner, he drives to Sluggers.

Just being shirtless in the cage on a warm night with the sound of baseballs smacking off wooden bats relaxes him. Here, he's in control. The baseballs fire his way at a speed of his choosing. He either hits or misses. No one to cheer or blame but himself. The five cages carry the name of a Yankee great, each set to deliver fastballs at a set speed, from 60-mph Mantle to 90-mph Ruth. Gene starts in the middle with DiMaggio, like his last visit, but this time, he tries not to imagine Jake's face. After a few rounds alternating with other batters, he finds his timing, his groove, and moves up a speed to Gehrig.

He enters the cage and drops a quarter in the machine. The label on the box bears a photo of a smiling Gehrig and underneath reads *The Iron Horse*. Gene turns the dial, the quarter drops, and sixty feet away, the gears behind the pitching arm start to turn. Gene freezes, staring at the label. "I'm Wally Pipp," he mumbles. The first pitch smacks the side of his chest, doubling him over. The second sails over his head. He stumbles out of the cage and sits on the bench, grimacing and holding his side.

"Mister, you going in?"

He looks up at a floppy-haired kid. "No, I'm fine."

"What?"

"Take it. It's yours."

Gene straightens. Takes a deep breath. Nothing feels broken. He slow-walks to the snack shack, sits at a picnic table, and rests his forehead against his palms. As baseball lore would have it, Wally Pipp, the starting first baseman for the Yankees, skipped a game because of a headache, only to be replaced permanently by Lou Gehrig, the Iron Horse, the player who went on to set the Major League Baseball record for most consecutive games played. Gene is Wally Pipp. One lousy moment when he pulls himself from the game, a cowboy med-student from Wyoming takes his spot. Jeez.

"You okay, Gene?" The question comes from Pete, the owner, a balding man wearing a barbecue apron.

"Yeah."

"Saw you take one in the side. Got to be careful."

"Right."

"Need anything?"

"Plenty."

"I'm about to shut down the grill."

"Chocolate shake. Can you throw a couple eggs in it?"

When Gene pulls his wallet to pay, the square of napkin from St. James Infirmary falls to the table.

A dime later, Sandra's phone is ringing. Gene lets it ring long enough to dash all hope and then two rings more. Damn. What did he expect? She's probably out on a date. So, he grabs his bat and blisters fastballs in Gehrig, finally calling it a night when Sluggers turns out the lights.

At home, a message is waiting on his answering machine. "Gene, this is Sandra. Dr. Pereira wanted me to call you. We're taking Mr. Mead back. He crumped. I'm already here. Come if you can. Bye."

Chapter Nineteen

KEEP ON GROWING

GENE IS TYING his mask as he busts into the Heart Room.

"God dammit Rui," Dr. Harrington shouts. "I need the light here, not here."

Rui has one hand on the light and the other holding a suction wand. A torrent of blood slurps along the clear tubing, the level of red rising by the second into the cylindrical container along the back wall.

Sandra rips open instrument packs and flings the clanging steel onto Irene's Mayo stand.

"Come on. Stitch. Stitch," Dr. Harrington says. He backhands the air with his gloved hand. Irene snaps a needle holder with suture into his hand.

"I'm going to need two more units," Dr. Boz says. "Sandra, did you —?"

"I heard! Betty?"

Betty huffs through the door to center hall.

"Heparin's in," Dr. Boz shouts. Dr. Boz frantically pumps blood, using each hand to squeeze the bulb on two infusion sets. "His pressure's for shit." Then to Gene. "Squeeze this."

Gene takes over one of the blood infusions, squeezing to his heart's pounding rate. The drape, usually clipped across the two IV poles, is just thrown over Mr. Mead's face, offering no sterile wall between Dr. Boz and Gene and the surgeons.

"Should I clip this to the pole?"

"Just keep squeezing," Dr. Boz says, not looking at Gene but at the blood bags Betty just brought into the room.

"On bypass," Dr. Harrington says.

"Gene," Rui says. "Go scrub."

Gene glances at Dr. Boz, who nods toward the door. "Go."

"Wait," Rui says. "Tie us up first." Neither Dr. Harrington nor Rui's gown is tied in back. Rui's gown hangs off one shoulder.

When Gene returns (he only scrubbed three minutes at best), the tempo in the room hasn't slowed, but the air has calmed. He knows enough to know why — bypass. Mr. Mead is suspended, albeit temporarily, from calamity; safe for now while Roger's machine breathes for him and pumps oxygen to his vital organs. But whatever is wrong with Mr. Mead's heart, it will have to be fixed. He can't depend on Roger forever. Gene's fluttering gut tells him that not even the balloon pump will help.

As Sandra ties the back of his gown, she whispers, "Glad you made it. We might be here a while."

THE PROBLEM IS A LEAKING coronary graft. The team repairs it, but as Gene feared, the first attempt to wean Mr. Mead from bypass fails. "Damn. Full flow," Dr. Harrington says. "Give me the twenty-three," he says.

Sandra opens a small sterile container for Irene. To Gene, Rui says, "A little bigger valve."

Dr. Harrington clips away the valve from a few days ago and replaces it with a larger one. Gene understands: greater valve area equals less resistance Mr. Mead's heart has to pump against. They try to wean Mr. Mead again. Step by step, Dr. Harrington orders the pump flow reduced, allowing Mr. Mead's heart to do more of the work. Like climbing stairs, they pause at each tread while his heart catches its breath. The intra-aortic balloon pump is helping, taking some of the weight off the heart's back. Finally, Dr. Harrington says, "Off bypass."

Gene breathes.

The chest spreader is removed, and the stainless-steel wires looped in place. When the wires are cinched, pulling the sternum back together, Mr. Mead's blood pressure plummets.

"Christ Almighty," Dr. Harrington says. He loosens the wires and bends them out to the side. "Steri-drape!"

He tucks laps between the sternum and the heart. The natural recoil in Mr. Mead's chest narrows the gap between the sternal halves to a couple inches. Then he covers Mr. Mead's chest with the same semi-translucent, plastic drape they normally apply at the start of a case. It's sticky on one side and impregnated with Betadine to ward off bacteria.

Dr. Harrington backs away from the OR table, rips off his gown and gloves, and leaves the room with the chart.

"That's it?" Gene says. He's leaving him open!"

Irene hands Rui a stitch to secure a chest tube.

"The chest will not close because of tissue swelling. You saw how his heart complained when we tried. In a few days, we will bring him back and try again."

Mr. Mead's eyelids are swollen shut, his fingers so puffy Gene can't see the joints. "He looks like the Michelin Man," Gene says.

"Again, we have Dr. Boz to blame. All the blood and saline he gave him."

"Without me, we'd be waiting for the coroner," Dr. Boz says. He's organizing the tangle of blood lines and infusion pumps. "As long as his kidneys keep working, he'll pee himself back to size."

Gene stares at the narrow chasm of Mr. Mead's chest. The white shroud of laps gently rock to the heart's ghostly rhythm. Or is it Mr. Mead's soul, stirring? A prickly wave travels across Gene's neck.

Sandra was right. It's close to sunrise when the team parks Mr. Mead in the ICU. Walking stiffly and supported on the arm of a nurse, Mrs. Mead returns to his bedside. Dr. Harrington explains that her husband's tissues swelled so much that it was impossible to close his chest without squeezing the breath out of him. "My dear wife packs a suitcase the same way," he says.

Mrs. Mead listens, but her eyes are fixed on her husband's face.

While Dr. Harrington charts at the nursing station, Gene loiters at the bedside. Mrs. Mead steps as close to the bed as she can. She smooths a wayward silver hair across the dome of her husband's head. The white sheet covering Mr. Mead rises with the hiss of the ventilator. She looks to the nurse. "Could I see it," she says.

"See it?" The nurse tilts her head.

"His heart."

"There's really not much to see."

"I doubt that. Mr. Mead's heart is as big as the moon."

"I mean it's covered. There's not anything *to* see."

"I'd still like to."

"Are you sure? I don't want you to faint."

"My dear, the only time I felt the blood drain from my brain was in 1919, the day Mr. Mead descended the steps of a train in Norfolk, and I saw for the first time what the war had done to him."

"His eye?" the nurse says.

"In his letters he never mentioned losing an eye. Just said the Huns gave him a minor scrape, and he was coming home after a little R-and-R in an English hospital. That was right before the war ended."

Gene stands on the opposite side of the bed from Mrs. Mead and the nurse. He looks at Mr. Mead's closed eye lids. No wonder he doesn't know about a missing eye, he's never seen them open.

"I'm so used to it," Mrs. Mead says sweeping her thumb across Mr. Mead's right eyebrow, "that I don't give it a second thought." She laughs. "He used to have a grand time popping out the old eye, his 'shooter' I used to call it. He'd come home from Fort Norfolk… initially he was a draftsman and later an engineer with the Army Corps of Engineers, and quite the talent I tell you…anyway, he'd come home, and if Benji had a friend over and the two were playing marbles, Mr. Mead would ask if he could play. Benji of course knew what was coming, and a sly smile would spread across his lovely face. 'Sure Pops,' he'd say. Mr. Mead would lean down, put his palm over that eye, cough, and pop it right out. Oh my, the look on Benji's friend's face would send us into hysterics. This was back when Benji was around eight to ten."

Mrs. Mead sits and pulls a tissue from her purse and folds her hands in her lap. "Mr. Mead was later fitted for a better prosthetic. I think the one now is his fourth or fifth. I've lost track. But that first one he gave to Benji when our son shipped off to France in '44. Most boys were being drafted, but Benji enlisted. Wanted to be just like Pops. He entered the Army Specialized Training Program at VMI to learn engineering, expecting to build bridges in Europe. Said if he lost an eye to the Krauts, he'd have a spare in his pocket. I suppose most boys, particularly an only child like Benji, want to emulate their fathers." She looks at Gene. "I'll bet my rose garden your father is a doctor. Am I right Dr. Hull?"

The ways Gene can answer that question stretch in two directions. He chooses the shortest route, evading the hills and valleys. "Yes. He is."

"There you go." She holds Gene in her gaze. "Be glad your father is a doctor and wasn't a soldier. Following in a soldier's footsteps is fraught with danger. Mr. Mead didn't like to talk about the war. He'd just say the *glory* turns to *gory* once you're actually there. When he came back, he traded an infantryman's gun for a pencil and protractor. That didn't dissuade our son. Of course, I think Hitler's war was different. The whole world needed to be saved. Benji said, 'They'll teach me how to shoot, but I'm there to build bridges and docks. Didn't turn out that way though. He was assigned to an engineer combat group and landed in Normandy on June 11, 1944. I prayed every day for months as he moved through France and Belgium. He had no idea being an engineer could be so dangerous. He was killed while setting charges on a bridge during the Battle of the Bulge."

Mrs. Mead dabs her eyes. "We were talking about fainting and listen to me go on. I didn't faint when the telegram came. I suppose, even though I was only in my mid-forties then, life had thickened my shell. It's even thicker now."

Mrs. Mead turns to Gene. "So, can I take a peek?"

Gene looks to the nurse, who says, "You're the doctor."

Dr. Harrington is buried in his chart.

"Sure."

The nurse places an arm around Mrs. Mead's slim waist. When the nurse pulls back the sheet, Mrs. Mead stands firm. The motion of her husband's heart, hidden under the laps, keeps time with the *beep-beep* of the EKG.

"It's a wonder…" She takes a deep breath through her nose, her bony shoulders rising, and exhales. "…and a blessing. The same shy, strong heart I've known since I was sixteen. Thank you."

———

THE SUN IS UP and preheating the day as Gene drives home in his open Jeep. He's invigorated from the all-night experience of saving a life. The traffic is light, and as he cruises up Central Avenue, the drone of the engine and lack of sleep begin to work on him. He turns up the radio. KCAZ is playing "Keep on Growing" by Derek and the Dominoes. When he passes Central High School, the station fades into the next cut on the *Layla* album. Of course. They're playing the entire album. He's usually never up this early on a Sunday morning to hear "Album Hour."

Gene is turning onto Orangewood when "I Am Yours" plays. This song still reminds him of Patty, but now, he also thinks of Mrs. Mead, who at this very moment might be applying Chapstick to her husband's lips, a man she's loved since she was sixteen, a man she waited for through a world war.

He pulls into his drive, eager to collapse into bed. Apollo doesn't greet him at the door. The dog door is open, the panel he splintered yesterday morning still in a heap on the kitchen counter. He steps out back and calls: "Apollo." It can't be the trap. He didn't set it.

He checks the pool. Nothing. When he turns, he sees a headless bird under the lounger. He bends and fingers some dried blood near it. His eyes follow a line of similar stains across the Kool Deck toward the grove. He stands and hears a whine. Gene races toward the far corner of the grove. Apollo lies in the cool mud from yesterday's irrigation, curled under the canopy of a tree. His back haunch is covered in dried blood. He raises his head as Gene approaches and attempts to limp over.

"Jeez, Apollo."

The dog pants. When Gene touches the blood-soaked area, Apollo jerks his leg and yelps.

He scoops him up and hustles inside. His mother always tapes a list of phone numbers inside the cabinet door over the secretary. The number for the vet is scratched out. Above it she wrote retired. What about her sheet of instructions? He shoves books and papers and empty plates out of the way on the kitchen table until he finds it. He dials the number. They are closed. Of course. Sunday. The recording gives another number for emergencies. He doesn't get all of it, and when he calls back, he realizes the address is at least forty-five minutes away. Damn.

Then he hears slurping. Apollo is in the bathroom by the kitchen, drinking from the toilet. The nearby water bowl is empty. Gene curses himself for forgetting to leave water or block the dog door, and whatever else he ignored in his rush to the hospital last night. Apollo knows he's not supposed to drink from the toilet and hops down.

"Hey. You can stand."

Apollo wags his tail weakly. Gene carries him to the kitchen sink. He runs water over the blood and gently teases the hair until he can see a laceration, a couple inches long over Apollo's hindquarter. Apollo's tense body quivers. "Don't move." Gene takes a step away. "Apollo. Stay." Gene runs to the freezer and returns with ice. He rubs a few pieces over the wound for several minutes and gradually Apollo relaxes. Gene separates the wound with his fingers. The muscle looks bruised, but it doesn't look like it's been cut. "It was that fucking cat, wasn't it?"

If he'd trapped the damn thing like he'd promised his mother, this wouldn't have happened. He could drive across town to the animal hospital, an hour-and-half there and back, plus the time to be seen and stitched up, and after all that his mom will have a cow over the cost. *If you'd caught that cat like I told you....* Gene carries Apollo back to the kitchen. "Wait."

He retrieves his father's doctor bag from one of the boxes in the master closet. Visualizing the protocol Dr. Knudson used to close Rebecca's scalp wound, Gene searches the bag. Everything he needs is here — Lidocaine, syringes, needles, even sterile gloves, although they're a size too big. He already has the suture — and he's practiced on several grapefruit. He looks down at Apollo. "I'll sew you up."

Gene clears a spot on the kitchen counter. He lays a clean bath towel down and places Apollo on his side. He breaks up a Gaines-Burger and feeds Apollo pieces as he floods the wound with Lidocaine. Gene then injects Lidocaine through the lip of the wound all the way around. The skin puffs up. The dog's hair is getting in the way, but he can't find any suture scissors to trim it back. He opens the gloves. Shoot, other than rinsing the wound in the sink, he's not cleaned it. There's no hospital-type soap in the doctor bag either. No Hibiclens. No Betadine. Crap. He picks Apollo up under one arm and hustles to his mother's bathroom. No alcohol. No iodine. But he finds an almost empty bottle of hydrogen peroxide under the sink.

He returns to the kitchen and douses Apollo's wound with what's left of the peroxide. Then he squirts a little dishwashing soap on a gauze pad. This will have to do. When he scrubs the wound, Apollo doesn't react. Fantastic. It's numb. Then he fills a syringe with tap water and flushes the soap away several times.

It's a little tricky to slip into the sterile gloves without Irene's help, but he manages, extracts a straight needle and suture from a packet, and goes to work. His hands tremble slightly as he pierces Apollo skin for the first time. The dog doesn't react. "Good boy." Okay, think soft hands. He pierces the other side and ties a knot, five throws, and cuts the tag. Ten more stitches, evenly spaced, and he's done. What surprises him is that it was easier than sewing the hard rind of a grapefruit. Apollo looks up for a second and then flops his head back.

"Now, don't lick it." Gene doesn't know how he'll keep him from doing that. Then he remembers an elastic sleeve he made from support hose to cover his pitching arm between innings. He finds it in his closet, and after cutting holes for Apollo's legs, he discovers that it fits over Apollo's hindquarters like a tube sock. The dog twirls a few circles and nibbles at the material where it covers his wound, but by the time Gene has cleaned up, Apollo seems content to live with his new outfit.

Before trudging upstairs to bed, Gene carries his father's doctor bag back to the master bedroom. He catches his image in the bureau mirror. For a few seconds he turns side to side, examining the look of the bag in his hand. Nine years ago, it weighed a ton as he lugged it out to his father. Now, with a single finger under the handle, Gene holds the bag out. The leather is worn and dented where his father's fingers gripped the handle. Nothing in this black bag was going to save that little girl. And his father knew it. In the hotel that night, he even said, "There was nothing I could do. Nothing." How he didn't feel as helpless as Gene felt that day, he'll never know.

Chapter Twenty

BON APPETIT MOTHERFUCKER

GENE WAITS at the elevator outside the OR suites, hoping Jesse will show today. For most of last week, some drill sergeant tight ass manned the breakfast cart. Gene tried to cajole him into a free breakfast, but all he got was a speech beginning with "Kitchen regulations dictate..."

Jesse has become a part of the hospital routine. His whistle. His banter. The promise of breakfast. For Gene, their encounters substitute for coffee — a cup of Jesse at sunrise. Their few minutes together nearly always infuse him with a smooth energy. Jesse is part of what he loves about the hospital. Beginning his fourth week, Gene feels at home in this bustling mini city. He loves the sounds the overhead pages; the click of shoes on linoleum; the rustling of long white coats. He loves the smell of ethyl alcohol and floor wax and grilled ham and cheese. And he loves the rush of people: doctors and nurses, technicians in white coats pushing robotic looking devices used for breathing treatments; lab techs carrying baskets of syringes, needles, and blood vials; messengers pushing wire baskets, moving correspondence from floor to floor, orderlies carting patients in wheelchairs or gurneys for an X-ray, ultrasound, or surgery.

But at this early hour, the hospital is mostly quiet, the healing to be done just a promise.

"Well, there he is," Jesse says. Jesse brings the cart to a stop and leans a hand against it, like a man leaning on a lamp post. "What's shakin', Dr. Gene?"

"Where've you been?" Gene says. "I thought the hospital might have fired you for filling me up every morning."

"Ah, shit, they don't know. Besides, if you don't eat it, just ends up in the dumpster out back." Jesse takes his pencil from behind his ear. "Had me some sick days so I took my lady up north. Seven thousand feet of cool, pine country and hungry trout. You should try my trout. Mmmm. Tell you what. Another thing you should try if you haven't." Jesse glances side to side and then whispers. "Poontang in the pines. Oh my. If you never had poontang in the pines..."

If Gene guessed Jesse's meaning, then yes, he's made love in the pines. Thanks for the reminder. Jesse makes some notes on his clipboard.

"So, what ya serving, Jesse?"

"Ham and eggs...all you can eat."

"I'll take two."

Jesse hangs the clipboard on a hook behind the cart. He slides the accordion door up, pulls two trays halfway out, and loads the covered plate from one tray onto the other.

"I say, doubling up for that muscle you putting on" He examines Gene up and down. "Looks good on you. Know what I'm saying?" Jesse hands the tray to Gene. "What's her name?"

"Who?"

"Whoever pants you trying to get into?"

"Nobody."

"You are one sorry ass bullshitter."

Gene smiles.

"So, you did get Mary Jane's number."

"Rebecca Layne? No."

"You're interested though."

"I'm just trying to stay in shape."

"Must be a tiger."

"Can we drop it?"

"Gimme that." Jesse takes the overburdened tray and sets it atop his cart. He puts a hand on Gene's shoulder. "We all strike out, Man."

"I never even asked her out."

"Well, somebody done you wrong. The only real question is, Why?"

Gene has tested a six pack of answers to that question; blamed Jake, blamed Patty, blamed circumstances and even blamed his father. But one answer hurts the most, and it came from Patty: He missed a chance to be someone his father would be proud of. To be more like him.

"You gonna tell me, or we gonna play it like some game show?"

"Nobody did me wrong."

"Game show then. Did she catch you in bed with her sister?"

There's no staring Jesse down or feeding him bullshit. He's seen too much.

"It's worse."

"Her mother?"

Gene closes his eyes against that thought.

"It doesn't matter anymore. She's engaged."

"Oh shit, man. You listen." Jesse stares in like a hypnotist. The elevator door opens. A female custodian shifts her mop bucket and holds the door. Jesse waves her off. The door closes. "Doc. You listening?"

"Yes."

"Burn and turn. You got that? That's what you do — burn… and…turn. Burn everything that bitch ever gave you and turn the page. Especially if she's engaged."

"I burned her letters last spring."

"What else you got to burn?"

"That only made me feel worse."

"Okay. You done the burn. Now do the turn. Shit, I thought you'd been pokin' where you shouldn't, and you were looking for forgiveness, not that you'd have deserved it."

"It's not that simple."

"You ain't been dumped enough."

Jesse smiles and hands the tray back. "Nothing you can say gonna change my advice. Matter of fact, you know how much advice like that costs around here? Plenty. And when you get it, it don't come until after the third session. Then they hang a di-ag-nosis on you, making you feel all crazy and shit. But in the end, it all comes down to burn and turn. Shit, I should be charging you. What time is it? How long we been hanging here?"

The elevator returns. After Jesse loads the cart into the empty carriage, he points a long finger past Gene. "We should be having this conversation in there." He's aiming at the Consultation Room. "That's where hope meets the truth."

AT THE END of the first case, Rui moves to Irene's side and prepares to close the skin. "How was your weekend?" he says to Gene. "Aside from our all-nighter."

"Nothing special," Gene says

Just saw a photo of the love of his life with her fiancé. Decided not to key his truck 'cause that felt pathetic. Probably just another stage of grief. He'll have to ask Jesse, his psychotherapist.

"Hit some balls at the batting cage. And Apollo tangled with a cat."

Gene brings Rui up to date on his trap-the-cat crusade and Apollo's injury. "Sewed him up myself. Just like you taught me."

"Did you irrigate it well?"

"Pretty well."

"Betadine?"

"I looked. No Hibiclens either."

"I would suggest a course of antibiotics."

"I hadn't thought of that."

"Someday it will be second nature, and you will dispense antibiotics like candy."

"Gene," Boz says. "Let me get this straight. You've been trying to catch a stray cat, alive mind you, and so far, all you've got is an empty trap and dog with a gash on his butt. Seems to me, it's time to go *Dirty Harry* on this critter."

"I'd rather take it to the pound."

"When nobody adopts the cute little bird-eating dog-slashing feline, what do you suppose happens?"

Gene tries to ignore him, concentrating on dabbing away blood ahead of Rui's skin closure. Finally, he looks over to Boz who makes a slashing motion across his throat.

"Here," Boz says. He digs around in the bottom of his doctor bag and pulls out a bottle of pills. "Took this for a DVT last year." He holds the plastic container up to Gene. "Coumadin. A blood thinner. Same stuff that's in rat poison. Put a little in your bait but keep your damn dog away from it."

———

ANOTHER POSTCARD from his mother arrives midweek. It ends, *I hope you've taken care of my cat infestation.*

As far as Gene knows, it's only one fucking cat. The thing is like a ghost though, leaving trails of blood, headless birds, and now an injured dog. He's starting to wonder if it's a cat at all. So far, the trap's been a bust. After snagging Apollo, it hasn't caught anything. Gene baits it only at night and then closes Apollo inside with the new dog door panel he constructed out of Masonite. During the day, he leaves the dog door open and the trap closed.

Another long day complete, Gene rests on the lounger by the pool. The sun set hours ago on a 115-degree day, the third near record-breaker in a row. The hotter the day, the more gorgeous the night. He finishes his beer and closes his eyes.

From under him, Apollo emits a long deep growl.

"Shhh," Gene says. "It's okay."

Apollo growls again and bolts for the trees. His rabid barking disappears into the grove.

"Apollo, come!"

An animal screeches. The sound is catlike but deeper, followed by more barking, more screeching, and then a yelp from Apollo. Gene runs toward the sound, and through a break in the trees, he sees a dark form leap the wood fence. Gene ducks through the trees to reach Apollo, whose front paws scratch frantically up the fence.

"Apollo! Apollo!"

He reaches down with both hands to pull him back. Apollo wheels at the first touch and strikes his teeth onto Gene's forearm.

"Shit!" Gene pulls back. Apollo runs toward the dog door, ears back, tail tucked. Blood trickles down Gene's arm.

Inside, Gene washes his arm and finds scratch marks but no punctures. What did he think would happen? He grabbed the dog's wounded hip. Apollo lies under the kitchen secretary, shivering. His face has three shallow scratch marks across the snout. One just missed his eye. Gene cleans them off with a cloth. The sutures under the tube-sock look okay. He gives Apollo his bedtime dose of antibiotics wrapped in tuna fish. Apollo follows him as Gene walks toward the back door with the remaining can of tuna fish in hand.

"You stay inside."

Gene retrieves a small glass bowl and reads the label on Dr. Boz's medication.

Warning: COUMADIN can cause bleeding which can be serious and sometimes lead to death. Call your doctor or seek immediate medical care if you have signs or symptoms of bleeding.

He takes a few of the white pills and, using the wooden end of a hammer, crushes them into a mix with the tuna fish. Then he sets the trap in the grove. "*Bon Appetit*, motherfucker."

Sometime that night, Gene wakes and can't shake thoughts of the cat. He pictures it jailed in the trap, taking mincing bites of its last meal. Dr. Boz said it might take a day or two to work, but then that was the point. If the cat escaped the trap, it would bleed to death somewhere. Maybe in the alley, maybe on his back porch, maybe in the backyard of whomever owned the damn thing, blood dripping from its eyes and ears, the corner of its mouth. But as hard as Gene tries, he's not Boz. He can't muster enough anger to wish the cat dead. He throws the covers aside and pads out into the backyard in his boxers and flip-flops. The trap's door is wide open, but the bait is gone.

———

A PLATOON of help wheels Mr. Mead, and his entourage of hardware (IV poles, infusions, oxygen tank, and balloon pump) from the ICU to the Heart Room. Heavily sedated, he will never remember making this trip. Gene wonders how many days in the hospital will just be a blank for Mr. Mead. Dr. Boz performs his magic. Roger is on "stand-by," his heart-lung machine primed and ready to go. Dr. Harrington slips in the chest spreader and explores. He doesn't like the position of the left-atrial catheter and replaces it. Other than that, there's nothing more to do than close the chest.

Dr. Harrington and Rui cinch Mr. Mead's sternum back together in a flash of stainless-steel wires. Then Dr. Harrington orders the balloon pump's settings to remain the same and breaks scrub for a smoke in the lounge.

"Well that was a long run for a short slide," Dr. Boz says.

As Gene dabs away blood with a surgical lap, Rui moves to Irene's side and closes the subcutaneous tissue.

Irene unfurls 3-0 nylon on a straight needle from its packet, but instead of handing it off to Rui, she holds it out to Gene.

Rui's eyes smile over his mask. "Take it," he says. "I am calling you up to the *Show*."

Gene extends his other hand for tooth forceps. Irene slaps it in his palm.

"Soft hands," Rui says.

Gene grasps one edge of skin and passes the needle through its full thickness. He hesitates. "Running or interrupted?"

"Running. It is late."

Rui acts as Gene's assistant, holding the suture taught and out of Gene's way as Gene loops stitches in a continuous line, aiming for about a quarter inch apart the length of the incision.

"How is our patient at home," Rui asks.

"He got into another scrape with that cat."

"A little of that Vitamin C," Dr. Boz says, "and you can put a notch in your gun."

"I did. It took the bait." Gene glances up at Rui, ashamed that he followed Dr. Boz's advice.

"Like I said," Dr. Boz says. "A stray's a stray. A trip to the pound would have ended with the same result. Either way, you're a hero in your Mama's eyes."

Hero. Right. If the damn trap had worked at least he could have allayed the cat's suffering. Now the cat had gone off to bleed in the alley.

"I never should have used that stuff."

Rui says, "Try that one again."

Gene pulls the needle back and repositions it closer to the previous bite. It's hard to talk and suture at the same time.

"Excellent."

"I've got to see this thing," Boz says. "Sounds fancier than anything we used in Texas. All our traps end with a chopping sound or a blast. How about you Sandra? Gene shown it to you yet?"

Sandra is finishing the lap count with Irene. "...eight, nine... No, I haven't...and one on the floor." she says. "Count's correct."

Rui ties the finishing knot and snips the tag. He extends his gloved hand to Gene. "Superb. In time you will be faster." Then, with a sloppy wet lap, he wipes the wound clean. "Look at this."

Gene's work now stands out under the focused lights. The blood and Betadine are wiped away. Mr. Mead's chest was shaved days ago, and his smooth white skin looks like the cover of a baseball but with blue stitching instead of red. Blood droplets grow at several suture entry points. Rui points to Gene's perfectly spaced sutures. "Beautiful work. He will carry your signature for the remainder of his days."

"How long do you leave them in?" Gene says. He's thinking of Apollo.

"Ah, it is a balance. On average, about ten days. Two weeks or so for strength if you are less concerned about the scar."

In the ICU, Sandra gives her report and then wheels the portable oxygen tank toward the exit. She motions for Gene to follow.

"Have any plans for dinner tonight?" she asks.

"A couple things left in the freezer."

"That's what I thought." She removes her bouffant cap and shakes her hair free. "I've got nothing going tonight. Why don't you come over? I'll fix us something."

What was this about? Because he listened to the story of her dying almost-husband? That figures. Or maybe for admitting he screwed up with the coumadin. About time confessions get rewarded. "Sure. That's great."

"You like pesto?"

"Can't say I've ever had it."

"Well, let's take a chance." She pulls a pen and today's folded OR schedule from her breast pocket and, using her thigh as a writing table, writes her address. Scribbled across her tight-fitting pants are lab results and callback numbers.

"It's the Sunrise Apartments on Sixteenth and Camelback. How about seven o'clock?" She starts to hand him the paper and then pulls it back. "You still have my number, right?"

It's in his wallet and in his head.

Chapter Twenty-One

LONELY STAR

APOLLO KNEW something was up tonight. He stays closer on Gene's heels than usual, even abandoning his food to follow Gene upstairs while he showers and shaves. Gene dresses in jeans and doubles up on the antiperspirant (it's still 106 outside) before slipping on his favorite Polo. Not wanting Apollo to tangle with the cat, Gene locks Apollo in the house and sets the trap. At the last minute, he mounts one of his father's jazz reel-to-reel tapes. "This will keep you company," Gene says. "Who knows how late I'll be."

It didn't take long to find Sandra's place. Growing up in Phoenix, he's probably passed the Sunrise Apartments a thousand times. The once spindly ash trees have sure matured. Now, they completely shade the second-floor tenants battling the late afternoon sun. Gene eases his father's air-conditioned Saab into a parking space. Right on time — ten minutes early.

He walks past a small circle of people gathered on chairs and loungers by the rectangular pool. Dressed in swimsuits, sunglasses, and sunburns, they laugh and hoist beers. A young woman looks Gene's way, as does a man wearing a gold chain.

"I'm looking for 212," Gene says.

"Ah, nurse Sandra," the man says. He angles his thick body and points straight-armed, revealing an anchor tattoo. "You're right online. Tell her Cap'n Nick is still waiting for an answer."

The woman leans over, her fully loaded bikini-top on the brink of capsizing and smacks him on the shoulder. "He is not," she shouts and jumps onto his lap. "He's taken."

"Thanks."

SANDRA'S APARTMENT is on the second floor at the north end of the quadrangle.

"Gene!" she says when she opens the door. "Don't you look different with your clothes on! In broad daylight this time."

"Captain Nick says *hi*."

"What?"

"He's down by the pool."

She raises her eyes to the low ceiling. "Oh, him." She closes the door. "No trouble finding the place?"

"None." Gene looks around. Two couches at right angles. A corner table and lamp. A teak *etagere* for knickknacks. "Nice place," he says.

"It's okay."

"It's better than my apartment in SLO.

She tips her head.

"San Luis Obispo," he says. "SLO."

She twists left and right. "Grab a seat or follow me into the kitchen." She points to the kitchen on the other side of the pass-through counter. "Beer's in there."

"Kitchen it is."

In the kitchen, Sandra flames a burner under a pot of water, and stirs something simmering in another pot.

He sniffs. "Smells good," he says.

"You may be a pesto man after all."

It sounds funny, hearing her call him a man. Next to her he feels like a high school kid. He isn't sure how old she is — twenty-eight, twenty-nine — and she has a career, a fully furnished apartment with framed poster prints — the Eiffel tower, a French cafe, and a few paintings he vaguely recognizes as belonging to the Impressionists.

She opens the low oven door, grasps a tray of French bread halves, and leans over to slide them in the oven. In the kitchen the aroma of garlic is thick. When he sits at the small kitchen table behind her, he feels the oven's heat. She, too, looks different with her clothes on — in broad daylight. She wears white three-quarter-length, tight-fitting shorts and a flowered blouse that leaves her midriff exposed. She's not heavy per se, but she looked slimmer in scrubs.

"This a one bedroom?"

Peering into the oven, she says, "The first thing guys ask about — the bedroom."

"No, I didn't mean —"

"I'm kidding," she says. She closes the oven door. "Yes. One bedroom. Look at you blush." She opens the refrigerator. "You have a choice: Michelob, or Michelob."

"That's what I drink."

"Like father, like son, I guess."

She pops the cap with an opener screwed to the face of the cabinet and hands the bottle to Gene. Then she pops one for herself. "Cheers," she says and salutes Gene with the bottle. He braces for another toast to his father. "Let's see…to your summer of hearts."

He reaches out and clinks her bottle. "To the summer."

"Let's sit in the other room," she says. "It's too hot in here."

She stirs a pot, lowers the heat, and leads Gene into the main room. Gene sits on a couch and picks up a coaster. It's a Parisian scene. Sandra sits on the couch that extends out into the room, separating the seating area from the dining table. She's already put out plates, cutlery, and napkins.

Gene looks over again at the prints on the wall. "Are you from France?"

Sandra stifles a laugh with her hand. "I've gone a little overboard, haven't I." She looks around. "After I graduated high school,

I spent two months living with a beautiful family in Paris. Best summer of my life." She flips off her sandals, tucks her legs, and takes Gene on a virtual tour — the cafes, the architecture, and museums. He can taste the chocolate eclairs, feel the smooth granite of a garden sculpture. Eyes alight, she describes her favorite paintings in the Louvre, and marvels at the artists' handling of light, perspective, and proportion. "I once dreamed of working there. That would be the life — introducing the *Mona Lisa* by day, followed by strolls along the streets at night. The summer nights transform you."

And they do Gene. He floats atop her French-accented pronunciations as he strolls with her along the Champs-Élysées, past the brightly lit Arc de Triomphe de l'Étoile, from *arrondissement* to *arrondissement*, his arms tingling through the last liquid word — Sacré-Cœur. "You know," she says. "That means Sacred Heart."

She takes a sip of her beer. "It's a wonderful place to be in love."

Should he ask her about it? Gene, the good listener? He was hoping for something like a real date tonight, but he'd rather leave her apartment as he entered, the college kid in need of a meal, than risk misreading her signals and suffer the humiliation: Gene, you're a nice guy, but....

Yet, her caring, green eyes give him hope, a slim hope, that the evening might end with a nervous kiss and the chance of reciprocated affection, his heart reawakened from bypass.

Sandra grins. "We've talked enough about me." She stretches her legs. Wiggles her toes. "So, what's on your walls? What would I learn about you?"

Juan Marichal and a shelf-load of teenage trophies. How embarrassing. "I took everything down."

"Ah, a blank slate."

"Want to help me decorate?"

Sandra smiles and wiggles closer, the end table still between them. "Ooo, that sounds very close to 'Come on over, I'll show you my etchings.'"

If he only had etchings.

She sets her beer on a coaster and unfolds her legs. "You know what I would like to see?"

He takes a sip of his beer. She stands and looks down at him. He swallows hard against a rising belch.

"That engineering marvel of yours."

"The trap?" The word 'trap' ends with a release of malted barley-infused air, sounding something like a lion's growl.

She doubles over and puts a hand on Gene's shoulder.

"Jeez."

Her eyes are moist with laughter. "Don't fret. We're all friends here, right?" She wipes an eye. "I've got to check on dinner."

Gene's eyes follow her past the dining table and into the kitchen. Yeah. We're all friends.

She shouts from the kitchen. "You did well with your first skin closure. I was a little surprised Rui started you off with the Cabbage AVR."

"Mr. Mead?"

She returns to her couch and takes her beer. "That's been a hairy case."

"Did you know his wife met him when she was sixteen?"

"Isn't she a doll?"

"The nurses say she never leaves his side. Just sits there reading, like she's waiting for a bus."

"That kind of devotion is rare."

Gene thinks back to St. James Infirmary, the story of Sandra nursing her dying fiancé. He tips his bottle toward her. "Not so rare."

Sandra smiles gently. "Thank you." She looks down at the bottle she holds softly between her hands. Then back to Gene. "I can see you being that devoted."

Gene shakes his head. "Not like you."

"If you're anything like your father."

Gene drains his beer, his eyes closed against Patty's words from last spring.

"You ready for another?" she says.

He examines his empty bottle. "Absolutely."

"By the way," she says. "I never mentioned it before, but I like the new haircut. You look older."

When she returns with their beers she says, "Have you noticed how Dr. Harrington treats you."

"He hardly says a word to me."

"Right. He never screams at you."

"I've never heard him scream at you."

"Oh, he has. Especially when I first started."

"I have the feeling I'm a strike away from being tossed from the Heart Room."

"I doubt it."

Gene holds up one finger. "Crashing to floor on my first day — strike one." Second finger. "Using his name to get Rebecca Layne's chart — strike two."

"Yeah, why'd you do that?"

"Just curious about her echo."

"Anyway, Harrington's not tossing you from the team. You're Carl Hull's son."

Gene almost slams his beer onto the end table. The bottle catches the edge of the coaster and tips over.

"Hey!" Sandra shouts.

"Sorry. Sorry." Gene whips off his shirt and starts sopping the beer flowing onto the carpet and couch.

"Don't. I'll get something."

Sandra returns with a hand towel. "What was that all about?"

"Nothing."

"I'm not wiping up nothing."

Gene goes to the kitchen, rinses his shirt, and rings it out before putting it back on and returning to the family room. "I'm sorry to put you out. I should probably go."

"Leaving now will put me out." She stands, clutching the wet towel in one hand and extends her other hand. "Give me that."

Gene shrugs.

"Your shirt."

He pulls it over his head and hands it to her.

"I'm charging you for the electricity to dry this."

Sandra disappears into the bedroom.

Jeez, he's such an idiot.

Shirtless, Gene walks around the room, admiring her apartment's decor and the markers of a life further along than his own — the Parisian prints, of course, and under the paired windows, a low open stereo cabinet. She has a line of albums at least five feet across. He squats and fingers through a few of the covers. She's definitely into jazz, but there are a couple he's seen in his sister's collection — Elvis, Everly Brothers, the early Beatles.

She's collected her most personal memories on the freestanding teak *etagere* next to the entry door. Prominent is a photo of Sandra on nursing graduation day. She wears a white nurse's cap. Her parents, dressed in their Sunday best stand on either side, beaming. They have that old-for-their age Norman Rockwell look. On another shelf, the same man, but older still, poses languidly against a roll-top desk. He has a stethoscope hanging from his neck. What do you know?

When he hears the dryer start to rumble, Gene turns. He turns back and admires a cluster of small, graceful figurines, porcelain perhaps. There's one of a small child nuzzling a cat. Another of a small-town doctor offering a lollipop to a shy girl. Makes sense. Next to that, Sandra has placed a gold hinged frame. The left photo is of a thinner, younger Sandra, standing alone on a bright day, the Eiffel Tower slightly out of focus behind her, her windswept hair longer than it is now. Her face is centered in the photo, and her smile one of flat-out joy. The photo on the right is compositionally identical to the left but differs by season. She appears older. Her face a tad chubby. It's a cloudy day and this Sandra wears a long coat. She leans on an umbrella. The weather has affected her disposition, as betrayed by her plaintive expression.

Gene continues to drift along the shelves until a photo on the highest shelf stops him. It must be him. Her deceased fiancé. She's behind him, hugging his waist, her chin over his shoulder. His hair is Gene's color and the same length as Gene's before he cut it. The young man's hand rests on her arm. This is what two people look like who love each other with their whole heart. And later, she proved it.

"Here," she says from behind.

She tosses a sixties-era tie-dyed t-shirt to Gene. "Bitchin', don't you think?" She heads to the kitchen.

The shirt has a faint musty smell and fits perfectly.

She returns, hands him a beer, and nods up to the photo. That's Patrick."

"I thought so."

"I can't put it away."

She reaches up around Gene for the frame.

"He was the one," she says. "You know. That soul mate everyone hopes they meet. The one to share the rest of your life. It's been six years since his death. What does that tell you?"

Gene looks back to the hinged frame. "You never got to share Paris with him."

Sandra studies Gene for a moment. "You know what you are, Eugene Hull?"

"A good listener?"

"A good observer."

"That's a new one."

"The best doctors — the best men — are good observers."

She places the photo back on the shelf, aligning the frame just so. "And good listeners. How about some music? What do you like?"

"Whatever you think," he says.

She kneels and settles her hips back on her heels. Gene sits on the couch. "Did you move here right after you finished nursing school?"

Sandra looks at an album cover. "No. After Patrick died, I hung around Kansas City for a while. Got a job in a thoracic surgeon's office. But everything in town reminded me of Patrick, our good times, but also his suffering. I had to get away. I managed a ticket to Paris. My exchange family put me up. I don't know what I was looking for. Something different, I guess. A kick-start to happiness. The winter weather didn't cooperate."

"So you moved to Phoenix."

"I needed sun. I needed warmth. The surgeon I worked for knew Harrington. The stars seemed to align, and here I am." She tilts an album forward and pauses. "It's not easy watching someone die." She turns her head. "Especially someone you love."

Gene nods. It was hard just hearing about his father's death. But to be there? To have witnessed the moment.

The timer goes off.

"Looks like dinner's finally ready," Sandra says. "Let me put this album on first."

THE DINNER IS DELICIOUS. The garden salad, the garlic bread, the pesto, the conversation; it's all delicious. Gene is sure he's never had pesto, but it's now his favorite. Sandra selects a series of jazz albums, some of the same music his father listened to and some Gene heard rotating off the vinyl of his roommate's turntable. She says that jazz is something she took to when his father played it during surgery. At the one Christmas party she attended, he played a few jazz versions of holiday classics. She talks about how kind his father was when she first arrived. If she forgot to have an odd instrument ready to open or fumbled when trying to open the sterile package — any number of things like that — he deflected Dr. Harrington's attention. He was a kind of protector for her until she got her feet settled firmly on the Heart-Room ground. "I was struggling with Patrick's death," she says. "until your father recommended a psychologist."

She doesn't elaborate, and Gene doesn't press her.

They have two more beers during dinner, and she offers a fifth. "Why not," he says. "I've paced myself." They sit, side by side, on the couch, and nibble Pepperidge Farm cookies. "Pretty high-end cookies," he says.

"Goes well with the Michelob." She says this around a cookie section hanging from her lips. Then it falls. He snatches it away and pops it in his mouth.

She throws her head back and laughs.

Then her expression changes. It is the look people get when they finally work up the courage to say something that has been on their mind all night.

"Tell me something. You talk much with Dr. Boswell, outside the OR?"

Gene exhales, disappointed that she's not asked him something like: Could you think of me as a real date?

"Other than at St. James and in the doctor's lounge?" he says. "No."

"What do you think of him?"

"He seems like a good anesthesiologist."

"That's not what I mean."

"I hear he's got a reputation."

"The hospital is full of reputations. Has he said anything about me?"

"Like what?"

"You see how he flirts, and it's not just with me. I know his type, and he can have his fun in the OR."

"I kind of wondered if something was going on."

"Nothing's going on!"

That's a relief, but she says it like she's driving a stake through the heart of a rumor.

"Sorry," she says. "The beer I guess."

She rests her head back and bobs to the rhythm of the music. "Seems like all the attention I get anymore is from the married doctors." She taps her fingers on the bottle. "You know what that tune is?"

"No."

"It's Chet Baker. He's playing *Lonely Star*." She closes her eyes and sways. "Can you believe it? We're sitting here talking about reputations, and this comes on."

"Why do people like jazz?" Gene says. "I mean the music is fine, but no lyrics. No meaning."

"I see." She grins but keeps her eyes closed. "You like the poetry of the lyrics. You inject yourself into the narrative."

Inject yourself into the narrative? Is that the beer talking?

She rolls her head to the side and gives Gene the most serene smile, her olive eyes floating, unguarded. Here it is. A moment. He wants to kiss her…and more. Wants it so much, it feels like a need. In the morning he could claim innocence — I was so drunk, I didn't know what I was doing. That's not really me. But he's sober enough to know that's not who he wants to be, despite Sandra's beer-soaked, beckoning eyes.

"It seems like lyrics make the music," he says. "Without the words, what's the music have to say? I couldn't see writing a song without saying something."

Sandra moves from the couch to the turntable and kneels. She pulls a few albums from the bottom shelf and shuffles them front to back. She returns those and takes out a few more. Soon she finds what she's looking for and replaces the platter on the wheel with her new selection. She consults the back of the album jacket and carefully places the needle on a spinning groove about two-thirds of the way in. Maybe she wasn't as drunk as he'd thought. After two hissing seconds, the music starts, a jazz instrumental. She returns to the couch, next to Gene, and rests her head back again. "Don't say anything," she says. "Just listen. Listen all the way through."

He's heard this tune before, not that he can place it. It isn't the usual melody followed by improvisation handed off from one band member to another, closing with a final redux of the melody. This tune is played straight for the most part with a haunting brass instrument, a trumpet probably, although it could have been a coronet. Gene's never been sure of the difference between the two.

When it's over and just as the next cut begins, Sandra lifts the needle, clicks the turntable off and returns to the couch. "What do you think?"

"Nice."

"Oh, come on." She reaches over and playfully pushes his knee. "You can come up with more than 'Nice'."

"Very nice. No, very, very, very nice."

Sandra puts the tune back on and when she returns, she swings Gene's legs onto her lap and removes his shoes. "Lay flat and close your eyes. I'm going to tell you a story."

With the music as background, Sandra tells her story. But soon, the music is the story and Sandra a kind of transducer, converting the music's acoustic waves into moving images. In her story, a girl wearing a student nurse uniform stands in silence at the grave of a young man. After some time, she removes a heart-shaped pendant and repeats aloud the words inscribed, Forever my love. She places a bouquet of baby's breath at the base of the headstone, turns, and departs. She returns the next week, same day, same time, same words and flowers. As the weeks pass, the grass in the cemetery goes dormant, the leaves turn and fall, and when snow covers the ground, she clears the drift from the headstone. Weeks more pass and the leaves are budding. On her penultimate visit, dressed in shorts and his Kansas City Athletics jersey, she goes through her routine, but also reads a letter that she received that day — she has a job in Phoenix. Through tears, she tells him she has to take it, and she makes him a promise, actually, she affirms a promise he extracted from her a few days before his death — don't accept second best. She doesn't ever expect to find someone better than him.

Sandra stops speaking, but the music plays on. Gene keeps his eyes closed. He continues the movie in his head — his version now. He sees her driving alone in a car pulling a U-Haul trailer swaying left and right down the road. He sees her setting up her apartment, enduring her first days in the operating room, a nervous rookie, and then sees her gaining experience and responsibility and moving into the Heart Room, second only to Irene and the surgeons in prestige and power. And he sees her dating, innocent dates to dinner, movies, a kiss at the door. After each — and there is only, at most, two with the same man — she dresses in her nightgown and gives a photo of her deceased fiancé a kiss before turning out the lights. She sighs and thinks I keep my promises.

Gene has made the same promise, a silent promise only to himself, but he is afraid there will be no one better than Patty. She didn't die, and he feels small for even thinking his promise parallels Sandra's. But Patty's love for him died. And he killed it.

The remainder of the album plays until there's nothing but the sound of the hissing needle stuck in the last groove.

"Do you still love Patty, Gene? Are you in love with that beautiful girl?"

The question comes as much within him as at him. "Anymore, I'm not sure what to call my feelings for her." He stares at the ceiling.

"Isn't that the question of the ages — What is love?" She tips back the last of her beer and sets the bottle on the table. She rubs his ankles. "How can that ever be answered? You can have the most beautiful sex. You can make a baby with someone you love, and after a time there's another man, another love who replaces the one before, and the one after that. Does that mean you didn't love the first time? Or the second? Were they not all true loves?" She scoffs and shakes her head. "There's a bullshit term for you. But still, shouldn't there be some excu...exclu...excusivity to love? You know what I mean."

"You had a baby?"

"My life is confused enough. I meant in general." She hums to music playing in her head. "Shit. I'm twenty-eight, and I can't make sense of it. Here's a sad thing, but maybe it's true. Maybe it really is easier to know love when it's gone than when you have it next to you."

Gene's eyes are closed, hypnotized by her voice. He feels her move from the couch. The turntable hissing stops.

When her hand touches his, he opens his eyes. She's standing, staring at him with the sweetest expression of what looks like gratitude.

"See what I mean," she says, in a soft beer-slurred voice. "Lyrics are someone else's story. But with jazz, you can write your own." She gives a gentle tug on his thumb. "Come."

Their fingers entwined, Gene stubs his toe as he rounds the couch. The pain, if there, is soothed by the beers and his narrow thoughts as he follows her through the doorway into the dark coolness of her bedroom.

Chapter Twenty-Two

AFTER MIDNIGHT

APOLLO IS A PEST. Gene can't sweep the pool more than a few strokes before Apollo drops the ball at his feet and whines for him to throw it again. And he's making it hard to think. Gene swipes the ball away with his foot. "Cut it out."

A day has passed and he still hasn't called Sandra. He snugs his broad-brimmed hat to his head. Maybe he could say he was just too busy with jobs around the house.

He left her bedroom at four a.m. yesterday. She was sweet. When she heard him fumbling with the dryer door for his Polo, she flipped on a table lamp, and said, "You can just wear Patrick's."

"Thanks. That should stay with you."

She threw on a nightshirt and guided him to the front door. "You going to be okay?" she said.

His head was cloudy and his mouth as stale as St. James' floor at closing. He told her he felt okay to drive, knowing that wasn't the answer to the question she'd asked.

She turned on the porch light and opened the door.

In the amber glow filling the threshold, he read the writing on her nightshirt — *Nurses have what the doctor ordered.*

"Nice shirt," he said.

Tenting the fabric, she looked down, then gave a short, weary, laugh. She held his face between her hands, searching his eyes for a few seconds. Gene had the uncomfortable feeling that she was making some kind of choice. Then she kissed him on the lips in a way Gene can only describe now as companionable and said, "Get some sleep. Call me later. We can talk."

The rest of Saturday was a bust. He slept past noon, tried to at least sweep the pool, but felt lightheaded. He lay on the lounger and baked in the sun, frequently gulping from a jug of ice water. He needed to sweat out the beer. Flush his brain of the residue of hops and malt and the twisted feeling that he had betrayed his better nature. He imagined his guilt evaporating from his pores, rising to cooler air thousands of feet above his superheated neighborhood, where it condensed into a cloud and blew east across the raw desert.

Today had been better. As he mowed the lawn, his mind spun in circles. What could he say if he did call? How's your day been going? Back inside, he used muscle memory alone to add a half-dozen more strands of knots to the kitchen chairs. After each strand he picked up the phone. But he never dialed. He can't bear another lecture about being too young. He has no idea what the atmosphere in the OR will be like tomorrow. God, he hopes Boz doesn't find out.

Apollo barks twice. "Dammit, Apollo. Give it a rest." Gene heaves the ball into the orange trees. It sounds like it got stuck. Just as well. "That'll keep you busy." Gene continues to sweep.

The lovemaking with Sandra, if he could call it that, was fierce, both of them succumbing to needs with uninhibited zeal. Whether the deeper nature of her needs had been satisfied, he didn't know. But in the end his had not, at least the need that at one unrestrained point felt like revenge. His orgasm shot through him like an angry fastball aimed at someone's head. Maybe his own. And in the next instant…remorse…and nausea.

Sandra pushed him aside and ran to the toilet first. The sound of her retching triggered Gene, and he purged in the sink in the bedroom alcove. There was no languishing in bed, gazing into each other's eyes, or laughing about keeping their socks on — nothing had stayed on. He padded back to the bed and sat on the edge, bent over, elbows on knees, his mouth and heart sour. The toilet flushed. Naked as a patient in the Heart Room, she walked into the soft light over the sink and lifted handfuls of water to her face. Whereas once he saw only her eyes, last night he was privileged to all of her beauty, from her generous heart-shaped bottom to her full breasts. But her most beautiful feature was her concern. She sat beside him until his breathing finally idled. She placed a chilly, folded washcloth across the back of his neck. "Better?"

"Dizzy."

"Lay down."

He did and she put the cloth on his forehead.

She was silent for a moment.

"Look…Gene…" She held his eyes.

"Yeah, me, too."

"You should know something —"

"I understand."

For a minute or two, with the air conditioner humming and its cool air skimming across his bare chest, their gazes mingled in silence.

She patted his hand. "Tomorrow, in case you wonder, I'm on the pill."

In case you wonder. I'm on the pill. From what he remembers, protection never entered his mind. He was too hungry, or just assumed all women who readily undressed were on the pill. Patty had been on the pill. Lot of good that did.

After storing the pool brush, he goes inside and sits at the secretary. He lifts the telephone receiver and taps it against his forehead. There will be no more nights with Sandra. That's what she meant by "We can talk." Fine. It was lust, his longing for the past. She too, he supposed. But why the shame? What normal guy wouldn't be proud this morning, celebratory, instead of feeling disgraced.

He hangs up. Maybe later. Now what.

He takes the plush Saab to What-a-Burger and, while steering, resets one of the radio's pushbuttons to KCAZ. They're playing "Liberation" from Chicago's debut double album. At the conclusion, the DJ comes on and reminds her listeners that the group will be performing at Big Surf.

> Bring your blankets for the Thursday-in-the-Park concert. That's right, not Saturday-in-the Park, but Thursday-in-the-Park. And plan to stay late for a special star-spangled-fireworks celebration. Looks like the weather will cooperate this time. The forecast is for a much cooler day. Ninety-seven for the high, with a chance of afternoon thunderstorms. I'll see you there.

There is no doubt. If his life had moved along the straight line he once projected, Patty and he would be attending that concert.

When he returns, there's a postcard in the mail from his mother. So soon? This one is a 1950s' drawing of Hampton Beach with couples strolling hand in hand along the boardwalk, multicolored umbrellas in the sand, and a child making a castle while the mother, who wears a bathing cap, tilts her head and smiles that solid, bright white smile.

He grabs the water jug and sits at the patio table. Apollo drops the ball in his lap. "You're insane, you know." Gene heaves the ball into the grove and reads.

What a glorious day at the beach. Suzanne and I slipped away mid-week. After, we had a long talk. She thinks I should move here to be near. I don't know. What do you think? All my friends are there. But the memories. So many things I'd like to forget. Suzanne's right about one thing. I don't need that big house. Time to sell. She thinks I should get it on the market before schools start. People always relocate before school starts. So, I'll be flying home August 1 to get the ball rolling. It's taking a bit to get used to the bugs back here, but it's so nice to be out of the Arizona oven. Don't worry about the cat. He won't have me to pester anymore. But you probably caught it already. Miss you. Love, Mom

No. He poisoned it, though.

August 1. That's when Dr. Harrington is scheduled to go on vacation and Gene does what? Paint trees? Sit alone on his deck at night? He flips the postcard onto the patio table, removes his t-shirt, and runs across the Kool Deck, diving into the pool, ten feet down to the bottom. When he shoots to surface, Apollo is waiting at the pool's edge with a gift. Not the tennis ball, but a dead rat, bloated and bleeding.

———

Gene hustles Apollo inside, and returns with his mother's kitchen gloves. Using them, he examines the rat. It wasn't a cat that took the coumadin-laced tuna. It was this fucking rat. As far as he can tell, Apollo didn't pierce the skin. He rinses out Apollo's mouth anyway. He disposes of the rodent, washes the gloves, and heads outside.

Why didn't the damn rat spring the trap? Systematically he tests and inspects it on the patio table. There's the problem. One of two wires on the outside of the cage is chewed through.

The repairs take no time at all. Some engineering marvel. So far, he's caught Apollo and killed a rat. He taps the pencil on the table's edge. The opening is now too small for Apollo, but if he makes it even smaller to exclude rats, the cat won't be able to get in. Then it hits him. Maybe the opening is already too small. It's been too small from the start. This creature might be bigger than Apollo.

He checks his watch. He'll just make it. Gene speeds to Entz-White for some sheet metal, and by the time the Milky Way is pouring across the sky, he has enlarged his trap to the size of a small doghouse. He makes a cheese crisp and eats on the patio while watching Apollo sniff his way into the cage. The enlarged door drops behind him. He wheels around and whines.

Through a full mouth, Gene says, "That's probably the safest place for you." He opens the trap's door. Apollo scurries to Gene's feet. The largest cat in the neighborhood will fit in there now.

He picks up his mother's postcard. Don't worry about the cat? What did his father say when Gene took over painting the trees or cleaning the pool? *Own it?* He's not catching the damn cat for his mother's sake anymore.

He clears the patio table, sets the plate in the kitchen sink, and returns the hot sauce to the refrigerator. When he closes the door, his eyes settle on Patty and his graduation-night photo.

Jesse's right. It's time.

Gene slides the photo from under the magnet for one last look. "Congratulations Bobcat Graduates," the sign says in the background over their heads. His father had them move a little, and then a little more, to get the banner positioned in just the right place in the photo. He was detailed that way. When he gave Gene and Patty the photo, he explained that he didn't want the banner's growling mascot-face "perched" atop Gene's head as if the bobcat were attacking him.

"Shit." He tosses the photo onto the counter.

In his father's study, he pulls out the B volume of the *World Book Encyclopedia*. He sits on the floor and reads about bobcats. They're endemic to Arizona. It's possible.

Gene thaws a palm-sized serving of ground beef. While Apollo does his business, Gene positions and arms the trap in the grove. A lightning flash breaks low on the eastern horizon. The weather's changing.

Inside, turning off lights as he goes, he heads upstairs with Apollo. Not until he brings the lawn chair in from his deck does he remember. He could wait until morning, but he's delayed long enough. Back in the kitchen, Gene picks up the tattered and bandaged photo from the counter. He steps to the trash bin and presses his foot on the lever. The lid flips up. Over the open pail, he suspends the last tangible proof that Patty once loved him. After a deep breath, he releases his grip.

Chapter Twenty-Three

BEGINNINGS

Monday morning, the moment Gene opens the back door to check the trap, he smells rain. According to the morning DJ, the first rain in ninety-five days. It rolled in last night in thunderous sheets, and with it, a drop in temperature from blistering to just warm. The monsoon season, as it is so lovingly called by the desert dwellers, has arrived and the shift in weather gives Gene hope that a corresponding shift in his luck is in the offing. But once he weaves through the grove to the far back corner, he finds the trap empty, the door still open, and the bait untouched.

In the Heart Room, as Sandra ties his gown, Gene tries to gauge his standing with her. She doesn't stab his waist or whisper in his ear that he was a bastard for not calling her and that he should grow up. She's the same Sandra he met the first day. Focused. Efficient.

Once the case begins, Gene's mind falls in line with the routine of a three-vessel CABG. In a fast-paced two-and-a-half hours, Rui tells his jokes, Gene slurps the blood and smoke, and Boz flirts with Sandra behind his back during bypass. Through it all Dr. Harrington's hands perform their magic, with Irene always a step ahead of him.

The team sails through the second case as well, a single vessel bypass, although it's a left main blockage. Rui points out the precarious nature of a blockage affecting two-thirds of the heart's blood supply. During the chest closure, Boz quips that there is only one organ whose blood supply he's worried about. The team is in such a lighthearted mood that even Irene smiles at the joke. At least the outside edge of her eyes crinkle.

As with the first case, Rui assists while Gene closes the skin.

"Ever find that cat you poisoned?" Boz says.

"Turned out to be a roof rat."

"See? The vitamin C worked though. You'll get it."

Rui dents the skin where he wants the next stitch. "A little closer together *por favor.*"

"Did y'all smell the air this morning?" Boz says. "Should be a perfect afternoon to open up the Harley."

"On wet, oil-slick streets," Rui says. "I will make a reservation for you in the Emergency Room."

"Sandra, how about a quick spin out to the Superstitions," Boz says. "I know you love the smell of creosote after a rain."

"No thanks."

"We can stop by Gene's and help him poison the cat."

"Definitely not," she says.

Gene looks over. Her back is turned as she sorts instruments.

"I get it. You want to sneak over there alone."

Sandra rattles one tray down on the other and carries both through the door into center hall.

"Sorry, Gene-o. I guess that's a no."

Gene wants to foul this conversation off into the stands. When Sandra returns, he says, "I'm not sure it's a cat. I think it might be a bobcat."

"That's gonna require a whole different approach," Boz says. "You might need a little help from a Texas rancher's son."

"A bobcat?" Sandra says.

"Brinkerhoff had a big bob drinking out of his pool." Boz says.

"Not surprising with the drought we've had. There's thousands of kidney-shaped watering-holes in the suburbs."

"So, my good Gene," Rui says, "Be patient. If indeed you have a bobcat taunting poor Apollo, the monsoons may send him back to the hills."

"Don't listen to him, Gene-o. Sniper on the roof is what you need."

"You must be practicing," Rui says.

"What?" Gene says.

"Your sewing."

"Yeah…all weekend."

"It shows."

"Hey, Gene-o," Boz says from behind the ether screen, "Ever heard the expression, 'All work and no play makes Gene a dull boy?'"

"I play."

"On this, I must admit Boz is correct," Rui says. "Balance in life is a necessity."

"I go to the batting cage. I swim. I run. I don't just sit around the house and study. I do other things."

"That's what I'm interested in," Boz says. "The other things."

"Well, I spent all of yesterday afternoon enlarging my trap."

Boz shakes his head. "You're killing me. Here you are, living my dream scenario — single, recently dumped, and home for the summer in an empty house — and you're playing 'Trapper Gene'." Boz turns and begins drawing medication from a vial into a syringe. "Missed opportunity Gene-o. On weekends you should not be sleeping alone."

Gene places the last stitch and looks past Rui to Sandra who carries another tray of instruments toward center hall. When she backs through the door, her eyes speak to him, and he doesn't like what they're saying. She's disappointed. Damn. Why was he such a chickenshit?

He should have called her.

Mrs. Mead looks up from her book as they wheel the single-vessel CABG past her. She smiles and nods to Gene. After the patient is settled, Gene follows Dr. Harrington to the bedside of the day's first patient. Dr. Harrington milks the chest tube and checks the drainage in the bottle. He seems satisfied and asks the nurse a few questions. Gene looks for Sandra and finds her talking to Dr. Boz near the code cart midway down the length of the Unit. Dr. Boz catches Gene looking, gives him a sly smile, and then playfully massages Sandra's shoulders before walking toward him. As he passes, heading for the exit doors, he leans in and whispers, "Careful, Chief."

Stuff it, Gene thinks. What he's mainly worried about is Sandra, standing with her arms folded and foot tapping. Was she waiting for him or waiting by the code cart in case Mr. Mead took a sudden dip?

Dr. Harrington ambles to Mr. Mead's station and checks the numbers on the clipboard hanging from the balloon pump console. Gene follows. The machine hisses, its rhythm disconnected from that of the ventilator's higher pitched hiss, creating a kind of discordant jazz beat.

Mrs. Mead holds her husband's hand through the bedrail. His wrists are tied to the rail with a soft, cotton strap. According to the night nurse, he's been groping for his endotracheal tube. But now the straps tether his arms to his side, and an increase in the IV sedation tethers his mind to another world. Mrs. Mead hums something to him.

Dr. Harrington raises the covers so as to block Mrs. Mead's view and examines her husband's chest.

"How does he look, Doctor?" she says.

"Like a man on the mend," Dr. Harrington says.

"Might I ask when Mr. Mead will be free from all these contraptions?"

Gene and the ICU nurse look at each other, mutually acknowledging Mrs. Meads' sweet innocence.

Dr. Harrington places a hand under her elbow. "I do believe

we'll remove that contraption at the foot of the bed later tomorrow."

"Must he be confined?"

"It's best I think," he says in his hypnotic tone.

"I see."

She takes Mr. Mead's hand in both of hers and stares at his face: his closed lids, now much less swollen; the sparse hair she keeps neat with her small black comb; his mouth pulled slightly to the left by the endotracheal tube. She sighs and shakes her head. "It will be a joy to see him again. To hear him again. In fifty-five years, this is the longest Mr. Mead and I have been apart."

When Dr. Harrington moves off to the nurse's station, Sandra, who still loiters by the code cart, motions to Gene. He gives Dr. Harrington a glance and then approaches her. Before she can say anything, he whispers: "I know, I should have called you."

She tugs his coat sleeve and motions for him to follow her to the hallway.

He looks toward Dr. Harrington again.

"It'll just take a second," she says.

Out in the hall, she overlaps her white coat around her as if she's cold. "Gene, I need to tell you something."

Here it comes. He needs to grow up. Gene plants his feet and straightens. All that's missing is the blindfold and the bullet-riddled wall.

The right side of her mouth curls to a half-smile. "Relax." She looks down the hall and steps closer. "I need to apologize for Friday night. I don't want you to get the wrong idea." She sighs. "About me. I don't want you to think I planned all that."

"I don't."

"The beer got the best of me."

Gene thinks of something and grins.

Sandra's eyes narrow. "What?"

"Nothing."

"You don't believe me."

"No. No. I just thought of the Michelob ads."

Her expression softens a little.

"You know. 'Michelob, an unexpected pleasure.'"

After a second, she smiles. "You are too much."

"Actually, I'm pretty cheap."

Sandra smiles again and shakes her head in a look of admiring disbelief. Gene feels giddy. He likes the flirtation, but mostly he's relieved, although a little surprised that he'd read her wrong.

"Boz thinks I've been looking at you," she says.

"How?"

"How do you think?"

"Have you?"

"I thought I wasn't being so obvious."

Gene thinks she wasn't obvious at all. But now, knowing she's eying him while he works in surgery, Jesse's advice comes back to him again. *Turn and burn, man. Turn and burn.* But for the memories, tossing the graduation photo completed the burn. Now, he's turning toward Sandra, and it feels like a cure of some kind.

"What'd you tell Dr. Boz? I mean, just now."

"To pay more attention to his wife than to the way I look around the room."

"What'd he say?"

Sandra nods over Gene's shoulder. "Looks like you've got to go."

Dr. Harrington stands in the hallway. He waves to Gene to follow and lumbers on.

"I'm indispensable," Gene says. He takes a step and then turns back. "You like Chicago?"

"The city?"

"The band."

"Sure."

"They're giving a concert Thursday."

"Is this a date?"

Gene walks backwards down the hall. "Could be."

BY MIDWEEK, he's still not caught the bobcat. It matters not. As he follows Dr. Harrington on afternoon rounds, Gene's mind is occupied with thoughts of Sandra and their date tomorrow. Perhaps the change in weather did bring him a little change in luck.

"What a momentous day." Mrs. Mead says, as Gene and Dr. Harrington gather at her husband's ICU bed. She's standing, holding a Styrofoam cup in one hand and a plastic spoon in the other. "My prayers have been answered." She tips a small portion of ice into Mr. Mead's waiting mouth. The breathing tube is gone.

"How's our patient," Dr. Harrington says.

"Stubborn," Mrs. Mead says. "The nurses say not too much ice, but he keeps opening his mouth like a little bird."

Mr. Mead widens his eyes and swallows. For the first time, Gene notices they are light blue, even his glass eye, like the blue of the sharply tailored sundress Mrs. Mead wears today. And for the first time since Gene first saw him, Mr. Mead seems alive. Weak, but alive.

"I have to pee," he says in a hoarse whisper.

"Henry," she says. "The nurses keep telling you. It's that catheter in your bladder. Try to forget about it."

Mr. Mead shoots his natural eye skyward.

"Is there something you can give him?"

"I'll instruct the nurses," Dr. Harrington says.

"Thank you. I'm afraid with that tube out of his throat you're going to have a time with him."

"When was he extubated?" Gene asks.

"This morning."

Gene wants to leap. All summer, he's been happy for patients who've cleared this hurdle, but Mr. and Mrs. Mead are different. They feel like family.

"Oh, gracious. My manners," Mrs. Mead says. "Dear, this is Dr. Hull. Dr. Harrington's assistant."

Gene nods.

Dr. Harrington pulls Mr. Mead's gown down, examines the incision and listens to his heart. Gene helps him lean forward and take deep breaths while Dr. Harrington listens to his lungs. When Mr. Mead rests back, he coughs, grimaces, and coughs some more. He places a red, Valentine's heart-shaped pillow over his chest and holds tight until the coughing spasm subsides.

"You look good, Henry," Dr. Harrington says. "We'll send you up to the floor in the morning."

Dr. Harrington moves on to the nursing station.

"I'll see you upstairs tomorrow," Gene says.

Mr. Mead taps his chest and frowns. He motions for his wife to come closer and then whispers.

"How long will he have this pain?" she asks.

"Could be several more days. He's been through a lot."

"I see."

"But the worst is over."

THE FORECAST for the concert has not changed. Chance of a thunderstorm or dust storm. Whether a five-minute torrent of rain or a fifteen-hundred-foot wall of dust, the inside of his soft-top-protected Jeep would have been a mess. But not the Saab.

The radio is tuned to KCAZ and plays Led Zeppelin's "Whole Lotta Love". But Gene's tuned in to Sandra and her strong profile in the passenger seat. He presses the button for the jazz station. "There."

She gives him a gentle smile.

"What?" he says.

"Nothing."

They drive along Van Buren past the mental hospital and cheap motels until the desert blooms into Papago Park, the Phoenix Zoo, and Phoenix Municipal Stadium. Sandra lowers the window and extends her arm. Warm air buffets her hand. She inhales. The aroma of creosote swirls around them. He points to the darkened stadium. "Ever been there?"

She looks out and shakes her head.

"It's where the Giants play spring training. In fourth grade my dad took me to my first game." He sighs. "I almost saw Willie Mays hit a home run."

"Almost?"

"I was focused on some peanuts or something. Heard the crack of the bat. When Willie connects, it's a sound that stops your breath. I stood on my seat and looked in the direction of the other fans, but never picked up the flight of the ball."

"That had to be disappointing."

"My dad was so excited. 'Did you see it! Did you see that!' He was slapping me on the back and pointing past center field. 'That must have landed in the lagoon.' He was so happy. You'd have thought I'd hit the ball."

Gene looks toward the zoo. "So, I lied. 'I saw it! I saw it!'" His eyes return to the road as it winds toward the lights of Big Surf. "I couldn't disappoint him."

THE FIRST NOTES from Chicago don't blast from their renowned horn section, but strum from an acoustic guitar. One syncopated measure in, Gene recognizes "Beginnings," a perfect choice, not just because of the name, but also its laid-back summer vibe. Seduced by the music and a gentle breeze, the concertgoers stretch out on beach chairs and blankets along every square foot of sand fronting the wave pool. Heads bob and toes tap to the rhythm. Many sway and lip sync to the music — including Sandra.

Gene leans back onto his elbows so he can watch the words trickling from her silent lips. Are the lyrics reminding her of Patrick? About the beginning that ended tragically.

When Gene spread the king-sized blanket on the sand, he half-hoped Chicago wouldn't play "Just You 'N' Me" — his song for Patty. But he never thought this evening might be hard for Sandra. Gene was only dumped. Patrick had died. How do you turn from that?

Chicago is nearing the song's end, weaving a repeated phrase in and around and over and under each member's brief solo. Sandra mouths every refrain. From behind her, Gene can't see her expression, but there's a mournful, almost pleading look to the way she sways.

Finally, the band ends on a hard stop, pauses a beat, and in perfect a cappella harmony belts, "Only the beginning."

The crowd leaps and roars, many thrusting their warming beers into the air. Sandra stands. She spins around, levels her eyes at Gene, smiles, and sings the last line to him. She reaches down and coaxes him to his feet. As they clap, she says, "That was fabulous." Pulling him close by the waist, she leans her temple to his shoulder. "I'm so glad you asked me."

His life used to ride a straight line. Now it swerves month to month, day to day, and even minute to minute. "Beginnings". Who knows? Maybe it will become their song.

The remainder of the first set crescendos right up to the break, when the band, fists pumping to the whoops of the audience, hustles offstage. Even the stars overhead seem to dance with approval.

"Wow," Gene says.

"Amazing."

Gene looks over Sandra's shoulder at the concession line — four wide and ten deep at least.

"How about a beer?"

"Is this a plan to get me drunk?"

Before he can answer she says, "Forget I said that."

In line, he turns and faces the past. Behind Sandra, the water is calm. The wave machine isn't running tonight. He was here with Patty a few times after she collapsed in the water. She worked the concession stand as late as last summer. The decor hasn't changed since they played that silly game: who can swim the farthest. Still the same grass shacks, palm trees fluttering in the breeze, and the hundred-foot coastline of fine white sand sloping to the water. But it all seems smaller. If it wasn't for Chicago and Sandra, he wouldn't be here. Not because of painful reminders, but because as he watches Sandra bury her toes in the sand, he feels that he's outgrown the place.

———

GENE RETURNS with two beers in plastic cups.

"Michelob?" Sandra says.

"We can pretend."

Her legs are bent, and her toes dig into the sand. She takes the cup in both hands and sips.

"Delish," she says. "What do I owe you?"

"My treat. We're on a date. Remember?"

She leans over and kisses him. A more than companionable kiss. "Now it's official." She tips her beer toward him. "

"*Santé!*"

"I assume that's French for 'Cheers'," he says, and takes a long draw. Her hair looks great pulled behind her ears.

"*Oui.*"

"I was wondering what it would be like to kiss you without being loaded."

"And?"

"Pretty nice."

"And what else might you be wondering about?"

Gene blushes. "Nothing. Honest." He takes a quick sip.

"Gene, I don't know what's going to happen tonight. Just don't be like other guys I've been with who, like Boz, feel the night's a failure if I don't go home with them."

"Boz?"

She holds a hand up. "That's not what I mean."

"So, what other guys?"

"Just dates."

"Many?"

She reaches over and touches his bare knee. "We're not keeping score."

A gust of wind sweeps across the concertgoers, blowing Sandra's hair over her head and spraying sand in Gene's face. He turns his head to the night sky. Still a few stars are blinking around the passing clouds.

Sandra brushes her hair back. "I guess a kind good-looking guy like you must have been with other girls besides Patty."

"Nope." He tries to say it with pride, but in truth he feels like a rookie next to her. "Only you. And I didn't plan on it either...but I'm glad. It...well...it helped."

She pulls back.

"Oh no. It's not like I thought you were some kind of therapy... I mean, after, when we were lying there —"

Sandra puts a finger to his lips. Then she slides next to him and kisses his cheek before intertwining their fingers. She points with her other hand. "They're coming back."

Chicago opens the set with "Wishing You Were Here" from their new album. The songs come one after another, saving Gene from saying some other stupid thing.

The band is midway through "I'm A Man" when the wind, which has been blowing across the stage, suddenly stiffens, and a mic stand topples. The air fills with dust. Pete Cetera stops singing and tells the audience he was warned this might happen. One of the promoters comes on stage and tells everyone the concert is on hold until this dust storm passes.

As sand cuts horizontally through the air, the band hustles off stage and a half-dozen crew members begin collecting instruments. Many in the crowd scamper for cover to the concession stands or the covered picnic areas. Gene knows what to do. Sand bites his face as he yells over the wind, "Get up."

Sandra looks puzzled.

"Sit on the edge. The blanket."

He pulls it over her back and then sits cross-legged, facing her and pulling the blanket over himself. The sand whips against the blanket as if it were being pulsed from a fire hose. "We're safe," Gene says.

The floodlights cast enough light through the blanket for Gene to see Sandra's eyes. She studies him for a minute, and then she takes his hand and holds his palm to the cleavage above her tube top. Inside the blanket's cocoon, the storm vanishes. There is only their breathing, the aroma of beer, her soft skin and the beat of her heart. It is as if she dipped into his memories and is playing make believe: You be Gene and I'll be Patty.

"I don't want to fall for you, Gene." The statement stuns him like fifty joules to his naked heart. "But you're making it difficult."

He drops his hand. "I don't mean to be difficult."

"Oh, you are. You're sensitive for one, and you listen. Small things, like tuning the radio to jazz when we drove over here."

"I don't always listen. Trust me."

She leans in. Forehead to forehead, her arms at his waist, she says, "You know, that first song made me think of Patrick. You probably sensed it."

"No. Not really."

"Come on."

"Maybe a little."

"I don't fight it anymore. I kind of hug the memory, feel blessed for having it, and try to look forward. You know, to a new love. A new beginning. But you can't force love to happen. That much I've learned. If it comes, it comes, regardless of having sex. So, last Friday night…" She takes a deep breath. "…I didn't plan, or even hope, our evening would end in bed. Well, maybe subconsciously I did. I guess I needed you, and now I know you needed me as well."

She's right. If she can treasure her memories and look toward a new beginning, then why can't he? He dips the fingertips of one hand under her tube top and waits. She guides his hand along her warm, moist skin, until he presses his palm flat against the pounding apex of her heart. Her pulse surges through his fingers and up his arm. He feels something else. Something they share, and Gene knows what it is before she says it. "We're both lonely, Gene. We miss someone we can't get back. We're searching for their love, but every love is unique."

He removes his hand from under her shirt and kisses her knuckles. The wind and sand continue to pelt the blanket.

"I'm nearly ten years older than you, Gene. Is that a problem?"

He enjoys hearing her talk. If he speaks, that will ruin the moment.

"Am I right? If I'm wrong, tell me now, but I think I'm right. You are lonely?"

"Eight. You're only eight years older."

After the storm passes, the band returns on stage. "Far out," Robert Lamm says. "What do you say we blow the sand out of our horns and rock!"

Near the end of their rollicking post-storm set, Pete Cetera comes to the mic. He shades his eyes from the lights and looks into the crowd. "Anybody in love out there?"

A female voice in the crowd shouts, "With you."

The horn intro is unmistakable. Here it comes. Sandra leans back against Gene's chest. As Pete sings "Just You 'N' Me," Gene wraps his arms around her, ready to hug his memories but look forward.

Midway in the song, Sandra squeezes his hand. She was responding to a lyric. He kisses the top of her head and squeezes back in agreement. His life does feel easy with her beside him. Just like it once did with Patty. Sandra was right. He is lonely. But maybe it's not, or never was, from missing Patty's love as much as missing their lovemaking. He used to be so sure.

The post-concert fireworks begin sometime after eleven and end with the usual rapid-fire starbursts of color. Gene's as relaxed of mind and body as he's been all summer, suspended in an interlude of hopeful resignation.

Back at Sandra's apartment, she unlocks the door and turns to him. "See you this weekend?"

"How about a movie?"

"Saturday?"

"Perfect."

She leans in and kisses him.

He pulls her close.

"We have to work tomorrow," she says.

"It's a short day."

Standing by her bed, he lifts her top over her head and kisses the notch above her sternum. A month ago, he would have thought of it as her breastbone. Now it's her sternum, and the notch above it, that soft vulnerable depression, is where one gains access to another one's heart. He kisses her there again. Then he courses his fingertips between her breasts, the length of her chest, along her tensing abdomen, to the waistband of her pants. He never speaks. She gives him a grin that says she too will not speak. And they don't. Not as she removes her clothes and not as he removes his. As she guides him to her bed, she presses her full figure against his wiry frame, rises up on her toes and whispers in his ear, "You know, it's not cold in here. You can take your socks off."

"You're right." He sits on the bed's edge and looks up. "I don't need these."

Chapter Twenty-Four

ANGER MANAGEMENT

IN THE DOCTOR'S LOUNGE, Gene devours Jesse's oatmeal and toast while Dr. Boz sleeps curled on the couch. His boots are toppled on the floor. Rui walks in, sits next to Gene, and slips his shoe covers on. "Look at that," Rui says. He nods toward Dr. Boz. "Poor bastard." He stretches his foot out and nudges the couch's curved metal armrest. "Boz!"

"What?" Boz says, his voice in low gear.

"You live here now? It is Friday, *senhor.* A new day. Time for you to wake and your patients to sleep. Then you can get home to that beautiful wife of yours."

"Go fuck yourself."

"Oh, Boz. That is no way to talk. My young apprentice here is quite impressionable."

Boz twists his head and upper body towards them, shading his squinting eyes from the fluorescent lights. "How'd you get stuck with the Portuguese piece of shit?" He flops onto his back and places the crook of his arm over his eyes.

"What was it, Boz?" Rui says. "What brought you in? The pull of the ER or the push of your lovely lady?"

Boz flips Rui the bird.

"Wake now. Pour your coffee, *amigo minho*. I will report your fidelity to your wife, should she ask."

"Thoracic aneurysm," Boz says. "Replaced his valve, too. All fucking night. He looks like crap in the Unit." Dr. Boz raises his head and looks over to Rui. "Where were you? We had to grab a general surgery resident to help us."

"On a well-deserved night off with my wife at the Cloud Club. A most memorable celebration of ten years together."

"She deserved more…sticking with you."

"On that point, I concur. However, therein lies her beauty. She doesn't think she deserves more."

"Give her time."

"I hear you lost power."

"A full-metal Harrington fuck-storm until the gennies kicked in."

"I wish you could have observed the cause of your consternation from the twenty-first floor. Like a scene from *Lawrence of Arabia*." Rui extends his gaze to the ceiling. "A wall of dust, perhaps three to four hundred meters high, swept over us. Down below, the street disappeared. Then the power failed. We finished dinner by candlelight. And then, just to add a touch more magic, as we lingered over our cappuccini, a firework's show erupted to the east. Spectacular evening."

"Well, yippee ki yi yo."

Rui turns to Gene. "Our pool, it was a disaster this morning. Did yours survive?"

Gene has no idea. His spectacular evening didn't end until drove home about two a.m.

"That reminds me," Rui says. "Alicia had a grand idea. Please join us Tuesday night to watch the All-Star Game. Burgers, beer, and baseball. A beautiful thing."

"What time is it?" Dr. Boz says.

Gene had hoped to watch the game with Sandra.

"First pitch at five-forty," Rui says. "But you hate baseball, *amigo minho*."

"Shoot," Gene says. "I've already made plans."

"Not the fucking game," Boz says. "What time is it now?"

Rui eyes the analog clock over Boz's head. "Six twenty."

"Shit." Boz swings his feet to the floor and sits up. He runs his hands through his riotous hair and yawns. "How about you, Gene-o? Any fireworks fill your night?"

Gene takes another bite of oatmeal.

"Noticed Sandra had the night off," Boz says. He's got that self-satisfied grin aimed at Gene.

Gene shakes his head and downs a pint carton of milk.

"Smart kid. Take the fifth."

Boz slips a boot on, tugging until his heal thuds into place. "I need coffee." He stands, loosens his pants' drawstring, and tucks in his scrub top. "Shit, look at this." There was a large rust-colored blood spot above his heart. "Goddamn resident."

Boz pours his coffee. He leans against the counter by the dressing room door. The coffeepot rattles. "Come on, Gene. What's going on between you two. You can trust us. We're family."

Rui has found the Jumble and pens the first word. "Perhaps you should finish your coffee and change," he says. He glares at Dr. Boz. "We're running late."

"I'm just saying if you're digging Sandra, so to speak, I'm all for it."

"That is quite enough."

"I admit, I'd love to be one of the notches on her bedpost."

Rui sets the paper on the table. Taking his coffee, he rises and walks toward Boz.

"You have to agree, Rui, there's a lot she could teach a young bull."

Rui elbows Boz into the counter. "Excuse me. I need a refill."

"Hey!" Boz looks down at his scrub shirt. A coffee spill now overlaps the one of blood.

Rui throws the dressing room door open. "On second thought, I shall check on a patient."

Gene has seen them kid each other for weeks, but this is different.

"I'll give him a minute to face the urinal," Boz says. "He gets a little high and mighty sometimes." He sets his mug down and dries the coffee spill. Then he leans against the counter and takes a careful sip. "I'm sure you heard all about the hospital from your dad. It's a real *Peyton Place.*"

Gene steps over to Boz, faces him, and waits. Boz shrugs and moves aside. Not knowing what else to do, Gene pours a cup of coffee, his first since starting here.

"No harm telling you I guess." Boz says.

Gene loads his coffee with sugar and Coffee-Mate. "Tell me what?"

"Rui had a fling with Sandra." Gene takes a step back. "Shocker, isn't it? But true."

"How would you know?"

"Word gets around."

"Whose word?"

"No one's in particular. Just stories from long before I showed up. Honestly, if you ask me, she's a real prick tease."

"No one's asking you."

Boz grins. "Easy there, cowboy. I've seen this before. Sure, she had it tough with her boyfriend dying and all, but don't be fooled. If you're going to sleep with her, don't think this will end with you two riding off into the sunset."

"How'd you know about her fiancé?"

Boz studies Gene for a second. "How'd you?" He taps Gene's chest with the coffee mug. "She'll use you, buddy. Listen…."

One more tap, and Gene will backhand this shit-fuck's coffee to the wall.

"You can't save everyone," Boz says.

"So, what's your story?"

"Whatever do you mean?"

There's that conceited grin again. "I see the way you are with her."

Boz slurps a sip of coffee, ending with a satisfied *ahhh.* "Hey, I'm a flirt. I admit it. But I sure as hell am not going to get drunk some night like Rui and do the dirty dance with Sandra. And you know why?"

Bullshit. Gene refuses to play.

"Alimony. Oh, I've had dreams about her, believe me. But the best advice I ever got from my old man was financial. He said, 'You want to save for retirement…don't get divorced. The alimony will drain you.'"

Gene's heart is about to rocket from his chest. He doesn't believe Boz's claim of financial morality and doesn't want to believe, doesn't want to think of Rui and Sandra together. What he does want is to slam this self-serving cowboy son of a bitch into the wall.

"Anyway, as far as I know Alicia never found out. That's a miracle around here." Boz drains the rest of the mug. "Oh, by the way. That young lass you saved in the lobby —"

Rebecca. He hasn't thought of her in days. "I didn't save her."

"That may be, but believe me, you need to take the points when you can get them. Anyway, she's on my schedule. I circled that one — July 31st."

Gene stiffens with the thought of Boz ogling Rebecca's naked body.

"…ASD repair. Twenty-two. Can't wait. I've not had a patient younger than fifty-five in months. Then I'm off to Cabo."

Boz tips his coffee back, forgetting it's empty, and frowns. "For now, I've got to get some fat-assed, bull-necked banker off to sleep so we can unclog his last forty years of hard living."

He backs his weight into the dressing room door. "I like her name — Rebecca Layne. Has a kind of southern quality that rolls off your tongue. Just thinking about her perky breasts is waking me up. How about you, Gene-o?"

Gene turns and drains the scalding beverage in three defiant gulps. When Boz passes back through on his way to the heart room, Gene pretends to read the paper. Several minutes later, Sandra calls in, "Gene?"

"Yes."

"We're ready."

Gene closes his eyes and clenches his jaw. *She'll use you, buddy.*

"Gene?"

"Sure."

GENE LUGS his anger and exhaustion into the Heart Room, greeting Sandra's bright "Good morning" with a another curt "Sure." She returns a quizzical look and continues to set up. At the head of the bed, Dr. Boz curses as he struggles with placement of the arterial line. Good. At least for the time being Boz's attention isn't on Sandra and him.

After the patient is asleep, Gene pulls the cath tray up to the OR table, dons his gloves, and preps the patient's scrotum and penis for the bladder catheter. He's performed this task enough in the last two weeks that the steps are automatic. Sandra and Rui? Boz must be full of it.

The catheter isn't going in. He angles the penis this way and that. He tries all the maneuvers Sandra has taught him. "Gene, if it won't go, don't force it," Sandra says from behind him.

"I can get it."

"Try the stylet."

"I know what to try." He looks back at her and her wide-open eyes. With Rui's help, he used the stylet once before on another patient. He runs the stylet down the catheter opening and then bends the whole thing to the shape that worked the last time. He passes the catheter into the penis and still, somewhere near the base of the penis, he meets resistance.

"I'll get Rui," Sandra says.

Gene doesn't want his help. He puts some hurt behind the catheter and it passes the obstruction and slips into place. "I don't need him. I got it." Gene turns and stares at Sandra. When he removes the stylet, blood pours from the catheter opening.

Sandra nudges Gene aside and, with a saline-filled syringe, inflates the balloon inside the bladder. She adds more saline than usual and pulls on the catheter until it's snug. The bleeding slows, but it doesn't stop. "Betty, get Dr. Harrington."

Gene's heart is pounding.

Rui rushes in with Dr. Harrington. They eye the blood oozing from the end of the catheter. As he looks over to Gene, Rui's shoulders sink. Dr. Harrington deflates the balloon, watches the blood rush out, then inflates it, pulls the catheter taught and snaps a clamp across it, tight against the tip of the penis. He slams the syringe to floor. "Cancel the goddamn case. Call Frazier to see him."

Cancel? Why? Gene turns his palms up to Rui and shrugs. Rui moves next to him. He whispers, "If he is bleeding from anywhere — bladder, prostate, urethra — we cannot anticoagulate for bypass. Once we give him the heparin, he will just continue to bleed."

Gene drops his head. Dr. Harrington might as well have said *and cancel Gene's admission to medical school!*

"Sandra, what in the Sam Hell happened?" Dr. Harrington shouts.

She looks at Gene and back to Dr. Harrington. "I met a little resistance, but honestly I didn't put that much pressure behind it, and it slipped in. I'm sorry. I guess I should have stopped."

"You're goddamn right you should have stopped." He grumbles something more and kicks the door as he leaves.

The room is silent. Gene expects Boz to open his trap first. He does, but it isn't what Gene expects. "I'll keep him asleep until you talk with Frazier. He may want to scope him here."

"Sandra," Irene says. "His number's in my book."

Sandra dials and makes arrangements. Dr. Frazier will be right over.

As Sandra, Irene, and Betty break down the room and prepare for the urologist, Rui walks over to Sandra. He places his healing hands on her shoulders and says something Gene can't hear. She nods. Gene leans against the counter, feeling as lost and alone as the night he drove home after his father died. As Rui passes him and opens the door, he gestures for Gene to follow. Before the door closes behind him, he hears Dr. Boz speaking to Sandra. "Darlin', I've never seen a woman throw herself on a grenade like that."

AT HOME, the pool is a mess. The entirety of the last night's dust storm seems to have settled at the bottom. As Gene vacuums in overlapping lines, the white of the plaster returns. He thinks of what Rui told him in the doctor's lounge after the case. Although Dr. Harrington gives Gene some slack, still, there are limits. As much as Gene might feel like a doctor, he has to remember he isn't one. Harrington can forgive Gene's lack of experience. He could forgive him for not knowing what to do. He can forgive him for cutting a knot or contaminating the light handle as long as Rui or Dr. Harrington are monitoring him. But pushing on with the catheterization when he should have stopped and requested Rui's help? That was over the line.

"What did you say to Sandra?" Gene asked.

"I told her she probably saved your admission to medical school."

"That wasn't like me," Gene said,

But maybe it was.

With the pool clean, Gene backwashes the filter and checks the water's pH and chlorine level. A little later he opens the irrigation valve. Apollo romps in the gushing water until Gene remembers the dog's wound. "Apollo! Out of there." Apollo bounds the length of the grove. "Now!"

Apollo finally submits and follows him to the lounge chair. Gene removes the dressing-sleeve and uses the towel to wipe Apollo's hind leg. From what he can see the stitches are holding. "We'll leave these in another few days. Better safe than sorry, huh?"

While waiting for his irrigation run to end, Gene lifts Apollo and walks into the grove. Compared to other trees in the neighborhood, the fruit on his are large. Even now, they approach the size of handballs. A sad thought comes to him. If his mother sells the house, he loses these trees. For years, they've been his responsibility. How could he trust anyone else with them?

He looks at his watch, then down to Apollo. "Come on in while I make a call."

When Sandra answers, he throws out the pithy opening he'd planned — How do you know an elephant has catheterized your bladder? — and just says, "Sandra. It's Gene."

"Why were you in such a pissy mood today? And don't tell me you were tired."

Damn, that was exactly what he was going to say. "Boz and I got into an argument before the case."

"About what?"

"You know how he is. Mining for a scandal."

"About us I suppose."

"He thinks we've gone out together."

"You mean that I fucked you."

"No. Not exactly."

"What exactly?"

"Nothing really."

"Nothing or something, you don't take it into the Heart Room. That's how patients get hurt."

Gene's eyes roam the kitchen, landing on the refrigerator where Patty's photo used to be. "He knew about your fiancé."

"That's all?"

"He says I shouldn't try to save you."

Sandra's voice softens. "I see." Her breathing feels close. "Patrick is no secret. But you know what? Like I said last night…or kind of said…you are saving me. At least, a little."

"You saved me today. Thank you. That was brave."

"I can take the heat."

"Wish I was like that." Gene looks at his watch. He's late closing the irrigation valve. "I hope we're still on for the movie tomorrow."

"Let me sleep on it."

"I'll throw in the popcorn."

"Maybe."

"Please. There's something I need to ask you."

"What's that?"

"After the movie."

Chapter Twenty-Five

IN THE STILL OF THE NIGHT

SANDRA INSISTS on paying for her ticket to *Chinatown*, the late afternoon discount showing, as well as her meal at Los Compadres, although she allows him to buy a round of margaritas.

At Gene's house, Apollo greets them at the back door, contorting his body in frantic tail wagging.

"Aren't you cute," Sandra says. She kneels, pats the tube dressing and looks up to Gene. "You make this?"

He nods.

"Nice work." She spins Apollo around and pulls the dressing back. "Operating without a license, I see. How long have these been in?"

"Almost two weeks."

She stands. "I'd get them out."

"He's so active, though."

"It's hard to see through his hair, but it looks like he's healing fine."

"Yes, nurse."

He apologizes for the state of the kitchen. The texts and dictionary are open, stacked atop one another next to the heart model. The grapefruit are dry and shriveled, looking like shrunken heads from Borneo. And the ladder-back chairs have been taken over by vines of knotted suture.

Sandra takes a moment to survey the mayhem and says, "I like what you've done with the place, Dr. Frankenstein."

Gene opens the refrigerator and offers her a beer.

"Just water for now."

She steps over to the refrigerator and examines the menagerie of photos, postcards, and advertising magnets on the door. The old OR schedule with her handwritten address is front and center. Suzanne's face peeks out from behind. "So, what's this question you need to ask me?"

"It can wait." It can't, but her answer might spoil the evening.

"Big surprise, huh?" She lifts the schedule to fully reveal the photo of his father clowning around with Suzanne.

Sandra pinches her lips.

"Hey." Gene puts his arm around her.

"I thought coming over here might be tough."

He presses gently at her waist. "Come out back. I'll show you the trap."

Apollo follows them out to the grove. The trees' long shadows stretch to the pool's deck. Between the recent rain and yesterday's irrigation, a few small water puddles remain. "Here it is," he says, resting his foot on the brick border.

Sandra kneels and touches the trapdoor. "This is something, Gene. It's bigger than I thought."

"I'm going after big game now."

She flips her hair behind her ear and looks up to him. "Quite the invention. How does it work?"

"Like any other trap." He kneels beside her. "Instead of having a mechanical means of tripping the door closed, mine uses an infrared beam. Here's the transmitter, and here's the receiver. When the beam's interrupted, a relay is tripped, which releases the spring, which pulls back this pin, which allows the door to fall."

"How's this better than a regular trap."

"To be honest, it's not. It was just a class project. But it works, at least when I haven't screwed up. Ask Apollo."

Apollo rests his front paws on Sandra's bare knees. She places her hand under his chin and brings her face close to his. "Poor boy. You should live with me. It's safer."

Gene unplugs the nine-volt battery. "Power source."

"I see."

"I'll be right back." Gene runs inside and returns with a small Baggie of ground beef and a fresh battery. He changes the battery every couple of days now to be sure. Carrying the trap and bait, he dodges the few remaining pools of water to the far corner, near the fence, where Apollo had his most recent encounter. Sandra and Apollo follow. Gene places a dollop of raw meat in the trap.

"So that's what's been attracting me," Sandra says.

Gene smiles, endeared more and more by her sense of humor. He reconnects the battery and sets the pin in the door. "We'll check it in the morning."

"Oh, will we?"

GENE GIVES Sandra a tour of the house. With Apollo zigzagging along, they walk through the living room, the family room, and his father's study. He turns on the bedroom light to the master bedroom. She sticks her head in, says, "Just as I remember," and turns off the light before retreating back through the study to the family room. She starts up the stairs and Gene follows.

"You seem to know your way around here," he says.

"Your dad gave me the tour years ago at a Christmas party." She stops before reaching the landing and points back over Gene, two treads below her. "That's where I met you. You were lying right there on that couch watching television. You said *hi*, but you never looked up. I thought, nice manners."

"I've matured."

She walks down the upstairs' hall and through the open door on the left. "Master Gene's lair, if I'm not mistaken."

Apollo jumps onto the bed and settles in. She pats his head and then, while looking around the room, runs her hand along the forest-green corduroy bedspread Gene's had since grade school.

"You really don't have anything on your walls."

"Suggestions?"

"Hmm." She walks to a rolled poster in the corner. "I'll have to get to know you a little better." She unfurls the poster. "I remember this."

"Juan Marichal?" he says.

"Your dad said he was your hero. That you wanted to be the next Juan Marichal." She points to a light spot on the wall where, until this morning, the poster had hung. "It was right there."

"I was a kid."

"I told him I thought you'd be a doctor. Doctors' kids are always growing up to be doctors."

Gene laughs. "What'd he say to that?"

Sandra starts to say something, but then looks past Gene to the window. "Is it still out there? That cute little deck you built?" She leans across the desk, drawing her forehead as close to the window as she can. The sun has long set.

"You know about it?"

"Carl made a point to show me. He was very proud of your work. Said you could build anything." She squints and peers out again.

He turns off the room lights. "That should help."

"Oh my." She laughs. "It is out there. You listened to baseball games or something."

"The Giants."

"Aren't you the all-American boy."

"Hardly."

She puts a knee on the desk and hoists herself up. "I'm not waiting for an invitation." She cranks the window open and crawls out.

Gene follows.

"Look at this view," she says. "Those lights? What's that?"

"Ballfields at the grade school."

"And what's this?"

"A chin-up bar."

She looks around. "You could sleep out here."

"Yeah. There's an amazing view of the stars."

"It's been christened I assume?" She kneels and runs her fingertips over the plywood. "Gritty."

"Sand in the varnish," he says. "So I don't slide off into the pool." He gestures with a swooping motion of his hand.

"You didn't answer my question."

"No. It's not been christened."

She looks at him and smiles. "A lie so kind, it feels true."

"Honest."

"You and Patty didn't do it like bunnies up here on prom night? I know why you built this."

Gene stands. "Don't be so sure."

"Hey, don't get bent. I approve. God, in high school though, I was such a prude."

"Really. Is that so." It's not the impression Boz has.

Sandra stands. She takes Gene's waist and presses up against him. "What's with you? Sorry if I hit a nerve, but don't try to be mean. It's not you."

She looks left and right.

"I'm a little disappointed," she says.

"Look, I didn't mean anything by it. It's been a tough week."

She puts a finger to his lips. "Relax. I'm disappointed I don't see any sleeping bags out here."

She's always a step ahead.

"Go. Go," she says. "I'll wait."

Downstairs, Gene collects the blue ice-chest and fills it with Michelob. While Apollo dances around him, Gene adds ice. He tosses a cube to the dog. "Nice catch." Apollo crunches away in the kitchen as Gene opens the back door, flips on the light to the pool, and checks the big outdoor thermometer on the wall. He runs back upstairs with the ice chest and passes it through the open window, then retrieves the sleeping bags from his closet and chucks them onto the roof.

Sandra's clothes hang from the eaves. In only her bra and

panties, her naked back faces him as she sits on the deck, knees pulled to her chest, looking out over the neighborhood roofs and citrus trees. "The pool looks great. You ever leap in from here."

"And lose my roof privileges?"

"Want to try it?"

"It's almost nine feet to the edge."

"You'd probably make it."

"Probably!"

"What if I was down there drowning, and you had to save me?"

Gene loses his smile. "Why'd you say that?"

Sandra looks surprised. "Sorry. I mean you're always coming to the rescue."

Gene kneels and starts to untie the sleeping bag. "I'd take the stairs."

Sandra helps Gene lay the sleeping bag out and sits back down. "Aren't you a little warm." She tugs at his pants.

It's almost ten. The ballfield lights will be going off soon. He removes his clothes except for the boxers and sits next to her. He hands her a beer. "This is a switch," he says. "Clothes off first, then the beer."

She clinks her bottle against his. They scan the stars and listen to the night. A loud cheer explodes from the ballfield. "Somebody scored," Gene says. Simultaneously they look at each other and smile. "Don't say it," he says. Several minutes later, the lights go out.

"This is nice," Sandra says.

"Lay back and close your eyes."

"I know where this is going."

"You don't. Trust me." She shimmies to a comfortable position. "It might be better if you take your bra off."

"Oh, you are smooth." She complies and lies back down. He lies next to her.

"Now try to feel the air against your skin."

He gives her a minute. "Do you feel it?"

"I don't feel anything."

"Precisely. It's ninety-nine degrees out here. I checked. Essentially body temperature. And with practically no humidity tonight, it feels like the air passes right through you. It's like being invisible."

"Wait. I do feel something…sweat. Running down my chest."

He rolls over and with his finger, dries the valley between her breasts. "There."

"I have heard of and been the subject of many attempted ploys, and this, my young man, is the most original."

"I'm serious."

She reaches over and runs her palm over the front of his boxers. "I see that." Then she kisses him.

After the sex, Sandra rises. "I'll be right back."

Gene drinks a second beer, remembering when Patty said about the same thing the day they met. His mind tallies the similarities between Sandra and Patty. They both could be funny at surprising times. They both surprised him with their exuberance. They appreciate art and music. And they both liked to linger. Patty demurely under cover, her modesty returning in the afterglow, whereas Sandra seems to feel most at ease with her clothes off. Her body isn't perfect, but Gene guesses she's seen enough of the naked human race to know she is miles ahead of most of womankind. He is no Atlas, as much as he wants to be. The sex is great, as great as it was with Patty. Perhaps better because of Sandra's…experience. That, he tries not to think about. And still, he feels empty. Maybe not empty, but at least not full of what Patty once gave him — a future. But why no future with Sandra? Why couldn't that change?

Sandra comes back and sits by him. She hugs his arm.

"I thought you'd skipped out on me," he says.

"I took a stroll."

"I'm sure the neighbors loved that." He hands her another beer.

"No, I wandered your house. It's strange."

"How so?"

"To think how much has changed." She clinks his beer with hers. "To better days."

"For you as well."

They sit in silence until she inhales deeply and says, "I see what you mean now." She holds her arms out. "The air does seem to pass through you. Makes you feel invisible. Kind of invulnerable." She drops her head.

"You okay?"

"I was thinking how nice this has been…not just tonight…but meeting you. But have you thought of something? I wouldn't be here if your father hadn't died."

Gene stares out to the once-lit ballfield across from Patty's house and back to the night of the memorial service, when he escaped to the safety of Patty's blanket after the argument with his mother, back to the classes he missed, the poor grades, and Patty's call for help…Gene, I'm pregnant. If not for his father's death, he would have saved Patty, would have dropped everything at SLO and sped to Tucson. He's almost sure.

"I pitched a game in high school where I completely fell apart. Two strikeouts to start the inning. Then on the third batter, I threw a 3-2 pitch for a perfect strike. A curve ball that started outside and swept in to catch the outside of the plate. Our catcher pumped his fist, and I was headed off the mound. But the shitty ump called it a ball. I walked the next batter. The one after hit an infield dribbler to load the bases. All I could think about was how the ump had screwed me. How close I was to a one, two, three inning. Then their light-hitting shortstop laced a triple down the line. Three runs scored, and I was pulled from the game.

"My dad knew what happened. He knew the bad call knocked me off course. The ump's call was out of my control, and I let it fester and affect my concentration for the rest of the inning. He said I was lucky to get this lesson in a meaningless baseball game. That stung. It didn't seem so meaningless to me. He said someday you'll be dealt a bad call, and not in a baseball game, and that all you can do is reset. Recognize the new situation, accept it, and set a new course. It's the hardest thing."

She leans her head to his shoulder and squeezes his arm. "I hope you know, I'd easily trade this night, this summer, to have your father back."

"Me, too."

When they finish their beers, Gene opens the cooler's lid.

"Okay. Enough stalling," she says. What's the big question you want to ask me?"

He deposits the empties and sits back down.

"I need you to be honest."

She shifts her eyes and frowns. "Sounds serious."

"It's something Boz told me."

"I knew you were hiding something."

Gene tries to steady his voice, "He said you had a fling… with a doctor."

She pulls her knees to her chest, looks up to the sky. "Christ."

Well, here it is.

"Does it matter to you if I did?"

"It changes things."

"And how's that? Because I've had sex with others than with you?"

It's not rational, but that does hurt a little. "No. It makes me feel used."

"Used? So, you think I'm a prick tease."

"No!" He touches her arm, and she pulls it away.

"If anyone's being used, it's me," she says. "Get your ya-ya's off first tonight and then ask me the question that could change things."

Gene shakes his head. "I was afraid to ask you."

"You were selfish."

"Maybe so, but still, I was afraid. I needed to know, but I didn't want to know. I like this." He gestures back and forth between them.

"You like the sex." She looks left and right. "Where's my underwear."

"Yes. I like the sex. But I also like you."

"Name one thing."

It's a question he could easily answer with Patty. And it surprises him a little, how easy it is to answer Sandra. "I've already told you."

Sandra's eyes narrow.

"Your toughness. Your courage."

Sandra's eyes relax and sparkle in the still, quiet night.

"Your kindness."

As she reaches for his hand, a low growl cracks the evening.

They freeze and then turn toward the orange grove. Sandra looks back to Gene. He puts his finger to his lips.

Another sound crescendos — the wail of a cat. A big cat.

"Get dressed."

Apollo greets them with an aggressive bark until he recognizes the two humans stepping through the window. In the kitchen, Gene grabs a flashlight. He hustles to the backyard, Sandra braless under her blouse and Gene shirtless in his cutoffs and flip-flops. Apollo bolts for the trees. Gene starts to call him back but recognizes the futility. After a moment, Apollo's barking turns to crazed attack sounds mixed with feline hissing. As Gene approaches, the caged animal snarls and shrinks away from the light. The shape of the head and the pinned back ears. He was right. It's a bobcat.

"Look at the size of that," Gene says. "Apollo. Stop." He picks up the dog, runs him back inside, and then returns. Without Apollo, the big cat has settled down, looking frightened and wary. Sandra is kneeling, holding a finger against the cage, encouraging the animal to sniff her. Gene quickly pulls her hand back. "Watch it!"

"It's okay."

"Do you know what that is?"

"A Maine Coon."

"A raccoon?"

"Maine Coon. A breed of cat. I had one growing up." She sticks her finger through the bars and makes soft clicking sounds with her tongue. "It's okay. I won't hurt you." The cat hisses, sniffs, and then hisses again.

"Are you sure? It looks like a young bobcat."

She looks up at Gene as if he's sweetly demented and then turns back to the cat. "They all have that feral look. You're a big boy, aren't you?"

"It's a male?"

"Just a guess." She stands. "Now what?"

Gene folds his arms. "He goes on trial for attempted murder."

Sandra kneels down again for an instant. "I don't see a tag."

"I'll take it to the pound in the morning."

"On a Sunday?"

"I can't take it inside with Apollo. And I can't leave it out here. It'll fry."

"I'll take it home. We'll check the papers. You look for posts in the neighborhood. If nothing comes up, maybe I'll keep him."

Gene lifts the trap. "Jeez, he must weigh thirty pounds." The cat crouches and hisses. "You sure about this?"

"No more dangerous than working with Boz."

That's right. Gene never got an answer. Sandra with Rui? Boz is a jerk, but he wouldn't invent that rumor. Spread it, sure. And he certainly opened some kind of wound in Rui that morning in the doctor's lounge.

Sandra stands. "There, there, there," she says to the cat while rubbing a finger along the bridge of its nose. It turns on its side and purrs. Her universal kindness and concern squeezes Gene's heart. Rui is unabashedly devoted to Alicia. He's just the kind of person Sandra would protect if they'd made a one-time drunken mistake. Someone a little like Gene.

"Before you go," Gene says. He lowers the trap to the ground. "I need to know."

"Gene —"

"Did you have an affair with Rui?"

Sandra places her palm against Gene's cheek. In the low light shining from the far-off patio, she gazes from one eye to the other. There's practically a relieved look on her face "No, Gene. I… did…not."

"I had to ask."

Her answer was what he expected. A lie so kind, it feels true. Perhaps Rui's invitation for burgers, beer, and baseball is still open.

Chapter Twenty-Six

TEAMMATES

WEARING a multi-colored bikini and extending her arms, Alicia Pereira opens her front door "Gene," she says. "About time you came over." Gene stoops and accepts her exuberant hug. Her lacy cream-colored wrap falls from her shoulders. Still the physique from her days as a UCLA gymnast. "Look at you," she says, retrieving the wrap. "Did you bring a swimsuit?"

He looks down at his cutoffs. "Just these."

"Matters not."

God, he hopes Boz's rumor is false. Somehow, he'll ask Rui tonight. Gene steps inside the remodeled foyer. "Wow. This turned out great."

Rui and Alicia live in a rambling ranch-style home off the bridal path that parallels Central Avenue. Last January, before heading back to Cal Poly, he called and thanked her for spending the night with his mom. He should have stopped by earlier this summer. But before now, they were Dr. Pereira and Mrs. Pereira, part of his parents' generation, and no one he knew just dropped in on their parents' friends. Not that he dropped in on anyone from high school. No time, but also no one he particularly wanted to see.

Gene follows Alicia past the living room. "We just finished the kitchen. Bathrooms are next." She points out the large island and a restaurant-style gas cooktop. From the kitchen, rustic double doors open to the patio. Through the glass panes Gene spies Rui, holding barbecue tongs, stacking coals in a grill. He wears plaid swim trunks and a short-sleeved white-collared shirt. When the door hinges squeak, Rui turns.

"Excellent," Rui says. "You made it. Dr. Harrington must have skated through rounds today."

"Smells good out here." The smell of lighter fluid and flaming charcoal brings back summer. No particular moment. Just peaceful feelings.

"Wait until Alicia's burgers are releasing their flavors to the air." Rui makes that kissing motion with his fingers.

Gene associates the gesture with someone from France, not Portugal.

"Grab a beer." Rui nods toward a red cooler resting on a rolling table pushed back against the slump-block wall. "We shall eat outside." Rui stirs the coals, sending sparks into the superheated air.

Under the shade of the overhang, Gene takes a seat at one of the three places set at the glass patio table. A lazy Susan with condiments rests in the center.

Alicia hands Rui a tray of burgers. Rui balances the tray on one hand and closes the barbecue with the other. "Not quite ready." He sets the tray on the table.

On the small TV mounted on a shelf in the corner, Joe Garagiola is interviewing Sparky Anderson in the dugout prior to the start of the All-Star Game. "Best manager in baseball," Rui says. He slides a chair next to Gene and looks up at the TV. "Did you read what Sparky's father once told him?"

"No."

"He said, 'Remember, just because you make a lot of money, doesn't mean you can't be nice.' More baseball players should remember that. More doctors, too. A wise admonition for us all." He takes a swig of beer. "How is our patient?"

For the last two days, Gene has meant to ask Dr. Harrington

about the case he mangled. "I don't know. I haven't seen him back on the schedule yet."

"I understand the man is healing from your misadventure, but I was speaking of Apollo."

"Shoot, I need to get his stitches out."

"How many days?"

"About two weeks."

"That's plenty of time."

On the TV, the American League players run from the dugout and stand along the third base line. "You are rooting for the National League, no doubt," Rui says.

"*Sim*," Gene says.

"Then I will take the American League even though my Reds dominate the National's roster. What shall we bet?"

Gene points to his beer.

"Ah, a fine choice." Rui runs his fingers across the wording on his bottle — *Super Bock*. "Six-pack shall we say?"

Alicia opens the door a crack. "Rui, dear." She motions to the burgers sitting on the table. You're going to have to move those a little closer to the coals. The beans are almost ready."

In the bottom of the eighth inning, Rollie Fingers walks Mike Schmidt. Don Kessinger then rips a triple scoring Schmidt, giving the National League a 6-2 lead. Rui, Alicia, and Gene have pulled their chairs around to one side of the table. Alicia is in on the bet, and when Schmidt scores Alicia cheers. She high-fives Gene and bends over laughing. After burgers, beans, two kinds of salads, a cooler full of beer, and a baseball contest between the best players in the world played out on a gloriously warm Phoenix night, Gene is floating with a congenial buzz. He thinks back to three nights ago, lying with Sandra on the roof. Thinks of a couple days before that when she took the hit for him after he caused the cancellation of a case. And last night on her patio. Her beer was only half empty when she said something that makes Gene smile now: "To the roof?" she asked. He knew immediately what she meant. They now shared a code. The sex that followed, for the first time, felt close to love.

Alicia rises and pulls another beer from the cooler.

Rui gestures toward her. "*Por favor.*"

"Gene?" she asks.

"*Gracias,*" he says.

"We say *obrigado*," she says, smiling. "But never mind."

"*Obrigado*, then," he says, "but, can I use your bathroom first?"

"Of course," she says. "You know where it is. Down the hall on your right. Wait. It's torn up. There's no sink. Use ours. Just keep on going. You'll find it."

On his way down the darkened hallway, Gene turns on lights. On his way back, he clicks them off, but pauses at what must be Rui's study. He's never been in here. The room is dark but for a soft glow from the low-wattage lamp on the desk in the center of the room. Gene walks in. The room feels heavy and smells of leather and oiled hardwood. Floor to ceiling bookshelves cover two walls. The shelves are filled with medical books, novels, and baseball history. Interspersed are small kachina dolls, woven baskets, and photographs. There are pictures of Rui from long ago looking no different, except for his ink black hair. A couple photos include Gene's father, one from what looks like their days as residents.

"Look how young they are." Alicia's voice startles Gene, and he turns.

"Sorry. I didn't mean to sneak up on you." She steps forward, close enough for Gene to smell the beer on her breath. "I didn't know Rui…or your father then." She runs her finger slowly across the top of the wood frame. "Those faces…so, so confident."

She picks up another framed photo. Taken at one of the Christmas parties. Gene recognizes his living room from the painting in the background. Sandra's standing between Rui and Gene's father. Her hair is permed into curls. Her arms are around each man's waist. She has that two-drink smile. Her eyes sparkle. She looks young but was probably about Gene's age then.

"They were quite the trio. Always having so much fun it seemed in the Heart Room." She looks up to Gene. "You've gotten a little taste of that, I guess. It's not all blood and guts. It's like a family." She puts the photo back on the shelf. "I'll be honest. I'm a little jealous." She releases the tiniest belch. "Excuse me."

"Like a baseball team."

"You might hear rumors, Gene. Don't believe them. Small people make themselves look big by spreading rumors."

Is she talking about Rui and Sandra? "I haven't heard anything."

"Good."

Alicia turns and leans against the built-in counter below a wall of shelves. "Tell me something." She looks to the door, and then swings it mostly closed. She hugs herself. "Does Rui seem okay at work?"

He nods.

"Is he happy?"

"He's always telling jokes."

"I told him, I think everyone told him, there was nothing he could have done for your dad. You understand that, don't you Gene?"

"Of course."

"Deep down, Rui's afraid you or your mother blame him. You don't, do you?"

"No. Absolutely not." She steps forward and grasps Gene's hand. Squeezes it. "He won't admit it but hearing that from you would mean the world to him. I mean if you ever have the chance."

"Sure." Although he told him some weeks ago.

She releases his hand and turns to the photo once more. She takes it from the shelf and turns back, looking from the photo to Gene and back again. "You have his eyes, you know."

"I hear that a lot."

She looks at the framed photo once more and sets it on the shelf behind her.

"Honest," he says. "Rui seems fine."

"He saw someone a few times. But even now, some nights he can't sleep. He has dreams. Dreams? Nightmares. Sometimes he stays up late, or gets up at night, and I'll find an extra bottle or two…or three…of that Super Bock in the trash.

"I'm sure he'll be fine."

"I couldn't have done what he did."

"He said it was his worst day."

She looks up to the ceiling. "God forbid. If the tables had been turned, Carl would have stayed strong." She looks back to Gene. "Don't get me wrong. Not that Rui isn't strong in his own way, but he can't put it behind him."

"Nobody blames him. I'll tell him."

She pats Gene's thigh. "Thanks. I just wish he could get your father's last words out of his head. I mean that tortures him more than having to open Carl's chest right there in the emergency room."

Suddenly, Gene feels faint. He steps to the side and sits on the leather ottoman.

Alicia reaches for him. "I'm sorry. I'm sorry. I shouldn't have said that." She places her hand on his forehead.

Gene closes his eyes and tries to slow his breathing. "Bathroom," he says.

She grabs his elbow and hustles him to the toilet, where he falls to his knees. He hears her move away for a few seconds and then feels the coolness of a washcloth on the back of his neck.

"What happened?" It's Rui's voice.

Gene vomits into the toilet. Rui crouches beside him. A hand on Gene's lower back.

"That Portuguese beer," she says.

Gene heaves again.

"Straight to the brain, I am afraid," Rui says.

"You stay with him."

"Where are you going."

"To cover up dessert."

After a minute or two with Rui's hand patting Gene's upper back, and Rui's lightly accented voice offering reassurance, the nausea subsides, and Gene's breathing slows. "I'm better."

"Come, sit over here."

Rui flushes the toilet and guides Gene to the bathtub ledge. He moves a large vase of artificial flowers and sits next to him.

"I didn't think you had that much beer."

"I didn't."

Rui soaks the washcloth, wrings it out in the sink, and then hands it to Gene as he sits down.

"Thanks," Gene says. He wipes his mouth, neck and hands.

Rui looks down at the dripping washcloth. "Here." He takes it from Gene and shoots it, basketball style, into the sink.

Gene leans forward, elbows on knees.

"Even in this light your color is better," Rui says.

Gene looks over. "Remember that first day when I fainted in the Heart Room."

"Ah, yes. You have come a long way."

"I thought maybe I wasn't doctor material."

"Because you fainted?"

"I can't imagine my father was ever that way. Was he?"

"I did not meet Carl until we were both residents." Rui studies Gene. "Why?"

"I used to think we were close. But now I'm not so sure. He never talked about his cases. I didn't really know what he did in the Heart Room until I watched Boz."

Rui pats Gene's knee.

"Ah, well, that is Carl for you."

"I suppose."

Rui screws up his mouth. "I always told him, 'Carlton, you are not one to tip your pitches.'"

Gene smiles at the analogy.

"Steady as a rock, Carl. Even keel."

Gene could just as well be sitting here in near darkness with his father, content within the physical closeness, feeling no need to fish for words, but allowing them to rise to the surface. He shifts his weight on the tub's edge. The sconces over the double sinks are dimmed to an evening glow.

"I feel horrible," Gene says.

"Do you need the toilet?"

"Not that. About lying about the bleeding I caused."

"You did not lie."

"I didn't tell the truth."

"No. But you are still in Dr. Harrington's good graces."

"Because of Sandra."

Rui nods. "Yes. She is special."

"And because of you and Boz, Betty and Roger. Even Irene. None of you told him."

"We are teammates are we not?"

The pipes hiss, signaling that Alicia is probably still in the kitchen. "I have to say something," Gene says.

"What is done is done."

"No. Something else. I'm seeing Sandra. Dating her."

"Ah."

"Did you know? Is that why you got so upset with Boz in the doctor's lounge?"

"His nose does not belong in your matters."

"And yours?" Gene swallows hard.

Rui squints.

"Boz said you and Sandra —"

"It is only a rumor. One I have heard before."

"And Alicia?"

"Yes."

Gene stares and waits.

"And completely false. On that you will have to trust me. I say this on your father's soul."

Gene closes his eyes and exhales. "Thank you."

"I must ask. Are you sure about Sandra?"

"What do you mean?"

"I do not want to see either of you hurt."

"I understand."

"You can confide to me. Anytime."

That was something his father never said, but that was always understood. If only Gene had taken advantage when it mattered most.

"Shall we join Alicia for dessert?"

"There is one more thing."

"Si."

"My father once told me he would have made a good pilot."

"Indeed."

Gene nods. "I came away feeling that he'd wanted to be a pilot his whole life. My mother said he became obsessed with the idea after the little girl died.

"He talked about it at times."

"Really?"

"About being a pilot."

"See, I never knew except for that one conversation. He said that being an anesthesiologist was a lot like being a pilot. You have a takeoff, you cruise for a while, and then you land. It was the most he'd ever talked to me about what he did. After he died, when I was driving home, I kept thinking about something else he'd said: 'When a pilot crashes, he goes down with the plane. When a patient crashes, I survive.' I thought he meant that was a good thing."

Rui is silent. Looking down at the floor.

"Now, I'm not so sure," Gene says.

He gives Rui a steady look. "It must be hard," Gene says, "even when you've done your best."

Rui drops his forehead to his hands. His elbows rest on his knees and his shoulders shake.

"Rui, you did what you could. No one blames you."

Rui turns his head. It's a face Gene doesn't recognize. The anguish is unbearable, and Gene wraps an arm around Rui's shoulders. Under the linen shirt, the muscles of his father's closest friend ripple beneath Gene's touch. Rui takes a few shuddering breaths.

"My mom, Suzanne, we all know there was nothing you could do."

Rui's face contorts. He shakes his head. "I failed him."

He crumbles against Gene and pounds the edge of the tub with his fist. The thudding reverberates through the marrow of Gene's bones. Gene wishes Alicia would return. Rui's grief is more than mourning. It's killing him.

Rui straightens, turns away, and wipes his face with open palms.

Gene rinses the washcloth from the sink and hands it to him.

Rui wipes his face and neck. "I need to move." He sits on the cream carpet and rests against the tub, his long legs bent at the knees.

Gene squats down like a catcher. "You didn't fail him."

Rui tosses the washcloth over his shoulder into the tub. He stretches one leg out. "We were on bypass when we heard a survivor from an Air Rescue crash was coming over. I knew Carl was on the flight. I scrubbed out and met the ambulance in the trauma room. It was a mad scramble. Carl looked right at me. He begged, 'Don't let me die. Don't let me die'."

Rui swallows hard. Gene moves closer, sits and rests a hand on Rui's knee. "It's okay."

Rui looks down and fingers the carpet pile. "Then Carl's eyes rolled back, and his heart stopped. I started chest compressions, but we could not feel a pulse. He was dying. I had to open his chest. As I suspected, his aorta was dissecting. I tried to keep him alive by pumping his heart, but we couldn't keep up with the bleeding. What was I supposed to do? He needed to be on bypass. The Heart Room was busy, and our backup heart-lung machine wasn't primed and ready."

Rui's voice squeaks. "Gene, he needed the Heart Team, and all he got was me."

Gene smears tears from his own cheeks.

Rui stares at his trembling palm. "Then I felt something. A warmth. It left his heart and moved up my arm." Rui's lips quiver. "It was like his soul…the warmth of his soul…moved through me. And was gone. Just gone." His voice cracks again. "I've never felt so alone."

Rui pulls his knees to his chest and sobs. "I tried. I tried." Gene's about to drape himself over Rui, when Alicia opens the door and rushes to her husband. She pulls Rui's face to her chest and kisses the crown of his head. Tears flood her cheeks. She mouths a pained *thank you* to Gene.

Gene squeezes Rui's shoulder. "You didn't fail him."

In his own way, Gene understands Rui's tortured, helpless feeling. The day the little girl died, he, too, felt helpless. And useless. He wanted so badly to help his father, but what was a little kid supposed to do? What was Rui supposed to do without a bypass machine, without the rest of the Heart Team? Out in the desert, on the edge of the freeway, Gene's father had even less support. No equipment. No nurses. Despite his brave face, he must have felt helpless, even useless. He must have.

Harder this time, as if giving him an order, Gene squeezes Rui's shoulder. "Rui, you are not alone."

Without looking up, Rui pats his hand. Then Gene retraces his steps, past the office, past the kitchen where a cherry cobbler remains uncovered, and exits through the front door.

Chapter Twenty-Seven

DAZED AND CONFUSED

Dr. Harrington and Gene come upon Mr. Mead shuffling down the fourth-floor hallway. He's been out of the ICU almost a week. Two nurses support his heavy arms and another aide trails with an oxygen tank and IV stand. That's what I could use, Gene thinks, oxygen and someone to lean on. He didn't sleep well last night. He had a dream that he was in the Heart Room and Rui had his hand in the patient's chest, squeezing the heart, and Gene's father was where Boz usually stands, telling Rui to squeeze harder, squeeze faster, and it doesn't make sense, now that Gene's awake, but in his dream he knew it was his father's heart, and Gene was trying to tell everyone to just go on bypass, but for some reason they weren't thinking of that, and he couldn't get the words out until finally he blurted "on bypass." But he actually said those words and it woke him.

Mr. Mead stops. He is breathing heavily, but smiles. "Bet you're looking for me."

"Indeed," Dr. Harrington says. "Perhaps you young ladies can guide my friend to his room."

"My wife calls them my harem."

"I'll return in a moment."

With Gene trailing, Dr. Harrington rounds on his other patients and then returns to Mr. Mead's room. When they enter, his wife closes her book. Mr. Mead is in bed, dozing.

"How's he look today," Dr. Harrington asks.

"Like a different man," Mrs. Mead says. "Henry, the doctor's here."

Mr. Mead's eyes open and his good eye darts about. When it lands on his wife, she hands him a cup of water. "Henry, tell Dr. Harrington how well you're doing."

Mr. Mead sips through a straw. "Not breaking any speed barriers yet."

"Day at a time," his wife says.

"Tell me one thing," Mr. Mead says and then clears his throat. "Will I be able to play the piano when I get out of here?"

Gene has heard this ancient joke at least twice this summer, and each time Dr. Harrington goes along with it.

"I see no reason why not."

Mr. Mead looks at his wife — a questioning look — then back to Dr. Harrington. "That's funny, I couldn't play the piano before surgery."

"Oh, Henry," Mrs. Mead says. "Doctor, is there anything you can do for his tired old jokes?"

"Who you calling a tired old joke?"

"See?" she says.

Dr. Harrington smiles through the whole exchange and comes around to one side of the bed. He listens to Mr. Mead's chest and abdomen and then pulls back the single layer dressing over Mr. Mead's incision site. "Eugene," Dr. Harrington says. "Fine work."

Gene steps around to the other side, close to where Mrs. Mead sits. A little rough, really. It was the first time Gene closed the skin. Dr. Harrington is just planting the idea that this is normal.

"Another couple days and we'll take these out."

"So, this is your handiwork, young man," Mr. Mead says. "Wish I'd talked with you ahead of time. I'd preferred a zipper. Take a look, dear."

Mrs. Mead settles back in her chair. "It's lovely, dear. I needn't look again."

Dr. Harrington replaces the dressing and pulls Mr. Mead's gown back down. "Any questions?"

"Can I get a celery stick with my Bloody Mary?"

Mrs. Mead extends her hand. "Don't listen to him. Thank you, Doctor. I know you're busy."

Mr. Mead coughs and winces. "Ooh. I was going to ask. What'd you fellas leave in there? Someone drop their teeth in the soup?" He starts to laugh and winces again. "Feels like someone's taking a bite out of the back of my heart."

Dr. Harrington has Mr. Mead lean forward. He places his stethoscope to his back and says "Cough…and again. That feel the same?"

"Not so bad that time."

Dr. Harrington presses along Mr. Mead's ribs. No pain. Then he has Mr. Mead lean back and presses along each rib on both sides.

"That hurts where you buzz-sawed me, but that's different than that other thing," Mr. Mead says.

"Let's see how you are in the morning."

Mrs. Mead stands and extends her hand. It disappears between Dr. Harrington's enormously soft hands. "I'll leave you in charge," he says.

She blushes and shakes Gene's hand as Dr. Harrington turns for the door. "Thank you, doctor. You've been so kind. She holds his hand a second longer that Gene expects. "I have to tell you, you have the kindest eyes. They remind me so much of Henry's at your age."

"Watch it there, Doc. She's taken."

She continues to hold Gene's hand and looks at her husband. "Oh, hush now." Then she looks back to Gene. "Some young lady is going to fall in love with those eyes, if she already hasn't. You have your Chapstick ready?"

Gene pulls it from the pocket of his white coat.

Mr. Mead laughs and then cringes. "Look at that. I sleep for a few days, and my wife gives away my secret."

She waves off his comment. "Don't listen to him. Now scoot. You're busy."

AT THE NURSING STATION, Gene stands next to Dr. Harrington, who scribbles notes in his charts. He's not mentioned anything about the case he had to cancel last week. Nobody's spilled the beans.

"Dr. Harrington? The patient you canceled last week. Is he doing okay?

"Mmm?"

"The three-vessel cabbage who Dr. Frazier saw. The man who was bleeding. Is he okay?"

"Far as I know."

If Gene had Sandra's courage, he'd risk Dr. Harrington's recommendation and admit that he, not Sandra, caused the patient's urethra to bleed. It's what his father would do.

"Your concern is admirable," Dr. Harrington says." He closes Mr. Mead's chart, swivels toward Gene, and locks on with his bearish eyes.

"You're doing an exemplary job, Eugene. I'm certain that whoever reads my letter of recommendation will be suitably impressed with your performance so far. Although —"

A nurse clears her throat. "Dr. Harrington, I'm sorry to interrupt."

He gives a heavy sigh. "I suppose you are."

"You forgot to sign this order this morning and the tech is here now."

Without a word, he scrawls his name on the page.

"Thank you, sir."

Gene waits for the *although*. But he's already completed it in his head, and he feels sick: Although, since I learned of your irrational behavior in the Heart Room…

Dr. Harrington swivels back to Gene. "I was about say, with my recent appointment to the admission committee in Tucson, I suspect your acceptance there will be a mere formality."

He stands and claps Gene on the shoulder. "Let's just call the remainder of your time here, your interview."

Gene disguises the guilt in his smile. "Thank you."

"Anything else?"

"No, sir. Not at the moment."

THE FIRST CASE THURSDAY, an AVR and four-vessel CABG does not go well. The vein graft which Dr. Brinkerhoff harvested seems to leak at every tributary when Dr. Harrington repeats the pressure test with a syringe of saline. Brinkerhoff has scrubbed out by then, so Dr. Harrington's curses fall on everyone else's ears. Irene, as efficient as ever, still can't pass the instruments to him fast enough. Rui's hands or head is always in Dr. Harrington's way, and the patient's squatty, deep chest makes aiming the light difficult. That turns out to be Gene's fault. "Dammit Gene, the light is horrible, just horrible."

Gene feels the eyes of the room on him. It's the first time Harrington has yelled at him during a case. "Sorry," Gene says.

Dr. Harrington reaches for the light handle and adjusts the light himself. "Here is where we're operating. You understand."

"Yes, sir."

"Stop with sirs. Concentrate."

The bypass time runs longer than most, and when they allow the heart to start beating again, it looks as sluggish as Mr. Mead's had. Then pinhole arcs of blood leak in two places along the vein grafts, requiring Dr. Harrington to over-sew them with hair-thin suture. Twice the suture tears through, causing Dr. Harrington to fling the needle holder and suture to the floor. "Stitch. Stitch!" he says, shaking his open palm to Irene. She's already motioned to Sandra to open another needle holder. Sandra has trouble separating the edges of the packaging. "Today, Sandra," Dr. Harrington says.

The package tears through the middle instead of the seams, contaminating the instrument. "I'll get another," she says, running toward the door to center hall. "God Almighty," Dr. Harrington says.

BETWEEN CASES GENE escapes to the diner for a takeout lunch. In the doctor's lounge, as Rui and he power down a meal, Gene asks, "What's with him today?"

"Who can know?" Rui looks around the empty room and lowers his voice. "By the way, Alicia and I enjoyed your company the other night. Thank you again." He squeezes Gene's knee.

Gene can only nod.

Dr. Boz strides in from the dressing room. He sits and whips off the napkin covering his burger. "You're gonna love this, sports fans," he says. "We've got an add-on after the VSD."

"Do not kid us, please," Rui says.

Dr. Boz pretends to put a microphone to his mouth. "Mr. Mead. Come on down!"

"We saw him yesterday," Gene says. "He was fine."

"Turns out, he's been hiding something from you."

While holding up a finger for Gene to be patient, Boz takes a bite and chews with purpose. "Harrington thinks he's got a couple four-by-fours in his chest."

"The post-op film was clean, was it not?" Rui says.

"Yesseroo, but apparently someone fucked up when stocking the OR. A few packs without the radiopaque strip got mixed in. Looks like one pack may have been used on our bring-back. At least the ultrasound is suspicious."

"What about the count?" Gene asks.

"What count? We had a DEFCON 1 crash-and-dash going before you arrived. That's one reason for the post-op film. Check for anything that might have been left behind. These garden variety four-by-fours are easy to lose and invisible on x-ray."

"I TOLD YOU, you should have used a zipper," Mr. Mead says. He's awake on the OR table, the first time Gene has seen a patient more or less conscious in the Heart Room.

"I'll see what I can do this time around," Gene says.

Mr. Mead's eyes look around the room. Sandra and Irene are busy opening instruments. Dr. Boz has his back turned to Mr. Mead and is drawing up drugs in syringes and laying them out on his anesthesia cart.

"That gas-passer right behind me?"

"Dr. Boswell. Yes."

"It's like a meat locker in here. Must feel good to get outside after a day in the cooler."

"You need another blanket while we get things set up?"

"Nah. I'll be dreaming soon enough."

"This isn't going to take long. Overnight in the ICU and then back to your room."

"You fellas have some kind of loyalty card, like at the car wash? I must be getting close to my free look under the hood."

"I'll check on it."

Mr. Mead takes a deep breath. "The wife's worried, you know, but I told her this was going to be an open and shut case. Open me up. Wash me out. Shut the doors. Sounds pretty simple."

"Simple as it goes around here."

"She wants me to tell you to take good care of me. There. I told you."

"I'll do that."

"She's got a good feeling about people. She can see a winner, and she thinks you're a winner. I guess that makes two of us." He reaches his hand out. It trembles slightly. "Just a quick little nap, right?"

Gene takes the hand. "You're going to be fine." He doesn't let go until the Pentothal relaxes Mr. Mead's grip.

Irene hands the scalpel to Dr. Harrington. He slices down the center of Mr. Mead's chest. Rui, right behind, cauterizes the bleeders. No words have been exchanged between the team since Dr. Harrington entered the room. Only Mr. Mead's beeping pulse dares break the silence. This is, as Mr. Mead pointed out, literally going to be an open and shut case. No bypass. Still, Roger and his machine are standing by. Gene notices that twice Sandra checks the position of the pedal Dr. Harrington uses to control the air-powered saw. Not that they're going to need it for Mr. Mead — he's already been cut open — just that today, the slightest perturbation will set Dr. Harrington off. Gene can imagine the surgeon's embarrassment at having to explain to Mr. Mead and his wife that some gauze pads had been left in Mr. Mead's chest. Not the kind of mistake the most respected and feared surgeon at MVH ever makes.

Dr. Harrington holds his hand out, and Irene slaps the wire cutters in his palm. One by one, Dr Harrington clips the stainless loops. Gene is reaching for the sterile light handle to adjust the light's beam toward the bottom of the incision when the OR phone's blaring ring causes him to flinch. His hand grazes the non-sterile base. Gene tips his face to the ceiling and curses with a barely audible, "Shit."

"Betty," Irene says. "Seven-and-a-halves."

Gene steps back from the table and waits for Sandra to remove his gloves.

Sandra has her hand cupped around the phone's mouthpiece. After a mumbled exchange, she covers it.

"Dr. Harrington?"

Dr. Harrington clips the last two wires.

"Dr. Harrington?"

"I'm right here, Sandra."

"It's the Unit. They think the first patient's chest tube may be clogged."

Dr. Harrington sighs deeply, sucking all the oxygen from the room. "Eugene," he says, "Since you're contaminated anyway, go down and milk the goddamn tube. Those nurses couldn't milk a cow."

"Yes, sir." Gene rips off his gloves and gown, relieved to be separating himself from the tension in the room. When he steps toward the hamper with his gown, his foot catches on one of the cords snaking along the floor. Sandra lunges for his arm, and he regains his balance. "I'm okay," he whispers. She rolls her beautiful green eyes to the ceiling and takes the gown from him.

As Gene opens the door, he hears foot stomping and turns. "God, Almighty," Dr. Harrington shouts, "Pedal. Where's the goddamn pedal?"

Sandra slides to her knees and reaches around the OR table's pedestal to reposition the chest-saw pedal, but the cord is hung up behind her, and the pedal won't reach.

"Sandra you are single-handedly trying my patience today."

"Betty," Irene says, "Give her a hand, please."

Why was Dr. Harrington so hung up about the saw? Maybe just because everything in the OR had its place. Not the feeling pedal beneath his toe was throwing him off.

"Dr. Harrington," Gene says. "I think I —"

"Eugene, please don't think. Just get down to the Unit."

From her knees, Sandra looks at Gene and mouths, "Tell him."

"Dr. Harrington —"

"Eugene. Now!"

Gene shrugs, and using only his eyes, projects his best "I'm sorry" before opening the door. The sound of the last wire holding Mr. Mead's chest together follows Gene through the door.

In the ICU, two nurses crouch by the AVR-four-vessel CABG from this morning. The man is heavily sedated, his chest rising with each breath from the ventilator. The head nurse taps on the tubing with a Kelly clamp. "There's got to be a clot," she says.

"Let me try," Gene says.

He kneads and stretches the tubing like Dr. Harrington has shown him and then repeats it twice more. But nothing.

"I swear, there must be a kink up high," she says. "Under the tape or just under the skin."

Gene examines the bottle containing the drainage from the two tubes. Less than fifty mils. "Maybe he's just not bleeding."

"After heart surgery? That would be a first."

She peels the tape from the man's skin to reveal the suture holding the tube in place. After putting on some sterile gloves, the nurse examines the tube where it exits the patient's chest. She palpates the skin. "Ah. I thought so. Put some gloves on. Feel this."

Gene follows her lead, holds the tube, and pushes the skin back to reveal a kink.

"I'll get some scissors." She returns and cuts and removes the suture. Gene expects her to reposition the tube and find the kink, but she says, "Your patient, Doctor."

Gene pulls the tube back a centimeter or two. There's the kink!

She squeezes the tubing counter to the bend, and blood, along with a few clots, begins to flow. "That's more like it," she says. "I'll get a suture."

Dr. Harrington's mood is sure to improve when he learns Gene solved the problem. The nurse returns with some supplies. "I've got to check on a patient," she says. "Holler if you need anything."

He should admit he's never done this, but who else is going to secure it? Visualizing Rui's technique, he sutures the tube in place. He gives it a slight tug. Perfect.

As he's applying the new dressing the nurse returns. "OR just called. They should be down with Mr. Mead soon."

Gene reaches for another gauze pad.

"Hopefully, he won't be here long," she says.

"Just overnight," Gene says.

"His wife's a dear. Always at his bedside. Like a little pilot fish."

The nurse flattens the tape over the patient's chest where the tube exits.

"I'll be taking care of him tonight," she says. "I'm sure Mrs. Mead will sit by him until late. I never have the heart to kick her out when visiting hours are up."

Gene looks at the clock. He should report to Dr. Harrington. "Anything else?"

She doesn't seem to hear him as she throws away the wrappers and collects the tape and instruments. "It's a shame though that you had to open his chest again just to take out a blood clot. He's been through so much already."

"That's what they found?"

"I thought you came down from his case."

"I left just as they were opening."

She unfolds a piece of paper from her skirt's pocket. "That's what was scheduled."

Writing appended at the bottom of the OR schedule reads: Mead, Howard. Evacuation of pericardial hematoma.

The nurse looks past Gene. "Barb's waving at you."

Behind the glass at the far end of the ICU, the unit secretary holds a telephone receiver up and points to it. He walks over. "Sandra's on the line," she says.

"Hey, San. The schedule says —"

"Irene wants you to stay there. He'll be down soon."

"How'd it go?"

"He'll be down soon."

She hangs up.

When Boz arrives with the patient, he looks as pissed as Sandra sounded on the phone.

"Where's Sandra?" Gene asks.

"Heading home."

Boz gives his report, not mentioning anything about a hematoma or anything else about the surgical procedure, only that Mr. Mead is stable. He jots down the vital signs on his record, and leans over the bed to Mr. Mead, who's just starting to stir. "You did great, Hank."

Gene pulls Boz aside. "The schedule said evacuation of hematoma. What about the four-by-fours?"

"Four-by-fours or hematoma. What does it matter? It was a slam dunk case. Besides, we're a fucking family, right? And guess who's slicing the turkey."

Boz then rushes past Dr. Harrington, as the big man dictates at a desk, flipping him off behind his back.

Gene stops Betty, who, instead of Sandra, accompanied Mr. Mead.

"What happened?" Gene says.

"The man's a bastard," Betty says. "Sandra quit."

"Eugene," Dr. Harrington shouts.

"You better go." Betty says.

GENE STOPS for gas on the way home. He leans his back against the Saab as the pump dings through the gallons rolling on the dial. The heat of the door handle penetrates his thin shirt, causing him to shift away. Sandra quit? This had to be about the foot-pedal hose he tripped over on the way out of the OR. He wishes now that he'd been more forceful. If he'd just shouted, *Dr. Harrington, it's my fault.* Sorry. Taken the heat instead of Sandra. But he didn't. Harrington didn't say a word to Gene on rounds. And any word from Gene would have been like lighting a match while pumping gas.

Across the street, a sign painted on the 7-Eleven window reads, *Michelob $3.00/case.* Stylized fireworks explode in the background. When the pump clicks off, Gene has already decided to purchase a peace offering. He owes her much more than that, but it's a start.

Gene waits in the station office to settle up. No sign of Jerry. He thought he might have recovered from his back surgery. J.J. comes in from the garage. "Hey, haven't seen you in weeks. What gives?"

"Don't drive that much."

"You ain't been buying that filth at Gemco, have you?" He smiles as wide as a Chrysler grill, the gap between his front teeth practically widening.

Gene returns the smile. "How's your dad?"

"He's fightin'."

"What do you mean?"

"He's got an infection now. He'll come back from it."

"Oh, I'm sorry. Tell him I wish him well. Tell him Gene Hull's tired of his son short-changing him."

"Oh, he'll love that."

The bell dings. A white Mustang has pulled up to the pump opposite Gene's Saab.

"You driving the Saab?" J.J. asks.

"Yep."

"One like that used to come in here years ago."

"Same one probably. It's been on the DL."

J.J. looks perplexed.

"Disabled list," Gene says. "Kind of a baseball expression." He wonders for a second if he should mention his father.

"Don't work on 'em. Whole different animal." He hands Gene his change. "You may want to count that."

Gene smiles and pockets the coins.

"How's surgery?" J.J. asks.

"Busy."

"Tell me. You seen anybody die in surgery?"

The question nearly knocks Gene off balance. There's death in the desert, death in the ER, and names crossed out on Jesse's clip-board. But everybody makes it out of the Heart Room. "No. We have a good team."

J.J. leans his bony elbows on the counter. "My patients come in dead all the time. But I bring 'em back." He straightens and nods to the Mustang. "Had a bitchin' Mustang hauled in dead a couple days ago. Bad starter. She thought it was the battery, and I told her that was certainly possible with this heat and all, but my money was on the starter."

Nine months ago, Patty's battery had died in the parking lot of a Tucson hospital. About the same time Gene's father died at MVH. One brought back to life. The other not.

"She said the car was fine on the drive up from Tucson. But the next morning, she turned the key and nothing. Dead."

Gene feels the prickly rush of adrenaline. Hoping to see Patty's car, he looks around J.J. to the garage.

"I told her if it weren't the battery, I might not be able to get to it for a couple days. I point to five cars ahead of her...all dead from the heat by the way —."

"What'd she look like?"

"A gorgeous deep blue with —"

"I mean the girl."

"Shoot, I can do better than that." J.J. thumbs through a stack of invoices and pauses at one. "McLellan. Patricia McLellan."

"When did she pick it up?"

"This morning. But it wasn't her. It was her mother. The girl rode in with the tow truck Saturday. You know her?"

Gene sat down in a cold metal chair. "I used to."

"Those eyes of hers could boil a radiator."

"Who picked her up...after she dropped it off?"

J.J. looks disappointed. "Yeah, I offered her a lift, but good ole mom showed up."

Gene rises and pulls the keys from his pocket.

"I was hoping the girl would be back today," J.J. says, "but Mom said she headed back to Tucson already. I guess her fiancé drove down to get her. Lucky guy. I'd a done the same thing in a minute."

Gene looks out to the white Mustang. "Most guys would."

He looks back to J.J. and taps the counter. "Say hi to your pop."

Gene drives across the street to the 7-Eleven and buys two cases of Michelob. Sandra's apartment is only two blocks away. This is going to be perfect. He has the conversation all planned out. She'll open the door, probably wearing her robe, her eyes red from crying, maybe a tissue in her hand. Sure, she'll want to be alone, and she'll probably look a little miffed. But when she spies the case of Michelob at his feet, their beer, she'll bite her lower lip, and before she can squeak out a thank you, he'll say Dr. Harrington's an ass. She'll understand that Gene has filled in the blanks. She'll be melting — the Swiss on his ham and cheese, curling at the edges. She'll invite him in...no, take his hand and lead him inside and tenderly wrap her arms around his neck. I apologize, he'll say. I should have taken the heat for moving the pedal. But I told him later. In the ICU. Not true, but he'll enlist Irene tomorrow to explain. He is, indeed, sorry. He knows he should tell the truth, but his instincts guide him toward self-preservation. He doesn't know why he's this way. He doesn't like it. But instincts are instincts and hard to escape.

He hauls one case up to her door, lays it down quietly, and hustles back for the second case and stacks it atop the first. Three doorbell rings later the door opens.

"Gene-o," Dr. Boz says. He holds a glass of red wine in his hand. He's bare-chested. "I thought you were the pizza." He looks down at the beer and taps the box with his stockinged toe. "That's what I call a full court press. All I brought was a cheap Chianti."

Gene hears Sandra's voice: "How much is it?" She comes up behind Boz, fingering bills in her wallet. Her hair is wet and combed back. She wears a bathrobe. The fear in her eyes tell the story.

"Fuck," Gene says.

"Gene, wait." She pushes around Dr. Boz.

Gene feels small and is shrinking by the second.

"Fuck you," he says, hoping that will energize a little growth spurt, but it only makes him feel smaller. He kicks a hole in the side of the bottom Michelob case, startling the chilled beer. "You know where you can put these. You too, Boz."

Sandra reaches for his arm, "Gene. Listen." But he twists away. She screams or pleads other things, but he's not in a listening mood.

He passes Boz's Harley in the parking lot. He must have been too love-struck or lust-struck or eager to be a hero to notice it on his jaunty two-treads-at-time scamper up the stairs when he thought Sandra would be alone and miserable. Being in a kicking mood, he kicks the Harley's back tire. A full force, blunt-toed kick, like he's going for a sixty-yard field goal. The bike doesn't budge. The pain reaches his groin, which seems apt. He limps at a run to the waiting Saab.

On the drive home, he flips the radio from jazz to KCAZ and pumps up the volume. Then he opens the windows and turns off the A/C, eager to bake in the black heat rising from the asphalt. "The monsoons look to be leaving us for a few days," the DJ says.

"Things are going to be heating up. Record breaking heat. Speaking of record breaking, here's…"

Yeah, Gene thinks. The hotter the better. He cranks the volume even more so that Zeppelin's "Dazed and Confused" fills his head with Plant's agonizing lyrics.

At home he strips to his boxers and dives into the pool. Afterward, he uses an Ace bandage to wrap a bag of ice around his foot. He feeds Apollo, fills the water bowl, and rewarms yesterday's pizza, all while Apollo nips at the ice bag like it's a game.

"Knock it off," Gene says.

In certain situations, his instincts run strongly toward self-pity, and tonight he doesn't have the energy to change course. There will be no studying or knots or grapefruit reconstruction. No push-ups or pull-ups or Giants' game, even though they're playing tonight. So, to the roof he goes with a lawn chair, a pizza box, a bucket of ice, and his mother's gin. The heat, even at night, raises sweat on his skin and softens his muscles. Despite the ice his foot aches. But that's okay. He wants his toes to be broken. It would serve him right. The air is still, the neighborhood quiet except for the occasional cheer, lifting over the trees from the ballfield.

Long after the games are over and his ice has melted, he's drinking gin straight from the bottle, one section of lights continues to illuminate the far, southeast backstop. He can see the top of it, imagine the stanchion cables angling back and behind the aluminum bleachers. That's where Patty laid it out to him — the whole thing — over Spring Break. And across the street, maybe in her driveway, maybe at the curb, is her Sapphire Blue Mustang, waiting for her to return.

"Hey, Patty," he shouts. The ballfield lights kiss the dark outline of her roof. "It happened again." He swigs from the bottle. "Same old story. Gene fucks up and gets screwed by an older guy. This time, a real doctor, not your fucking medical student or intern or whoever the fuck he is." Gin trickles down a corner of his mouth. "Good news, though. She's not pregnant."

Chapter Twenty-Eight

FIRST CLASS FOOL

GENE WAKES from a bilious dream and vomits in bed. He wavers in the dark to the toilet. Several times he retches until it feels like he's turned inside out. Back in his room, he notices that the window is open. How or when he crawled back through is a mystery. Cleaning up will have to wait. He crashes on the floor.

Later, he rises to consciousness again, but this time to Irene's voice. At first, he thinks he's fainted in the Heart Room, but it's coming from downstairs — the answering machine. He fumbles for the extension in his room.

"Irene." He covers the receiver and tries to clear the gravel from his throat. "Sorry, it's Gene."

"You should call if you're sick."

"I was going to. I slept through my alarm." He checks the clock on the desk. It's twelve-thirty.

"I assume you're ill. That's what I told Dr. Harrington."

"Thanks."

"This isn't college, Gene. No excuses."

"Really. I meant to call."

"If we'd really needed an extra hand, we'd been scrambling.

"Sorry."

Now that he's awake, his head throbs and the smell of vomit hangs in the room.

"Are you okay?" she says. "Do you need anything?" For a second, she sounds like his mother.

"Just a twenty-four-hour stomach bug I think." He looks over at the Texas-shaped stain covering his bedspread. Like tumbleweed, little balls of pepperoni are scattered across the landscape. "I'm pretty empty now."

"Ginger ale," she says. "Start with that."

It's exactly what his mother would have said. "Will do."

"Wait a second."

It sounds like she covers the receiver with her hand. She's talking with someone.

"Gene."

"Yes."

"Sandra wants to know if you have any ginger ale. She'd be happy to pick some up and bring it by."

"She's there?"

"Of course."

For a moment, Gene wonders if he'd dreamed the whole thing or misunderstood the part about Sandra quitting.

"Ginger ale or not?"

"I thought she quit."

Irene sighs. "Just a minute."

Gene hears Irene speaking. "The small chest spreader's in the autoclave. Get it before I forget? Thanks."

After a second, she comes back on the line. "Gene. Families fight. We're no different. One of my jobs is to hold it together."

Yeah, and the Heart Room family lies to protect each other.

"I'll be in Monday."

"No excuses."

The ginger ale was a good idea, but he has none. "Tell Sandra no thanks on the ginger ale. I've got plenty." He wants to say, Maybe Boz needs her delivery service.

After he hangs up, he stumbles into the bathroom where Apollo is curled around the cool base of the toilet. The dog, his tail doing his little pitter-patter thump, backs into the hall. His head and body are matted with the contents of Gene's stomach, but his eyes say it all — Am I in trouble for this?

"Oh, Apollo." Gene leans against the counter and cries.

When he picks Apollo up, the dog yelps.

The stitches look a little red. He should have removed them days ago. When he's steady, he'll take them out.

Together, they wash in the shower. He hugs his dog and asks for his forgiveness, knowing that forgiveness is something dogs don't give. They don't have to. They don't blame you for anything.

Gene spends the rest of Friday in bed, runs to the toilet twice, and swears off gin for life. Apollo sleeps behind the commode and doesn't even lift his head when Gene rushes in. That evening Gene limps out to get the paper. The garage door is open. He forgot to close it after his little show at Sandra's. At the mini-mart, while hobbling around for ginger-ale, dog food, and aspirin, his foot throbs. If he's no better by Monday, he'll get an x-ray. At home, he reads the sports page and solves the Jumble. It's silly, but working the Jumble makes him feel guilty that he was at home while Rui worked today.

Work. What did Irene say on the phone — *If we'd really needed an extra hand*. Gene's always known he wasn't indispensable in the Heart Room, but he thought he was at least being useful. The team works fine without him.

He's not watched TV all summer but gives it a try while nursing a Ginger Ale. Every channel of evening news is focused on the panel investigating Nixon's troubles. So maybe they kick him out of office. Then what? The VP takes his place. No one is indispensable. That cheers Gene enough to bolster his appetite and make a couple fried eggs for dinner. He's soaking the last of his toast in the yolk when the phone rings. It's probably Sandra. No way he's picking up.

After the fourth ring, Sandra's voice fills the kitchen. "Gene, I hope you're feeling better. I'd like to talk to you. I think I know why you didn't come in today. Please call me."

She doesn't know. She couldn't know he got wasted on the roof. He steps to the phone and erases her message. No more jazz. No knot tying or reading about heart surgery this weekend. He decides to spend the remainder of the weekend transferring his cassettes to an empty reel-to-reel he found among his father's music. When completed, he can listen to all the music that reminds him of Patty, uninterrupted, all day and night. Poor, pitiful me.

Saturday morning, he watches cartoons, his old favorites — *The Jetsons, Johnny Quest, The Roadrunner*. He and his father used to howl as the Coyote plummeted off cliffs or was beaned with an anvil. Another postcard, actually two postcards (labeled I and II), arrive from his mother Saturday afternoon. He fixes a sizzling steak sandwich, props his ice-wrapped foot on a chair, and eats at the kitchen table while he reads. His toes are less swollen, and he can bear more weight. Dr. Hull's diagnosis: severe sprain.

> Dear Gene, seems like I just wrote. Suzanne and I had a fight. The details aren't important. We patched things up. But I'm not sure moving out here is such a good idea. I don't know, one day I want to move, the next day I don't. Suzanne thinks I'm afraid to sell the house because it's like admitting once and for all he's never coming back. That sounds silly when I write it out, but when I can't sleep at night it feels true. What do you think?

On the second post card…

> Maybe if I just found a little place in Flagstaff for the summers. You know, to get out of the heat. How am I going to afford two houses? I remember when we thought we couldn't afford the one. We waited two years before we added the pool and landscaped the backyard. Remember what the trees looked like before you painted them? Have the monsoons started yet? I admit, I do like the monsoons there. Not so much the dust storms. Out of room. Love, Mom xo. PS: Hope the first card arrives with this one.

"Apollo, let's get those stitches out."

Apollo is sound asleep under the kitchen secretary. Gene retrieves his father's doctor bag but doesn't find any fine-tipped scissors. He checks a couple other places before giving up. Monday, he'll borrow some from the hospital.

Before heading out back to vacuum the pool, he sets up *Every Picture Tells a Story* to record. Using long, languid strokes, a foot at a time he works his way around the perimeter of the pool. In the blistering afternoon air, Rod Stewart's raspy voice drifts from the patio speakers, telling Maggie May she stole his heart and made a fool of him.

Gene stops vacuuming and stares at his stubby shadow rippling in the water. He played this song over and over on the drive back to Cal Poly last spring, substituting Patty for Maggie Mae...but now the song speaks of Sandra.

LATER IN THE afternoon she leaves another message. He doesn't hear her words, only the pleading cadence of her voice as he carries freshly washed sheets up to his bedroom.

Eventually, he settles into the lounger by the pool with a tumbler of ginger ale. After an hour he gets more ice from the kitchen, takes a dip in the pool, and settles again in the lounger. The heat, even at dusk, is searing. He's turned down the music and can hear the traffic from the nearby intersection. Apollo whimpers through a dream under the patio table. Gene would love to go to the cage later to sweat out the alcohol and clear his mind. But his toes, although better, aren't up to it.

The doorbell rings. Gene twists toward the sound. If it's somebody selling encyclopedias or religion, he isn't interested. He ignores it and then ignores the next two rings.

A few minutes later, the side gate slams, and he sits up to see Sandra charging toward him. Her thighs ripple with each angry stride.

"This might have been an apology," she shouts. "But not anymore."

"I was just going to call you."

"Bullshit."

"No, really."

"Grow up, Gene." She gives him a hard look, and he doesn't know how to respond. For the second time in four months, a girl is telling him to grow up. "Tell me. What do you think happened between Boz and me?"

"I don't need to tell you."

Her jugular veins bulge. Her nostrils flare like a cartoon bull, and for an instant, he grins.

"Oh, so this is funny now?" she says. "Well, plenty happened."

"I'm sure it did."

He braces for a dose of sour medicine.

"Harrington raked me while you were diddling in the ICU. He blamed me for the Bovie pedal you tripped over. He blamed me for the four-by-fours left in Mr. Mead's chest. Then you know what he did?"

Gene waits her out.

"He threw them at me. The whole bloody clump of gauze. Right in the face. And then he tells me to get out and send somebody in who can count. Boz told him to back off, and Harrington almost flung a scalpel over the screen. I said, 'Do it yourself. I quit,' and drove home. I'd just gotten out of the tub when Boz came by with a bottle of wine. He told me I was the best nurse he'd ever worked with. Boz said this. He sat on the opposite couch and never made a pass. Boz. How do you explain some people? To tell you the truth, I was feeling so low and so angry that had he reached for my robe, I might have dropped it. But he didn't. Not even close."

"He'll be back."

"That's all you have to say?"

"You should hear him in the doctor's lounge. He's on your scent."

Sandra gives Gene a pitying look, walks close, and cups her hand under his chin.

"You certainly have your father's eyes. Maybe when you're a little older you'll have his insight."

None too gently, he bats her hand away. "Well, I don't. I'm not perfect like he was. Okay. I never will be. I'm not him. I'm me." He stabs his chest. "I'm tired of women telling me to grow up. And I'm tired of everyone expecting me to be just like him."

Sandra cradles her wrist. Her face tightens, and he assumes she's going to belt him. But her hateful expression ebbs to one of concern. She walks two steps away and turns, extends her arms and lets them drop to her side. "What happened, Gene. How'd we get here?" She walks back to him and gestures for him to move over. She sits. Their shadows wave over the pool.

"This probably wasn't a good idea," she says.

"I should have answered your calls."

"No, I mean, our relationship."

When she says *relationship*, it sounds clinical, like a diagnosis.

"Is that what we had?"

Gene knows it's over, has ignored the feeling that their relationship wasn't much more than a beautiful skin closure — that his wound underneath still hadn't healed. The look on Sandra's face tells him she's relieved he's crossed that line on his own.

"When Patrick died, everyone told me the first two years would be the toughest. My therapist said in time I'd find a place for him in my heart and another place for someone new. Each special. Each separate. No competition. People tell you these things, and you nod and agree, but all you can think about is how much you hurt now. Two years. It seemed like two years would never come. And it's past, and I still haven't found a place for someone next to Patrick." She takes in a deep breath. "I hoped it might be you. But I was kidding myself. And what's worse, I was not true to you. He's still with me… in my head…when I'm with you."

He places his hand on her knee.

She places her hand atop his.

"I know what you mean," he says. "It's hard. But worlds harder for you."

"Sorry about that comparison to your father."

"I shouldn't have hit you."

"No."

He massages her wrist lightly. "I used to think I was more like my father. Now I think I'm more like my mother."

"How's that?"

"More selfish. Less perfect."

Sandra looks at Gene. "You have your father's best qualities, I think."

"I doubt that." Gene picks at the lounger's webbing.

"I can see how it would be tough — the son trying to live up to his father's legacy."

"I'm not trying to live up to anything."

"Sure, you are. But you're better than a cliché."

"How could I? Everywhere I go in the hospital, he's a saint. He was a rock. He even died a hero."

Sandra stretches her tan legs. She looks in Gene's eyes for an uncomfortably long time.

"What?" he says.

"Your father. He made mistakes, too."

"Not many."

"He gave a patient the wrong drug once."

"Once? That's all?"

"As far as I know."

"Big deal."

She looks down and then turns her head to Gene. "To Patty."

Every molecule of air escapes his lungs.

"Before bypass," Sandra says. "Instead of giving her heparin, he accidentally gave her cardioplegia."

Gene closes his eyes. Slowly, he shakes his head. He slumps, elbows on knees.

"Here, drink this," she says and offers the Ginger Ale.

He refuses. "So that's why her heart stopped?" he says. "It was his fault?"

"Yes."

"Well, that's no big deal. You just put her on bypass."

"Most of the bypass lines weren't in yet."

"Then massage her heart until you can get on bypass."

"That's the one thing you don't do with an atrial myxoma. The tumor might break free."

Gene begins to sway.

"Come on," she says. "Let's get inside. I'll explain."

She leads him into the cool kitchen. He sits at the big oak table and drops his forehead onto his arms. Sandra dumps the ginger ale and brings him ice water.

Using his thumb, Gene rubs condensation from the side of the glass. "So?"

Sandra pulls up a ladder-back chair to face Gene. "Here's what happened. The case is proceeding normally. Dr. Harrington has placed the first bypass line. He asks for the heparin. Your father injects a syringe of what he thinks is heparin but is actually cardioplegia. Several seconds later, Patty arrests. At the time, he thinks… we all think…a piece of the tumor has embolized to a coronary artery or is blocking the outflow through the mitral valve. Rui doesn't perform open chest massage because, as I said, a piece of the tumor might break off and go to her brain. So, everyone is hustling to get her on bypass."

Gene looks up, picturing himself in the room, scrubbed in for the case, realizing now what no one knew at that moment, not even his father. "Shit. She's not anticoagulated."

"Right."

"If they start bypass now, her blood will clot in the bypass machine. It will seize. Flow will stop. She will die."

Gene imagines Harrington barking orders, Rui and Irene's hands flying to keep up, all of them concentrating on Patty's stilled heart. But on the other side of the blood-brain barrier, Gene's father works alone, mostly out of sight from the surgeons' controlled chaos.

"You know why she didn't die?" Sandra says.

Gene shakes his head.

"He gave her heparin. The real thing, this time."

Gene looks at all the books and notes on the kitchen table. "How'd he know to do that?"

Sandra turns her hands up and shrugs. "He told me it was all a hunch. He had a sick feeling, he'd messed up. There wasn't time to think. Any second, Harrington was going to shout, 'On bypass.'"

Gene rubs the cool, slick glass against his forehead.

"Then during bypass, he hands me a blood-test tube, but there is no blood in it, just a little clear fluid. He says he needs a potassium level. At the time, I didn't know where it came from. The result comes back sky high."

Gene sighs. "It was from the syringe, right? The one he thought was heparin."

Sandra nods.

"What did Harrington say?" Gene asks. "He must have blown a gasket."

Sandra shakes her head. "He never knew."

"Rui?"

"No."

"Jeez."

"At first, I didn't know. None of us but your father knew the reason she arrested, but we all thought, whatever the reason, her heart…or brain…might have suffered damage. She was a little slow coming off bypass, but gradually she came around."

Gene squeezes his eyes tight, trying to push away the thought of Patty dying in the Heart Room. Her naked body motionless. Everyone silent. No whirl of the bypass machine. No hiss from the ventilator. No *beep, beep, beep* from the EKG monitor — only a long, straight, green line extending beyond the edge of the screen to forever.

The air conditioner surges on. A cool breeze glides over Gene's warm neck. "How did you find out?"

"I came back down to the Heart Room to set some things up for the next day. Your father was in the room sitting next to his anesthesia cart. He had a medication vial in each hand. He looked up at me and said, 'I don't know how it happened. I picked up the wrong one. I looked right at it. I was so sure it read 'heparin'. Then he showed me the other vial labeled cardioplegia. He stocked his own cart. The top drawer was a checkerboard of dividers. He said he must have mixed a vial of potassium in with the heparin. He said, 'I can't explain it. I always read the label before I draw the drug.' Gene, when he looked at me, I wanted to cry. He said, 'I nearly killed her. I can't do this anymore.'"

"Oh, Jeez." Gene covers his face. When he looks up, he reaches to the center of the oak table and holds up his mother's house-sitting instructions and her postcards. "My mother rambles on about this and that…catch the cat, don't air-condition the backyard, irrigate the trees." He shakes his head. "Yet, anything important, and she…I mean, we're a family, right?" He slams the papers and postcards onto the table.

The air conditioner shudders off. From the refrigerator, new ice cubes make a faint tumbling sound.

"I don't know any family that doesn't have secrets," Sandra says.

He takes a sip of ice water. Glass in hand he holds his arms wide. "I lived here, too. I thought I was his little buddy. I thought we were a team."

He slams the glass onto the table. It slips from his hand and spills. "Shit."

Sandra rockets to her feet. "I'll get it." She finds a dish towel and sops up the water coursing around his books and dripping onto the floor.

From her knees, she rests back on her heels and looks up at Gene. "It's hard to admit your mistakes, your flaws, especially to those you care for or love the most. You don't want to disappoint them and risk losing their respect."

Sandra rises and tosses the soaked towel into the sink. She returns with another glass of ice water.

"I'm fine," Gene says.

"Drink it."

He takes a gulp and strums his fingers on the glass. His father's strum.

She nods to his toes. "How'd you do it?"

He straightens his leg out on the chair. "You saw it. I kicked the case of beer."

"I thought it might have been when you kicked Boz's tire."

Shit.

"You didn't notice, but I chased after you. That's some temper you have."

"You mean, some flaw."

"I mean, it's okay that you're not perfect."

"Like my father."

"Yes, you're both perfectly not perfect."

Gene guzzles half the ice water. Takes a breath, then finishes it off. "My mother resents that he tried to be everyone's hero."

"Gene, there are some things you can't become and some things you can't un-become. Carl was born to be hero."

"I suppose so," he says. "Maybe I wasn't."

"First, you don't have to be someone's hero. Second, I'm adding self-pity to your wonderful flaws."

"And now you know all of my secrets." But of course, she doesn't. If she knew the selfish way he treated Patty and the things he said to her, he'd lose her respect like…just like he did Patty's.

"Time for me to go," she says.

When she takes Genes empty glass to the kitchen, her foot knocks a tennis ball across the floor. She turns back to Gene. "How's your patient? Any trouble getting the stitches out?"

Gene sighs. "My mind's been other places."

"Okay. Where is he?" she says. "I'll take them out."

"He was outside under the patio table."

Sandra walks to the sliding glass door. "Not there."

"He probably came in the dog door. Check the pool bath."

She checks. "Not there."

Gene limps to the sliding door and steps out. "Apollo."

He bounces the tennis ball on the patio cement. "Apollo." He bounces it again and then throws it into the pool. He expects Apollo to dash from the grove and dive into the water. But he doesn't. "Apollo!"

THEY FIND Apollo in the coolest, darkest corner of the grove. He's on his side, panting. Gene falls to his knees. "Oh Jeez. Apollo."

Sandra pushes Gene aside. "Shit." She picks Apollo up in her nurse's arms and races toward the patio. Not since Mr. Mead crashed in the ICU has he seen her this alarmed.

He rushes along beside her. "What?" That's all he can squeeze out.

"Look at his leg," she says.

"I can't see it."

"It's swollen." She starts to lay him on the table. "Grab the towel."

He doesn't know what she means at first.

"Over there. On the lounger. The lounger." Her voice rises.

Gene spreads the towel on the table.

"Get some scissors." Again, he freezes. "To clip these sutures."

"I don't have any."

"Stay with him."

Sandra runs out the side gate and returns with a small folded bag, like a heavy cloth apron used for tools. She fumbles with the ties. "Dammit."

Apollo's tongue, pale and fissured, hangs from his mouth. He's breathing like a hummingbird.

Sandra clips through the sutures.

"These should have been out by now."

"I meant to."

"Oh, God." Sandra's head recoils from the smell accompanying the pus gushing from Apollo's open wound. Gene's never seen or smelled such a river of pus. She swaddles Apollo in the towel and practically pitches him to Gene. "Let's go. I'll drive."

"My shoes? I need a shirt."

"Gene!"

IT MAY BE A DODGE DART, but Sandra drives it like Richard Petty. Gene sits in the passenger seat with Apollo on his lap. They are racing down Orangewood and heading toward Central when she says, "Which way do I turn?"

"I don't know."

"Where's your vet?"

"I don't know. I can't remember."

She accelerates right. A box of tissues slides from the dash to the floor.

"Wait," he says. "There's an animal hospital. I was going to take him there for the laceration. What was it? Missouri and 15th…19th?"

"It doesn't matter. We're going to mine. God, I hope they're open."

She honks and weaves though traffic. She pounds on the steering wheel, shouting, "Move. Will you fucking move?" At the first stop light she looks over at Apollo and says, "How is he?"

"I don't know," Gene says. He doesn't know anything. He's helpless.

At the next intersection, the car in front stops suddenly when the light turns yellow. Sandra slams on the brakes. Gene makes the same motion with his foot. Lightening blazes up his shin. He screams out.

"You okay?"

"My toes."

Apollo doesn't stir. His breathing seems to slow. That's got be a good sign. It has to be a good sign.

They make the next two lights, but the one after that narrows to one lane between construction cones. The cars crawl through the intersection.

"Come on. Come on," Sandra shouts.

The light goes yellow to red.

"Shit."

Gene points a block ahead. "There it is." Cars are in the parking lot. "They're open!"

"How's his pulse?"

Gene's trembling hand searches Apollo' neck.

"I don't know." Apollo takes a deep breath.

Sandra looks over. "Fuck."

She steers around honking cars gridlocked at the intersection, and a block later, makes a hard left and follows an Emergency sign to the side entrance.

Gene looks down at Apollo. "We're almost there, buddy." Apollo's eyes loll toward Gene. He leans in to meet them. He expects to see what he always sees in Apollo's eyes, unconditional gratitude. But he sees nothing. Not gratitude. Not pleading. Not accusation. His eyes are like marbles. "Apollo. Please. Apollo."

"Gene, is he breathing? Gene!" The car screeches to a sideways stop in the parking lot. A moment later, his door flies open. "Give him to me."

When Sandra reaches in, Gene blocks her arm. He doesn't need a monitor with a flat green line. He doesn't need a stethoscope. Or even a finger on a pulse. Apollo is gone.

Gene folds over him and sobs. "I'm sorry. I'm sorry. I'm sorry." When he looks up, Sandra is biting her lower lip, failing to fight back tears. "What did I do?" he cries.

"Oh, Gene." Sandra rests her hand on his bare shoulder. She leans in, and with Apollo limp on his lap, they cry their goodbyes.

When she pulls back, she reaches for the box of tissues by his feet and wipes her eyes. "Do you want me to take him in?"

"No." He takes a tissue. "I'll do it."

It is no longer an emergency, but he limps toward the side entrance anyway. The cement practically burns his feet. The air conditioning inside cools his bare back. He hands blanket-covered Apollo to a tech, who seems as uncertain of Gene as if he were homeless.

"I'm sorry," Gene says, his voice stumbling. "His name was Apollo."

Sandra drops him off at home.

"You going to be okay?"

"I don't know."

"You want me to stay?"

"Best not."

She gives him a brave smile. "Call me later."

The front door is locked. He has to go around back. But for the hum of the pool pump, the yard is quiet. He sits in the shade of the patio, protected from the late afternoon sun's ricocheting heat. He feels surprisingly calm, composed…

…until he notices a tennis ball drifting in the pool.

Chapter Twenty-Nine

THE TRUTH

THE STALE QUIETNESS of the house is suffocating, and he can't bear to be alone in his room. It is Sunday morning, and he watches the last star blink away, relinquishing the darkness to a new day. He lugs his thoughts inside. It's two hours later on the east coast. They're probably up.

Suzanne's surprised he called. Actually, she'd meant to call him today.

"This isn't working," she says. "I think she and I are too much alike."

"Is she there?"

"Sure, what's the matter?"

"There's been an accident."

"Are you okay?"

"Not me. Apollo."

"Apollo?"

He hears his mother's voice in the background. Susanne says, "Apollo's had an accident."

After a pause, his mother comes on the line. "Gene, what's going on? What happened?"

Sandra and Gene dissected just that on the phone late last night.

She'd called to check on him. Specifically, he assumed she called to see if he'd kicked his foot through anything else or jumped off the roof. She thought it was pretty clear that Apollo had been septic — a raging blood infection. It came from the laceration on his leg. He said, "San, I need to know what I did wrong. The truth. Please."

She laid it out in honest, sterile terms. Perhaps he didn't clean the wound well enough. Maybe his technique was lacking, and he introduced a pathogen while sewing. Or maybe, later, when Apollo ran through the irrigation water, the wound became contaminated. "Who knows?" she said. "That's the way it is in medicine. You often never know the reason, for sure." He asked Sandra why he never saw any pus. She was gentle but didn't hold back. "You strangled the wound closed pretty tight," she said. "It couldn't get out."

So much for soft hands.

"Gene," his mother says, "Please, is he okay?"

He has a story all ready to protect himself. But sitting at the secretary, he can see Apollo's tennis ball still circling around the pool. He can't betray him a second time.

"He died yesterday."

His mother gasps.

"It was my fault."

"Gene, surely you —"

"The cat you wanted me to catch put a gash in his hip. Instead of taking him to the vet, I tried to take care of it myself. The wound became infected. I didn't notice, and it killed him. I killed him."

She starts to whimper.

"I thought about lying. Tell you it was rat poison or something."

"I'm glad you told me. It's who you are."

"That's a laugh."

"You're as honest as the day is long."

"You hardly know me. Do you?"

"Gene!"

"Tell you what. I'll tell you a past lie, if you tell me one."

"You're being ridiculous."

"Okay. I'll start." He swings around to face the refrigerator menagerie. "I told you Patty broke up with me because she fell in love with an older guy."

"Her mistake."

"Here's what really happened. I got her pregnant. She wanted me to come to Tucson to talk to the doctor. Decide what to do. But I didn't. I told her I was too busy. That my grades were a disaster, and I couldn't miss any more classes. A week later she had a miscarriage."

"You should have said something."

"You are right about that. I should have said something. I should have been her hero and walked across the desert if I had to. But I didn't. And for one simple reason…I was too embarrassed. I didn't want to be that guy. And I got what I deserved. She found someone better. Someone she could count on. So there. Tell Suzanne. Tell Rodney. Send your friends a postcard and tell them your perfect little boy knocked up a girl and then abandoned her because he was afraid of the way it would look."

"Okay, just stop it. I'm coming home as soon as I can get a flight."

"Come home. Don't come home. It doesn't matter. Just tell me your secret."

"I'm not playing this game."

"I know it anyway."

"We'll talk when I get back."

"Sandra told me."

There's a long silence.

"She told me everything," he says.

"That slut."

"You can't call her that!"

"You're on her side?"

"I'm glad she told me the truth. Dad didn't."

His mother laughs. "Like he's going to tell you he slept with a nurse."

Gene's mind goes flat. Slept with a nurse? "Sandra, you mean?"

"Wait. You didn't know?"

Gene shakes his head. "He had an affair with Sandra?"

"If you call two nights an affair."

"When did this supposedly happen?"

"Does it matter?"

Gene leans forward. Twists the receiver away and clenches his jaw. What a sap. Boz's rumor was true, but it wasn't Rui. "I need to know."

"I hope nothing's going on between you two."

"Nothing's going on."

Speaking to Suzanne, his mother says, "No. Sit down. I'm not done."

Then to Gene: "If you must know, it was after our big fight. He didn't stay at the hospital. He ran to her."

"Shit."

"He said, 'If you can't give me the emotional support I need, maybe I'll find someone who can.' Dammit, I gave him nothing but support…medical school, residency, when cases didn't go well or Harrington chewed him out. And then after that little girl died. Especially then. That just tore him up."

Stretching the coiled phone cord, Gene sinks to the cool tile and lies down.

"Gene?" his mom says.

"About the little girl."

"What about her?"

"It really bothered him."

"I know," she says. "He couldn't sleep for weeks."

"I thought I was the only one not sleeping."

"He wanted to be brave for you kids."

Gene stares at the ceiling. Tears trickle toward his ears. "I felt so alone."

"And you shouldn't be alone now."

"Why are we like this? Why do we hide?"

"He never wanted to disappoint you."

"He seemed so strong."

"Gene, he was. He truly was…with most things. He just couldn't cope with failure. And he rarely ever failed with anything."

"There was nothing he could have done for her."

"He knew that. But it still bothered him tremendously."

"I know why," Gene says. "He felt helpless."

In the background, Suzanne is saying something.

"Gene," his mother says. "Are you going to be okay?"

"How did he cope?"

"What do you mean?"

"You said he didn't sleep for weeks."

"Maybe I was exaggerating."

"Did you know how helpless Rui felt trying to save Dad? It still bothers him. Even after seeing a therapist. Alicia says at times he still escapes with a few beers. What did Dad do?"

"We should talk later."

"No more secrets! What did he do?" Gene closes his eyes.

His mother's deep sigh into the mouthpiece sounds like a gust of wind from an approaching storm.

"He started taking my leftover Percodan to sleep."

"Jeez."

"Eventually I figured it out."

"How?"

"I found the near empty bottle in his doctor bag."

"What'd you do?"

"What any nagging wife would do. I read him the riot act. I told him, 'This stops now,' and made him see someone."

"A therapist?"

"Psychologist. The same one I recommended to Alicia for Rui."

Gene can hear what sounds like Suzanne crying, her face near the phone's handset.

"We didn't want anyone to know," she says. "It was our secret. Just like his two nights with that nurse."

"But he came back."

"Of course."

"Why?"

"Same reason I didn't pack my bags. You kids. We would never abandon you over that or anything else. And I think it scared him, the thought of a failed marriage."

Gene sits up, eye level with the space under the secretary. Apollo's dog bed is no longer underneath. It's in the trash with his dog bowl, the empty antibiotic vial, the Gaines-burgers. All but the coumadin. That he flushed down the toilet, but only after thinking, maybe I should take the whole damn thing.

"I know why he quit the Heart Room."

His mother is silent.

"He gave Patty the wrong drug."

"That nurse told you."

"The secrets never cease, do they?" he says.

"Go get his black bag," she says.

"Why?"

"Go get it."

Gene throws the receiver onto the counter. He returns with the bag.

"Dump everything out."

Gene piles it on the kitchen table.

"Now get a paperclip from the drawer by phone. Use it to pull out the bottom."

Gene sets the phone down, bends the clip, and loosens an edge inside the bag. With his finger, he lifts the bottom out. A false bottom.

"There's nothing there."

"Every day Carl went to work he worried that he might make a mistake that would kill a patient. The night of Patty's surgery, I woke and saw him just sitting on the edge of the bed. I said, 'Carl, you okay?' He didn't turn. He just said, 'I almost killed Patty today. If she doesn't wake up, I'm afraid what I might do.' Then he opened his doctor bag and lifted the bottom. Underneath were six vials of Demerol and syringes. Gene, he always thought if he ever killed a patient, he would send me on an errand, write a note, and quietly, painlessly end his life."

Gene slumps back into his chair. "Jeez."

"And to think, he once called me selfish."

"But he was asking for help."

"Yes, for the first time. I said, 'Carl, I don't care if you have to dig ditches for a living. You've done enough. It's time for a change.

I can't have you trying to save everyone if it's going to kill you.' He started seeing the psychologist again and left the Heart Room."

Gene blinks away tears.

"Mom."

"Hmm."

"Dad didn't want me to be a doctor, did he."

"Yes and no."

"On that first drive up to Cal Poly, he told me not to become a doctor just because he was. I thought he didn't think I was smart enough or had, I don't know, the right stuff."

"Smarts wasn't the issue. He was afraid that a medical career might be as hard on you as it was on him."

"Why didn't he just tell me?"

"Because he also thought you were stronger than him. That, as much as you cared for others, as much as you were a perfectionist like he was, you might handle failure better, and the fear of failure."

"He should have just explained all this."

"Probably so."

Gene looks around the kitchen. Her kitchen.

"Since Dad died, I've said some things to you —"

"Gene," she says. "We both have."

"You saved him."

With a cracking voice she says, "Here's Suzanne."

A few seconds later, Suzanne comes on the line. "She's gone outside. God, Gene. I called her selfish the other day."

"I heard."

"You think you know your parents."

"And they think they know you."

LATER THAT NIGHT, Gene drives to Sandra's. From behind her door, she says, "Who is it?"

"It's me," Gene says. The door chain rattles, and the dead bolt slides. And there's Sandra, concerned and fearful for all the wrong reasons. Once again, wearing her *Nurses Have What the Doctor Ordered* nightshirt. How perfect was that.

"Gene, are you okay? It's after eleven."

"I haven't been okay in months."

"What happened?"

"That's what I want to know."

The door opens.

"Gene, come on in." She sits on the couch, folding her legs to the side. Gene closes the door behind him and just stands, steadying himself. There's no good way to ask her. Sandra's expression changes. "This isn't about Apollo, is it?"

"Not entirely." Though that wound is still raw and just mentioning his name is like rinsing it with alcohol. "I called my mother."

"How'd she take the news?"

"I told her it was my fault."

"Don't be hard on yourself."

"Then we traded lies."

"Lies?"

"Sure. We all lie. You know that. Harrington lies about the four-by-fours left in Mr. Mead. My father lies about why Patty arrested in the OR. Then he lies to me about why he quit the Heart Room. My mother lies about her perfect marriage. Not so long ago, during my fairy tale life, my father secretly took a flying lesson. She told him if he did it again, she hoped he crashed and died. He told her she no longer supported him. So, who does he run to? Who does he stay with for two nights?" His voice shakes.

Sandra leans and pats the cushion an arm's length away. "Sit. Please."

"This the same move you used on him?"

"There were no moves."

"No. You just led him into your bedroom, like you did me, and fucked him."

"No."

"Then my mother is lying again. He didn't stay with you."

She places her feet firmly on the carpet and looks down. "She's not lying."

With the cocktail table between them, Gene, fists clenched, paces back and forth. "Jesus," he says. "Jesus."

She reaches forward with one hand. "Gene, we didn't have sex."

He jerks away. "I should have listened to Boz."

Sandra shakes her head. "He just slept here."

"More lies!" Gene turns and pounds the front door with his fist.

"Gene!"

He hears her, but he's not listening. She lurches toward him, grabs his arm and whips him around. "Listen." She's in his face. Then the color from her face recedes. "Listen," she says softly. "He slept on the couch."

"Oh, please!" Gene turns the doorknob.

"That's what you do!" Sandra shouts. "Run." She grabs his wrists. "You owe it to yourself, if not to your father. You need to read something."

Sandra moves around the couch and disappears into her dark bedroom. A light brightens the bedroom doorway. In a few seconds it goes off and she returns. "Please…sit."

Gene exhales and flops onto the couch. She stands over him and holds out a letter. He doesn't move, doesn't look at her. "Please. Your mother never believed him either."

Gene raises his eyes. He snaps the cream-colored page from her. It's the same three-quarter-size heavy stock his father used to pen the occasional letter to Gene at Cal Poly. This page has the rough creases of a letter that has been unfolded and folded several times.

May 27, 1969

Dear Sandra,

Where do I begin? With an apology, I think. I was distraught when I arrived at your door two weeks ago. And I took advantage of you. Not forcibly in a physical sense. But emotionally. I took advantage of our friendship by fleeing to you after Dee and I had that terrible fight. I knew you were still vulnerable. I knew there was a chance we would end up in bed. I admit I had fantasized about you. But I never expected I would try to act on that fantasy. We do things, we say things, in moments of anger and resentment that we would probably not do or say otherwise. If not for you, we would have had sex and that would have ruined our friendship and probably my marriage.

But you let me stay, and I told you things that no one but Dee has ever known. At times I have felt trapped in my work by my own success and trapped in my marriage by Dee's reluctance to share what she considers my silly passion to be a pilot. For those two nights with you, I felt oddly free. And in the clarity of our conversations, you reminded me how special Dee has been. If not for her tough love three years ago, Percodan might have ruined my life. Or killed me. Regaining her respect and trust again will take time.

They don't know it, but I feel as if I've let my children down. They both look up to me, but Gene in particular. He wants to be just like me. I hope his better nature surpasses mine. He's so young, just entering high school, with so much compassion for others. In one important way, he's more like his mother than he is like me — he's resilient. I hope that doesn't change. Gene would make a great doctor, but it's his life, his decision.

Thank you for being a friend and trusted colleague. You are right, Dee is a truly beautiful woman. But so are you, in every sense. You deserve an equally beautiful man to share your life. I look forward to meeting him someday and telling him how lucky he is.

Fondly,

Carl

Gene hands the page back to Sandra. "I think he overestimates my resilience."

She sits on the couch opposite him. "Now you know why I

wasn't at any of the other Christmas parties at your house, other than that first one in 1968."

"I can't say I really noticed you in 1968."

"I guess I deserved that."

"I didn't mean it that way."

Sandra scoots closer to Gene. "As you can see, your mother would never accept me into your life. I was foolish."

Gene looks around Sandra's apartment, not able to quite imagine his father sitting on this couch.

"My mother made him quit the Heart Room." He glances at Sandra. "But I suppose you knew that. And the psychologist."

She cringes and nods. "It was the right thing."

WHEN GENE OPENS her front door to leave, the Maine Coon darts in, slithers between Gene's legs, and meows. "What did you name him?"

"Bypass."

"Of course." Gene raises the toes of one foot and watches the cat rub his jaw against them, eyes closed. He hasn't seen the cat since Apollo died. "I'd like to take him home."

Sandra tips her head. "Really."

"Take him up to my roof deck and give him a flying lesson."

She looks hurt. No. Disappointed. She picks up the cat and strokes his head. "It's not his fault," she says.

"Whose was it then?"

"Not yours either."

"Now, that is a sweet lie."

"Go home. Try to sleep. If you don't make it in tomorrow, I'll tell Irene you're still contagious."

"It's what families do. Right?"

Gene remembers to check the irrigation board on the way home. Only twenty minutes to spare. He opens the valve. The blast of water furrows the moonlight-speckled ground and races toward the thirsty trees. Had he missed a week, they wouldn't have died. Suffered, yes, from the brutal temperatures expected over the next few days, but not died from his neglect. That thought sends him tumbling into tears again.

At the appointed time he closes the valve and treads up to his room. Out on the roof with a beer and the stars, he strips to his boxers and sits in the lawn chair. The pool pump surges on, breaking the silence. The sound reminds him of the bypass machine.

Down below, light from the kitchen skims the pool's surface. Next to the steps, bougainvillea petals swirl in an eddy. He remembers his first household responsibility years ago: netting the debris before he met Patty; before he could daydream of her stepping from the water, her bikinied hips tilting seductively from side to side as she ascended the steps; the way she gathered her hair to the back, water sheeting off her brown arms like a fall of grateful tears.

He leans back and remembers other things too: Watching cartoons on Saturday morning dressed in his dad's white t-shirt, the hem to his knees; laying out five hundred hard-earned dollars for the Jeep and learning how to drive a clutch on the way home from the seller's house; Fourteen years old and the full bottle of beer his dad handed him on the patio after he finished painting the trees' brown trunks. "Have your first beer with your ole Dad," he said. "It is your first?"

It was. Gene still remembers that beer. He can taste it. He can feel the pride of sharing that moment, the desire to be this man someday. And now he is. And now he isn't. In ways both good and bad. As much as he wishes he could tell his father how much the little girl's death bothered him; tell him that knowing his father wasn't perfect makes him feel better, not worse; tell him the responsibility for another person's life, even if he's your dog, can't be explained, only experienced; tell him that for all her passive-aggressive ways, Gene's mother was truly beautiful when it mattered; tell him that he may have given Patty the wrong drug, but so did Gene — he gave her excuses when she needed a good listener and a man by her side. As much as he would like to tell him all these things and more, what he would most like to tell him is this: how much it meant to read the words *Gene would make a great doctor* in his father's handwriting.

He imagines himself in the future, sitting on the brain side of the blood-brain barrier, double checking the heparin vial before drawing it up and then telling a young girl, I'll take good care of you, or maybe standing on the blood side, calling out, On bypass, and then plucking a pearl from a young girl's heart.

Either of those Genes are years and years away. Tonight's ninety-eight-degree air passes through his exposed heart. His aching heart. It's like being on bypass. What did Boz say? "You can't stay on bypass forever. At some point, it's sink or swim."

He steps to the edge of the roof and eyes the deep end of the pool below. For the next girl who asks him, *If I was drowning, would you save me?* He has an answer.

Gene walks back to far edge of the deck and readies for a three-yard sprint. He takes a deep breath. "Clear!"

When his pedaling legs hit the water and a million bubbles rush past his ears, he goes limp, drops to the bottom and fires to the surface, breaking free with a gasping breath and pounding heart. He strokes to the side and hangs on. Looking up to the roof, he smiles through water gliding down his face and quietly announces, "Off bypass."

Chapter Thirty

OFF BYPASS

On Monday, Gene skips Jesse's breakfast, arriving later so he doesn't have to wait in the doctor's lounge before surgery. Sandra welcomes him back as she ties his gown, saying to him and the rest of the Heart Team, "I hope you've recovered from that stomach flu." During bypass, she banters with Dr. Boz. She must have cautioned him about the beer kicking incident because Boz says nothing about it. Not even a pointed hint.

The MVR needs a little extra coaxing from Dr. Boz's magic elixirs to get off bypass, but the two-vessel CABG revs his engines the moment Roger starts warming the heart. As Gene closes the skin with Rui and Irene, he says, "I have some sad news."

The whole Team pauses for an instant, as if the power just flickered. "More sad news, you do not need," Rui says.

Gene looks up. "Apollo died over the weekend."

"I'm so sorry," Irene says.

"What happened?" Rui says.

Gene feels Sandra place her hand on his lower back. "Sepsis, the vet thinks. I strangled the wound and then left the sutures in too long." He makes the last loop of the stitch, cuts the needle off and passes the strands to Rui. "I was careless and didn't pay close enough attention."

Gene looks up at Rui. He has stopped tying the knot. "It is hard," Rui says. "You are young. You did your best and will learn from it. We have all been there. I, for one, do not blame you."

THE NEXT DAY, Jesse greets Gene at the service elevator on Four. "Man, where you been? Not like you to take a sick day two days in a row."

"You waited?"

"Course I waited."

Gene loosens his tie. "I've been a little preoccupied."

"Shit, Doc, when you gonna make the turn?"

"I'm making it, Jesse. Honest."

"Bet you are. You ever look out the window?"

"What?"

"Come here." Jesse leaves the breakfast cart by the elevator and pulls Gene over to the alcove window. "Look out there. What do you see?"

"Jesse, I've got to get to the OR."

"Okay, okay, I'll tell you what you see…heartache. See that kid waiting for the bus. I bet that boy found his girl in bed with her old boyfriend. How about that nurse running across the street? Her boyfriend probably told her he needs his space. Oh, and that car turning left, he's coming home from a night with his mistress. What he don't know is that his wife *do* know and she's waiting at home to give him a twenty-two-caliber ass-kicking." Jesse extends both arms to the horizon, the low sun casting a harsh orange tint across his brown latex skin. "Thousands of heartaches out there, man. You ain't the only one, and most of them are bigger than yours."

"Mine's pretty big."

"Always feels that way from the inside."

"Unfortunately, that's where I live."

"Not forever, Doc. Not forever. Let me tell you a secret. That kid waiting for the bus down there?"

"Yeah."

"That's me. That's me when I got back from 'Nam, and my sweet Lorraine, who would never ever leave me, who kissed my picture every night, who would be waiting for me when I got back from dodging bullets, told me face to face, that for six months she'd been scratching her itch with Melvin. But I'm over that."

"Sounds like it."

Jesse smiles and shakes a finger at Gene. "Okay, okay. A little scar maybe. But you don't get through 'Nam without some scars. Let me show you something."

"Jesse, I'm going to be late."

"Won't take long." He pulls out a thin well-worn leather wallet. "No cash in here so don't get any ideas." He opens it and hands it to Gene. "If Melvin hadn't moved on my lady…my ex-lady…I'd had none of this."

Gene pages through five small photos in plastic sleeves. The first is one of Jesse, a woman, and two preschoolers, all dressed for church, Jesse's wide smile as genuine as Gene has ever seen. There's also a department store glamour shot of the woman, the kids standing beside her slightly older.

"That," Jesse says tapping the first photo, "is my wife and our two kids. Her kids really. Twins. Boy and girl. She'd already had them when I met her. The father said he needed his space."

Gene smiles. "I see."

"Life's like that, Doc. One day you're living a pain on the inside, and next thing you know, you been blessed. Have everything a man could want."

Gene folds the wallet and hands it back.

"What if she'd carried your baby?"

"Who?"

"Lorraine. Was that her name?"

"Shit. You a daddy, too?"

"No, I mean she was pregnant, but then —"

"Jesse knows what you mean. You knocked her up, though. Right?"

"Guess I did."

Jesse gives Gene a smile as bright as the sunrise. He leads him back to the breakfast cart and slides out a tray. "Man, you are a case. We'll talk more tomorrow."

"Tomorrow's my last day," Gene says in a tone that, even to him, sounds apologetic.

"You ever come back, you know where to find me. Now here. Eat. It's good for your heart. Especially yours, Doc. You care too much."

Gene smiles. Just like that, Jesse has confirmed who Gene is and where he's going. He loops the tie around his neck and accepts the covered plates of food despite his lack of appetite. The elevator opens. Jesse presses the hold button, begins his whistle, and pulls the cart inside. "Don't you worry. Young, handsome Doc like you, you'll be fine. Just fine."

Gene blocks the door with his foot. "Thanks, Jesse. Thanks for everything."

After the morning's cases, Gene changes into his shirt, tie, and white coat again before going down to the diner. The waitress slides a Dr. Pepper across the counter. "Usual?" she asks.

"Grilled ham and cheese."

"Swiss. Got it."

Gene twists the icy drink between his palms. This is where he sat, what now seems like months ago, when he ran toward the Code Blue in the lobby. And tomorrow Rebecca will have surgery, and after that, Dr. Harrington will go on vacation. And after that? Who knows? Maybe Gene can find a way to follow her recovery.

He rotates on his stool to look toward the lobby and catches Rebecca smiling at him from a corner booth. She gestures with a little half wave. Across from her, a guy about her age dips his stubbled chin in acknowledgment.

Gene takes a sip of Dr. Pepper and walks over. "Dr. Hull," Rebecca says, "This is Alan."

Alan extends a hand.

Rebecca smiles into Alan's eyes. "He drove nine-hundred miles from Houston to be here."

"Who wouldn't? Right?" Alan says.

"Right," Gene says.

"I told you about Dr. Hull, Dr. Harrington's assistant. The one who saved my life."

"Hardly."

"Well, my mother thinks so, and mothers know best."

Alan raises his eyebrows. "Especially yours."

Rebecca spanks Alan's hand.

"Hey, easy," he says. "Remember, no exertion."

She leans in. "Hey, easy. The no exertion rule can be continued after surgery, too."

Alan blushes. He glances up at Gene.

She scoots over. "Have a seat."

In a summer of revelations, this one seems fitting. Of course — a boyfriend. Gene's disappointment stabs for a moment, but it's not a crushing blow. Although he cares for her well-being, he barely knows her. Perhaps this sudden turn is his last penance for deserting Patty. The slate is clean.

"No thanks," Gene says. "I've got rounds to make with Dr. Harrington." He looks at Alan. The guy seems worried.

"We're just hanging here until my room's ready." Rebecca reaches over and squeezes Alan's hand.

"Tell me," Alan says. "is Dr. Harrington as good as everyone says?"

"Alan!"

"It's okay," Gene says. "You want the TV answer, or you want my honest opinion?"

"Which will make me feel better?" Alan says.

Gene places his hands on the table and leans forward, giving them his best doctor-look. Both pairs of nervous eyes lock onto him. "Honestly, if my girlfriend were having heart surgery, there is no one I would rather have than Dr. Harrington and his team."

THAT AFTERNOON, waiting for Rebecca Layne to come out of the bathroom, Gene looks out the fourth-floor window. Behind him, Mrs. Layne and Dr. Harrington sit across from each other; he, writing in the chart; she, legs crossed, foot bouncing. Alan pulled a chair to the head of the bed.

"My husband should be right up," Mrs. Layne says. He's trying to find some shade for the car. This is so unusual for late July. The heat, I mean."

Gene turns. Dr. Harrington is still engrossed in the chart. "Yes," Gene says. "One last heat wave. Then the monsoons will be back."

Below, in the parking lot, employees on the day shift head for their cars. Nurses, custodians, techs and secretaries grasp car door handles with their shirttails, one lady springing out of the front seat when the vinyl sears the back of her legs.

"You grow up here, Dr. Hull?"

"Indeed."

"How do you take this heat?"

Gene looks out to the dry haze in the distance, to the approximate location of his home. The morning DJ said tomorrow's temp will not just push the envelope. It will spontaneously combust it. It is the kind of heat that will desiccate and yellow the outer citrus leaves and shrivel and blacken the weakest of the young, green orbs. Even so, by December, his trees will be bursting with succulent fruit. "I think I just accept it," he says. "It's a part of me."

She laughs. "You are lucky. Fortunately, or unfortunately, I know who I am, and Phoenix summers are not a part of me."

"You could be my mother."

"Well, she's a lucky woman."

Gene is working hard to steer his thoughts from all that transpired the last few days — the secrets he learned from Sandra and his mother, the shifting images and opinions of his father, and, of course, there's Apollo. But when you come off bypass, you don't just walk out of the Heart Room to your car and a normal life. There's a period of recuperation.

Gene thinks recuperating from betraying Apollo may never happen. Not feeding him is tough. Not being pestered with the tennis balls the toughest. Gene flexes his toes. They're better. He walks without a limp, but he tried to jog Monday morning and returned after a few hundred feet. Today was better. He ran the old loop by Patty's house and, glad to see her car still there, never stopped. He hopes she doesn't return from Tucson before tomorrow to pick it up.

Behind him, the bathroom door opens. Gene turns as Rebecca hops onto the bed. She looks to the window and squints. Gene stifles a yawn and narrows the slats on the shade.

"Thanks," she says.

Gene moves around the foot of the bed and leans against the sink. Rebecca wears the same loose ASU t-shirt and maroon and gold gym shorts she'd worn at the diner. Her golden legs stretch the length of the bed. Alan strokes her hand.

"Dr. Harrington," Mrs. Layne says. "I can't tell you how nervous I am." She places her magazine on the bed and squeezes Rebecca's foot.

"Not to worry," Dr. Harrington says. He closes the chart, crosses his legs, and sits back in the chair. "Rebecca, my dear, are you ready to close that hole in your heart?"

"Yes," she says.

It is a *yes* so brave and irrevocable in its tenor that Gene's throat tightens as if he has a boyfriend's stake in her well-being. He doesn't. She is just another patient with a patient's history: Previously healthy. No allergies. No medications. Lab work negative, including her pregnancy test. Five-foot ten. One hundred and forty-five pounds. Her eyes are brown.

"How long will it take?" Rebecca says.

"For you." Dr. Harrington says. "A single breath."

"I wish I could be there," Alan says. "If just to hold her hand as she falls asleep."

"Perhaps Eugene can fill in."

A single breath. She falls asleep…she wakes up. That's all she will know. That's all Patty knew. That's all Gene knew about open heart surgery back when he was the boyfriend in the waiting room. But he knows the in-between now. He's peered into the open chests for the hour or two of each case when patients like Mr. Mead, Mrs. Perkins, and Patty entrusted their lives to the Heart Team, their hearts stilled, opened, and repaired on bypass, before being shocked back to life. Rebecca's heart will be no different. It just has to be.

After rounds, Dr. Harrington heads to the lounge to smoke, and Gene returns to Rebecca's room. He never told her that tomorrow's his last day, and he probably won't see her after surgery. Or she won't see him. She'll be too drowsy.

"You know how to pick 'em, Gene-o," Boz says. He's come up behind Gene.

"What do you mean?"

"Rebecca Layne." He says her name as if he's sipping a fine wine. "Pre-opped her earlier. I was going to put in a good word for her hero, not that you need it, when her boyfriend walked in."

"I met him."

Boz looks back toward Rebecca's room. "That's one lucky cowboy who gets to saddle her up."

"He seems nice." Gene taps Boz's chest with the back of his hand. "Thanks for today. For not mentioning the beer-kicking and all."

"Gene-o, I'm not going to bash you when you're down. At least not intentionally. I know what it's like to lose a dog. Accidentally shot mine while hunting. Talk about a guilt trip."

"I'm sorry."

"Don't worry about it. That was three dogs ago. Rattler's the only remains I ever kept, though."

The guy does have a heart.

Boz offers his hand. "In case we don't catch up after the case tomorrow."

Gene looks down and accepts Boz's hand, feeling bad that he'd always assumed the worst.

"After you fainted that first day, I didn't think you'd last the week, much less be trusted by the old man. College student? You shittin' me!"

"Thanks."

Boz heads down the hall, stops, and calls back. "Look me up when you're a gas passer. After all those years with Harrington, if I'm still alive, I'll need a partner to share the pain."

"Maybe I'll be a surgeon."

"Nah. It's not in your DNA."

Gene decides against visiting Rebecca. All he really wanted was another pat on the back. What a dope. Sandra said, Some things you can't unbecome. He hopes not all things.

He walks down to Mr. Mead's room. Mrs. Mead looks surprised when he enters. Dr. Harrington and Gene rounded on them earlier. Mr. Mead snores, mouth agape, while Mrs. Mead holds his dangling hand. She whispers, "This is an unexpected surprise. Is anything wrong?"

Plenty, he wants to confess. "No. I didn't have a chance to tell you that tomorrow is my last day. In case I miss you on rounds, I wanted to wish you well. You've had a tough road."

"Sit," Mrs. Mead says.

Gene moves a chair next to her.

"If you don't mind," she says. "I won't wake Mr. Mead."

"No need. I can't stay long."

"So, you are in training," she says.

"Yes, very early in my training."

"Well, you've been wonderful. Such a comfort to me. Dr. Harrington is a wonderful surgeon. He inspires confidence. But he feigns closeness. I probably shouldn't say that. You'll think I don't appreciate the man."

"No. Not at all."

"With you, it's different. You're genuine."

"Not as much as you may think."

"No. I have met a few people in my life, and I can tell the charlatans from the rest. It doesn't mean we genuine folk — and I include myself in your club — don't hide a thing or two. And perhaps you do. No matter. The core of who you are comes through." She carefully releases Mr. Mead's hand. He doesn't move. She grasps both of Gene's hands, and, with her gray eyes, looks straight into his soul. "Don't ever change. Promise me that."

"I don't think I can."

"I mean it." She squeezes his hands.

"Me, too."

"Good." She takes Mr. Mead's hand and strokes the fat vein under his thin, speckled skin. "I've held this hand for over sixty years," she says. "To think I almost lost it." She looks at Gene, her eyes full pools. "Nobody holds hands anymore." She looks to the door and then leans into Gene and whispers. "It's all free love. Sex with whomever you want. I know you look at me and think, What does this old lady know about sex? It may not have been so out in the open in my generation, but that's a good thing. There's more to intimacy than sex. Just holding hands is so very intimate. When Mr. Mead walks with me in public and takes my hand, it's like he's holding my heart. Think about what it means. He's saying to the world 'I'm proud to be with this woman. I'm grateful that I am hers and she is mine.' You may think that sounds possessive. Well, so be it. Because it's mutual. I guess in a way, every time we held hands it was like a little renewal of our vows — for better or worse, for richer or poorer, till death do us part. So, I will hold Mr. Mead's hand to the very end, knowing that he would hold mine."

She straightens. "I've never told anyone my little secret. See what I mean? You have a way that relaxes people."

Gene leans in and kisses her on the cheek.

"Oh, my," she says. "Now, we have our own little secret."

"I'll make sure to stop by tomorrow and see Mr. Mead."

"Please do."

ONE LAST STOP on his penultimate day of Hearts. Gene enters Dr. Harrington's cool, empty waiting room. Irene sits at the secretary's desk. "Gene?" she says. "I thought you'd be home by now."

"I didn't want to forget this." He places the heart model on the counter. "Thanks. It helped a lot. And thanks for teaching me how to scrub, and, well, for being patient."

She walks around the counter. Gene readies for a hug, but she shakes his hand in her perfunctory way, and it sends a chill through him.

"Can you wait here a second," she says. "I think Dr. Harrington would like to speak to you."

Oh, shit. The bladder catheter. He found out.

"Gene?" Irene stands at the door leading to the inner office. She's not smiling. "Follow me."

One day left and he's being cut loose.

Signing papers, Dr. Harrington, dressed in white shirt and tie, sits behind a large teak desk. He looks up. "Gene, I'm glad you stopped by." He points to an isolated chair in front of the desk. "Have a seat."

As Gene sits, the chair's stiff leather complains. This is where Dr. Harrington's patients wring their hands as he explains how he will cut into their chests. A model of the heart, identical to the one Gene has just brought back, rests on the uncluttered desk. Behind Dr. Harrington, medical books, certificates, and awards line the wall-to-wall shelves. In the center, a decades-old photo of the doctor and his young family looks out into the wood-paneled room. Dr. Harrington looks as if he's about to bolt from his wife and three young girls to the comfort of the hospital.

"First, let me say, it's been an honah and a privilege to have you by my side these past six weeks."

What?

"A bit of a rough start, but you persevered. I dare say, your father would have been proud."

Dr. Harrington rotates a piece of paper on his desk and pushes it toward Gene. Gene leans in and reads the contents of a glowing recommendation, ending with Dr. Harrington's dominating signature. It's Gene's golden ticket for admission to just about any medical school he chooses.

Gene sits back and takes a deep breath. His father, faults and all, would not be proud. He pushes the letter back.

"You need to know something." Gene looks forcefully into Dr. Harrington's eyes. I caused that patient to bleed from the bladder catheter. The case you had to cancel. It was me. Not Sandra. I should have told you sooner. I was stupid."

Dr. Harrington tilts his chin up. "Hmm. I guess that changes things." He takes the letter and opens a desk drawer.

"I understand." Gene's disappointed that he won't be a part of Rebecca's surgery tomorrow, but he's more ashamed and disappointed in himself. "I'm sorry." Gene stands to leave.

"Sit down, please." From the drawer Dr. Harrington removes a signed check, attaches it to the letter with a paper clip, and pushes it all back to Gene.

Gene reads the check. "Eight hundred dollars. I don't understand."

"Let's just say you passed my final exam."

Gene flexes the letter in his hand.

Dr. Harrington adds, "It's hard to admit a mistake."

"You knew?"

"I know everything…eventually."

"But eight hundred dollars?"

"You earned it. Use it for school, applications, interviews, travel. Whatever you decide."

"Thank you."

This still doesn't feel right.

"When you learned it was me, why didn't you fire me?"

"I thought about sending you home, except for one thing."

"My father."

"No. Your patients."

"My patients?"

"They love…Dr. Hull.

"Someone called me doctor and I —"

Dr. Harrington raises his hand to silence him. "Uniformly, they gave you high marks. The nursing staff as well. Regardless of your title, you earned their respect. I would have been a fool not to give you another chance."

WITH A CHECK in his wallet and one of his goals for this summer in a manila envelope, Gene jogs from the office.

As he approaches the Saab, he looks up to the fourth-floor windows. He's not sure, but that looks like Rebecca's silhouette gazing toward the sunset. He'd like to ease her mind. A thought will have to do. *We'll take good care of you.*

Chapter Thirty-One

HERE COMES THE SUN

GENE WAKES before the sun and stares at his ceiling, collecting and rearranging thoughts. The radio alarm clicks on.

> …is expected to reach 119. That would shatter the previous record of 112 set on this date in 1946. Currently it's ninety-nine degrees. Here's a cut from Neal Young's album *After the Gold Rush.* Purportedly, Young wrote this song after Joni Mitchell and Graham Nash broke up. And to think I always thought he wrote it for me…but that's another story. One of my favorites: "Only Love Can Break Your Heart".

Gene dresses in running shorts and shoes, tests his toes with a few calf raises. Not quite healed but getting there. Before he leaves the house, he searches through the boxes in his father's closet until he finds the mahogany desk set and Mount Blanc pen Rui gave his father. His mother had wanted Gene to take it back to school last winter, but it seemed pretentious then. Now the pen feels natural in his hand.

At the desk in the mostly empty study, he retrieves a sheet of his father's stationary. He turns on the single desk lamp, sits, and listens for the right words before writing:

Where do I begin …

OUTSIDE, he runs east. The sun crouches behind the rooftops, its faint glow a warning, like a deep growl. Not a molecule of water hangs in the air. By the end of the first mile, sweat drips from every hardened angle of his body. At the turn onto Third Place, the lawn sprinklers pop up at the corner house. He walks into the spray and then kneels like a dog, lapping a mouthful of water before heading on.

At Patty's house, he stops. As hoped, her Mustang is still there. But the truck is back, Jake's piece-of-shit truck, with the Wyoming cowboy riding his filly on the front plate. Gene circles the truck and peers inside. The guy's a slob. The same crumpled napkins and dog-eared journals litter the front seat. Gene would have cleaned up by now. Maybe there's an explanation. Maybe, like Boz, there is something more to Jake. He hopes so. As painful as it is to lose Patty, it's more painful to think she's settled for second best. She certainly sees something in him. It's evident by her adoring look in the photo that still hangs from the rear-view mirror.

Gene removes his Central High baseball cap. He takes the sealed envelope from inside, walks over to Patty's Mustang, and places it under the windshield wiper. Resting his hands on the open driver's window for absolutely the last time, he drops his head and closes his eyes. There. The familiar fragrance of Estée Lauder. Probably only a single, stubborn molecule, but he was bound to discover it.

GENE ARRIVES at the hospital a little later than usual. He's glad he saw Jesse yesterday, because he missed him and his breakfast offering this morning. Not that Gene could eat. He's too nervous.

The first case of the day, a complicated AVR-triple vessel CABG runs over four hours. Instead of following the patient to the ICU, on Irene's orders, Gene runs down to radiology to retrieve Rebecca's films. Someone forgot to send them up. Then it takes forever to find them. God, he hopes this isn't an omen. When he finally returns to the heart room, Boz is just about finished setting up for Rebecca.

"Hey Gene-o," Boz says. "This is going to be a slam dunk. Our easiest case all summer. Wham bam, thank you ma'am, and then I'm going to sleep for a week. How about you?"

"I suppose."

"Okay, Sandra. Bring her in."

Rebecca is heavily sedated, her eyes closed and her breathing easy. While Boz and Sandra attach the EKG leads, Gene stands at her side. "Rebecca," he says. "It's me. Dr. Hull."

Sandra looks up at Gene, a slight smile in her eyes.

He shrugs and then places his hand atop Rebecca's. "We'll take good care of you."

"See," Boz says, "You're a natural gas-passer." He places a mask over Rebecca's face. "Say goodnight, Irene."

After a carefully timed ten-minute scrub, Gene backs into the operating room, water dripping from his elbows. Irene hands him a sterile towel.

Rebecca lies, naked and anesthetized on the table. He can see all of her, except for her eyes. They are taped closed, her head wrapped in a turban. An endotracheal tube angles from her mouth. With each ventilator hiss, her chest rises, her small, pale breasts flattening.

Sandra has already inserted the bladder catheter. Now she spreads a cloth drape over Rebecca's lower legs and begins the prep. She lathers Rebecca from her thighs to her neck. With Irene's assistance, Gene gowns and gloves and then waits with arms folded across his abdomen. He looks to Boz, whose attention is exactly where he hopes it stays — on his anesthesia machine and the green trace of Rebecca's pulse across the monitor.

Gene expected to find Rui already here. "Where's Dr. Pereira?"

"Seeing a patient in the ICU," Irene says. "I'm surprised he's not back." Irene gestures with the folded towels.

"Sure" Gene says.

Together they frame a long rectangular window from the notch at Rebecca's neck to a few inches below her sternum. Irene hands Gene the folded drape. They unfurl it from head to foot like a bolt of fabric. Boz clamps the drape to paired IV poles.

Dripping sudsy water, Rui backs in the door. "Sorry I'm late. I made a quick jaunt to the office. It's like a pizza oven out there."

Rui moves to his position next to Gene, and together they secure the cautery, the suction tubing, and the bypass tubing. Once again, Roger sits at his post, tap, tap, tapping away the last few bubbles lurking within the artificial circulation of his machine. Errant bubbles could convert a beautiful life to a tragedy. A misplaced stitch or knot tied incorrectly could cause bleeding. The wrong drug at the wrong time could stop the heart. Sometimes they don't restart. A hundred things could go wrong. It's not as simple as Gene once thought — close the hole, game over, Rebecca wins. It's not simple at all.

"You are quiet," Rui says. "How about a joke?"

"I'm okay."

"How do you know elephants have been making love in your alley?"

"I've heard it…the first day, remember?"

"Nice shot, Gene-o," Boz says. "We've finally looped back to the beginning. No more elephant jokes. We've heard them all."

Rebecca, completely covered, but for a narrow window of skin, looks like any other patient oblivious to the jokes and noise and lights. Gene hopes he can handle seeing her chest opened, her heart exposed. Maybe he should drop out and wait in the lounge. But he's part of the team. You don't always get to choose your patients. It was like that for Rui when his father arrived in the ER. It was that way for his father when a little girl lay dying in the desert. No matter how insignificant Gene's task or how replaceable he is, he's still part of the team. And he'll own that, right up to the last stitch, which he'll place with extra care, leaving Rebecca his thin, anonymous signature.

Dr. Harrington lumbers in. Irene suits him up. He walks to the x-ray box and studies the film, the screen's light turning his glasses opaque. Rui reaches up and focuses the lights on the stripe of skin. "Shame about Mr. Mead," he says.

Gene feels the blood drain to his feet.

"Horrible, just horrible," Dr. Harrington says while studying the films.

Steadying his voice, Gene asks, "What happened?"

"Stroke. Last night," Rui says. "He's back in the Unit."

Gene pictures Mrs. Mead's frail hand holding her husband's through the bedrail.

"Is it bad?"

Rui gives him a long look. "He's on a vent."

Dr. Harrington takes his position at the OR table. He adjusts the lights and then, using a dry lap sponge, wipes the excess Betadine from Rebecca's skin. Irene hands him the scalpel. In a swift, deep stroke, he makes an incision the length of Rebecca's chest. For a second, the edges of the skin are dry, as if the startling intrusion has caught the vessels napping. Then they bleed. Red, copious blood flows from her skin. Rui cauterizes while Gene robotically suctions the smoke.

The first part of her surgery proceeds sharply, efficiently, like the others Gene has assisted on. Dr. Harrington saws the length of her sternum and spreads her chest. Deep in the cavity her naked heart rocks behind the sheer pericardial veil. A feeling of privileged intimacy rises as gooseflesh down Gene's arms. Rui helps spread the translucent membrane, and they tie the edges back like they always do, suspending her heart in its hammock. But something is different. This isn't Mr. Mead's heart or any of the other feeble hearts Gene has seen limping through the dusk of life. Rebecca's heart is young.

Sleek and athletic, a throbbing, ruby muscle with none of the fat of old age. Its beats are crisp and powerful, its vigor a sign of rebellion at being exposed. Just as Patty's heart must have looked. But instead of assuring Gene, convincing him that Rebecca will glide through the surgery, the contrast grips him under the ribs. She has so much more to lose.

"Heparin's in," Dr. Boz says.

Gene looks over to him and then back to Rebecca's heart, imagining the shock of it suddenly, unexpectedly ceasing to beat. But it never wavers while Gene's heart beats faster.

They saddle her heart to Roger's bypass machine, one tube taking the blood away, the other returning it to her body. Dr. Harrington pronounces, "On bypass" and fills the bowl of her chest with iced saline.

"Potassium," Irene says and hands him a syringe.

Like a plunge into a frigid lake, Rebecca's heart quivers for a moment. Its beats slow from a run to a jog to an unstable walk and then stop. Only the bypass machine keeps her alive now.

Sandra starts the clock.

Gene has read the texts, seen the still photos of this simple operation: Repair of Atrial Septal Defect. Dr. Harrington uses angled scissors to enter Rebecca's heart through the thin, atrial wall—just as he would have done to pluck the pearl from Patty's heart. He adds stay sutures, just a few, to hold it open. Rui suctions the chamber dry of blood. Dr. Harrington refocuses the light. In this vast green-tiled room, filled with dozens and dozens of instruments laid out on stainless tables, amid the hums and beeps and whirls of machinery, Gene peers into the depth of Rebecca's chest, down into a private corner of her heart, where the edges of a small hole glisten. He could plug it with his finger. Gene whispers, "That's all it is?"

Suddenly, the room goes black.

"Christ Almighty," Dr. Harrington shouts.

A few seconds later two flashlight beams streak across the room. Boz shines one onto Roger's bypass machine. "I'm on battery," Roger says. "Coming back up to flow."

Sandra aims her flashlight over Gene's shoulder. The narrow beam offers a tenth the light they had before. "Give me the patch," Dr. Harrington says. "Where are the generators?"

"Betty," Irene shouts.

"I'm coming." Betty aims another flashlight from the head of the table.

Darlene's voice blasts from the intercom. "Power's out downtown. Generators aren't starting up. Maintenance is on it. What do you need?"

"More goddamn light," Dr. Harrington says.

"Couple of headlamps," Irene says.

"I'll get them," Darlene says. "Dr. Boswell?"

"The monitor's on battery for now. I'll need respiratory to hand ventilate when we come off bypass."

Dr. Harrington tries to place the first interrupted suture. "I can't see a goddamn thing."

Arms extended, Betty and Sandra blindly aim their lights.

"How's the flow?" Dr. Harrington says.

Roger has found his own flashlight and scans it across the bypass machine. "I think we're good. Drawing gases now."

"Gene, suction," Rui says

"I can't see."

"Sandra, aim down…a little more…there."

"That's better."

Darlene charges into the room. "Headlamps. The batteries even work."

Dr. Harrington and Rui pause long enough to bend down. Darlene crowns them with the headlamps.

Rui turns back to the field. "Let there be light."

Betty and Sandra now use their flashlights for their own work.

Boz looks over the screen. "Like watching a couple burglars crack a safe in the basement."

"Aim here, Rui," Dr. Harrington says.

With only two narrowly focused lights, there's an eerie feel to the surgery. Like driving in the desert on a moonless night, wary of what lies beyond the periphery of the high beams.

Using a long, double-armed suture, Dr. Harrington takes a bite through the patch and the edge of the hole. He hands the strands to Rui, who ties a knot, but doesn't cut the strands. They are equal in length, each with a curved needle still attached.

"Shit," Roger says. "My battery's down."

Gene looks over. He can't hear the whirl of the bypass machine. What's happening.

"Gene, suction," Rui says. "Stay with us."

"Okay," Roger says. "I'm hand cranking. Pressure looks good. I'll need another battery for warming. Sandra, check the machine in the hall."

Loop by loop the surgeons run one strand halfway around the patch. Rui holds it taught, while Dr. Harrington begins with the other strand in the opposite direction. Midway, their headlights collide, knocking Dr. Harrington's lamp off-kilter. "This is why I hate these goddamn things." He twists and leans away from the field, and Betty redirects the beam.

Then it happens again. "Mother of God!"

Sandra busts in the room. "Got it."

Sandra cranks the bypass pump, and Roger switches out the battery.

Finally, opposite the first knot, the two strands meet. The patch covers the hole. Rebecca's nearly home.

Rui cuts the needles off, and Dr. Harrington ties the final knot, securing the patch in place.

"Surgery by braille," Rui says. He whips the scissors around and snips away the waste. "For me, a new experience."

"Start warming," Dr. Harrington orders.

"Warming, Lee. Back on battery."

"Wait!" Gene shouts.

The eyes of the Heart Team bear upon him. He has to say something now. He looks up to Dr. Harrington's blinding light.

Gene clears his throat. "That last knot," he says. "I'm not sure, but I think you better check it."

Irene snaps a Mayo Forceps to Dr. Harrington's palm. With the tips he tugs lightly on the knot. Nothing. Then a firmer tug. The knot unravels.

Gene looks up at Rui. He hopes his eyes convey the apology he's feeling. Rui holds the tips of scissors in front of his face and angles them slightly. Dr. Harrington is already repairing the break with a suture Irene had quietly passed to him. It takes only minutes, and the repair holds.

Rui leans into Gene. "You saved the game on that one." He pats Gene's hand, glove to glove, teammate to teammate.

"Warm her up," Dr. Harrington orders.

He sutures Rebecca's atrial wall closed. Rui ties the knots, and Gene clips the waste, leaving a perfect tag. The last suture pair is left untied. Inserting a large syringe into the remaining small opening, Rui fills the chamber with blood.

"Dr. Pereira," Dr. Harrington says. "If you'll have Eugene do the honors on his last case."

"What do you mean?" Gene says.

"Give me your hand." With only the two headlamps lighting the way, Rui guides Gene's hand under Rebecca's heart. "Time to bring her back."

"Who me?"

"You have earned it."

The heavy chill of the flaccid heart surprises him. It's lifeless and cold. He shudders: This is what his father's heart would have felt like. Rui's shadowed glance conveys that he knows where Gene's mind has wandered.

"Concentrate. First, you'll evacuate the air."

Dr. Harrington accepts a pitcher of warm saline from Irene and pours the contents into Rebecca's chest, submerging Gene and his charge. The well of the cavity glows in the darkened room.

"Now squeeze, gently," Rui says. "Soft hands."

While Dr. Harrington tents the opening in the atrium by pulling up on the sutures, Gene flexes his fingers. A few bubbles spill from the heart's opening. He squeezes again and a few more glistening bubbles appear. Slowly and repeatedly, as if trying to gently awaken her from a deep slumber, he massages Rebecca's heart. With each caress, fewer and fewer bubbles rise from the warm bath until none appear at all.

Dr. Harrington loosens the ribbons around the vena cava, allowing her heart to fill with warming blood. "A couple breaths if you will, Boz," Rui says. Rebecca's pink lungs expand, curling like a blanket around the heart nestled in palm of Gene's hand.

"Cross clamp off," Dr. Harrington says.

"Do the work for her now." Rui says. "Squeeze firmly but gently. Her heart needs warmth and oxygen."

Even in the limited light, the blush begins to return to the muscle. The channels of arteries and veins fatten on the surface. But still her heart lies limp in his hand.

Rui suctions the saline bath. Dr. Harrington pours more warm saline into the cavity. Gene squeezes faster.

"Patience," Rui says.

It's hard to be patient when your pulse pounds behind your eyes. "Am I doing something wrong?"

"Just stay with her. She depends on you."

Come on, come on! "Should Boz give her something?"

"You're doing fine."

With the first startling contraction, Gene gasps. When the second beat leaps in his palm, he exhales with a rush. Now a third beat, and another. The pace is still slow, but picking up, her heart waking, stretching its arms to the dawn. Faster and faster it beats, as if racing to catch up with the pulse pounding in his ears. Her heart is charging now.

"Flow down," Dr. Harrington says.

"Pressure's good," Boz says. "Didn't even need any epi."

"Down some more."

"Looks strong here."

"You did it, my young Gene," Rui says. "She is back in this world."

"Off bypass." Dr Harrington says.

Gene suddenly feels hot and weak. There's a rush in his ears like a desert wind. His vision narrows to the sight of Rebecca's heart, dancing in his palm.

"Gene," a voice calls. He looks up and squints against the bright, hot sun. It's shining just over his father's silhouetted face.

Gene beams. "We did it," he says, just as a surge of heat spreads across his face and explodes into a thousand glittering shards of glass.

———

When he wakes, Gene is sitting on the Heart Room floor, his back against the wall. He is still wearing his gown and gloves, but his mask has been removed. Sandra kneels and places a wet rolled washcloth on the back of his neck. Her expression is sweet, and for a moment he thinks he's back in her bedroom and has just vomited. "Your color's coming back," she says. She places her hands at the sides of his face. He wants to kiss her.

She removes his gloves, opens the end of a small carton of orange juice and says, "Drink."

He sips and wipes his eyes, his head slowly clearing. Above and around are bright lights and hushed voices, the sound of slurping blood, and the odor of burning flesh — the Heart Team at work.

"When did the lights come back on?" he asks.

"Just after yours went out," Boz says, standing beyond the ether screen.

"She okay?"

"For a second, we thought maybe you were going to take her heart home with you."

"Jeez. I didn't hurt her, did I?"

"No. You didn't even rip out her IV."

Before the end of the case, Sandra walks him to the doctor's lounge. "You remember anything?"

Gene looks down at his hands. "I saw my father."

She places a hand against his cheek. "You didn't eat breakfast, did you?"

"I needed to go for a run this morning."

"In this heat?"

"I love the heat."

"Go home. Rest…and rehydrate! Give me a call tomorrow."

He hopes that wasn't an offer. He can't circle back now. He's off bypass.

"Just so I know you're okay," she says.

"I will."

THAT NIGHT GENE drives back to the hospital. It is late. He takes his Jeep. The top is down, and KCAZ fills the superheated evening with the music of his youth. That's how he thinks of it now.

The DJ repeats the big news of the day—one hundred and twenty degrees. An all-time record. So off the charts, the airport closed for several hours. Earlier in the day, Desert Valley Hospital lost power for a time. Even now, after ten p.m., the pavement is a hot skillet. He loves the heat, a backdrop for the finest summers of his life. Maybe tomorrow, before his mother's plane arrives, he'll touch up his trees. It will feel good.

In the ICU, the nurses are huddled in the nursing station giving report at the change of shift. The lights are dimmed. He tiptoes from one curtained partition to another until he finds Mrs. Mead nodding off in a chair. When he pulls the curtain, her head pops up, and her eyes blink open. "Oh, doctor, I'm afraid I was dreaming."

"How is he?"

She pats her husband's unconscious hand. "He is beautiful. The most beautiful man."

Gene looks up to the EKG and its steady beat. The ventilator hisses, and Mr. Mead's chest rises. Then Gene notices a flower in a vase behind her.

She turns. "Do you like it?"

"It's beautiful."

"Mr. Mead had a nurse bring that to me last night. Before the stroke." She swivels and fingers the stem. "It's an iris. My name is Iris. He always said, 'A dozen roses have nothing on his single Iris.'" She laughs bravely, retrieves a tissue from her waistband, and dabs her eyes. "This is our last night," she says.

"Don't say that. I'm sure he'll be fine."

"You are sweet. The neurologist was in. He thinks otherwise. He will check again in the morning, and then I think I will release his hand." She dabs her eyes again. "I'm sure I won't be far behind."

Gene can't speak.

"I always wondered how I would go. I'm sure now it will be from a broken heart." She looks up to the clock.

"Do you need a ride home?" he asks.

"No, the nurses are bringing in a chair that lays back a little. They say I can stay here tonight."

"That's nice."

"But you should go home. You look tired."

Gene takes her hand and can't say what he feels — I hope someday, I die from a broken heart.

He excuses himself and finds Rebecca. Concealed by the curtains, he stands by her bedside. Her endotracheal tube has been removed. One of the perks of being young. The quick upstrokes of the EKG match its crisp tone. He reads the numbers on the clipboard hanging from the bedrail as if he knows what it all means. Then he does the one thing he knows how to do: he milks her chest tube. What drains is a pale rose color. A good sign, a sign of recovery.

He watches her breathe, the contented way her chest rises and falls beneath her gown. After a few minutes, his breathing falls in sync with hers, a kind of summertime breathing that has eluded him. He didn't close her skin. He remembers that now. She will not bear his signature, and that is probably best. He cares for her in a unique way. It is based on far less than he had with Patty, or even Sandra, but it feels like something more. As far as he knows, it's central to the same trait that made his father a wonderful doctor but became the heaviest of weights to bear.

He brushes a stray hair fluttering at the corner of Rebecca's mouth. Her lids open, heavy blinds revealing a sweet, morphine gaze. Unable to sustain their weight, her lids close. "I almost stole your heart," he says with a smile.

"Me, too," she says with a slur through parched lips.

He knows she doesn't mean anything by it. They are just words bubbling up from her own half-known world.

Very softly, she begins to snore.

"Doctor Hull?" a voice says from outside the curtain. "Is that you in there?"

"No," he says. "It's just me. Eugene."

Chapter Thirty-Two

I WILL

Late September 1974

Gene sits on the paint-spattered *Johnny Quest* sheet under the shade of an orange tree in his backyard. He leans against the trunk and throws small stones, imaginary tennis balls, toward the other trees. It's summer in September, and the stubborn desert plans to hold onto its identity for a few more days until the first cool mornings of Fall. He is heading back to Cal Poly in a few days. Apollo will be coming with him this time. Gene's not able to articulate a simple reason he's bringing the remains of his buddy. Maybe it's an apology. Maybe a reminder of the best and worst of his nature. Maybe it's his way to turn and burn.

He faces the last trunk to be painted. With a screwdriver he levers the lid open, dips the broad brush in the white paint and begins at the base. His strokes are precise and deliberate. This may be the last time he cares for these trees. His mother has once again made noises about moving, but Gene senses this isn't so much about escaping the heat as accepting that she can take all the good memories with her.

"Gene. Telephone," his mother calls out.

Jeez, he's almost done. Only an hour till sunset. He wipes the dripping sweat from his face. "Who is it?" he shouts and then goes back to painting.

She must not have heard him. "Who is —"

"I don't know," she says. She's at the edge of the grove now. "It's a woman's voice."

Gene tamps down the paint-can's lid. He'd snuck a call to Sandra and left a message, telling her he'd come by one last time. She knows his mother is back and wouldn't call unless it was important.

Gene walks toward the sliding door. His mom is silent.

"It's probably a nurse from the ICU," Gene says. "I told her I'd stop by."

"That's nice."

Inside, he waits until she leaves the kitchen.

"Hey," he whispers into the mouthpiece. "You got my message?"

"Gene?"

His breath falters, and he drops into a chair.

From behind him, his mother kisses the top of his head.

"Gene? Are you there?" the voice says. "It's Patty."

WHEN HE PULLS the Jeep up to the curb, she's sitting on the low brick wall in the shadow of an orange tree. It has been six months since he's seen her, and her hair is longer than he remembers. She's not wearing the *Bear Down Arizona* nightshirt he spent so many nights dreaming about, but a lavender top and cutoffs. He'd changed out of his paint clothes into a green-and-gold Cal Poly Engineering t-shirt. As he steps from the Jeep and walks over, she smiles. She has a folded square of paper in her hands. "How are you?" she says.

"Busy. I leave for school in two days."

"I know."

Gene frowns.

"I mean, I remember it was always late September. I took a chance you might still be home."

Patty's Mustang rests in the drive where he last saw it two months ago.

"Hasn't your semester started?"

Patty looks down at the paper and then up. "I'm taking a little break."

"For what?"

She pats the spot next to her. Gene looks toward her front door. "He's gone," she says.

"For how long?"

Patty doesn't speak. Once again, it's her eyes that tell him what *gone* means — out of her life.

He sits. She's sucking a peppermint and offers him one. Surprised, he takes it.

"Thanks," he says, "but what happened?"

Patty holds the paper up. "This."

Gene recognizes the color and weight of his letter.

"You got it, then. When you didn't ring me, I thought maybe it spontaneously combusted. It was so hot that day."

Patty grins. "No, it was fine. But Jake caught fire."

"You read it to him?"

"Hardly. He read it to me."

"I didn't mean for him to see it."

"I know."

"So, he left you?"

"No. He hit me."

Gene turns full on toward her, examining every detail of her beautiful face. "I'll kill him." Fists clenched, he stands.

Patty shakes her head. "No, you won't."

"I will."

"No. My mother gets the first shot. Besides, that's not *you* in here." She raises the letter again. "Please, sit next to me."

And, of course, he sits and moves over close enough to feel her skin against his arm.

Patty clears her throat.

Dearest Patty,

Where do I begin? With an apology, I think. From the moment I first saw you standing by your swimming pool I've wanted to save you. That's a funny way to express my affection but that's how I felt. Then, when you needed me most, I betrayed you. Not in the way I thought you betrayed me, but something worse. You were drowning. I should have driven to Tucson that night. I should have been with you emotionally as well as physically. But I was selfish. And it had less to do with my grades, than that I was embarrassed. Embarrassed to be the kind of guy who could get a girl pregnant. You were right. I needed to grow up. I can't say that I have yet, but I have been told that I have a good core and that I should never change. That doesn't absolve me from my mistakes, and I've made plenty this summer. But none top the mistake I made that lost you.

For the last three months I've asked myself: What if my father hadn't encouraged you to be a nurse? What if he hadn't died? You never would have met Jake, and we would have lived happily ever after. Perhaps. Perhaps not. I'll never know. But I also wouldn't have spent the summer with the Heart Team and learned the naked truths about my father and myself. He's still my hero, but I don't have to follow him. Maybe just be myself and learn from his successes and his failures.

I won't be applying to medical school. Instead, I'll continue with engineering. Biomedical now. I've always wanted to build things. Who knows, maybe someday I'll invent a mechanical heart. But I won't be a doctor. It's too hard on me. More than one person has told me: I care too much. Isn't that ironic? I can be both selfish and caring.

One last thing. I was angry last spring. I did not mean what I said. I know the baby was mine. I was scared. Being an unwed father wasn't part of plan A for my life. Someday, I hope to have a child and I hope I am as good a father as mine was to me and that he knows and accepts my flaws.

I wish you only the best in life.

My love forever,
Gene

It is strange hearing his words read back to him in her voice. Patty folds the letter.

"Jake went out for the paper that morning and came back to our bedroom fuming. He's always been jealous of you. I told him he had no right to read a letter meant for me, snatched it from him, and ran to the kitchen. He followed. He backed me against the counter and told me to never mention your name again. I shook the letter at him and said, 'You could learn a little from this.' That's when he hit me…across the face."

Gene closes his eyes and clenches his jaw.

"My mother heard it all and rushed in with one of Dennis's bats. 'Out,' she said. 'My daughter will not marry a man who acts like her father.' He held his hands up and said, 'No problem, I wouldn't marry your daughter when she's still getting love letters from a guy who knocked her up.'"

"Gene, I had never told her about that. She took a wild swing at him. Thank God she missed. I haven't seen him since."

Gene drops his head. "Patty, I am so sorry."

"Don't be. Your letter saved me."

"He hasn't tried to reach you?"

"Oh, he has. But my mother told him if he shows up at my door, she'll call the police first and his residency program second. It was the second time he hit me. I hadn't told my mother until this happened."

"What was the first time?"

"Remember that photo of your father and me in the bleachers?"

Gene nods.

"He asked who the old guy was. When I explained and the reason your father meant so much to me, well, he didn't want any reminders of you around. Push came to shove so to speak, and it ended badly. But like an idiot, I forgave him."

Gene points to the ballfield. Grant Elementary started up three weeks ago, but the ballfield is empty. Little Leaguers won't be back at it until the end of the school year.

"My house key's out there somewhere."

"What?"

"Early this summer, I ran by your house and saw Jake's truck. I was going to key our initials on it. But I didn't. I chickened out and threw the key into the field."

"Doesn't sound like a chicken. Sounds like someone with a good core."

"So, what now?"

Patty stands and stretches. "Like I said, I just wanted to thank you for your letter. I will treasure it."

"Treasure it?"

"Yes. Always. I should go in."

"Oh."

Patty steps forward. "Gene, we've changed."

He picks a brown withered grapefruit from the ground. It's the size and weight of a golf ball. He tosses it from hand to hand.

"You said that once before."

He looks up and down the street. Her house casts a shadow across the lawn.

"I learned something this summer," he says. "My father had a secret."

Gene overhands the hard, dead fruit toward the ballfield.

"He nearly killed you."

Patty's eyes widen. She takes a step back, her hand over her mouth.

"Sit," he says. "I'll explain."

He holds nothing back and when he's finished, tears streak Patty's cheeks. He wipes them with his thumb.

"Only your mother and the nurse knew?" she says.

"Sandra. Yes."

"Why he quit? The hidden drugs?"

"Everything."

"That must hurt. To learn all this."

"It did. But also, because he kept it a secret from me. I'd like to think he would have told me eventually. At a time when I needed to know. Turns out that time was now."

Gene stands and gazes at the white trunks of the trees next door. "I was painting those trees the day I met you." He turns back to her. "Neither of us knew you had a secret then."

Patty gives him a wary look.

"That pearl in your heart."

She smiles. "Even then I knew something wasn't right."

He extends his arm to her, his palm skyward. She places her hand in his.

"Tell me, Patricia. What's your secret now?"

Patty stiffens. "My secret?"

"The thing you don't want me to know."

She stares at him, her eyes betraying her thoughts.

"The thing you need me to know."

Patty bites her lip.

Gene takes the last step between them. "I knew nothing about pregnancy until your call last February. Then I read it all." He examines the wrapped candy she gave him. "You never liked peppermint. It made you sneeze. But I understand it's supposed to help with morning sickness."

Patty grins. "It does."

"Does your mother know?"

She nods. "And we agree. I'm keeping it…her."

"Does he know?"

"Not if I can help it. I didn't have the test until a few days after he left."

"He'll find out."

"Jake didn't believe in contraception. Said, as a doctor he could time it. Now, I think it was just an excuse to get me pregnant, so I'd have to stay with him."

Gene looks across the street to the bleachers where they sat six months ago and Patty told him *Things change.*

"Let's take a walk."

"Where?"

"I don't know. Just walk. We'll turn back when you get tired." He reaches into his pocket and offers his Chapstick. It's hardly used.

"Thanks," she says, uncapping the tube and then handing it back. "I like the haircut. You gain some weight?"

"Some."

"Me, too." She rolls her eyes. "And more to come."

Side by side they walk down her street. His army of mature trees cast stepping-stone-like shadows onto the sidewalk.

She looks up to him with her squinting blue eyes and says, "And what secrets do you have from this summer."

From shade to shade, Gene tells her about the Heart Room and the types of surgeries he witnessed and the skills he learned, but none of that seems as important anymore. He speaks glowingly of the Heart Team and the precision of their work. He tells Patty about Rui's torment. He tells her about Sandra and his father and what didn't happen. And then he tells her about his own complicated relationship with Sandra and what did happen. A summer thing, he calls it. Finally, he breaks the news of Apollo's death and the guilt he'll have to live with.

She stops and grasps his arm. "I'm so sorry. That must have been the hardest thing."

"There are harder things." He tells her about the sixty-year marriage of Iris and Henry Mead, tells her as much of their life as he knows, right up to his last conversation after Mr. Mead's stroke.

"Sandra called me and said he died that next day. Mrs. Mead passed away a week later. They'll call it heart failure."

Finally, he tells her about his last case. Rebecca Layne. The only girl whose heart he actually held in the palm of his hand. The girl he "saved" by simply lifting her chin so she could breathe.

"Kind of like me," Patty says.

Gene studies her eyes. "Kind of like you."

He offers his hand. As dusk falls, they walk on, far past the Big Tree, far past his summers of old: painting trees, sitting on the roof deck, skinny-dipping with Patty at two a.m., coupling in the shallow end, drying on loungers in the hypnotizing air. Simple and free. A life together. Nursing for her. Medical school for him. His father alive. A long-ago plan A.

"What was it like?" she says.

"What?"

"Holding someone's heart in your hand."

Gene stops. He faces her and moves his thumbs across her knuckles' moist ridges. "It's like being trusted with the most sacred secret a person could have."

She reaches hard into his eyes and asks, "Like touching her soul?"

"More." He places his palm lightly on her abdomen. "Like vowing to protect it."

She covers his hand with hers.

"You must be scared," he says.

She blinks a few times and gives the slightest nod.

"I can't stay," he says. He kisses her forehead, their first kiss in his grown-up world. "You're right. We've changed, and I belong at Cal Poly."

"I understand. I belong here with my mom." Patty shivers. "Maybe we should head back."

"It is a little cool. I guess summer is about to pass the torch after all." Gene places an arm around her shoulders. He feels slightly taller next to her now. Over the summer he has grown.

As they approach her walkway, Mrs. McLellan waves from the lit front porch. Gene smiles and nods. She smiles back and returns inside.

Patty turns to face him. "Will you write?"

"I'll want to know how you're doing."

She smiles, steps forward, and hugs him.

Goodbyes have always been hard, but this isn't goodbye. He pats the Jeep's hood, walks around to the driver's side, and buckles in.

Before turning the key, he looks once again at the eyes that captured him what seems like an eternity ago. "I'll probably be back for Thanksgiving. I earned a little extra cash this summer."

"That would be nice."

"Will you be here?"

"I will."

Gene smiles and turns the ignition.

The tachometer leaps and the engine purrs. As he turns toward home, the headlights rake across the ballfield's backstop and the Big Tree's silhouette. The warmth of the late summer evening makes him feel as if his skin isn't even there.

Acknowledgments

Over the years and in many workshops, I've benefitted from the wisdom of writers whose work I admire: Robert Boswell, Nancy Packer, and Ron Carlson, to name but a few.

Help with this manuscript came from Phoenix writers who read early drafts. These include Polly Baughman, Deborah Bauer, Ann Bergin, Judy Taylor, and Bhira Backhaus. Particular thanks are due to Chandra Graham Garcia whose insightful comments shaped the final draft, and also to retired orthopedic surgeon, Ron Sandler, retired cardiac surgeon, Neale Cogswell, and cardiac nurse Liz Williams. Their careful reading saved me from technical missteps.

Most of all thanks to my four amazing children and my wife Linda, whose unwavering support made me believe in this novel during the many episodes of self-doubt that every writer faces when confronting the gap between the story they want to tell and the story that eventually winds up on the page.

About the Author

Gregory D. Williams, M.D. is the winner of Georgia College's 2008 *Arts and Letters* Prize for Fiction. His fiction, essays, and poetry have appeared in *Blue Mesa Review, Elysian Fields, American Fiction, Bosque,* and the *Journal of the American Medical Association*. A graduate of Stanford University and the University of Arizona Medical School, he grew up in Phoenix, Arizona. Dr. Williams' specialty was anesthesiology, and he was the son of an anesthesiologist. The author passed away in 2020.

Also by Gregory D. Williams

Playing Doctor and Other Stories

When We Were Twelve

Guilt, Grief, and Other Things We Don't Talk About

Grand Canyon Press

Grand Canyon Press is a small, independent press based in Arizona. The press specializes in quality books in the following categories: memoir, how-to books about the craft of writing, narrative non-fiction, and literary fiction. Their mission is to find talented writers with something interesting to say. The press provides book-group discussion guides and coordinates author appearances, either in person or online.

www.grandcanyonpress.com

If you enjoyed *Open Heart,* you might also enjoy the author's chap-book, *When We Were Twelve and Other Stories.*